For Adults

ALFRED HITCHCOCK PRESENTS

Stories Not for the Nervous

Alfred Hitchcock
Presents:

STORIES
NOT
FOR THE
NERVOUS

Random House · New York

FIRST PRINTING

© Copyright, 1965, by Random House, Inc.

All rights reserved under International and Pan-American
Copyright Conventions. Published in New York by Random House, Inc.,
and simultaneously in Toronto, Canada,
by Random House of Canada Limited.

LIBRARY OF CONGRESS CATALOG CARD NUMBER: 65–21262

Manufactured in the United States of America

ACKNOWLEDGMENTS

TO THE FUTURE, by Ray Bradbury. Reprinted by permission of The Harold Matson Company, Inc. From *The Illustrated Man*, by Ray Bradbury. Copyright, 1950, by The Crowell-Collier Publishing Co.

RIVER OF RICHES, by Gerald Kersh. Reprinted by permission of Willis Kingsley Wing. © Copyright, 1958, by The Curtis Publishing Company.

LEVITATION, by Joseph Payne Brennan. Reprinted by permission of Arkham House. © Copyright, 1958, by Joseph Payne Brennan.

MISS WINTERS AND THE WIND, by Christine Noble Govan. Reprinted by permission of the author. Copyright, 1946, by Creative Age Press, Inc.

VIEW FROM THE TERRACE, by Mike Marmer. Reprinted by permission of the author. © Copyright, 1960, by *Cosmopolitan Magazine*.

THE MAN WITH COPPER FINGERS, by Dorothy L. Sayers. Reprinted by permission of A. Watkins, Inc. From *Lord Peter Views the Body*, by Dorothy L. Sayers. Copyright, 1928, by Anthony Fleming, renewed © Copyright, 1956, by Anthony Fleming.

TWENTY FRIENDS OF WILLIAM SHAW, by Raymond E. Banks. Reprinted by permission of the author and *Mike Shayne Mystery Magazine*. © Copyright, 1960, by Raymond E. Banks.

THE OTHER HANGMAN, by Carter Dickson. Reprinted by permission of William Morrow and Company, Inc. From *The Department of Queer Complaints*, by Carter Dickson. Copyright, 1940, by William Morrow and Company, Inc.

DON'T LOOK BEHIND YOU, by Frederic Brown. Reprinted by permission of the author and the author's agent, the Scott Meredith Literary Agency, Inc. Copyright, 1947, by Davis Publications, Inc. (formerly Mercury Publications, Inc.). Originally appeared in *Ellery Queen's Mystery Magazine*.

NO BATH FOR THE BROWNS, by Margot Bennet. Reprinted by permission of David Higham Associates, Ltd., London. Copyright, 1944, by Margot Bennet.

THE UNINVITED, by Michael Gilbert. Reprinted by permission of the author. © Copyright, 1960, by Popular Publications, Inc.

DUNE ROLLER, by Julian May. Reprinted by permission of The Condé Nast Publications Inc. Originally appeared in *ASTOUNDING Science*

The editor gratefully acknowledges
the invaluable assistance of Robert Arthur
in the preparation of this volume

A BRIEF MESSAGE FROM OUR SPONSOR

The title of this volume is *Stories* Not *for the Nervous.* There are those who will argue that this title could apply to any of the various tomes of terror, sagas of suspense, or groupings of grue which I have, from time to time, gathered together for the delectation of my readers. And indeed the point is well taken.

For I am not a man to cater to the nervous. If you are in the habit of chewing your fingernails, jumping from your chair when a door slams, or swooning when someone playfully shouts "Boo!" in your ear, I have only two words of advice—pass on.

If, however, you have nerves which are under good control, nerves which are pleasantly tickled by a touch of terror or agreeably stimulated by a *soupçon* of suspense, then I invite you to join me.

Take a seat, any seat, and start wherever you wish. Break for an intermission whenever you choose and return when you are ready. Informality rules in your enjoyment of this smörgåsbord of stories. There is, I think, something for every taste.

Except, that is, for the nervous.

And now my sixty seconds are up.

ALFRED HITCHCOCK

CONTENTS

ALFRED HITCHCOCK PRESENTS

Stories Not for the Nervous

RAY BRADBURY

To the Future

The fireworks sizzled across the cool-tiled square, banged against adobe café walls, then rushed on hot wires to bash the high church tower, while a fiery bull ran about the plaza chasing boys and laughing men. It was a spring night in Mexico in the year 1938.

Mr. and Mrs. William Travis stood on the edge of the yelling crowd, smiling. The bull charged. Ducking, the man and wife ran, fire pelting them, past the brass band that pulsed out vast rhythms of "La Paloma." The bull passed, a framework of bamboo and gunpowder, carried lightly on the shoulders of a charging Mexican.

"I've never enjoyed myself so much in my life," gasped Susan Travis, stopping.

"It's terrific," said William.

"It will go on, won't it? I mean our trip?"

He patted his breast pocket. "I've enough traveler's checks for a lifetime. Enjoy yourself. Forget it. They'll never find us."

"Never?"

Now someone hurled giant firecrackers from the bell tower. The bull was dead. The Mexican lifted its framework from his shoulders. Children clustered to touch the magnificent papier-mâché animal.

"Let's examine the bull," said William.

As they walked past the café entrance, Susan saw the strange man looking out at them, a white man in a white suit, with a thin, sunburned face. His eyes coldly watched them as they walked.

She would never have noticed him if it had not been for the bottles at his immaculate elbow; a fat bottle of crème de menthe, a clear bottle of vermouth, a flagon of cognac, and seven others bottles of assorted liqueurs; and, at his fingertips, ten small half-filled glasses from which, without taking his eyes off the street, he sipped, occasionally squinting, pressing his thin mouth shut upon the savor. In his free hand a thin Havana cigar smoked, and on a chair stood twenty cartons of Turkish cigarettes, six boxes of cigars and some packaged colognes.

"Bill—" whispered Susan.

"Take it easy," William said. "That man's nobody."

"I saw him in the plaza this morning."

"Don't look back, keep walking, examine the papier-mâché bull—here, that's it, ask questions."

"Do you think he's from the Searchers?"

"They *couldn't* follow us!"

"They might!"

"What a nice bull," said William pleasantly to the man who owned it.

"He couldn't have followed us back through two hundred years, could he?"

"Watch yourself!" said William.

She swayed. He crushed her elbow tightly, steering her away.

"Don't faint." He smiled to make it look good. "You'll be all right. Let's go right in that café, drink in front of him, so if he *is* what we think he is, he won't suspect."

"No, I couldn't."

"We've *got* to—come on now. And so I said to David, that's *ridiculous!*" He spoke this last in a loud voice as they went up the café steps.

We are here, thought Susan. Who are we? Where are we going? What do we fear? Start at the beginning, she told herself, holding to her sanity, as she felt the adobe floor underfoot.

My name is Ann Kristen, my husband's name is Roger, we were born in the year 2155 A.D. And we lived in a world that was evil. A world that was like a great ship pulling away from the shore of sanity and civilization, roaring its black horn in the night, taking two billion people with it, whether they wanted to go or not, to death, to fall over the edge of the earth and the sea into radioactive flame and madness.

They walked into the café. The man was staring at them. A phone rang.

The phone startled Susan. She remembered a phone ringing two hundred years in the future, on that blue April morning in 2155, and herself answering it:

"Ann, this is René! Have you heard? I mean about Travel In Time, Incorporated? Trips to Rome in 21 B.C., trips to Napoleon's Waterloo, any time, anyplace!"

"René, you're joking."

"No. Clinton Smith left this morning for Philadelphia in 1776. Travel In Time, Inc., arranges everything. Costs money. But *think*, to actually *see* the burning of Rome, to see Kublai Khan, Moses and the Red Sea! You've probably got an ad in your tube-mail now."

She had opened the suction mail-tube and there was the metal foil advertisement:

ROME AND THE BORGIAS!
THE WRIGHT BROTHERS AT
KITTY HAWK!

Travel In Time, Inc., can costume you, put you in a crowd during the assassination of Lincoln or Caesar! We guarantee to teach you any language you need to move freely in any civilization, in any year, without friction. Latin, Greek, ancient American colloquial. Take your vacation in TIME *as well as Place!*

René's voice was buzzing on the phone. "Tom and I leave for 1492 tomorrow. They're arranging for Tom to sail with Columbus—isn't it amazing?"

"Yes," murmured Ann, stunned. "What does the government say about this Time Machine Company?"

"Oh, the police have an eye on it. Afraid people might evade the draft, run off and hide in the Past. Everyone has to leave a security bond behind, his house and belongings, to guarantee return. After all, the war's on."

"Yes, the war," murmured Ann. "The war."

Standing there, holding the phone, she had thought: Here is the chance my husband and I have talked and prayed over for so many years. We don't like this world of 2155. We want to run away from his work at the bomb factory—from my position with disease-culture units. Perhaps there is some chance for us, to escape, to run for centuries into a wild country of years where they will never find us and bring us back to burn our books, censor our thoughts, scald our minds with fear, march us, scream at us with radios. . . .

The phone rang.

They were in Mexico in the year 1938.

She looked at the stained café wall.

Good workers for the Future State were allowed vacations into the Past to escape fatigue. And so she and her husband had moved back into 1938. They took a room in New York City, and enjoyed the theaters and the Statue of Liberty which still stood green in the harbor. And on the third day, they had changed their clothes and their names, and flown off to hide in Mexico.

"It *must* be him," whispered Susan, looking at the stranger seated at the table. "Those cigarettes, the cigars, the liquor. They give him away. Remember *our* first night in the Past?"

A month ago, on their first night in New York, before their flight, they had tasted all the strange drinks, bought odd foods, perfumes, cigarettes of ten dozen rare brands, for they were scarce in the Future, where war was everything. So they had made fools of themselves, rushing in and out of stores, salons, tobacconists', going up to their room to get wonderfully ill.

And now here was this stranger doing likewise, doing a thing that only a man from the Future would do, who had been starved for liquors and cigarettes too many years.

Susan and William sat and ordered a drink.

The stranger was examining their clothes, their hair, their jewelry, the way they walked and sat.

"Sit easily," said William under his breath. "Look as if you've worn this clothing style all your life."

"We should never have tried to escape."

"My God," said William. "He's coming over. Let me do the talking."

The stranger bowed before them. There was the faintest tap of heels knocking together. Susan stiffened. That military sound—unmistakable as that certain ugly rap on your door at midnight.

"Mr. Kristen," said the stranger, "you did not pull up your pant legs when you sat down."

William froze. He looked at his hands lying on either leg, innocently. Susan's heart was beating swiftly.

"You've got the wrong person," said William, quickly. "My name's not Krisler."

"*Kristen*," corrected the stranger.

"I'm William Travis," said William. "And I don't see what my pant legs have to do with you."

"Sorry." The stranger pulled up a chair. "Let us say I thought I knew you because you did *not* pull your trousers up. Everyone does. If they don't the trousers bag quickly. I am a long way from home, Mr.—Travis—and in need of company. My name is Simms."

"Mr. Simms, we appreciate your loneliness, but we're tired. We're leaving for Acapulco tomorrow."

"A charming spot. I was just there, looking for some friends of mine.

"They are somewhere. I shall find them yet. Oh, is the lady a bit sick?"

"Good night, Mr. Simms."

They started out the door, William holding Susan's arm firmly. They did not look back when Mr. Simms called. "Oh, just one other thing." He paused and then slowly spoke the words:

"Twenty-one fifty-five A.D."

Susan shut her eyes and felt the earth falter under her. She kept going, into the fiery plaza, seeing nothing. . . .

They locked the door of their hotel room. And then she was crying and they were standing in the dark, and the room tilted under them. Far away, firecrackers exploded, there was laughter in the plaza.

"What a damned, loud nerve," said William. "Him sitting there, looking us up and down like animals, smoking his damn cigarettes, drinking his drinks. I should have killed him then!" His voice was nearly hysterical. "He even had the nerve to use his real name to us. The Chief of the Searchers. And the thing about my pant legs. I should have pulled them up when I sat. It's an automatic gesture of this day and age. When I didn't do it, it set me off from the others. It made *him* think: Here's a man who never wore pants, a man used to breech-uniforms and Future styles. I could kill myself for giving us away!"

"No, no, it was my walk, these high heels, that did it. Our haircuts, so new, so fresh. Everything about us odd and uneasy."

William turned on the light. "He's still testing us. He's not positive of us, not completely. We can't run out on him, then. We can't make him certain. We'll go to Acapulco, leisurely."

"Maybe he *is* sure of us, but is just playing."

"I wouldn't put it past him. He's got all the time in the world. He can dally here if he wants, and bring us back to the Future sixty seconds after we left it. He might keep us wondering for days, laughing at us, before he acted."

Susan sat on the bed, wiping the tears from her face, smelling the old smell of charcoal and incense.

"They won't make a scene, will they?"

"They won't dare. They'll have to get us alone to put us in the Time Machine and send us back."

"There's a solution then," she said. "We'll never be alone, we'll always be in crowds."

Footsteps sounded outside their locked door.

They turned out the light and undressed in silence. The footsteps went away.

Susan stood by the window looking down at the plaza in the darkness. "So that building there is a church?"

"Yes."

"I've often wondered what a church looked like. It's been so long since anyone saw one. Can we visit it tomorrow?"

"Of course. Come to bed."

They lay in the dark room.

Half an hour later, their phone rang. She lifted the receiver. "Hello?"

"The rabbits may hide in the forest," said a voice, "but a fox can always find them."

She replaced the receiver and lay back straight and cold in the bed.

Outside, in the year 1938, a man played three tunes upon a guitar, one following another. . . .

During the night, she put her hand out and almost touched the year 2155. She felt her fingers slide over cool spaces of time, as over a corrugated surface, and she heard the insistent thump of marching feet, a million bands playing a million military tunes. She saw the fifty thousand rows of disease-culture in their aseptic glass tubes, her hand reaching out to them at her work in that huge factory in the Future. She saw the tubes of leprosy, bubonic, typhoid, tuberculosis. She heard the great explosion and saw her hand burned to a wrinkled plum, felt it recoil from a concussion so immense that the world was lifted and let fall, and all the buildings broke and people hemorrhaged and lay silent. Great volcanoes, machines, winds, avalanches slid down to silence and she awoke, sobbing, in the bed, in Mexico, many years away . . .

In the early morning, drugged with the single hour's sleep they had finally been able to obtain, they awoke to the sound of loud automobiles in the street. Susan peered down from the iron balcony at a small crowd of eight people only now emerging, chattering, yelling, from trucks and cars with red lettering on them. A crowd of Mexicans had followed the trucks.

"*Qué pasa?*" Susan called to a little boy.

The boy replied.

Susan turned back to her husband. "An American motion picture company, here on location."

"Sounds interesting." William was in the shower. "Let's watch them. I don't think we'd better leave today. We'll try to lull Simms."

For a moment, in the bright sun, she had forgotten that somewhere in the hotel, waiting, was a man smoking a thousand cigarettes, it seemed. She saw the eight loud, happy Americans below and wanted to call to them: "Save me, hide me, help me! I'm from the year 2155!"

But the words stayed in her throat. The functionaries of Travel In Time, Inc., were not foolish. In your brain, before you left on your trip, they placed a psychological block. You could tell no one your true time or birthplace, nor could you reveal any of the Future to those in the Past. The Past and the

Future must be protected from each other. Only with this hindrance were people allowed to travel unguarded through the ages. The Future must be protected from any change brought about by her people traveling in the Past. Even if Susan wanted to with all of her heart, she could not tell any of those happy people below in the plaza who she was, or what her predicament had become.

"What about breakfast?" said William

Breakfast was being served in the immense dining room. Ham and eggs for everyone. The place was full of tourists. The film people entered, all eight of them, six men and two women, giggling, shoving chairs about. And Susan sat near them feeling the warmth and protection they offered, even when Mr. Simms came down the lobby stairs, smoking his Turkish cigarette with great intensity. He nodded at them from a distance, and Susan nodded back, smiling, because he couldn't do anything to them here, in front of eight film people and twenty other tourists.

"Those actors," said William. "Perhaps I could hire two of them, say it was a joke, dress them in our clothes, have them drive off in our car, when Simms is in such a spot where he can't see their faces. If two people pretending to be us could lure him off for a few hours, we might make it to Mexico City. It would take him years to find us there!"

"Hey!"

A fat man, with liquor on his breath, leaned on their table. "American tourists!" he cried. "I'm so sick of seeing Mexicans, I could kiss you!" He shook their hands. "Come on, eat with us. Misery loves company. I'm Misery, this is Miss Gloom, and Mr. and Mrs. Do-We-Hate-Mexico! We all hate it. But we're here for some preliminary shots for a damn film. The rest of the crew arrives tomorrow. My name's Joe Melton, I'm a director, and if this ain't a hell of a country—funerals in the streets, people dying—come on, move over, join the party, cheer us up!"

Susan and William were both laughing.

"Am I funny?" Mr. Melton asked the immediate world.

"Wonderful!" Susan moved over.

Mr. Simms was glaring across the dining room at them.

She made a face at him.

Mr. Simms advanced among the tables.

"Mr. and Mrs. Travis!" he called. "I thought we were break-fasting together, alone?"

"Sorry," said William.

"Sit down, pal," said Mr. Melton. "Any friend of theirs is a pal of mine."

Mr. Simms sat. The film people talked loudly and while they talked, Mr. Simms said, quietly, "I hope you slept well."

"Did you?"

"I'm not used to spring mattresses," replied Mr. Simms, wryly. "But there are compensations. I stayed up half the night trying new cigarettes and foods. Odd, fascinating. A whole new spectrum of sensation, these ancient vices."

"We don't know what you're talking about," said Susan.

Simms laughed. "Always the play acting. It's no use. Nor is this stratagem of crowds. I'll get you alone soon enough. I'm immensely patient."

"Say," Mr. Melton broke in, "is this guy giving you any trouble?"

"It's all right."

"Say the word and I'll give him the bum's rush."

Melton turned back to yell at his associates. In the laughter, Mr. Simms went on: "Let us come to the point. It took me a month of tracing you through towns and cities to find you, and all of yesterday to be sure of you. If you come with me quietly, I might be able to get you off with no punishment—if you agree to go back to work on the Hydrogen-Plus bomb."

"We don't know what you're talking about."

"Stop it!" cried Simms, irritably. "Use your intelligence! You know we can't let you get away with this escape. Other people in the year 2155 might get the same idea and do the same. We need people."

"To fight your wars," said William.

"Bill!"

"It's all right, Susan. We'll talk on his terms now. We can't escape."

"Excellent," said Simms. "Really, you've both been incredibly romantic, running away from responsibilities."

"Running away from horror."

"Nonsense. Only a war."

"What are you guys talking about?" asked Mr. Melton.

Susan wanted to tell him. But you could only speak in

generalities. The psychological block in your mind allowed that. Generalities, such as Simms and William were now discussing.

"Only *the* war," said William. "Half the world dead of leprosy bombs!"

"Nevertheless," Simms pointed out, "the inhabitants of the Future resent you two hiding on a tropical isle, as it were, while they drop off the cliff into hell. Death loves death, not life. Dying people love to know that others die with them; it is a comfort to learn you are not alone in the kiln, in the grave. I am the guardian of their collective resentment against you two."

"Look at the guardian of resentments!" said Mr. Melton to his companions.

"The longer you keep me waiting, the harder it will go for you. We need you on the bomb project, Mr. Travis. Return now—no torture. Later, we'll force you to work and after you've finished the bomb, we'll try a number of complicated new devices on you, sir."

"I've got a proposition," said William. "I'll come back with you, if my wife stays here alive, safe, away from that war."

Mr. Simms debated. "All right. Meet me in the plaza in ten minutes. Pick me up in your car. Drive me to a deserted country spot. I'll have the Travel Machine pick us up there where there won't be any witnesses."

"Bill!" Susan held his arm tightly.

"Don't argue." He looked over at her. "It's settled." To Simms: "One thing. Last night, you could have got in our room and kidnaped us. Why didn't you?"

"Shall we say that I was enjoying myself?" replied Mr. Simms languidly, sucking his new cigar. "I hate giving up this wonderful atmosphere, this sun, this vacation. I regret leaving behind the wine and the cigarettes. Oh, how I regret it. The plaza then, in ten minutes. You wife will be protected and may stay here as long as she wishes. Say your good-byes."

Mr. Simms arose and walked out.

"There goes Mr. Big-Talk!" yelled Mr. Melton at the departing gentleman. He turned and looked at Susan. "Hey. Someone's crying. Breakfast's no time for people to cry, now *is* it?"

At nine-fifteen, Susan stood on the balcony of their room, gazing down at the plaza. Mr. Simms was seated there, his neat legs crossed, on a delicate bronze bench. Biting the tip from a cigar, he lighted it tenderly.

Susan heard the throb of a motor, and far up the street, out of a garage and down the cobbled hill, slowly, came William in his car.

The car picked up speed. Thirty, now forty, now fifty miles an hour. Chickens scattered before it.

Mr. Simms took off his white Panama hat and mopped his pink forehead, put his hat back on, and then saw the car.

It was rushing sixty miles an hour, straight on for the plaza.

"William!" screamed Susan.

The car hit the low plaza curb, thundering, jumped up, sped across the tiles toward the green bench where Mr. Simms now dropped his cigar, shrieked, flailed his hands, and was hit by the car. His body flew up and up in the air, and down, crazily, into the street.

On the far side of the plaza, one front wheel broken, the car stopped. People were running.

Susan went in and closed the balcony doors.

They came down the Official Palace steps together, arm in arm, their faces pale, at twelve noon.

"*Adiós, señor,*" said the mayor behind them. "*Señora.*"

They stood in the plaza where the crowd was pointing at the blood.

"Will they want to see you again?" asked Susan.

"No, we went over and over it. It was an accident. I lost control of the car. I wept for them. God knows I had to get my relief out somewhere. I *felt* like weeping. I hated to kill him. I've never wanted to do anything like that in my life."

"They won't prosecute you?"

"They talked about it, but no. I talked faster. They believe me. It was an accident. It's over."

"Where will we go? Mexico City?"

"The car's in the repair shop. It'll be ready at four this afternoon. Then we'll get the hell out."

"Will we be followed? Was Simms working alone?"

"I don't know. We'll have a little head start on them, I think."

The film people were coming out of the hotel as they approached. Mr. Melton hurried up, scowling. "Hey, I heard what happened. Too bad. Everything okay now? Want to get your minds off it? We're doing some preliminary shots up the street. You want to watch, you're welcome. Come on, do you good."

They went.

They stood on the cobbled street while the film camera was being set up. Susan looked at the road leading down and away, at the highway going to Acapulco and the sea, past pyramids and ruins and little adobe towns with yellow walls, blue walls, purple walls and flaming bougainvillaea. She thought: We shall take the roads, travel in clusters and crowds, in markets, in lobbies, bribe police to sleep near, keep double locks, but always the crowds, never alone again, always afraid the next person who passes might be another Simms. Never knowing if we've tricked and lost the Searchers. And always up ahead, in the Future, they'll wait for us to be brought back, waiting with their bombs to burn us and disease to rot us, and their police to tell us to roll over, turn around, jump through the hoop. And so we'll keep running through the forest, and we'll never ever stop or sleep well again in our lives.

A crowd gathered to watch the film being made. And Susan watched the crowd and the streets.

"Seen anyone suspicious?"

"No. What time is it?"

"Three o'clock. The car should be almost ready."

The test film was finished at three forty-five. They all walked down to the hotel, talking. William paused at the garage. "The car'll be ready at six," he said, coming out.

"But no later than that?"

"It'll be ready, don't worry."

In the hotel lobby they looked around for other men traveling alone, men who resembled Mr. Simms, men with new haircuts and too much cigarette smoke and cologne smell about them, but the lobby was empty. Going up the stairs, Mr. Melton said, "Well, it's been a long, hard day. Who'd like to put a header on it. Martini? Beer?"

"Maybe one."

The whole crowd pushed into Mr. Melton's room and the drinking began.

"Watch the time," said William.

Time, thought Susan, if only they had time. All she wanted was to sit in the plaza all of a long, bright day in spring, with not a worry or a thought, with the sun on her face and arms, her eyes closed, smiling at the warmth—and never move, but just sleep in the Mexican sun . . .

Mr. Melton opened the champagne.

"To a very beautiful lady, lovely enough for films," he said, toasting Susan. "I might even give you a test."

She laughed.

"I mean it," said Melton. "You're very nice. I could make you a movie star."

"And take me to Hollywood?"

"Get the hell out of Mexico, sure!"

Susan glanced at William, and he lifted an eyebrow and nodded. It would be a change of scene, clothing, locale, name perhaps, and they would be traveling with eight other people, a good shield against any interference from the future.

"It sounds wonderful," said Susan.

She was feeling the champagne now, the afternoon was slipping by, the party was whirling about her, she felt safe and good and alive and truly happy for the first time in many years.

"What kind of film would my wife be good for?" asked William, refilling his glass.

Melton appraised Susan. The party stopped laughing and listened.

"Well, I'd like to do a story of suspense," said Melton. "A story of a man and wife, like yourselves."

"Go on."

"Sort of a war story, maybe," said the director, examining the color of his drink against the sunlight.

Susan and William waited.

"A story about a man and wife who live in a little house on a little street in the year 2155, maybe," said Melton. "This is ad lib, understand. But this man and wife are faced with a terrible war, Super-Plus Hydrogen bombs, censorship, death, in that year and—here's the gimmick—they escape into the past, followed by a man who they think is evil, but who is only trying to show them what their Duty is."

William dropped his glass to the floor.

Mr. Melton continued. "And this couple take refuge with a group of film people whom they learn to trust. Safety in numbers, they say to themselves."

Susan felt herself slip down into a chair. Everyone was

watching the director. He took a little sip of wine. "Ah, that's a fine wine. Well, this man and woman, it seems, don't realize how important they are to the future. The man, especially, is the keystone to a new bomb metal. So the Searchers, let's call them, spare no trouble or expense to find, capture, and take home the man and wife, once they get them totally alone, in a hotel room, where no one can see. Strategy. The Searchers work alone, or in groups of eight. One trick or another will do it. Don't you think it would make a wonderful film, Susan? Don't you, Bill?" He finished his drink.

Susan sat with her eyes straight ahead.

"Have a drink?" said Mr. Melton.

William's gun was out and fired three times, and one of the men fell, and the others ran forward. Susan screamed. A hand was clamped to her mouth. Now the gun was on the floor and William was struggling with the men holding him.

Mr. Melton said, "Please," standing there where he had stood, blood showing on his fingers. "Let's not make matters worse."

Someone pounded on the hall door.

"Let me in!"

"The manager," said Mr. Melton, dryly. He jerked his head. "Everyone, let's move!"

"Let me in. I'll call the police!"

Susan and William looked at each other quickly, and then at the door.

"The manager wishes to come in," said Mr. Melton. "Quick!"

A camera was carried forward. From it shot a blue light which encompassed the room instantly. It widened out and the people of the party vanished, one by one.

"Quickly!"

Outside the window in the instant before she vanished, Susan saw the green land and the purple and yellow and blue and crimson walls and the cobbles flowing like a river, a man upon a burro riding into the warm hills, a boy drinking orange pop. She could feel the sweet liquid in her throat; she could see a man standing under a cool plaza tree with a guitar, could feel her hand upon the strings. And, far away, she could see the sea, the blue and tender sea; she could feel it roll her over and take her in.

And then she was gone. Her husband was gone.

The door burst wide. The manager and his staff rushed in.

The room was empty.

"But they were just here! I saw them come in, and now—gone!" cried the manager. "The windows are covered with iron grating; they couldn't get out that way!" . . .

In the late afternoon, the priest was summoned and they opened the room again and aired it out, and had him sprinkle holy water through each corner and give it his cleansing.

"What shall we do with these?" asked the charwoman.

She pointed to the closet, where there were sixty-seven bottles of chartreuse, cognac, *crème de cacao,* absinthe, vermouth, tequila, 106 cartons of Turkish cigarettes, and 198 yellow boxes of fifty-cent pure Havana-filler cigars. . . .

GERALD KERSH

River of Riches

About the man called Pilgrim there was a
certain air of something gone stale. "Seedy" is the word for it,
as applied to a human being. It was difficult to regard him except as a careful housewife regards a pot of homemade jam
upon the surface of which she observes a patch of mildew.
Sweet but questionable, she says to herself, *but it is a pity
to waste it. Give it to the poor.* So, as it seemed to me, it was
with Pilgrim.

He was curiously appealing to me in what looked like a
losing fight against Skid Row, and maintained a haughty reserve when the bartender, detaining him as he abstractedly
started to stroll out of MacAroon's Grill, said, "Daddle be a dollar-
ten, doc."

Pilgrim slapped himself on the forehead, and beat himself
about the pockets, and cried, "My wallet! I left it at home."

"Oh-oh," the bartender said, lifting the counter flap.

Then I said, "Here's the dollar-ten, Mike. Let the man go."

But Pilgrim would not go. He took me by the arm, and said in the old-fashioned drawling kind of Oxford accent, "No, but really, this is too kind! I'm afraid I can't reciprocate. As a fellow limey you will understand. One's position here becomes invidious. You see, I have only just now lost two fortunes, and am in the trough of the wave between the second and the third—which I assure you is not farther off than the middle of next month. I must get to Detroit. But allow me to introduce myself by the name by which I prefer to be known: John Pilgrim. Call me Jack. In honesty, I ought to tell you that this is not my real name. If some plague were to wipe out the male members of my family in a certain quarter of Middlesex, in England, I should be addressed very differently; and ride my horses, to boot. As matters stand, I am the younger son of a younger son, cast out with a few thousand pounds in my pocket, to make my fortune in Canada."

I asked, "Was that your first fortune?"

"Heavens, no! Man on the boat had an infallible system shooting dice. I arrived in Canada, sir, with four dollars and eighteen cents—and my clothes. I roughed it, I assure you. Clerk in a hardware store, dismissed on unjust suspicion of peculation; errand boy at a consulate, kicked out for what they called 'shaking down' an applicant for a visa, which was a lie; representative of a wine merchant, wrongly accused of drinking the samples. I went through the mill, I do assure you. And now I am offered a lucrative post in Detroit."

"Doing what?" I asked.

He said, "Checking things for a motor company."

"What things?"

"A word to the wise is sufficient. This is strictly hush-hush. Less said the better, what? But I can put you in the way of a few million dollars if you have time and money to spare."

"Pray do so," I said.

"I will. But not being a complete fool I will not be exact in my geography. Do you know Brazil? I know where there is a massive fortune in virgin gold in one of the tributaries of the Amazon. . . . Oh, dear, it really is a bitter fact that men with money who want some more insist on having the more before they lay out the less! Yet I tell you without the least reserve that I got about ten thousand ounces of pure gold out of the people who live by that river."

"How did you manage that?" I asked.

Pilgrim smiled at me, and said, "I dare say you have heard of the tocte nut? No? . . . Well, the tocte nut comes from Ecuador. It is something like an English walnut, only perfectly oval, almost. As in the case of the walnut, the kernel of the tocte nut resembles in its lobes, twists and convolutions, the human brain. It is bitter to eat, and is used generally by children for playing with, as we used to play with marbles.

"Ah, but this is in Ecuador. Go into Brazil, into a certain tributary of the Amazon, and I can show you a place where these nuts—or close relations of theirs—are taken very seriously indeed. The tribesmen do not call them tocte, but tictoc, and only adults play with these nuts in Brazil—for extremely high stakes too. Fortunes—as they are counted in these wild parts—are won or lost on one game with the tictoc nuts. The savages have a saying there: 'Tictoc takes twenty years to learn.' To proceed: . . ."

From vicissitude to vicissitude is the destiny of the younger son (he said). I could, of course, have written to my elder brother for money. In fact I did. But he didn't answer. In the end, I shipped as cook on a freighter bound for South America. I suspect it was running guns. The crew was composed of the offscourings of Lapland, Finland, Iceland and San Francisco.

I jumped ship first opportunity, with nothing in my pockets but the papers of an oiler named Martinsen which I must have picked up by accident, and looked, as one does, for a fellow countryman. Luckily—I have the most astonishing luck—I overheard a man in a bar ordering whisky and soda without ice. Blood calls to blood. I was at his elbow in a trice.

He was a huge fellow, and was about to go to the place—which, if you'll forgive me, I won't mention—prospecting for rubies. Desirous of civilized company, he invited me to come along with him—said he would make it worth my while—offered me a share in the profits. He found the equipment, of course: quinine, rifles, trade goods, shotguns, soap and all that.

His idea was that, the market being good just then, if the worst came to the worst we might make our expenses out of snake skin and alligator hide. His name was Grimes, but he knew a gentleman when he saw one. But he was accident prone. Exploring mud for rubies, Grimes stood on a log to steady himself. The log came to life, opened a pair of jaws, and carried him off—an alligator, of course. They tell me that a mature alligator can, with his jaws, exert a pressure of nearly one thousand pounds' weight. It upset me, I don't mind telling you. Ever since then I have never been able to look at an alligator without disgust. They bring me bad luck.

The following morning I awoke to find my attendants all gone. They had paid themselves in trade goods, leaving me with only what I slept in—pajamas—plus a rifle, a bandoleer of .30-.30 cartridges, my papers and some dried beef.

Goodness only knows what might have happened to me if I had not been rescued by cannibals—and jolly fine fellows they were too. Sportsmen, I assure you. They only ate women past marriageable age. They took me to their chief. I thought I was in a pretty sticky spot, at first, but he gave me some stew to eat—it was monkey, I hope—and while I ate I looked about me. Anyone could see with half an eye that the old gentleman wanted my rifle.

Now I reasoned as follows: I am outnumbered about two hundred and fifty to one by savages armed with spears and poisoned arrows. In the circumstances my rifle must be worse than useless. Better make a virtue of the inevitable and give it to him before he takes it away. Be magnanimous, Jack!

So, expressing delight at the flavor of the stew, I gave him the rifle and the bandoleer. He was overwhelmed with joy and gratitude and wanted to know what he could do for me. He offered me girls, more stew, necklaces of human teeth. I conveyed to him that I might prefer a few rubies. Heartbroken, he said that he had none of the red stones, only the green ones, and handed me a fistful of emeralds to the value, conservatively, of a thousand rifles at a hundred and twenty dollars apiece.

I thanked him politely, controlling my emotions as our sort of people are brought up to do. But he mistook my impassive air for disappointment. He was downcast for a moment or two. Then he brightened and said to me, "Wait. I have something that will make you very rich. It has made me chief. But now I am too old to play. I will give it to you."

Then he fumbled in what might laughingly be described as

his clothes, and produced—guess what—a nut! Upon my word, a common nut, something like a walnut, but smooth and much larger in circumference at one end than at the other. Through years of handling, it had a wonderful patina, like very old bronze. "You know tictoc?" the old boy asked.

"I know tocte," I said. "It is a game played by children in Ecuador."

"You play?" he asked.

"Never. In Ecuador I have seen it played. In England we call it marbles."

"Of these places," said the chief, "I have never heard. Here, it is tictoc."

Then he went on to explain—it took all night—that the tictoc nut was not like other nuts. Everything, said the chief, everything could think a little. Even a leaf had sense enough to turn itself to the light. Even a rat. Even a woman. Sometimes, even a hard-shelled nut. Now when the world was made, the deuce of a long time ago, man having been created, there was a little intelligence left over for distribution. Woman got some. Rats got some. Leaves got some. Insects got some. In short, at last there was very little left.

Then the tictoc bush spoke up and begged, "A little for us?"

The answer came, "There are so many of you, and so little left to go around. But justice must be done. One in every ten million of you shall think with a man, and do his bidding. We have spoken."

So, the old geezer affirmed, the kernel of the tictoc nut came to resemble the human brain. Stroking his great knife, he assured me that he had many times seen one, and the resemblance was uncanny. Superficially, you understand.

To only one tictoc nut in ten million was vouchsafed the gift of thought. And the nuts, being very prolific, grew in the jungles in great profusion. Anyone who could find the ten-millionth nut, the thinking nut, was assured of good fortune, the old savage told me, because this nut would obey its master.

"Now play tictoc," he said.

I said, "But I don't know how."

He did not answer, but led me to a strip of ground stamped flat and level, and polished by innumerable feet. At one end someone had described a circle drawn with ocher. In this circle were arranged ten nuts in this pattern:

```
                    o

            o               o

        o                       o

                o

        o                   o


                o       o
```

The object of the game was to knock the ten nuts out of the circle in the fewest possible shots. As a game, I should say that tictoc was much more difficult than pool, pyramids or snooker. You shot from a distance of about seven feet. It was a good player who could clear the circle in five shots; a remarkable one who could do it in four; a superlative one who could do it in three, flipping the oval tictoc nut with a peculiar twist of the thumb.

Several young fellows were playing, but more were betting their very loincloths on the champion, who had recently made a Three.

"Now," the old codger whispered, "rub the tictoc between your hands, breathe on it and shout without sound—shout at the back of your mind—telling it what to do. Challenge the champion. Stake your shirt."

The top of my pajamas could be no great loss. Furthermore, I had the emeralds, you know. So I took it off and offered my challenge. The young buck felt the cotton and put down against it a necklace of good nuggets, the largest of which was about as big as a grape.

He played first. On his first shot, out went five. Second, out went four. The last was easy. He had scored a Three.

And now it was my turn. Caressing my nut I said to it, without talking, "Now, old thing, show them what you can do. Try for a One, just to astonish the natives."

Without much hope, and with no skill at all, I flipped my nut. It seemed to stop halfway, gyrating. Everybody laughed, and my opponent reached for my pajama top—when, suddenly, my nut kind of shouldered its way forward into the circle, and with something devilishly like careful aim, spun its way into the ten and pushed them, one by one, beyond the bounds of the ring.

You never heard such a shout! I had broken a record. Picking my nut up, I caressed it and warmed it in my hand.

The chief said, "This I have never seen. Two, yes. One, no. I know what it is—the markings inside that nut must exactly match the markings of your brain. You are a lucky man."

Feeling the weight of the necklace I had won, I asked, "Is there any more stuff like this hereabout?"

He said no, they didn't regard it especially. The ex-champion had won it downstream, where they picked it out of the river bed and gave it to their women for ornaments. A string of your enemy's teeth meant something. But the yellow stuff was too soft and too heavy. "If you want it, take your tictoc nut and you can win as much of it as you can carry away—you and ten strong men."

I promised him that when I came back I would bring more guns and bullets, hatchets, knives, and all his heart could desire, if he would lend me a good canoe and the services of half a dozen sturdy men to paddle it, together with food and water. He agreed, and we took off.

In fine, I cleaned out that village and went on downstream with two war canoes, all loaded with gold and other valuables, such as garnets, emeralds, et cetera. I should have left it at that. But success had gone to my head.

On the way I stayed the night in the shack of a petty trader, a Portuguese, from whom I bought a whole suit of white-duck clothes, a couple of shirts, and pants and some other stuff. "Your fame has gone before you," he said, looking enviously at me and then at the gold nuggets I had paid him with. "They call you the Tictoc Man up and down the river. Now I happen to know that no white man can play tictoc—it takes twenty years to learn. How do you do it?"

I said, "A mere knack."

"Well, give me another nugget and I'll give you some good advice. . . . Thank you. My advice is, make straight for the big river, and so to the coast. Don't stop to play at the next village—there is only one—or you may regret it. The Esporco are the most villainous Indians in these parts. Don't push even your luck too far. Four ounces of gold, and I'll let you have a fine weapon, a revolver, all the way from Belgium."

The revolver I took, but not his advice, and we went on at dawn. In the late afternoon several canoes came out to meet us. My men spat and said, "Esporco, master—very bad."

"What, will they attack us?" I asked.

"No." They indicated that the Esporco Indian was the worst trickster and cheat in the Mato Grosso. But I fondled the tictoc nut, while observing that in every canoe sat a girl wearing a necklace of raw rubies, and little else. The men—big fellows, as Indians go—had an easy, cozy way with them, all smiles, no weapons, full of good humor. They hailed me as Senhor Tictoc, while the girls threw flowers.

My leading paddler, the stroke, as it were, growled, "When Esporco bring flowers, keep your hand on your knife"—a savage version of *Timeo Danaos et dona ferentes*.

Still, I gave orders to land, and was received with wild delight. The chief ordered several young goats killed. I presented him with a sack of salt, which is highly prized thereabout. There was a banquet with a profusion of some slightly effervescent drink in the nature of the Mexican mescal, only lighter and breezier.

In a little while we started to talk business. I expressed interest in rubies. The chief said, "Those red things? But they are nothing." And, taking a magnificent necklace from one of the girls, he tossed it into the river—I was to learn, later, that he had a net there to catch it. "I have heard that you are interested in stones," said he, while I gaped like a fish. And he went away and came back with an uncut diamond of the Brazilian variety, as big as your two fists.

I displayed no emotion, but said, "Interesting. How much do you want for it?"

He said, "It has no price. I have been around, and know the value your people set on such stones. I also know—we all know on this river—what would happen if the news got about that there was gold, rubies, emeralds and diamonds hereabout. Your people would come down on us like jaguars, and drive us off the face of the earth. As it is, we have enough, we are contented, we regard such stuff as this as pretty for unmarried girls. No, my friend, it is not for sale. But I tell you what. It being a plaything, let us play for it. You have a great reputation as a tictoc player. As it happens, so have I. Now what have you to stake against this stone?"

"Three canoeloads of treasure," I said.

At this, one of his sons chimes in with, "Don't do it, father! The man is a wizard. All the river knows it. He has a thinking nut!"

Apparently tipsy, the chief shouted, "Silence, brat! There is no such thing. It is a superstition. Tictoc is a game of skill, and I am the best man on this river." He became angry. "Who questions my skill?"

Nobody did. The circle was made, the ten nuts arranged at their proper distances. I begged my host to shoot first. There was a breathless hush as he went down on his knees and shot a perfect Two—at which there was a murmur of applause.

Then I stroked my nut and asked it for a One. Out it went, spinning like a little whirlwind, and a One it was.

It is etiquette, in the tictoc game, for the winner to pick up the fighting nuts and bring them back to the base. Loser shoots first. This time the chief shot a Three. I was feeling warm-hearted. Who wouldn't, if he was certain to win a diamond that would make the Koh-i-noor and the Cullinan diamonds look like stones in a fifty-dollar engagement ring? So I said to my nut, "This time, for the sport of the thing, get me a Five. But last shot we'll have another One and the best out of three games."

It did as it was bid, and I lost with a Five. The Chief, much elated, got our nuts and handed me mine with grave courtesy. I shot with perfect confidence. Imagine my horror when, instead of moving with grace and deliberation, it reeled drunkenly forward and barely reached the periphery of the circle! I wondered, could that mescal-like stuff I had drunk have gone to its head through mine? Thinking with all my might, I shot again—and knocked one nut out of the ring. A third time, and I finished with an Eight.

The chief went to pick up our nuts. I was numb with grief. He handed me the nut I had played that last game with. I looked at it—and it was not my own!

Then the truth dawned on me. The old rascal had swapped nuts after the second game! Simple as that. But I kept my temper, because in a split second everybody had stopped laughing, and every man had produced a machete, an ax, a bow or a spear. I said, "There is some mistake here, sir. This is not my tictoc nut."

"Then whose it it?"

"Yours. You are, no doubt inadvertently, holding mine in your hand. Give it back, if you please."

And driven beyond prudence, I made a grab at it. I was fast, but he was faster, and surprisingly strong. I, too, am tolerably strong in the fingers. We stood locked, hand to hand, for about twenty seconds. Then I heard and felt a sharp little crack. So did he, for he stood back, waving away his tribesmen who were closing in.

He held out his hand with dignity; it held the common tictoc nut that he had palmed off on me. In my palm lay my own true nut, but split down the center, exposing the kernel.

I looked at it, fascinated. You know, I studied medicine once—might be in Harley Street by now, only there was a bureaucratic misunderstanding about four microscopes I borrowed. Silly old asses! I'd have got them out of pawn and put them back where I'd found them, as soon as my remittance came in. But no, they gave me the sack.

However, I have read some anatomy, and I solemnly swear that the kernel of my poor tictoc nut definitely and in detail resembled the human brain—convolutions, lobes, cerebrum, cerebellum, medulla—in every respect.

Most remarkable of all, when I touched it affectionately with my finger tip, it throbbed very faintly, and then lay still. Whereupon some of the virtue seemed to drain out of me, and I cried like a child.

But I pulled myself together and said, "Well, the bet is off. The game is null and void. Let me get my men together and push off."

Then, in the light of torches, I saw bundles on the shore—very familiar bundles.

"To save your men unnecessary exertion," the chief said, "I had them unload your canoes for you. I wish you no harm, but put it to you that you go quietly back where you belong. Come, you shall not go empty handed. Take as many small nuggets as your two hands can hold, and depart in peace. You overreached yourself. I would have given you the diamond for the thinking nut, and gladly, in fair exchange. But no, you had to cheat, to do bad trade, to bet on a sure thing. In this life, nothing is sure."

I said, holding out the revolver, "And what will you give me for this?"

"Oh, two double handfuls of gold."

"May I suggest three?"

"If you will allow me to test it first."

I did. He fired one shot into the dark. I took the gun back and said, "First, the gold."

Down by the river I took the liberty of scooping up a handful of heavy clay and filling up the barrel of that revolver. It would dry like brick. That old rogue would never play tictoc again.

But in burying the remains of my thinking nut, I had a weird feeling that I was leaving behind a certain essential portion of myself. Gold and jewels I can get again. But that, never.

"So I got to the coast and took ship, as a passenger this time, on a heavy freighter bound for Tampa, Florida. What with one thing and another, I arrived with only a few nuggets left, which I keep as . . . I don't know, call it keepsakes. You have been very kind to me. Let me give you one—a very little one—and then I must be on my way. Have this one."

He dropped a heavy gold pellet on the wet table. It was not much larger than a pea, but shaped, or misshapen, beyond human conception. Fire and water had done that.

"Have it made into a tie pin," said Pilgrim.

"But I couldn't take a valuable thing like this," I cried, "without doing something for you in return!"

"Not a bit of it. We limeys must stick together, and I'm on my way to Detroit. About seven days from now, John Pilgrim, at Detroit's leading hotel, will find me. Help me on my way, if you like, but—" He shrugged.

"I have only ten dollars," I said, deeply moved by a certain sadness in Pilgrim's eyes. "You're welcome to that."

"You're very obliging. It shall be returned with interest."

"I must go now," I said.

"So must I," said he.

Marveling at the intricacies of the human mind, I walked until I found myself on Sixth Avenue, near West 46th Street, in which area congregate those who, with pitying smiles and a certain kind of shrug, can flaw a diamond carat by carat until you are ashamed to own it, and with a shake of the head depreciate a watch until it stops of its own accord. On impulse I went into a shop there and, putting down Pilgrim's nugget, asked what such a bit of gold might be worth.

His reply was, "Ya kiddin'? Tickle me so I'll laugh. What's the current price of printer's metal? . . . Worth? Kugel's Kute Nov-

elties sell those twelve for fifty cents, mail order. I can get 'em
for ya a dollar for two dozen. A teaspoonful lead, melt it and
drop it in cold water. You can honestly advertise 'no two alike.'
Gild 'em, and there's a nugget. A miniature gold brick. That
manufacturer, so he puts out loaded dice 'for amusement only'
—he sells 'em too. Seriously, did you buy this?"

I said, "Yes and no." But as I dropped the nugget into my
pocket and turned to go, the shopman said, "Wait a minute,
mister—it's a nice imitation and a good job of plating. Maybe
I might give you a couple bucks for it!"

"Oh, no, you won't," I said, my suspicions aroused. I fondled
the nugget in my pocket; it had the indescribable, authentic
feel of real gold. As for that trick with melted lead and cold
water, I suddenly remembered that I had played it myself about
thirty years ago, with some broken toy soldiers, just for the
sake of playing with fire. Recently-melted lead has a feel all its
own, and is sharp at the edges. But my nugget felt old and
worn.

"It could be, after forty years, for once I made a mistake," the
man said. "Let's have another look."

But I went out, and visited another shop a few doors away:
one of those double-fronted establishments, in the right-hand
window of which, under a sign which says OLD GOLD BOUGHT,
there lies a mess of pinchbeck bracelets, ancient watch chains,
old false teeth and tie pins. In the other window, diamonds
carefully carded and priced at anything between two thousand
and fifteen thousand dollars. The proprietor, here, looked as if
he were next door but one to the breadline.

I put down my nugget and said boldly, "How much for this?"

He scrutinized the nugget, put it in a balance and weighed
it; then tested it on a jeweler's stone, with several kinds of
acid. "Voigin gold," he said. "Where'd you get it?"

"A friend gave it to me."

"I wish I had such friends." He called, "Oiving, come here a
minute," and a younger man came to his side. "What d'you make
of this?"

Irving said, "It ain't African gold. It ain't Indian gold. It
ain't a California nugget. I say South America."

"Good boy. Correct."

"How can you tell?" I asked.

He shrugged. "You loin," he said. "How d'you tell the differ-

ence between salt and sugar? You loin. . . . The market value
of this little bit voigin gold is about forty dollars. I got to make
a buck—I'll give you thoity-five."

"Eh?"

"Thoity-six, and not a penny more," he said, counting out
the money. "And if your friend gives you any more, come to me
with 'em."

I took the money, caught a taxi, and hurried back to Mac-
Aroon's place. The bartender was gazing into space.

"That man I was sitting with," I said, "where is he?"

The bartender, with a sardonic smile, said, "He put the bite
on you, huh? I can smell a phony a mile off. I didn't like the
looks of him as soon as he set foot in my bar. If I was you—"

"Which way did he go?"

"I didn't notice. Soon after you left he ordered a double, no
ice and put down a ten-dollar bill—left me fifty cents, and went
out."

"Here's my telephone number," I said. "If he turns up again,
call me any hour of the day or night, and hold him till I get
here. Here's five dollars on account; another five when you call."

But Pilgrim never came to MacAroon's again.

I inquired high and low—mostly low—but found no trace of
him. A British-sounding man with an insinuating air, a ma-
larial complexion and a misleading eccentric manner, who
talks about the River Amazon and its tributaries—I will pay a
substantial reward for information leading to his rediscovery.

JOSEPH PAYNE BRENNAN

Levitation

Morgan's Wonder Carnival moved into Riverville for an overnight stand, setting up its tents in the big ball park on the edge of the village. It was a warm evening in early October and by seven o'clock a sizable crowd had made its way to the scene of raucous amusement.

The traveling show was neither large nor particularly impressive of its type, but its appearance was eagerly welcomed in Riverville, an isolated mountain community many miles from the motion picture houses, vaudeville theatres and sports arenas situated in larger towns.

The natives of Riverville did not demand sophisticated entertainment; consequently the inevitable Fat Lady, the Tattooed Man and the Monkey Boy kept them chattering animatedly for many minutes at a time. They crammed peanuts and buttered popcorn into their mouths, drank cup after cup of pink lemonade, and got their fingers all but stuck together trying to scrape the paper wrappers off colored taffy candies.

Everyone appeared to be in a relaxed and tolerant state of mind when the barker for the Hypnotist began his spiel. The barker, a short stocky man wearing a checkered suit, bellowed through an improvised megaphone, while the Hypnotist himself remained aloof at the rear of the plank platform erected in front of his tent. He appeared disinterested, scornful, and he scarcely deigned to glance at the gathering crowd.

At length, however, when some fifty souls had assembled in front of the platform, he stepped forward into the light. A murmur went up from the crowd.

In the harsh overhead electric glare, the Hypnotist made a striking appearance. His tall figure, thin to the point of emaciation, his pale complexion, and most of all his dark, sunken eyes, enormous and brilliant, compelled immediate attention. His dress, a severe black suit and an archaic black string tie, added a final Mephistophelean touch.

He surveyed the crowd coolly, with an expression betraying resignation and a kind of quiet contempt.

His sonorous voice reached to the far edge of the throng. "I will require one volunteer from among you," he said. "If someone will kindly step up—"

Everyone glanced around, or nudged his neighbor, but nobody advanced toward the platform.

The Hypnotist shrugged. "There can be no demonstration," he said in a weary voice, "unless one of you is kind enough to come up. I assure you, ladies and gentlemen, the demonstration is quite harmless, quite without danger."

He looked around expectantly and presently a young man slowly elbowed through the crowd toward the platform.

The Hypnotist helped him up the steps and seated him in a chair.

"Relax," said the Hypnotist. "Presently you will be asleep and you will do exactly what I tell you to do."

The young man squirmed on the chair, grinning self-consciously toward the crowd.

The Hypnotist caught his attention, fixing his enormous eyes on him, and the young man stopped squirming.

Suddenly someone in the crowd threw a large ball of colored popcorn toward the platform. The popcorn arched over the lights, landing squarely atop the head of the young man sitting in the chair.

He jerked sideways, almost falling off the chair, and the crowd, quiet a moment before, guffawed boisterously.

The Hypnotist was furious. He turned scarlet and literally shook with rage as he glared at the crowd.

"Who threw that?" he demanded in a choking voice.

The crowd grew silent.

The Hypnotist continued to glare at them. At length the color left his face and he stopped trembling, but his brilliant eyes remained baleful.

Finally he nodded to the young man seated on the platform, dismissing him with brief thanks, and turned again toward the crowd.

"Due to the interruption," he announced in a low voice, "it will be necessary to recommence the demonstration—with a new subject. Perhaps the person who threw the popcorn would care to come up?"

At least a dozen people in the crowd turned to gaze at someone who stood half in shadow at the rear of the gathering.

The Hypnotist spotted him at once; his dark eyes seemed to smoulder. "Perhaps," he said in a purring, mocking voice, "the one who interrupted is afraid to come up. He prefers to hide in the shadows and throw popcorn!"

The culprit voiced a sudden exclamation and then pushed belligerently toward the platform. His appearance was not in any way remarkable; in fact, he somewhat resembled the first young man, and any casual observer would have placed the two of them in the farm-laborer class, neither more nor less capable than the average.

The second young man sat down in the platform chair with a distinct air of defiance and for some minutes visibly fought the Hypnotist's suggestion to relax. Presently, however, his aggressiveness disappeared and he dutifully stared into the smouldering eyes opposite his own.

In another minute or two he arose at the Hypnotist's command and lay flat on his back on the hard planks of the platform. The crowd gasped.

"You will fall asleep," the Hypnotist told him. "You will fall asleep. You are falling asleep. You are falling asleep. You are asleep and you will do anything which I command you to do. Anything which I command you to do. Anything. . . ."

His voice droned on, repeating repetitious phrases, and the crowd grew perfectly silent.

Suddenly a new note entered the Hypnotist's voice and the audience became tense.

"Do not stand up—but *rise from the platform!*" the Hypnotist commanded. "*Rise from the platform!*" His dark eyes became wild and luminous-looking and the crowd shivered.

"*Rise!*"

Then the crowd drew in its collective breath with an audible start.

The young man lying rigid on the platform, without moving a muscle, began to ascend horizontally. He arose slowly, almost imperceptively at first, but soon with a steady and unmistakable acceleration.

"*Rise!*" the Hypnotist's voice rang out.

The young man continued to ascend, until he was feet off the platform, and still he did not stop.

The crowd was sure it was some kind of trick, but in spite of themselves they stared open-mouthed. The young man appeared to be suspended and moving in mid-air without any possible means of physical support.

Abruptly the focus of the crowd's attention was shifted; the Hypnotist clasped a hand to his chest, staggered, and crumpled to the platform.

There were calls for a doctor. The barker in the checkered suit appeared out of the tent and bent over the motionless form.

He felt for a pulse, shook his head and straightened up. Someone offered a bottle of whiskey, but he merely shrugged.

Suddenly a woman in the crowd screamed.

Everyone turned to look at her and a second later followed the direction of her gaze.

Immediately there were further cries—for the young man whom the Hypnotist had put to sleep was still ascending. While the crowd's attention had been distracted by the fatal collapse of the Hypnotist, he had continued to rise. He was now a good seven feet above the platform and moving inexorably upward. Even after the death of the Hypnotist, he continued to obey that final ringing command: "*Rise!*"

The barker, eyes all but popping out of his head, made a frantic upward leap, but he was too short. His fingers barely brushed the moving figure above and he fell heavily back to the platform.

The rigid form of the young man continued to float upward, as if he were being hoisted by some kind of invisible pulley. Women began screaming hysterically; men shouted. But no one knew what to do. A look of terror crept over the face of the barker as he stared up. Once he glanced wildly toward the sprawled shape of the Hypnotist.

"Come down, Frank! Come down!" the crowd shrieked. "Frank! Wake up! Come down! Stop! Frank!"

But the rigid form of Frank moved ever upward. Up, up, until he was level with the top of the carnival tent, until he reached the height of the tallest trees—until he passed the trees and moved on into the soft moonlit sky of early October.

Many in the crowd threw hands over horror-stricken faces and turned away.

Those who continued to stare saw the floating form ascend into the sky until it was no more than a tiny speck, like a little cinder drifting far up near the moon.

Then it disappeared altogether.

CHRISTINE NOBLE GOVAN

Miss Winters and the Wind

Miss Winters stood on the corner with her bus transfer held tightly in her hand and hated the wind. There had been a feud between Miss Winters and the wind for all the years that she had lived in this flat, dreadful city. It seemed to pick her out—a lone, forlorn little figure—to vent its nasty, playful vindictivenss upon. It pulled at her droopy felt hat and whipped her straggly hair about her face, grabbed up her skirt in bawdy mischief, exposing her black cotton stockings.

Once, when she had been coming home from her work, it had snatched the transfer from her hand and blown it under a passing bus. When the bus had gone, Miss Winters had peered through the dusk, searching everywhere; but the bit of yellow paper eluded her. People crowding about her had almost pushed her under a truck and had sworn at her impatiently. It had been the day before payday and she had only the fare back to work in the morning. She had to walk the rest of the way home—three miles, and all against the wind.

When she had lived in the South as a child, the wind had been a lovesome thing. The mountains kept it properly in hand and broke it as one breaks a mettlesome colt. It blew against the mountains tops and was parted into bits by the trees, which roiled and hummed with a sound like the sea. Over the fields, wild broom swept gently, making them rippling, molten seas of red-gold, liquid beauty. In school, when she read *Hiawatha,* her narrow face lighted momentarily at the lines:

> As in sunshine gleam the ripples
> That the cold wind makes in rivers.

She had not known what a cold wind really was.

But now she knew. It was what seeped in at the ledges and made her feet numb in spite of the fire she so assiduously tended. It got into bed with her at night so that even her striped cat which crept under the covers shivered, getting up all through the cold black hours to turn his aching bones and seek to warm another surface. It blew through her worn coat and crept into the jagged hole in her flannel bloomers, where she had snagged them on the wire clothesline on the roof. It tore at her fingers in their patched gloves until they burned in an agony of freezing.

Her mother had come from this unspeakable section. And after Miss Winters' father had died, the old lady had yearned to come home. The wind had been too much for her, Miss Winters remembered with grim satisfaction. Two seasons of it and the old lady had been carried off with pleurisy.

Miss Winters had had a fairly comfortable business then. She did "Fine and Fancy Sewing, Prices Reasonable." A flat-chested spinster, whose maidenly longings had burned to a black ash years before, she made babies' frocks with minute embroidered yokes as delicate as frost, bridal gowns, and perky pinafores for chubby little girls.

Her mother's illness and death was an expense. The depression came. She moved to meaner quarters, quarters evidently coveted by the wind, since it came in at every opportunity. She was lonely and anxious and sometimes afraid. Fear clutched at her throat like an actual hand, making it difficult to swallow.

Then the WPA gave her sewing to do. She made thick sacks and heavy work garments. Her hands grew stiff and raw at the clumsy work, and she thought of the women she had draped in

silk and and crepe de Chine, of the flounced embroideries of
her girlhood.

The worst blow came when the project was closed. Women
wore slacks and worked in factories and bought ready-made
things. They had no time to try on Miss Winters' meticulously
fashioned garments. Her old customers died or went to Florida
where the wind was less bitter. Miss Winters' fright crept over
her like a slowly rising tide. The hands which had once fashioned sprays of lilies of the valley on batiste and lawn had
grown arthritic with the cold and with coarse work. All she
could get was mending now, and occasional work at an alteration shop.

The bus was crowded, and Miss Winters had to stand. On the
street in which she lived, the cold had killed even the smell of
garlic and cabbage. But the wind was there blowing the papers
about, sending smoke and dust into her face and tugging at her
hat until her eyes filled with tears of vexation.

She had two flights of stairs to climb before she got to her
rooms. The cat was there waiting, curled up in the middle of
the bed. He jumped down, stretching his lanky, striped body,
and called to her—the only creature left who greeted her as a
friend. With the cat she could sometimes forget the clutching
fear. His confidence in her gave her a meager courage and
determination. Yet she feared for him, too; so many people
were unkind to cats, especially if they were homeless.

"Wuzee lonesome, muzzer's boofu puwussycat?" she asked
through chapped lips. "Muzzer'll build ums a fire. Muzzer'll
feed him."

The cat, as if in appreciation of such obviously idiotic devotion, writhed against her skirt and purred.

Miss Winters, still gloved, laid the sticks and the precious bits
of coal in the ashy grate and set a match to them. The damned
wind came down the chimney and blew out the flame, scattering ashes over the hearth and over her desperately polished
shoes.

At last she got the fire burning feebly. She set a pan of water
on the gas ring for tea. While it heated, she sat in the deep-
bottomed rocker before the hearth, her legs spread comfortably,
her hands folded against her body for warmth. The cat jumped
on her lap, nudging her with determined, silken buttings
under the chin, and she put her arms around him gratefully.

He was something alive in the bare room, something to make her forget a little the rising tide of her fright. The rent—it took all she made at the shop—there was the thirty-seven cents due the milkman—her shoe soles—the fear was always there. Haunted by it, she had bungled a garment at the alteration shop and had nearly lost her day's work there. Cold that was not from the wind filled her at the memory.

The cat stood on his legs, purring and sliding his velvety nose against her face, making a winning sound that was both a purr and a mew. In a sudden burst of tenderness she hugged him to her and he stared up at her smugly, his eyes green moons with mysteriously golden crevices in them.

She jumped up and made the tea, pouring a little milk from a can and some of the hot water into a saucer for the cat. From her purse she took a chop bone she had wheedled from one of her fellow workers. It had a sliver of meat upon it and gave forth an enticing fragrance of pepper and fried flesh. She pulled the meat off, looking about the bare room shamefacedly, and ate it slowly, tears of self-pity welling for a moment in her eyes. Then she stooped and set the bone with its ruffle of cold suet by the cat's saucer. The cat left the milk and began to gnaw fastidiously at the suet, the tip of his tail curling in and out with satisfaction.

Miss Winters took off her hat and drank her tea. She sat and sipped it and watched the cat, savoring the beauty of his gaunt grace and the wonder of his green and depthless eyes.

The wind was rising. The room grew colder and colder as the darkness deepened. Miss Winters took off her outer garments and brought her flannel gown and heated it by the fire. She heated more water and filled a fruit jar to slip between the frigid sheets. Then, armed with the cat and the jar, and banking the meager coals to hold the heat as long as possible, she crept into bed. The spotted bulb beside her bed gave scarcely enough light to read the sensational love-story magazine with which she escaped into forgetfulness each night.

Hours later she was awakened. The wind, not content to torment her by day, to make every waking hour a misery and a threat, must arouse her by night and bring her back to the grim knowledge from which in her dreams she had a brief escape.

It howled around the chimney, it battered the windows so that they rattled in their frames. The window that Miss Winters had patched with a wide piece of butcher's paper seemed to bulge as if at any moment it would burst and hurtle across the room.

Something blew down on the roof and continued to rattle and bounce, making it impossible to sleep. The cold seemed a tangible thing, raking her spine, nipping her face, pinching at her feet where the already chilly fruit jar mocked any idea of comfort. She turned on the light as though it might warm her. The cat crawled out and moved nervously about the bed.

There came a particularly vicious gust of wind. It screamed and threw itself at the cracked window. The glass ripped apart and was scattered like shrapnel. The cat leaped from the bed, meeting a spear of the glass in midair. He gave a scream and dropped wearily. Over the yellowish matting rug the bright splashes of his blood were blown like the petals of a rose.

Miss Winters rose from the intricate wrappings of the bed. She was cold, but with the cold of insensate fury. She went across the broken glass and picked up the limp body. The lovely green eyes were glazing and the blood dripped in warm splotches on her stockinged feet.

She stood there for a long, long time. At last she laid the cat down and said absently, "This has gone far enough."

She knew at last what she must do, and consequently felt calm. Going to the bed, she ripped off the covers, the coat she wore in the daytime, the quilt that was made of all the velvet and silks of her happier days. She got the sheet, a huge, patched affair, and she shook it out, looking at it thoughtfully.

It was so clear, so simple, that she wondered she had not thought of it before. She must catch the wind and tie it firmly in something so that never again could it get away, frightening and harassing poor old women, keeping them awake to the knowledge of their misery, killing their cats. She put on her shoes and, without giving the cat another look, opened the door and began to walk resolutely down the stairs.

"Who has seen the wind?" she sang in the treble of her childhood, as the wind tore at her long flannel gown and tried to take the sheet away from her.

"Ha! Ha!" she chuckled, holding the sheet closer to her. "Not this time, my fine friend! Not this time!"

"Who has seen the wind? Where does the wind go—up high— up high, high in the sky!"

She looked at the church steeple. It was the highest thing in sight. It shone there even on this dark night, a dull, gleaming spear. A spear had killed the cat. The wind had a spear. She would kill the wind.

"Q.E.D.," she chuckled, from some forgotten pigeonhole.

You got at the tower of the church through a little door in the rear. As she had expected, it was not locked, and without hesitation she began her purposeful ascent. Up and up, around and around, tripping over the sheet, stepping on the hem of her gown, stumbling, laughing and going on again. There was no wind inside the tower, but she was not deceived. It was waiting for her at the top—*and she was waiting for it!*

At last she reached the little room where the chimes were, a square room with open Gothic arches and a balcony off to one side. The wind was there, as she expected, ramping and growling about like a lion. But she was no longer afraid of it.

"We shall see!" she crooned happily. "We shall see!"

She shook out the sheet. Of course the wind tried to take it, but she caught the four corners together skillfully and stepped out on the little ledge. The lights in the town glimmered and twinkled far below. She looked at them placidly as if to say, "Just watch me! I'm fixing this devilish fellow once and for all!"

Just then the wind came at her. It gave a swoop and she caught it in the sheet which billowed like a huge loaf of rising bread. She had to leap to get it, but she had it there! She was so happy, so relieved, she felt as though she were simply walking on air!

She looked down and the lights rushed toward her. She had one icy moment before she died—one moment in which to know that the wind had won.

MIKE MARMER

View from the Terrace

The red-orange sun eased its way out of the
Jamaican sky, then suspended itself halfway into the Carib-
bean horizon as though holding still for some divine time ex-
posure. The late-afternoon shadows lengthened, gently splay-
ing a dusky tint over the brilliantly colored bougainvillaea and
hibiscus, and finally came to rest against the bright-white
façade of Montego Bay's luxurious Hotel Dorando. It somehow
seemed an effrontery to this picture-postcard setting when the
body of George Farnham, arms flailing wildly, descending
scream trailing behind, tore through the coconut palms and
plummeted to the patio below.

Twenty minutes later, in the twelfth-floor suite from which
the late Mr. Farnham had started his downward flight, his
widow sat quietly on the sofa, a portrait of stunned bereave-
ment.

Opposite her, Mr. Tibble, the slight, balding Assistant Manager of the Dorando, perched birdlike on the edge of a chair. He was suitably compassionate, despite feeling uncomfortable for the past quarter hour, since Mr. Farnham's widow had been placed in his charge.

Tibble shook his head. "Terrible," he said in the direction of the widow. "A terrible accident," he said again.

The widow looked up, acknowledged Tibble's commiseration with an almost imperceptible nod, and bowed her head once more.

An *accident*. It had not occurred to her that George's death would be considered an *accident*. In that brief moment on the terrace, she'd thought only of police, courts, a trial. But here, for the umpteenth time in the past fifteen minutes, Mr. Tibble referred to the *accident*.

And earlier, when she'd hastened down to the patio as quickly as the elevator could carry her, everyone had been murmuring about the *accident*. "Tragedy," they'd whispered. "Dreadful accident . . . lovely woman . . . two of the most beautiful children . . . a terrible accident."

Had no one seen what happened on the terrace?

Priscilla Farnham was a soft, almost-plump woman, still retaining a trace of girlish prettiness. Never having considered herself a particularly strong or resourceful person, she'd been surprised when she'd reached inside herself during these past minutes and discovered hidden iron. She was amazed at her ability to remain calm underneath, while wearing a mask of grief-stricken widowhood.

Her feeling for George had long since gone. She had felt only a touch of remorse, she recalled, when she looked down from the terrace and thought that George appeared strangely like an isolated piece of a jigsaw puzzle, framed on the flagstone.

The jangling of the telephone pierced her retrospection.

Tibble, his eyes apologizing for the desecrating peal of the phone, darted over to answer it. He announced himself, listened, then cupped a thin hand over the mouthpiece.

"It's Constable Edmonds. He says that the man from C.I.D. is in the lobby and, if you're up to it, he'd like to stop up here to make a few inquiries."

Tibble smiled assuringly. "Just routine, I'm sure. You're a visitor to the island, you know. And the Constable had already informed me that someone would be along to investigate."

There must have been a noticeable change in her expression, because Tibble was quick to add: "Of course, if you're not up to it . . ."

"No, it will be all right," she said.

Tibble relayed the answer, then turned back to her. "Five minutes?"

Priscilla nodded.

"Five minutes will do fine," Tibble informed Constable Edmonds, then hung up. Turning to Priscilla: "Is there anything further I can do?"

"I'd appreciate it if you'd look in on the children."

Grateful for the opportunity to leave, Tibble scurried into the bedroom.

The children: they were all that mattered now. What would they do without her? She pictured Mark, with his black, curly hair and long lashes. Only nine, but already showing signs of the lean good looks he would possess as a man. And Amy, two years his junior, with Priscilla's own blonde prettiness and saucerlike violet eyes. She couldn't bear the thought of being apart from them, and her new-found resourcefulness was suddenly edged with fear.

Five minutes. Five minutes to organize a defense. For what? If the inquiry was to be a mere formality, an investigation of an unfortunate accident, as Mr. Tibble had tried to assure her, there would be no need for preparation. But if the C.I.D. man intended to probe deeper, if he had uncovered any intimation of the truth, the investigation would proceed along quite different lines.

Murder!

She shivered at the word, but what else could it be called? Admittedly, George's death was not what might be considered "premeditated"; there had been no long-nurtured, cold-blooded plan. Still, there *had been* some five or ten minutes of thought behind it. *Manslaughter?* Perhaps. There could be many interpretations of degree, but each of them carried its own special punishment. No, she must take another tack. *Justifiable?* Had George's death been justifiable? Not legally; although in a simple, almost primitive way, she supposed it really had been justifiable. In a sense, it had been George's own fault. He had brought it on himself.

Tibble's return from the bedroom interrupted her rationalization. He reported that the children were doing fine. The staff housekeeper, whom he'd sent up earlier to stay with them, said that Mark and Amy were extremely well-behaved.

"They seem concerned only about you," Tibble added with a comforting smile. "I told them you'd be with them soon."

Priscilla nodded gratefully. "We're very close," she told the Assistant Manager as he took his perch on the chair again.

Now to the business at hand, she told herself firmly. The business of getting away with murder.

What would the C.I.D. man ask? Surely he'd look for a motive. Money? No, that would hardly apply here. Jealousy? She dismissed that quickly. Hate? Well, there had been arguments, of course, but didn't they take place in the best of families?

After all, the Farnhams were in a strange country; wouldn't the investigation have to be based on their behavior in Jamaica?

Her hopes sank abruptly. There *had* been an argument. A bitter argument. And she remembered that, at its climax, she had turned away from George and suddenly seen the children standing there, in the living-room doorway, their faces frozen in expressions of fear and concern. She had tried to caution George, but he'd ranted on, shouting all those perfectly horrible things at her. Then he had stalked off to the terrace, and the children had run to her, pressing close.

She'd needed five or ten minutes alone to collect her thoughts, to figure out some way to dissuade George from what he planned to do. So she suggested the Game. The fear and anxiety immediately disappeared from their faces and they ran into the bedroom to begin playing.

Strange, she thought abstractedly. If George had understood and participated in the Game, everything might have been different. If, in fact, George had participated in *anything* that involved love and sharing, he might not be lying down there, covered by that ridiculously colorful patio tablecloth.

The circumstances leading up to the scene on the terrace had begun, she reasoned, a long time ago, when George changed. He had been gay and considerate when he'd been courting her. But when her father had died, shortly after their marriage, and George took over the management of the many interests and investments Father left behind, the metamorphosis had taken place. George had become all business. No time for fun. No more unexpected gifts. No more unexpected flowers or candy. Not a surprise in a carload; that was George.

She had tried to get him interested in the Game and have him discover in it the joy and romance that her own family had found. George reluctantly agreed to try it once, she remembered. She snuggled up to him and said, "Guess what?" George replied according to the rules of the Game: "What?" And she said: "Guess what I did for you today?" George was then supposed to venture some silly guesses, like: "You found a million dollars in gold, and you're going to put it under my napkin." Or, "You just made the Taj Mahal out of toothpicks, and we're going downtown tomorrow to pick out furniture." Then, the guessing was supposed to get more serious until George eventually discovered what she had done to surprise him; or he'd give up and Priscilla would reveal the surprise.

But, naturally, George had quit right after asking, "What?" He found the Game "silly" and thought Priscilla even sillier for playing it.

Of course it was silly, Priscilla admitted, but it was fun. It was full of Surprises and Giving and Doing and Loving. And Romance, too, because her surprise that night had been the most diaphanous of negligees.

She and George had continued to drift, and only the arrival of the children had saved their marriage. Mark and Amy had inherited her looks and zest for life. They took to picnics and surprises and the Game and displays of love just as she always had. So, they'd become their mother's children.

Perhaps—she allowed herself a tiny pang of guilt—she'd concentrated too fiercely on Mark and Amy and not enough on George. But still, she felt defensively, if George had *wanted* to be part of it . . . if he'd wanted to share the wonderful understanding . . . if only—

Priscilla got no farther. A discreet knock broke her train of thought and brought Tibble off the edge of his chair. He went to the door, opened it, and admitted Constable Edmonds and a tall man in tropical civvies.

Edmonds, resplendent in his summer uniform with red cummerbund and white "Bobby" helmet, introduced his companion. He then about-faced smartly and stepped back into the corridor, closing the suite door behind him.

An efficient-looking man with piercing blue eyes and graying sandy hair, Detective-Sergeant Waring was ranking C.I.D. investigator for the Montego Bay area.

"Sorry to disturb you at this time, Mrs. Farnham," he said in a clipped British accent. "But if you feel disposed to answering a few questions, I'll try to take up very little of your time."

"I'll give you whatever information I can," she said.

The Sergeant eased into the chair beside Tibble's and removed a small notebook from a jacket pocket. Absently searching for a pencil and finding it, he flipped a few pages in the book, scanned his notes, then addressed her again.

"Perhaps we can start with your telling me, as best you can, what you recall just before . . . it happened."

"I can't remember too much, I'm afraid. I was lying here on the sofa—in a kind of fog. I don't know whether it was the scream that brought me out of it or the children. I just remember their shaking me, and I got up. We went to the terrace—I looked down"—she managed a little break in her voice—"and saw my husband."

Sergeant Waring rose, walked quickly to the terrace, gazed about for a moment, then returned to his chair.

"Had your husband been unnaturally depressed lately? Had he given you the feeling he might be thinking of taking his own life?"

"Oh, no!" Priscilla blurted, and regretted the denial the second it was uttered. She had not considered the possible deduction of suicide. Now the opportunity was gone.

Waring asked, "Was he all right?"

Priscilla looked puzzled.

"I mean," he explained, "was he in good health? Did he suffer from fainting or dizzy spells or anything of that sort?"

"Yes," she replied. "In fact, that was one of the reasons we took this vacation. My husband worked very hard. Much too hard, we all told him. And he'd mentioned headaches and dizzy spells every once in a while. I felt that he needed to get away for a while . . . to relax. And so we came to Jamaica."

It's amazing, she marveled, how easily one can lie when the stakes are so high.

The C.I.D. man made a note in his black book.

"I realize this is quite a strain for you," he said solicitously. "If you'll bear with me for a few minutes more, I'm certain everything will be cleared up. We must make inquiries in all cases of violent death." He paused for a moment, then continued. "There is, as you know, a three-foot railing that surrounds your terrace. It would seem difficult to conceive of a man just *falling* over a railing of that height . . ."

Priscilla felt the beginning of a nervous gnawing.

". . . unless he had suffered a dizzy spell and toppled over. You see, Mrs. Farnham, one of the waiters . . ." he consulted his notebook again ". . . a chap named Parsons, was setting up the patio tables for dinner. He happened to glance up, or perhaps it was your husband's scream—the one you said you heard—that attracted his attention. And he saw your husband pitch over the railing. But Parsons claims he had a distinct impression that your husband did not fall."

Sudden shock swept through her. Someone *had* seen what happened.

"Naturally," Waring said, "we asked Parsons if he had seen anyone on the terrace besides your husband. He admitted that he had not."

"Certainly you didn't think that—"

"Of course not," Waring cut in with a disarming smile. "But we have to follow up any information of that sort. We soon discovered that there was no substance to Parsons' statement, after all. In the first place, Parsons was almost directly beneath the line of terraces, and, as he was looking virtually straight up, he could not possibly have had a clear view of your terrace. And secondly, Parsons' statement was predicated on his impression that your husband seemed to be trying to catch his balance. His arms were rather clutching for air, as it were . . . as though he were trying to protect himself. It goes without saying that . . ."

Priscilla felt a sudden warm glow of confidence. Perhaps it was possible to get away with murder!

". . . probably mistook your husband's desperate attempt to save himself as something more," the Sergeant was saying. "And now that you've verified your husband's dizzy spells, we can see how he might have just toppled over the railing."

A rapping at the door interrupted him. He stepped to the door, opened it, and Priscilla saw Constable Edmond's white helmet bobbing as he spoke rapidly in a low voice.

Waring poked his head back into the living room. He looked

carefully at Priscilla before saying, "Would you excuse me, please? I'll only be a moment. There are, it seems, some other witnesses."

Her confidence ebbing away, she sat tight-lipped, questions tumbling over each other in her mind.

The answer came as Waring re-entered and moved swiftly toward her. He suddenly looked formidable.

"Mrs. Farnham," he said. "Did you and your husband have a row shortly before he died?"

"Yes," she answered in a tiny voice.

Waring pressed on. "The couple in the suite next door—the Rineharts—claim they heard you and your husband involved in a rather violent dispute. Your voices were quite loud, and they are certain they heard your husband say something about . . . dying."

"It seems like a silly argument now—"

The Sergeant looked at her inquiringly.

"I don't mean *silly*, exactly," she continued. "It just seems . . . well . . . unimportant now. My husband wanted to cut our vacation short and go home. The children and I wanted to stay. Our original vacation plans called for us to remain here for another week at least. The argument got out of hand, I'm afraid, and there were some harsh words. Then he said that when he was dead, I could do as I pleased, but right now, while he was head of the family, we were going home." She forced a brief facsimile of a smile. "That was one of his pet expressions."

She looked up at Waring. The silence was the longest she had ever known.

The Sergeant's face softened. "That seems to check in essence with the fragments of the argument which the Rineharts overheard." He consulted his notebook once again.

"There's just one more thing, Mrs. Farnham. You said that you were lying down on the sofa at the time your husband fell."

Priscilla nodded.

"And you also said," he went on, "that your children shook you right after you thought you heard your husband's scream."

She nodded again.

Waring wore the disarming look once more. "Would you mind, then, if we brought your children in here and asked *them* where you were when they called you? It's merely a routine

check. Naturally, I can't question them officially; and I must
have your permission, of course. But it would clarify my report
and end it all right here."

Priscilla drew up her shoulders. "All right," she said. "But,
please—"

Waring nodded appreciatively. He gestured to Tibble who
went into the bedroom and returned with Mark and Amy.

Priscilla didn't look up as the children entered. Then, as
they were led toward the Sergeant, she lifted her head slowly
and caressed them with a smile.

Waring resumed his seat, hunching a bit in order to be at eye-
level with them. He spoke softly, but directly. "Do you understand what happened today?"

Mark and Amy nodded gravely.

"I'm going to ask you something. Will you answer me?"

Their faces remained grave as they glanced questioningly at
their mother.

"You may answer the gentleman," she instructed gently. As
she directed the children to face Waring, she saw that his eyes
had been focused intently on her.

He turned his attention to Mark and Amy now, and began
gingerly. "A little while ago, when you heard your father—
yell . . . Do you remember?"

They returned the Sergeant's gaze.

Waring continued. "You shouted when you heard him. You
shouted to your mother . . . and shook her, is that right?"

They nodded solemnly.

"Where was your mother when you shook her, do you remember?"

Mark answered. "She was right there where she is now."

"Are you sure?" said Waring.

"Uh, huh," said Amy. "We were playing the Game."

"The game?"

Priscilla started to explain. "It's just a little game we play—"

She was stopped by the Sergeant's upraised, cautioning
hand. This was the moment Priscilla had dreaded. She had
somehow known that the final judgment would be found in the
Game.

"What about the game?" Waring inquired easily. "What kind
of a game?"

Mark took over. "It's a game we play with Mommy. It's a lot

of fun. We make up surprises. We buy things . . . or make things . . . or do things. . . . Then we say, 'Guess what?' "

" 'Guess what?' " Sergeant Waring echoed.

"Sure," chimed in Amy. "Mommy says, 'Guess what I did for you,' and we try to guess the surprise."

"Or we say, 'Guess what we did for you,' and Mommy tries to guess," Mark added.

"Go on," urged Waring.

"Well, after Mommy and Daddy"—his voice dropped—"had a fight, Mommy said let's play the Game." His voice brightened again, and he looked toward his sister. "So Amy and me went into the bedroom to figure out a surprise for Mommy. And Mommy stayed here figuring one out for us."

"Then, when you heard your father yell," Waring said carefully "you came right to your mother. And she was right here on the sofa?"

"Oh, yes," trilled Amy. "She was lying down. We came to tell her our surprise. Do you want to know what it was?"

"No," said the Sergeant, laughing. "A secret is a secret. I just wanted to see if you knew where your mother was."

He turned to Priscilla. "I think that takes care of everything, Mrs. Farnham. Of course, there will be an inquest after the post-mortem, but it will be routine."

"Must the children be brought into it again?" she asked.

"I hardly think so. It has been a trying enough experience for them as it is."

Waring shook hands with Mark and Amy and thanked them.

"I'm sorry, Mrs. Farnham," he said. "I hope this wasn't too much of an inconvenience. I realize that your husband's tragic accident was upsetting enough without my disturbing you with these questions. But, it's my duty."

"I understand, Sergeant Waring," she said, "And thank you for being so considerate with the children."

"Not at all," said Waring. "I'm a father myself." He motioned for Tibble to follow him and they left the suite, softly closing the door behind them.

Priscilla sat still for a long moment, not daring to believe it was all over. Then she smiled at the children, who were standing quietly once again.

Amy, a petulant look on her face, broke the silence. "Mommy," she said. "You didn't tell us your surprise."

Mark added his disappointment. "You never told us what you did. You forgot."

"No, I didn't forget," said Priscilla in a voice touched with sadness.

She would tell them soon what *she* had done. When it was time to sit down with them and explain how the Game had been played wrong that day.

No, she had not forgotten. Nor would she ever forget that moment when Mark and Amy had shaken her and shouted, "Guess what?" In a haze, she'd asked "What?" The children, their beautiful faces beaming with *their* surprise, had pulled her out to the terrace, pointed over the railing, and chanted, "Guess what we did for you today!"

DOROTHY L. SAYERS

The Man with Copper Fingers

The Egotists' Club is one of the most genial places in London. It is a place to which you may go when you want to tell that odd dream you had last night, or to announce what a good dentist you have discovered. You can write letters there if you like, and have the temperament of a Jane Austen, for there is no silence room, and it would be a breach of club manners to appear busy or absorbed when another member addresses you. You must not mention golf or fish, however, and, if the Hon. Freddy Arbuthnot's motion is carried at the next committee meeting (and opinion so far appears very favorable), you will not be allowed to mention wireless either. As Lord Peter Wimsey said when the matter was mooted the other day in the smoking-room, those are things you can talk about anywhere. Otherwise the club is not specially exclusive. Nobody is ineligible per se, except strong, silent men. Nominees are, however, required to pass certain tests, whose nature is sufficiently indicated by the fact that a certain distinguished explorer came to grief through accepting, and smoking, a powerful Trichinoply cigar as an accompaniment to a '63 port. On the other hand, dear old Sir Roger Bunt (the coster millionaire who won the £20,000 ballot offered by the *Sunday Shriek*, and used it to found his immense catering business in the Midlands) was highly commended and unanimously elected after declaring frankly that beer and a pipe were all he really cared for in that way. As Lord Peter said again: "Nobody minds coarseness, but one must draw the line at cruelty."

On this particular evening, Masterman (the cubist poet) had brought a guest with him, a man named Varden. Varden had started life as a professional athlete, but a strained heart had obliged him to cut short a brilliant career, and turn his handsome face and remarkably beautiful body to account in the service of the cinema screen. He had come to London from Los Angeles to stimulate publicity for his great new film, *Marathon,* and turned out to be quite a pleasant, unspoiled person—greatly to the relief of the club, since Masterman's guests were apt to be something of a toss-up.

There were only eight men, including Varden, in the brown room that evening. This, with its paneled walls, shaded lamps, and heavy blue curtains was perhaps the cosiest and pleasantest of the small smoking-rooms, of which the club possessed half a dozen or so.

The conversation had begun quite casually by Armstrong's relating a curious little incident which he had witnessed that afternoon at the Temple Station, and Bayes had gone on to say that that was nothing to the really very odd thing which had happened to him, personally, in a thick fog one night in the Euston Road.

Masterman said that the more secluded London squares teemed with subjects for a writer, and instanced his own singular encounter with a weeping woman and a dead monkey, and then Judson took up the tale and narrated how, in a lonely suburb, late at night, he had come upon the dead body of a woman stretched on the pavement with a knife in her side and a policeman standing motionless near by. He had asked if he could do anything, but the policeman had only said, "I wouldn't interfere if I was you, sir; she deserved what she got." Judson said he had not been able to get the incident out of his mind, and then Pettifer told them a queer case in his own medical practice, when a totally unknown man had led him to a house in Bloomsbury where there was a woman suffering from strychnine poisoning. This man had helped him in the most intelligent manner all night, and, when the patient was out of danger, had walked straight out of the house and never reappeared; the odd thing being that, when he (Pettifer) questioned the woman, she answered in great surprise that she had never seen the man in her life and had taken him to be Pettifer's assistant.

"That reminds me," said Varden, "of something still stranger that happened to me once in New York—I've never been able to make out whether it was a madman or a practical joke, or whether I really had a very narrow shave."

This sounded promising, and the guest was urged to go on with his story.

"Well, it really started ages ago," said the actor, "seven years it must have been—just before America came into the war. I was twenty-five at the time, and had been in the film business a little over two years. There was a man called Eric P. Loder, pretty well known in New York at that period, who would have been a very fine sculptor if he hadn't had more money than was good for him, or so I understood from the people who go in for that kind of thing. He used to exhibit a good deal and had a lot of one-man shows of his stuff to which the highbrow people went—he did a good many bronzes, I believe. Perhaps you know about him, Masterman?"

"I've never seen any of his things," said the poet, "but I remember some photographs in *The Art of Tomorrow*. Clever, but rather over-ripe. Didn't he go in for a lot of that chryselephantine stuff? Just to show he could afford to pay for the materials, I suppose."

"Yes, that sounds very like him."

"Of course—and he did a very slick and very ugly realistic group called Lucina, and had the impudence to have it cast in solid gold and stood in his front hall."

"Oh, that thing! Yes—simply beastly I thought it, but then I never could see anything artistic in the idea. Realism, I suppose you'd call it. I like a picture or a statue to make you feel good, or what's it there for? Still, there was something very attractive about Loder."

"How did you come across him?"

"Oh, yes. Well, he saw me in that little picture of mine, *Apollo Comes to New York*—perhaps you remember it. It was my first star part. About a statue that's brought to life—one of the old gods, you know—and how he gets on in a modern city. Dear old Reubenssohn produced it. Now, there was a man who could put a thing through with consummate artistry. You couldn't find an atom of offense from beginning to end, it was all so tasteful, though in the first part one didn't have anything to wear except a sort of scarf—taken from the classical statue, you know."

"The Belvedere?"

"I dare say. Well, Loder wrote me, and said as a sculptor he was interested in me, because I was a good shape and so on, and would I come and pay him a visit in New York when I was free. So I found out about Loder, and decided it would be good publicity, and when my contract was up, and I had a bit of time to fill in, I went up east and called on him. He was very decent to me, and asked me to stay a few weeks with him while I was looking around.

"He had a magnificent great house about five miles out of the city, crammed full of pictures and antiques and so on. He was somewhere between thirty-five and forty, I should think, dark and smooth, and very quick and lively in his movements. He talked very well, seemed to have been everywhere and have seen everything and not to have any too good an opinion of anybody. You could sit and listen to him for hours; he'd got anecdotes about everybody, from the Pope to old Phineas E. Groot of the Chicago Ring. The only kind of story I didn't care about hearing from him was the improper sort. Not that I don't enjoy an after-dinner story—no, sir, I wouldn't like you to think I was a prig—but he'd tell it with his eyes upon you as if he suspected you of having something to do with it. I've known women do that, and I've seen men do it to women and seen the women squirm, but he was the only man that's ever given me that feeling. Still, apart from that, Loder was the most fascinating fellow I've ever known. And, as I say, his house surely was beautiful, and he kept a first-class table.

"He liked to have everything of the best. There was his mistress, Maria Morano. I don't think I've ever seen anything to touch her, and when you work for the screen you're apt to have a pretty exacting standard of female beauty. She was one of those big, slow, beautifully moving creatures, very placid, with a slow, wide smile. We don't grow them in the States. She'd come from the South—had been a cabaret dancer, he said, and she didn't contradict him. He was very proud of her, and she seemed to be devoted to him in her own fashion. He'd show her off in the studio with nothing on but a fig leaf or so—stand her up beside one of the figures he was always doing of her, and compare them point by point. There was literally only one half inch of her, it seemed, that wasn't absolutely perfect from the sculptor's point of view—the second toe of her left foot was shorter than the big toe. He used to correct it, of course, in the statues. She'd listen to it all with a good-natured smile, sort of vaguely flattered, you know. Though I think the poor girl sometimes got tired of being gloated over that way. She'd sometimes hunt me out and confide to me that what she had always hoped for was to run a restaurant of her own, with a cabaret show and a great many cooks with white aprons, and lots of polished electric cookers. 'And then I would marry,' she'd say, 'and have four sons and one daughter,' and she told me all the names she had chosen for the family. I thought it was rather pathetic. Loder came in at the end of one of these conversations. He had a sort of a grin on, so I dare say he'd overheard. I don't suppose he attached much importance to it, which shows that he never really understood the girl. I don't think he every imagined any woman would chuck up the sort of life he'd accustomed her to, and if he was a bit possessive in his manner, at least he never gave her a rival. For all his talk and his ugly statues, she'd got him, and she knew it.

"I stayed there getting on for a month altogether, having a thundering good time. On two occasions Loder had an art spasm, and shut himself up in his studio to work and wouldn't let anybody in for several days on end. He was rather given to that sort of stunt, and when it was over we would have a party, and all Loder's friends and hangers-on would come to have a look at the work of art. He was doing a figure of some nymph or goddess, I fancy, to be cast in silver, and Maria used to go along and sit for him. Apart from those times, he went about everywhere, and we saw all there was to be seen.

"I was fairly annoyed, I admit, when it came to an end. War was declared, and I'd made up my mind to join up when that happened. My heart put me out of the running for trench service, but I counted on getting some sort of a job, with perserverance, so I packed up and went off.

"I wouldn't have believed Loder would have been so genuinely sorry to say good-bye to me. He said over and over again that we'd meet again soon. However, I did get a job with the hospital people, and was sent over to Europe, and it wasn't till 1920 that I saw Loder again.

"He'd written to me before, but I'd had two big pictures to make in '19, and it couldn't be done. However, in '20 I found myself back in New York, doing publicity for *The Passion Streak,* and got a note from Loder begging me to stay with him, and saying he wanted me to sit for him. Well, that was advertisement that he'd pay for himself, you know, so I agreed. I had accepted an engagement to go out with Mystofilms Ltd. in *Fake of Dead Man's Bush*—the dwarf-men picture, you know, taken on the spot among the Australian bushmen. I wired them that I would join them at Sydney the third week in April, and took my bags out to Loder's.

"Loder greeted me very cordially, though I thought he looked older than when I last saw him. He had certainly grown more nervous in his manner. He was—how shall I describe it?— more intense—more real, in a way. He brought out his pet cynicisms as if he thoroughly meant them, and more and more with that air of getting at you personally. I used to think his disbelief in everything was a kind of artistic pose, but I began to feel I had done him an injustice. He was really unhappy, I could see that quite well, and soon I discovered the reason. As we were driving out in the car I asked for Maria.

" 'She has left me,' he said.

"Well, now, you know, that really surprised me. Honestly, I hadn't thought the girl had that much initiative. 'Why,' I said, 'has she gone and set up in that restaurant of her own she wanted so much?'

" 'Oh! she talked to you about restaurants, did she?' said Loder. 'I suppose you are one of the men that women tell things to. No. She made a fool of herself. She's gone.'

"I didn't quite know what to say. He was so obviously hurt in his vanity, you know, as well as in his feelings. I muttered the usual things, and added that it must be a great loss to his work as well as in other ways. He said it was.

"I asked him when it had happened and whether he'd finished the nymph he was working on before I left. He said,

Oh, yes, he'd finished that and done another—something pretty original, which I should like.

"Well, we got to the house and dined, and Loder told me he was going to Europe shortly, a few days after I left myself, in fact. The nymph stood in the dining-room, in a special niche let into the wall. It really was a beautiful thing, not so showy as most of Loder's work, and a wonderful likeness of Maria. Loder put me opposite it, so that I could see it during dinner, and, really, I could hardly take my eyes off it. He seemed very proud of it, and kept on telling me over and over again how glad he was that I liked it. It struck me that he was falling into a trick of repeating himself.

"We went into the smoking-room after dinner. He'd had it rearranged, and the first thing that caught one's eye was a big settee drawn before the fire. It stood about a couple of feet from the ground, and consisted of a base made like a Roman couch, with cushions and a highish back, all made of oak with a silver inlay, and on top of this, forming the actual seat one sat on, if you follow me, there was a great silver figure of a nude woman, fully life-size, lying with her head back and her arms extended along the sides of the couch. A few big loose cushions made it possible to use the thing as an actual settee, though I must say it never was really comfortable to sit on respectably. As a stage prop, for registering dissipation it would have been excellent, but to see Loder sprawling over it by his own fireside gave me a kind of shock. He seemed very much attached to it, though.

" 'I told you,' he said, 'that it was something original.'

"Then I looked more closely at it, and saw that the figure actually was Maria's though the face was rather sketchily done, if you understand what I mean. I suppose he thought a bolder treatment more suited to a piece of furniture.

"But I did begin to think Loder a trifle degenerate when I saw that couch. And in the fortnight that followed I grew more and more uncomfortable with him. That personal manner of his grew more marked every day, and sometimes, while I was giving him sittings, he would sit there and tell one the most beastly things, with his eyes fixed on one in the nastiest way, just to see how one would take it. Upon my word, though he certainly did me uncommonly well, I began to feel I'd be more at ease among the bushmen.

"Well, now I come to the odd thing."

Everybody sat up and listened a little more eagerly.

"It was the evening before I had to leave New York," went on Varden. "I was sitting——"

Here somebody opened the door of the brown room, to be greeted by a warning sign from Bayes. The intruder sank obscurely into a large chair and mixed himself a whisky, with extreme care not to disturb the speaker.

"I was sitting in the smoking-room," continued Varden, "waiting for Loder to come in. I had the house to myself, for Loder had given the servants leave to go to some show or lecture or other, and he himself was getting his things together for his European trip and had had to keep an appointment with this man of business. I must have been very nearly asleep, because it was dusk when I came to with a start and saw a young man quite close to me.

"He wasn't at all like a housebreaker, and still less like a ghost. He was, I might almost say, exceptionally ordinary-looking. He was dressed in a grey English suit, with a fawn overcoat on his arm, and his soft hat and stick in his hand. He had sleek, pale hair, and one of those rather stupid faces, with a long nose and a monocle. I stared at him, for I knew the front door was locked, but before I could get my wits together he spoke. He had a curious, hesitating, husky voice and a strong English accent. He said, surprisingly:

" 'Are you Mr. Varden?'

" 'You have the advantage of me,' I said.

"He said, 'Please excuse my butting in; I know it looks like bad manners, but you'd better clear out of this place very quickly, don't you know.'

" 'What the hell do you mean?' I said.

"He said, 'I don't mean it in any impertinent way, but you must realize that Loder's never forgiven you, and I'm afraid he means to make you into a hatstand or an electric-light fitting, or something of that sort.'

"My God! I can tell you I felt queer. It was such a quiet voice, and his manners were perfect, and yet the words were quite meaningless! I remembered that madmen are supposed to be extra strong, and edged toward the bell—and then it came over me with rather a chill that I was alone in the house.

" 'How did you get here?' I asked, putting a bold face on it.

" 'I'm afraid I picked the lock,' he said, as casually as though he were apologizing for not having a card about him. 'I couldn't be sure Loder hadn't come back. But I do really think you had better get out as quickly as possible.'

" 'See here,' I said, 'who are you and what the hell are you driving at? What do you mean about Loder never forgiving me? Forgiving me what?'

" 'Why,' he said, 'about—you will pardon me prancing in on your private affairs, won't you—about Maria Morano.'

" 'What about her, in the devil's name?' I cried. 'What do you know about her, anyway? She went off while I was at the war. What's it to do with me?'

" 'Oh!' said the very odd young man. 'I beg your pardon. Perhaps I have been relying too much on Loder's judgment. Damned foolish; but the possibility of his being mistaken did not occur to me. He fancies you were Maria Morano's lover when you were here last time.'

" 'Maria's lover?' I said. 'Preposterous! She went off with her man, whoever he was. He must know she didn't go with me.'

" 'Maria never left the house,' said the young man, 'and if you don't get out of it this moment, I won't answer for your ever leaving, either.'

" 'In God's name,' I cried, exasperated, 'what do you mean?'

"The man turned and threw the blue cushions off the foot of the silver couch.

" 'Have you ever examined the toes of this?' he asked.

" 'Not particularly,' I said, more and more astonished. 'Why should I?'

"'Did you ever know Loder to make any figure of her but this with that short toe on the left foot?' he went on.

"Well, I did take a look at it then, and saw it was as he said—the left foot had a short second toe.

" 'So it is,' I said, 'but, after all, why not?'

" 'Why not, indeed?' said the young man. 'Wouldn't you like to see why, of all the figures Loder made of Maria Morano, this is the only one that has the feet of the living woman?'

"He picked up the poker.

" 'Look!' he said.

"With a lot more strength than I should have expected from him, he brought the head of the poker down with a heavy crack on the silver couch. It struck one of the arms of the figure neatly at the elbow-joint, smashing a jagged hole in the silver.

He wrenched at the arm and brought it away. It was hollow, and, as I am alive, I tell you there was a long, dry arm-bone inside it!"

Varden paused, and put away a good mouthful of whisky.

"Well?" cried several breathless voices.

"Well," said Varden, "I'm not ashamed to say I went out of that house like an old buck-rabbit that hears the man with the gun. There was a car standing just outside, and the driver opened the door. I tumbled in, and then it came over me that the whole thing might be a trap, and I tumbled out again and ran till I reached the trolley-cars. But I found my bags at the station next day, duly registered for Vancouver.

"When I pulled myself together I did rather wonder what Loder was thinking about my disappearance, but I could no more have gone back into that horrible house than I could have taken poison. I left for Vancouver next morning, and from that day to this I never saw either of those men again. I've still not the faintest idea who the fair man was, or what became of him, but I heard in a roundabout way that Loder was dead—in some kind of an accident, I fancy."

There was a pause. Then:

"It's a damned good story, Mr. Varden," said Armstrong—he was a dabbler in various kinds of handiwork, and was, indeed, chiefly responsible for Mr. Arbuthnot's motion to ban wireless—"but are you suggesting there was a complete skeleton inside that silver casting? Do you mean Loder put it into the core of the mold when the casting was done? It would be awfully difficult and dangerous—the slightest accident would have put him at the mercy of his workmen. And that statue must have been considerably over life-size to allow of the skeleton being well covered."

"Mr. Varden has unintentionally misled you, Armstrong," said a quiet, husky voice suddenly from the shadow behind Varden's chair. "The figure was not silver, but electro-plated on a copper base deposited direct on the body. The lady was Sheffield-plated, in fact. I fancy the soft parts of her must have been digested away with pepsin, or some preparation of the kind, after the process was complete, but I can't be positive about that."

"Hullo, Wimsey," said Armstrong, "was that you came in just now? And why this confident pronouncement?"

The effect of Wimsey's voice on Varden had been extraordinary. He had leapt to his feet, and turned the lamp so as to light up Wimsey's face.

"Good evening, Mr. Varden," said Lord Peter. "I'm delighted to meet you again and to apologize for my unceremonious behavior on the occasion of our last encounter."

Varden took the proffered hand, but was speechless.

"D'you mean to say, you mad mystery-monger, that you were Varden's Great Unknown?" demanded Bayes. "Ah, well," he added rudely, "we might have guessed it from his vivid description."

"Well, since you're here," said Smith-Hartington, the Morning Yell man, "I think you ought to come across with the rest of the story."

"Was it just a joke?" asked Judson.

"Of course not," interrupted Pettifer, before Lord Peter had time to reply. "Why should it be? Wimsey's seen enough queer things not to have to waste his time inventing them."

"That's true enough," said Bayes. "Comes of having deductive powers and all that sort of thing, and always sticking one's nose into things that are better not investigated."

"That's all very well, Bayes," said his lordship, "but if I hadn't just mentioned the matter to Mr. Varden that evening, where would he be?"

"Ah, where? That's exactly what we want to know," demanded Smith-Hartington. "Come on, Wimsey, no shirking; we must have the tale."

"And the whole tale," added Pettifer.

"And nothing but the tale," said Armstrong, dexterously whisking away the whisky-bottle and the cigars from under Lord Peter's nose. "Get on with it, old son. Not a smoke do you smoke and not a sup do you sip till Burd Ellen is set free."

"Brute!" said his lordship plaintively. "As a matter of fact," he went on, with a change of tone, "it's not really a story I want to get about. It might land me in a very unpleasant sort of position—manslaughter, probably, and murder possibly."

"Gosh!" said Bayes.

"That's all right," said Armstrong, "nobody's going to talk. We can't afford to lose you from the club, you know. Smith-Hartington will have to control his passion for copy, that's all."

Pledges of discretion having been given all around, Lord Peter settled himself back and began his tale.

"The curious case of Eric P. Loder affords one more instance of the strange manner in which some power beyond our puny human wills arranges the affairs of men. Call it Providence— call it Destiny——"

"We'll call it off," said Bayes, "you can leave out that part."

Lord Peter groaned and began again.

"Well, the first thing that made me feel a bit inquisitive about Loder was a casual remark by a man at the Emigration Office in New York, where I happened to go about that silly affair of Mrs. Bilt's. He said, 'What on earth is Eric Loder going to do in Australia? I should have thought Europe was more in his line.'

"'Australia?' I said, 'you're wandering, dear old thing. He told me the other day he was off to Italy in three weeks' time.'

"'Italy, nothing,' he said, 'he was all over our place today, asking about how you got to Sydney and what were the necessary formalities, and so on.'

"'Oh,' I said, 'I suppose he's going by the Pacific route, and calling at Sydney on his way.' But I wondered why he hadn't said so when I'd met him the day before. He had distinctly talked about sailing for Europe and doing Paris before he went on to Rome.

"I felt so darned inquisitive that I went and called on Loder two nights later.

"He seemed quite pleased to see me, and was full of his forthcoming trip. I asked him again about his route, and he told me quite distinctly he was going via Paris.

"Well, that was that, and it wasn't really any of my business, and we chatted about other things. He told me that Mr. Varden was coming to stay with him before he went, and that he hoped to get him to pose for a figure before he left. He said he'd never seen a man so perfectly formed. 'I meant to get him to do it before,' he said, 'but war broke out, and he went and joined the army before I had time to start.'

"He was lolling on that beastly couch of his at the time, and, happening to look round at him, I caught such a nasty sort of glitter in his eye that it gave me quite a turn. He was stroking the figure over the neck and grinning at it.

"'None of your efforts in Sheffield plate, I hope,' said I.

" 'Well,' he said, 'I thought of making a kind of companion to this, The Sleeping Athlete, you know, or something of that sort.'

" 'You'd much better cast it,' I said. 'Why did you put the stuff on so thick? It destroys the fine detail.'

"That annoyed him. He never liked to hear any objection made to that work of art.

" 'This was experimental,' he said. 'I mean the next to be a real masterpiece. You'll see.'

"We'd got to about that point when the butler came in to ask should he make up a bed for me, as it was such a bad night. We hadn't noticed the weather particularly, though it had looked a bit threatening when I started from New York. However, we now looked out, and saw that it was coming down in sheets and torrents. It wouldn't have mattered, only that I'd only brought a little open racing car and no overcoat, and certainly the prospect of five miles in that downpour wasn't altogether attractive. Loder urged me to stay, and I said I would.

"I was feeling a bit fagged, so I went to bed right off. Loder said he wanted to do a bit of work in the studio first, and I saw him depart along the corridor.

"You won't allow me to mention Providence, so I'll only say it was a very remarkable thing that I should have woken up at two in the morning to find myself lying in a pool of water. The man had stuck a hot-water bottle into the bed, because it hadn't been used just lately, and the beastly thing had gone and unstoppered itself. I lay awake for ten minutes in the deeps of damp misery before I had sufficient strength of mind to investigate. Then I found it was hopeless—sheets, blankets, mattress, all soaked. I looked at the arm-chair, and then I had a brilliant idea. I remembered there was a lovely great divan in the studio, with a big skin rug and a pile of cushions. Why not finish the night there? I took the little electric torch which always goes about with me, and started off.

"The studio was empty, so I supposed Loder had finished and trotted off to roost. The divan was there, all right, with a screen drawn partly across it, so I rolled myself up under the rug and prepared to snooze off.

"I was just getting beautifully sleepy again when I heard footsteps, not in the passage, but apparently on the other side of the room. I was surprised, because I didn't know there was any way out in that direction. I lay low, and presently I saw a streak of light appear from the cupboard where Loder kept his tools and things. The streak widened, and Loder emerged, carrying an electric torch. He closed the cupboard door very gently after him, and padded across the studio. He stopped before the easel and uncovered it; I could see him through a crack in the screen. He stood for some minutes gazing at a sketch on the easel, and then gave one of the nastiest gurgly laughs I've ever had the pleasure of hearing. If I'd ever seriously thought of announcing my unauthorized presence I abandoned all idea of it then. Presently he covered the easel again, and went out by the door at which I had come in.

"I waited till I was sure he had gone, and then got up—uncommonly quietly, I may say. I tiptoed over to the easel to see what the fascinating work of art was. I saw at once it was the design for the figure of The Sleeping Athlete, and as I looked at it I felt a sort of horrid conviction stealing over me. It was an idea which seemed to begin in my stomach, and work its way up to the roots of my hair.

"My family say I'm too inquisitive. I can only say that wild horses wouldn't have kept me from investigating that cupboard. With the feeling that something absolutely vile might hop out at me—I was a bit wrought up, and it was a rotten time of night—I put a heroic hand on the door knob.

"To my astonishment, the thing wasn't even locked. It opened at once, to show a range of perfectly innocent and orderly shelves, which wouldn't possibly have held Loder.

"My blood was up, you know, by this time, so I hunted round for the spring-lock which I knew must exist, and found it without much difficulty. The back of the cupboard swung noiselessly inwards, and I found myself at the top of a narrow flight of stairs.

"I had the sense to stop and see that the door could be opened from the inside before I went any farther, and I also selected a good stout pestle which I found on the shelves as a weapon in case of accident. Then I closed the door and tripped with elf-like lightness down that jolly old staircase.

"There was another door at the bottom, but it didn't take me long to fathom the secret of that. Feeling frightfully excited, I threw it boldly open, with the pestle ready for action.

"However, the room seemed to be empty. My torch caught the gleam of something liquid, and then I found the wall-switch.

"I saw a biggish square room, fitted up as a workshop. On the right-hand wall was a big switchboard, with a bench beneath it. From the middle of the ceiling hung a great floodlight, illuminating a glass vat, fully seven feet long by about three wide. I turned on the floodlight, and looked down into the vat. It was filled with a dark brown liquid which I recognized as the usual compound of cyanide and copper sulphate which they use for copper-plating.

"The rods hung over it with their hooks all empty, but there was a packing-case half-opened at one side of the room, and, pulling the covering aside, I could see rows of copper anodes —enough of them to put a plating over a quarter of an inch thick on a life-size figure. There was a smaller case, still nailed up, which from its weight and appearance I guessed to contain the silver for the rest of the process. There was something else I was looking for, and I soon found it—considerable quantity of prepared graphite and a big jar of varnish.

"Of course, there was no evidence, really, of anything being on the cross. There was no reason why Loder shouldn't make a plaster cast and Sheffield-plate it if he had a fancy for that kind of thing. But then I found something that couldn't have come there legitimately.

"On the bench was an oval slab of copper about an inch and a half long—Loder's night's work, I guessed. It was an electrotype of the American Consular seal, the thing they stamp on your passport photograph to keep you from hiking it off and substituting the picture of your friend Mr. Jiggs, who would like to get out of the country because he is so popular with Scotland Yard.

"I sat down on Loder's stool, and worked out that pretty little plot in all its details. I could see it all turned on three things. First of all, I must find out if Varden was proposing to make tracks shortly for Australia, because, if he wasn't, it threw all my beautiful theories out. And, secondly, it would help matters greatly if he happened to have dark hair like Loder's, as he has, you see—near enough, anyway, to fit the description on a passport. I'd only seen him in that Apollo Belvedere thing, with a fair wig on. But I knew if I hung about I should see him presently when he came to stay with Loder. And, thirdly, of course, I had to discover if Loder was likely to have any grounds for a grudge against Varden.

"Well, I figured out I'd stayed down in that room about as

long as was healthy. Loder might come back at any moment, and I didn't forget that a vatful of copper sulphate and cyanide of potassium would be a highly handy means of getting rid of a too-inquisitive guest. And I can't say I had any great fancy for figuring as part of Loder's domestic furniture. I've always hated things made in the shape of things—volumes of Dickens that turn out to be a biscuit-tin, and dodges like that; and, though I take no overwhelming interest in my own funeral, I should like it to be in good taste. I went so far as to wipe away any finger-marks I might have left behind me, and then I went back to the studio and rearranged that divan. I didn't feel Loder would care to think I'd been down there.

"There was just one other thing I felt inquisitive about. I tiptoed back through the hall and into the smoking-room. The silver couch glimmered in the light of the torch. I felt I disliked it fifty times more than ever before. However, I pulled myself together and took a careful look at the feet of the figure. I'd heard all about that second toe of Maria Morano's.

"I passed the rest of the night in the arm-chair after all.

"What with Mrs. Bilt's job and one thing and another, and the enquiries I had to make, I had to put off my interference in Loder's little game till rather late. I found out that Varden had been staying with Loder a few months before the beautiful Maria Morano had vanished. I'm afraid I was rather stupid about that, Mr. Varden. I thought perhaps there had been something."

"Don't apologize," said Varden, with a little laugh. "Cinema actors are notoriously immoral."

"Why rub it in?" said Wimsey, a trifle hurt. "I apologize. Anyway, it came to the same thing as far as Loder was concerned. Then there was one bit of evidence I had to get to be absolutely certain. Electro-plating—especially such a ticklish job as the one I had in mind—wasn't a job that could be finished in a night; on the other hand, it seemed necessary that Mr. Varden should be seen alive in New York up to the day he was scheduled to depart. It was also clear that Loder meant to be able to prove that a Mr. Varden had left New York all right, according to plan, and had actually arrived in Sydney. Accordingly, a false Mr. Varden was to depart with Varden's papers and Varden's passport furnished with a new photograph duly stamped with the Consular stamp, and to disappear quietly at

Sydney and be retransformed into Mr. Eric Loder, traveling
with a perfectly regular passport of his own. Well, then, in that
case, obviously a cablegram would have to be sent off to Mystofilms Ltd., warning them to expect Varden by a later boat than
he had arranged. I handed over this part of the job to my man,
Bunter, who is uncommonly capable. The devoted fellow shad-
owed Loder faithfully for getting on for three weeks, and at
length, the very day before Mr. Varden was due to depart, the
cablegram was sent from an office in Broadway, where, by a
happy Providence (once more) they supply extremely hard
pencils."

"By Jove!" cried Varden, "I remember now being told something about a cablegram when I got out, but I never connected
it with Loder. I thought it was just some stupidity of the
telegraph people."

"Quite so. Well, as soon as I'd got that, I popped along to
Loder's with a picklock in one pocket and an automatic in the
other. The good Bunter went with me, and, if I didn't return by
a certain time, had orders to telephone for the police. So you
see everything was pretty well covered. Bunter was the
chauffeur who was waiting for you, Mr. Varden, but you turned
suspicious—I don't blame you altogether—so all we could do
was forward your luggage along to the train.

"On the way out we met the Loder servants en route for New
York in a car, which showed us that we were on the right track,
and also that I was going to have a fairly simple job of it.

"You've heard all about my interview with Mr. Varden. I
really don't think I could improve upon his account. When I'd
seen him and his traps safely off the premises, I made for the
studio. It was empty, so I opened the secret door, and, as I
expected, saw a line of light under the workshop door at the far
end of the passage."

"So Loder was there all the time?"

"Of course he was. I took my little pop-gun tight in my fist
and opened the door very gently. Loder was standing between
the tank and the switchboard, very busy indeed—so busy he
didn't hear me come in. His hands were black with graphite, a
big heap of which was spread on a sheet on the floor, and he
was engaged with a long, springy coil of copper wire, running
to the output of the transformer. The big packing-case had been
opened, and all the hooks were occupied.

" 'Loder!' I said.

"He turned on me with a face like nothing human. 'Wimsey!' he shouted. 'What the hell are you doing here?'

" 'I have come,' I said, 'to tell you that I know how the apple gets into the dumpling.' And I showed him the automatic.

"He gave a great yell and dashed at the switchboard, turning out the light, so that I could not see to aim. I heard him leap at me—and then there came in the darkness a crash and a splash—and a shriek such as I never heard—not in five years of war—and never want to hear again.

"I groped forward for the switchboard. Of course, I turned on everything before I could lay my hand on the light, but I got it at last—a great white glare from the floodlight over the vat.

"He lay there, still twitching faintly. Cyanide, you see, is about the swiftest and painfulest thing out. Before I could move to do anything, I knew he was dead—poisoned and drowned and dead. The coil of wire that had tripped him had gone into the vat with him. Without thinking, I touched it, and got a shock that pretty well staggered me. Then I realized that I must have turned on the current when I was hunting for the light. I looked into the vat again. As he fell, his hands had clutched at the wire. The coils were tight around his fingers, and the current was methodically depositing a film of copper all over his hands, which were blackened with the graphite.

"I had just sense enough to realize that Loder was dead, and that it might be a nasty sort of look-out for me if the thing came out, for I'd certainly gone along to threaten him with a pistol.

"I searched about till I found some solder and an iron. Then I went upstairs and called in Bunter, who had done his ten miles in record time. We went into the smoking-room and soldered the arm of that cursed figure into place again, as well as we could, and then we took everything back into the workshop. We cleaned off every fingerprint and removed every trace of our presence. We left the light and the switchboard as they were, and returned to New York by an extremely roundabout route. The only thing we brought away with us was the facsimile of the Consular seal, and that we threw into the river.

"Loder was found by the butler next morning. We read in the papers how he had fallen into the vat when engaged on some experiments in electro-plating. The ghastly fact was commented upon that the dead man's hands were thickly coppered over. They couldn't get it off without irreverent violence, so he was buried like that.

"That's all. Please, may I have my whisky-and-soda now?"

"What happened to the couch?" enquired Smith-Hartington.

"I bought it at the sale of Loder's things." said Wimsey, "and got hold of a dear old Catholic priest I knew, to whom I told the whole story under strict vow of secrecy. He was a very sensible and feeling old bird; so one moonlight night Bunter and I carried the thing out in the car to his own little church, some miles out of the city, and gave it Christian burial in a corner of the graveyard. It seemed the best thing to do."

RAYMOND E. BANKS

The Twenty Friends of William Shaw

It isn't often that a butler calls at my house. Even less often is he carrying a lunch basket. But I admitted Higgins because he worked for William Shaw, and William Shaw once—well, he had done me a great favor.

Higgins was affably formal, and conveyed his employer's respects. I brought out a bottle of my best wine, still remembering my indebtedness—because William Shaw was an old and true friend.

"Bring me up to date," I said. "I haven't seen Mr. Shaw for a long time. Well, since he was—"

"Since his marriage," said Higgins quietly. I had always admired Higgins' firm jaw and precise manner of speech. He was the kind of butler who could competently direct the affairs of the moment by just the right kind of smile or frown. Now his face was absolutely set in stone—a man committed to a purpose. "Since his marriage," he repeated.

"Grace Shaw was rather—I mean, after the marriage her presence put a kind of damper on the old crowd," I said.

"Mr. Shaw had very few weaknesses," said Higgins. "His wife was one of them. An older man—a younger woman. His later years have been difficult."

Higgins moved his lunch basket delicately with the pointed toe of his conservative black shoe. "Because of Mr. Shaw's desire to help people he found himself in a bad position," said Higgins. "There is little left of what was once a large estate. Divorce was out of the question, since Mrs. Shaw would certainly have settled for no less than most of it."

I recalled the last time time I'd been to the Shaws'—the stunning sparkle of the necklace Grace Shaw had worn and the way she had caressed it against her white throat.

"Most certainly out of the question," I said, unconsciously imitating a little Higgins' extremely precise English. It was hard not to imitate that dry forceful voice.

"Deserting one's wife and going into hiding leaves much to be desired," Higgins went on. "Principally, it cuts a man off from his friends—and Mr. Shaw always lived for his friends."

"We had some great times," I said. "Before."

"Furthermore, accidents are hard to explain," Higgins went on.

I found myself staring now at the basket with a growing interest and distaste.

I shuddered, but it may have been the wine. It sparkled blood-red in Higgins' pale fingers as he lifted his glass to the sunlight. My picture window was open, and a strong earth smell, a smell of spring and flowers lingered in the room—a time of hope and reawakening.

"You have a fine home here," said Higgins, looking around. "You've done well. Mr. Shaw will be delighted to know that you have done so well."

"I was once at the point of killing myself," I said. There was something about him that invited confidence. "I was a pretty dismal failure. I was broke, without friends or family. I was also seriously ill, and I didn't even have enough money to buy drugs to ease my pain. I went up into the Hollywood Hills. To that big sign up there that spells out H-O-L-L-Y-W-O-O-D across the face of the hills. People used to jump off that sign, you know."

"But then you met Mr. Shaw," Higgins said, smiling a little.

"Turning point," I said. "He was a stranger—he owed me nothing. But he spent a great deal of time and money in getting me back on my feet. I shall never forget it."

"Of course you shan't," said Higgins. "Mr. Shaw has at least twenty friends like you. People who were in desperate circumstances when he found them."

Higgins edged the basket further from himself, and closer to me. His smile increased in warmth and understanding.

"I always hoped—I could repay him in some way," I said.

"Mr. Shaw never expects repayment when he helps people," said Higgins. "Still, there is a little matter in which you might be able to help him."

"Well, if there's anything—" I let the words hang, because the smile was no longer in evidence. He looked suddenly almost forbidding.

"Unfortunately the man who has been always the soul of kindness may well die at the hands of the state," said Higgins, his eyes clouded. "However, it is probable that Grace Shaw's disappearance will cause no great comment. She has disappeared before—once with a sailor for a two-week affair in San Diego. Another time, I believe, with a truck driver."

"I had heard she had her faults," I said.

Higgins' perfectly tailored shoulders shrugged. "This time—who knows? Butcher, baker, candlestick maker. She is gone and Mr. Shaw looks and acts twenty years younger—as if a great weight had been lifted from his shoulders. Of course, there is her pesky brother trying to make trouble. But Mr. Shaw won't have him around, now that Grace has gone."

He finished his wine and rose. "Mr. Shaw's best and closest friends are all helping him. Perhaps twenty or so—the ones who owed him the most. I trust we can count on you."

"I—I . . ."

But Higgins bowed, and moved to the door. "I wouldn't delay if I were you," he said. "The weather is warm and the dry ice won't last long. Good day, Mr. Benson. But not goodbye. Mr. Shaw will soon have one of his old-time get-togethers. A sort of celebration, and you and your wife are most cordially invited."

I walked him to the door. I accompanied him across the small porch, down the walk and to the door of the Rolls. "I haven't had much experience in these matters," I protested.

"Mr. Goodlace went fishing on a deep-sea boat," said Higgins.

"Mr. Al Drayton was putting in a brick patio. Eileen Wilson found her garden needed new rose bushes—the deep-rooted kind. One's mind can conceive of many possibilities." Higgins grasped my hand and smiled. "Take care of yourself, Mr. Benson. You look pale. I suggest you lie down and rest for a few moments. Mr. Shaw always considered you one of his staunchest—"

The Rolls was gone.

I have never been one to do much work in the yard. But the family was away, and it was a sunny afternoon, so I went out into the garden with the shovel, leaving the basket in the garage. The first patch of ground resisted any considerable digging, but I found another softer spot by a patch of hyacinths.

Soon I became aware of another presence at my side.

"What are you doing?" said the small child—a boy. He was watching me with serious eyes.

I thought of a possible range of replies but settled for a simple one. "Digging," I said.

"Digging what?" the neighbor's child asked. It was Danny, the curious one, already launched on a lifetime of gossip.

"A hole," I said, beginning to sweat even though I was barely more than six inches down.

This went on until he learned I was planting a rose bush.

"My mom doesn't plant rose bushes that deep," he said, hard and suspicious. Normally, he had an attractive young face full of intelligence. Today his eyes looked close-set, his mouth sneering.

"You may be right," I said abandoning the project. With thirty-five children loose in the neighborhood, it didn't seem precisely the right way to proceed. There wasn't much time left as my wife would be back at five, and my son Timmy at six.

Many persons do not know the virtues of the modern-day city dump. The old-fashioned dump with its shacks and its islands of rubble, some burning, surrounded by railroad tracks and inhabited by derelicts is a thing of the past.

The dump near my home is run by the JHK Construction Company. It's a tract of low land that is being slowly filled, and will eventually become the construction site for a long row of forty-thousand-dollar homes. It is surrounded by a high wire fence, and has a polite attendant who checks in the customers at the entrance. Beyond the gate are several winding roads, and a fresh site for the dumping activities of the day. As the trucks drive up, a bulldozer snorts, scrambles, whines and keens, mashing and crushing the discarded goods into the rich, black earth.

Beneath its blade, mixed into a permanent cocktail with the earth are old bedsprings, clippings from the gardeners' trucks, papers, bottles, clothes and furniture. After the bulldozer passes over there is nothing left but churned up ground with a leavening of mashed paper or wood or green branches. Tomorrow another layer will cover this layer, then another, and eventually still another. Archeologists of the future will have to take the twentieth century bulldozer into account.

Once inside the gate you join a procession of trucks, with a few plain cars with trailers moving to the dumping spot of the day. You back in a few feet from where the bulldozer works and deposit your stuff. There are always some coming in and dumping in the shadow of the bulldozer and as it eternally groans away, the dumping spot changes.

I had filled the car with the accumulation of the garage, which I had been promising to do for months anyway. Things that the weekly pickup service wouldn't touch. Higgins' basket looked innocent enough in the symphony of crud I carried.

I was about to back into a dumping spot when I took note of a car only one truck ahead of me. It looked disturbingly familiar. I hadn't seen Ben Jackson for a couple of years, but there was no doubt that the car was sporting one of Ben's distinctive paint jobs. And there was good old Ben himself, one of William Shaw's best friends, jockeying the vehicle into position to dump.

I parked out of the line and went over to see him. He wasn't glad to see me, and when I surveyed his trailer full of dumpings, I could understand why. Higgins had been going the rounds that Saturday.

"I thought of it first!" he cried.

"It is a large dump," I said. "A very large dump."

He was a fat, balding man with vague brown eyes. He waved at the three dump attendants who were busily engaged in picking over the materials left by the trucks.

"One could get by. Two—that would look suspicious," he said.

"I can't help it," I said. "There are only so many places."

That was when the accident happened. I don't know whether I slipped, or whether Ben stumbled against me. But there was a truck hurrying in alongside of him; it caught me and knocked me flat on the ground.

Things went whirly-whirly for a while. I heard voices and the large, kind face of William Shaw came down out of the sky and smiled and thanked me for the kind of assistance I was giving him. I tried to protest that I really couldn't help my bungling when I felt the strong fingers of the dump attendant pressing me into the seat behind the wheel of my car.

"Your friend helped you empty your stuff and left. You better go home now," said the attendant, wetting his lips nervously.

His nervousness wasn't hard to understand. I might be badly hurt. I might even require ambulance attention. Later I might sue the dump. On the whole, he thought it better if I left. So I did. The aspects of danger on my end were strong enough to get me out of there in a hurry.

Safe on the road, I looked in the back seat to be sure all the stuff had vanished. The dump stuff was gone, and that pleased me. But resting on the back seat were two baskets instead of my original one.

I tried to think but didn't get very far. I was still dazed and aching from the dump accident, although I had suffered no permanent damage. I decided to go on home and look up Ben Jackson's address and go calling on him with a crowbar.

My anger lasted all the way home, until I drove up in front of the house and saw, on my front porch, a too-familiar basket. The note attached to it was written in a flowing feminine hand:

"You'll remember," it said, "Sarah King, a good friend of William Shaw's. I haven't seen you for a long time, Mr. Benson, but I know you can help me. I am practically a shut-in these days and live in an apartment. I know you are a gentleman and will be glad to help an old lady who doesn't get around much. Would you please take care of Mr. Shaw's rose bush for me? You live closest to me of all his friends and have a nice, big yard." It was signed *Sarah King*.

I hurried into the house. I was panicky. True, William Shaw had saved my life, and helped start me on a useful career. But there were limits to gratitude.

The phone rang with a monotonous petulance which suggested it had been ringing for a long time. It was Charles Moriseau, Grace Shaw's brother. I recognized the defensively belligerent voice before he'd spoken three words.

"Have you seen Grace Shaw?" he asked.

"No," I said, trying to make my voice sound natural though fear kept tightening my throat. I had not seen her. I had seen only some white packages, securely wrapped and tied, in three baskets. So at least I wasn't lying.

"My illustrious brother-in-law claims she's disappeared," said Moriseau. "I suspect foul play by some of his crude friends."

I had a mental picture of Moriseau as I'd last seen him. The too-cultured voice, the moist hands, the balding head, the fish-pale blue eyes that peered suspiciously on all the human race. I remembered Shaw's gracious good humour and fun. I began to get a little angry.

"Your sister hasn't a very conspicuous reputation as a stay-at-home," I said.

"I think there's something odd going on," he said. "I may be coming to see you and some of his so-called friends—with the police."

"Any day, old man, any day," I said and hung up. That settled it. I wasn't going to be Moriseau's tool for destroying my good friend, William Shaw.

A week went by. I was ready for the expected visit of Moriseau and a heavy-footed policeman. I was completely ready, and even had an alibi for that particular Saturday afternoon. No one came; there was nothing in the papers. Once I drove by the Shaw place in Bel Air, one of the largest mansions. I saw only a uniformed Pinkerton man patrolling the grounds. I tried to call Higgins but the phone was answered by a professional guard who said nobody was home.

The tension lasted, but nothing disturbing happened. However, my wife complained about my peevishness and one night I threw an old shoe at my son.

Relief finally came. I received a note addressed by Higgins which read: "Mr. Shaw is taking a trip to Europe, after a trying winter. He will see all his old friends when he returns in the fall."

So that ended it. William Shaw was going to be all right, and I and the rest of us had nothing to worry about.

. . .

"Why do you swerve whenever you see a police car?" my wife asked. "Have you been cheating on your income tax again?"

Why, indeed, I wondered. To hell with waiting until fall! I wanted to be doubly sure that no policeman would come knocking at my door.

I bought a bottle of champagne and forced my way into the Shaw mansion. Again I met the imperturbable Higgins and told him about the call from Moriseau.

Higgins smiled his quiet smile. "We have nothing to fear, Mr. Benson. In fact, the trip to Europe was deliberately planned to put an end to Moriseau's staying here, now that his sister has—ah—run off with another disreputable man. There were just the four of us—Mr. and Mrs. Shaw, Mr. Moriseau and myself. Mrs. Shaw is gone. Now we we can close the house and he will have to leave. But there'll be good times for all of us again in the fall!"

I pointed to some luggage lined up in the hall—two large trunks, and several women's suitcases. "It looks as if I barely made it," I said. "Maybe I'd better give this champagne to William and be on my way."

Higgins shook his head. "That wouldn't be wise, Mr. Benson. We have convinced Moriseau that his sister has run off. It wouldn't look right if he saw familiar faces—faces of the old crowd—appearing so soon."

"I see your logic," I said, setting the bottle on the luggage. "Give my regards to William."

I stood at the dock in Los Angeles Harbor watching the departure of the big liner for Hawaii. It had been all too easy to discover the booking in the name of "Mr. and Mrs. Higgins." I saw them briefly at the rail, but took great care to make sure they wouldn't see me.

Charles Moriseau was there, grinning and waving up at his sister and his new brother-in-law. With William dead and buried by his twenty best friends, they had it made. Grace could support both Higgins and Charles in good style, because none of them spent with the generosity that poor William had displayed all of his life. Her necklace sparkled from her smooth throat, Higgins' teeth glistened in the sun as he hugged her and laughed a happy, unbutler-like laugh.

I left and sent my telegrams to the harbor police, telling them anonymously what they'd find in the three baskets in the Higgins' stateroom. Baskets that I'd kept on ice in a friendly butcher shop while wracking my poor, unimaginative brain in an unnecessary effort to get myself off the well-known hook.

Higgins had planned the murder well, and executed the removal of the body neatly—the practical butler to the end. Higgins had made only one slip—a slip he couldn't help. There were three men and one woman living in that mansion. The woman was supposed to be dead—yet in the luggage he'd prepared for the trip to Europe (and wasn't it obvious that they'd take reservations in the opposite direction?) Higgins had a set of women's luggage.

Now no proper butler of Higgins' ability would send two males, his master and himself, off to Europe with a lady's luggage!

The Other Hangman

Why do they electrocute 'em instead of hanging 'em in Pennsylvania? What (said my old friend, Judge Murchison, dexterously hooking the spittoon closer with his foot) do they teach you in these new-fangled law schools, anyway? Because that, son, was a murder case! It turned the Supreme Court whiskers grey to find a final ruling, and for thirty years it's been argued about by lawyers in the back room of every saloon from here to the Pacific coast. It happened right here in this county—when they hanged Fred Joliffe for the murder of Randall Fraser.

It was in '92 or '93; anyway, it was the year they put the first telephone in the courthouse, and you could talk as far as Pittsburgh except when the wires blew down. Considering it was the county seat, we were mighty proud of our town (population 3,500). The hustlers were always bragging about how thriving and growing our town was, and we had just got to the point of enthusiasm where every ten years we were certain the census-taker must have forgotten half our population. Old Mark Sturgis, who owned the *Bugle Gazette* then, carried on something awful in an editorial when they printed in the almanac that we had a population of only 3,263. We were all pretty riled about it.

We were proud of plenty of other things, too. We had good reason to brag about the McClellan House, which was the finest hotel in the county; and I mind when you could get room and board, with apple pie for breakfast every morning, for two a week. We were proud of our old county families, that came over the mountains when Braddock's army was scalped by the Indians in 1775, and settled down in log huts to dry their wounds. But most of all we were proud of our legal batteries.

Son, it was a grand assembly! Mind, I won't say that all of 'em were long on knowledge of the Statute Books; but they knew their Blackstone and their Greenleaf on Evidence, and they were powerful speakers. And there were some—the top-notchers, full of graces and book-knowledge and dignity—who were hell on the exact letter of the law. Scotch-Irish Presbyterians, all of us, who loved a good debate and a bottle o' whisky. There was Charley Connell, a Harvard graduate and the district attorney, who had fine hands, and wore a fine high collar, and made such pathetic addresses to the jury that people flocked for miles around to hear him; though he mostly lost his cases. There was Judge Hunt, who prided himself on his resemblance to Abe Lincoln, and in consequence always wore a frock coat and an elegant plug hat. Why, there was your own grandfather, who had over two hundred books in his library, and people used to go up nights to borrow volumes of the encyclopaedia.

You know the big stone courthouse at the top of the street, with the flowers round it, and the jail adjoining? People went there as they'd go to a picture show nowadays; it was a lot better, too. Well, from there it was only two minutes' walk across the meadow to Jim Riley's saloon. All the legal cronies gathered there—in the back room of course, where Jim had an elegant brass spittoon and a picture of George Washington on the wall to make it dignified. You could see the footpath worn across the grass until they built over that meadow. Besides the usual crowd, there was Bob Moran, the sheriff, a fine, strapping big fellow, but very nervous about doing his duty strictly. And there was poor old Nabors, a big, quiet, reddish-eyed fellow, who'd been a doctor before he took to drink. He was always

broke, and he had two daughters—one of 'em consumptive—
and Jim Riley pitied him so much that he gave him all he
wanted to drink for nothing. Those were fine, happy days, with
a power of eloquence and theorizing and solving the problems
of the nation in that back room, until our wives came to fetch
us home.

Then Randall Fraser was murdered and there was hell to
pay.

Now if it had been anybody else but Fred Joliffe who killed
him, naturally we wouldn't have convicted. You can't do it,
son, not in a little community. It's all very well to talk about
the power and grandeur of justice, and sounds fine in a speech.
But here's somebody you've seen walking the streets about his
business every day for years; and you know when his kids were
born, and saw him crying when one of 'em died; and you
remember how he loaned you ten dollars when you needed it
. . . Well, you can't take that person out in the cold light of
day and string him up by the neck until he's dead. You'd
always be seeing the look on his face afterwards. And you'd find
excuses for him no matter what he did.

But with Fred Joliffe it was different. Fred Joliffe was the
worst and nastiest customer we ever had, with the possible
exception of Randall Fraser himself. Ever seen a copperhead
curled up on a flat stone? And a copperhead's worse than a
rattlesnake—that won't strike unless you step on it, and gives
warning before it does. Fred Joliffe had the same brownish
colour and sliding movements. You always remembered his
cart through town—he had some sort of rag-and-bone business,
you understand—you'd see him sitting up there, a skinny little
man in a brown coat, peeping round the side of his nose to find
something for gossip. And grinning.

It wasn't merely the things he said about people behind their
backs. Or to their faces, for that matter, because he relied on
the fact that he was too small to be thrashed. He was a slick
customer. It was believed that he wrote those anonymous letters
that caused . . . but never mind that. Anyhow, I can tell you
this little smirk did drive Will Farmer crazy one time, and
Will did beat him within an inch of his life. Will's livery
stable was burned down one night about a month later with
eleven horses inside, but nothing could ever be proved. He was
too smart for us.

That brings me to Fred Joliffe's only companion—I don't

mean friend. Randall Fraser had a harness-and-saddle store in Market Street, a dusty place with a big dummy horse in the window. I reckon the only thing in the world Randall liked was that dummy horse, which was a dappled mare with vicious-looking glass eyes. He used to keep its mane combed. Randall was a big man with a fine moustache, and a horseshoe pin in his tie, and sporty checked clothes. He was buttery polite, and mean as sin. He thought a dirty trick or a swindle was the funniest joke he ever heard. But the women liked him—a lot of them, it's no use denying, sneaked in at the back door of that harness store. Randall itched to tell it at the barber shop, to show what fools they were and how virile he was, but he had to be careful. He and Fred Joliffe did a lot of drinking together.

Then the news came. It was in October, I think, and I heard it in the morning when I was putting on my hat to go down to the office. Old Withers was the town constable then. He got up early in the morning, although there was no need for it, and when he was going down Market Street in the mist about five o'clock he saw the gas still burning in the back room of Randall's store. The front door was wide open. Withers went in and found Randall lying on a pile of harness in his shirt-sleeves, his forehead and face bashed in with a wedging-mallet. There wasn't much left of the face, but you could recognize him by his moustache and his horeshoe pin.

I was in my office when somebody yelled up from the street that they found Fred Joliffe drunk and asleep in the flour mill, with blood on his hands and an empty bottle of Randall Fraser's whisky in his pocket. He was still in bad shape, and couldn't walk or understand what was going on, when the sheriff—that was Bob Moran I told you about—came to take him to the lock-up. Bob had to drive him in his own rag-and-bone cart. I saw them drive up Market Street in the rain, Fred lying in the back of the cart all white with flour, and rolling and cursing. People were very quiet. They were pleased, but they couldn't show it.

That is, all except Will Farmer, who had owned the livery stable that was burnt down.

"Now they'll hang him," says Will. "Now, by God, they'll hang him."

It's a funny thing, son, I didn't realize the force of that until I heard Judge Hunt pronounce sentence after the trial. They appointed me to defend him, because I was a young man without any particular practice, and somebody had to do it. The evidence was all over town before I got a chance to speak with Fred. You could see he was done for. A scissors-grinder who lived across the street (I forget his name now) had seen Fred go into Randall's place about eleven o'clock. An old couple who lived up over the store had heard 'em drinking and yelling downstairs. At near on midnight they'd heard a noise like a fight and a fall—but they knew better than to interfere. Finally, a couple of farmers driving home from town at midnight had seen Fred stumble out of the front door, slapping his clothes and wiping his hands on his coat like a man with delirium tremens.

I went to see Fred at the jail. He was sober, although he jerked a good deal. Those pale eyes of his were as poisonous as ever. I can still see him sitting on the bunk in his cell, sucking a brown paper cigarette, wriggling his neck, and jeering at me. He wouldn't tell me anything, because he said I would go and tell the judge if he did.

"Hang me?" he says, and wrinkled his nose and jeered again. "Hang me? Don't you worry about that, mister. Them so-and-so's will never hang me. They're too much afraid of me, them so-and-so's are. Eh, mister?"

And the fool couldn't get it through his head right up until the sentence. He strutted away in court making remarks, and threatening to tell what he knew about people, and calling the judge by his first name. He wore a new dickey shirt-front he bought to look spruce in.

I was surprised how quietly everybody took it. The people who came to the trial didn't whisper or shove; they just sat still as death and looked at him. All you could hear was a kind of breathing. It's funny about a courtroom, son. It has its own particular smell, which won't bother you unless you get to thinking about what it means, but you notice worn places and cracks in the walls more than you would anywhere else. You would hear Charley Connell's voice for the prosecution, a little thin sound in a big room, and Charley's footsteps creaking. You would hear a cough in the audience, or a woman's dress rustle, or the gas-jets whistling. It was dark in the rainy season, so they lit the gas-jets by two o'clock in the afternoon.

. . .

The only defense I could make was that Fred had been too drunk to be responsible, and remembered nothing of that night (which he admitted was true). But, in addition to being no defense in law, it was a terrible frost besides. My own voice sounded wrong. I remember that six of the jury had whiskers, and six hadn't, and Judge Hunt, up on the bench with the flag draped on the wall behind his head, looked more like Abe Lincoln than ever. Even Fred Joliffe began to notice. He kept twitching round to look at the people, a little uneasy-like. Once he stuck out his neck at the jury and screeched: "Say something, cantcha? Do something, cantcha?"

They did.

When the foreman of the jury said, "Guilty of murder in the first degree," there was just a little noise from those people. Not a cheer or anything like that. It hissed out all together, only once, like breath released, but it was terrible to hear. It didn't hit Fred until Judge Hunt was halfway through pronouncing sentence. Fred stood looking round with a wild, half-witted expression until he heard Judge Hunt say, "And may God have mercy on your soul." Then he burst out, kind of pleading and kidding as though this was carrying the joke too far. He said, "Listen now, you don't mean that, do you? You can't fool me. You're only Jerry Hunt. I know who you are. You can't do that to me." All of a sudden he began pounding the table and screaming, "You ain't really a-going to hang me, are you?"

But we were.

The date of the execution was fixed for the twelfth of November. The order was all signed. ". . . within the precincts of the said county jail, between the hours of eight and nine A.M., the said Frederick Joliffe shall be hanged by the neck until he is dead; an executioner to be commissioned by the sheriff for this purpose, and the sentence to be carried out in the presence of a qualified medical practitioner; the body to be interred . . ." And the rest of it. Everybody was nervous. There hadn't been a hanging since any of that crowd had been in office, and nobody knew how to go about it exactly. Old Doc Macdonald, the coroner, was to be there and of course they got hold of Reverend Phelps the preacher and Bob Moran's wife was going to cook pancakes and sausage for the last breakfast. Maybe you think that's fool talk. But think for a minute of taking somebody you've known all your life, and binding his arms one cold morning, and walking him out in your own back yard to crack his neck on a rope—all religious and legal, with not a soul to interfere. Then you begin to get scared of the powers of life and death, and the thin partition between.

Bob Moran was scared white for fear things wouldn't go off properly. He had appointed big, slow-moving, tipsy Ed Nabors as hangman. This was partly because Ed Nabors needed the fifty dollars and partly because Bob had a vague idea that an ex-medical man would be better able to manage an execution. Ed had sworn to keep sober. Bob Moran said he wouldn't get a dime unless he was sober, but you couldn't always tell.

Nabors seemed in earnest. He had studied up the matter of scientific hanging in an old book he borrowed from your grandfather, and he and the carpenter had knocked together a big, shaky-looking contraption in the jail yard. It worked all right in practice, with sacks of meal. The trap went down with a boom that brought your heart up in your throat. But once they allowed for too much spring in the rope, and it tore a sack apart. Then old Doc Macdonald chipped in about that fellow John Lee, in England—and it nearly finished Bob Moran.

That was late on the night before the execution. We were sitting round the lamp in Bob's office, trying to play stud poker. There were tops and skipping-ropes, all kinds of toys, all over that office. Bob let his kids play in there—which he shouldn't have done, because the door out of it led to a corridor of cells with Fred Joliffe in the last one. Of course the few other prisoners, disorderlies and chicken-thieves and the like, had been moved upstairs. Somebody had told Bob that the scent of an execution affects 'em like a cage of wild animals. Whoever it was, he was right. We could hear 'em shifting and stamping over our heads, and one colored boy singing hymns all night long.

Well, it was raining hard on the thin roof. Maybe that was what put Doc Macdonald in mind of it. Doc was a cynical old devil. When he saw that Bob couldn't sit still, and would throw in his hand without even looking at the buried card, Doc says:

"Yes, I hope it'll go off all right. But you want to be careful about that rain. Did you read about that fellow they tried to hang in England—and the rain had swelled the boards so's the trap wouldn't fall? They stuck him on it three times, but still it wouldn't work."

Ed Nabors slammed his hand down on the table. I reckon he felt bad enough as it was, because one of his daughters had run away and left him, and the other was dying of consumption. But he was twitchy and reddish about the eyes. He hadn't had a drink for two days, although there was a bottle on the table. He says:

"You shut up or I'll kill you. Damn you, Macdonald," he says, and grabs the edge of the table. "I tell you nothing can go wrong. I'll go out and test the thing again, if you'll let me put the rope round your neck."

And Bob Moran says, "What do you want to talk like that for anyway, Doc. Ain't it bad enough as it is?" he says. "Now you've got me worrying about something else," he says. "I went down there a while ago to look at him, and he said the funniest thing I ever heard Fred Joliffe say. He's crazy. He giggled and said God wouldn't let them so-and-so's hang him. It was terrible, hearing Fred Joliffe talk like that. What time is it, somebody?"

It was cold that night. I dozed off in a chair, hearing the rain, and that animal-cage shuffling upstairs. The colored boy was singing that part of the hymn about while the nearer waters roll, while the tempest still is high.

They woke me about half past eight to say that Judge Hunt and all the witnesses were out in the jail yard, and they were ready to start the march. Then I realized that they were really going to hang him after all. I had to join behind the procession as I was sworn, but I didn't see Fred Joliffe's face and I didn't want to see it. They had given him a good wash, and a clean flannel shirt that they tucked under at the neck. He stumbled coming out of the cell, and started to go in the wrong direction, but Bob Moran and the constable each had him by one arm. It was a cold, dark, windy morning. His hands were tied behind.

The preacher was saying something I couldn't catch, and everything went off smoothly enough until they got halfway across the jail yard. It's a pretty big yard. I didn't look at the contraption in the middle, but at the witnesses standing over against the wall with their hats off. But Fred Joliffe did look at it, and went down flat on his knees. They hauled him up again. I heard them keep on walking, and go up the steps, which were creaky.

I didn't look at the contraption until I heard a thumping sound, and we all knew something was wrong.

Fred Joliffe was not standing on the trap, nor was the bag pulled over his head, although his legs were strapped. He stood with his eyes closed and his face toward the pink sky. Ed Nabors was clinging with both hands to the rope, twirling round a little and stamping on the trap. It didn't budge. Just as I heard Ed crying something about the rain having swelled the boards, Judge Hunt ran past me to the foot of the contraption.

Bob Moran started cursing pretty obscenely. "Put him on and try it, anyway," he says, and grabs Fred's arm. "Stick that bag over his head and give the thing a chance."

"In His name," says the preacher pretty steadily, "you'll not do it if I can help it."

Bob ran over like a crazy man and jumped on the trap with both feet. It was stuck fast. Then Bob turned round and pulled an Ivor-Johnson .45 out of his hip-pocket. Judge Hunt got in front of Fred, whose lips were moving a little.

"He'll have the law, and nothing but the law," says Judge Hunt. "Put that gun away, you lunatic, and take him back to the cell until you can make the thing work. Easy with him, now."

To this day I don't think Fred Joliffe had realized what happened. I believe he only had his belief confirmed that they never meant to hang him after all. When he found himself going down the steps again, he opened his eyes. His face looked shrunken and dazed-like, but all of a sudden it came to him in a blaze.

"I knew them so-and-so's would never hang me," says he. His throat was so dry he couldn't spit at Judge Hunt, as he tried to do, but he marched straight and giggling across the yard. "I knew them so-and-so's would never hang me," he says.

We all had to sit down a minute, and we had to give Ed Nabors a drink. Bob made him hurry up, although we didn't say much, and he was leaving to fix the trap again when the courthouse janitor came bustling into Bob's office.

"Call," says he, "on the new machine over there. Telephone."

"Lemme out of here!" yells Bob. "I can't listen to no telephone calls now. Come out and give us a hand."

"But it's from Harrisburg," says the janitor. "It's from the Governor's office. You got to go."

"Stay here, Bob," says Judge Hunt. He beckons to me. "Stay here, and I'll answer it," he says. We looked at each other in a queer way when we went across the Bridge of Sighs. The courthouse clock was striking nine, and I could look down into the yard and see people hammering at the trap. After Judge Hunt had listened to that telephone call he had a hard time putting the receiver back on the hook.

"I always believed in Providence, in a way," says he, "but I never thought it was so person-like. Fred Joliffe is innocent. We're to call off this business," says he, "and wait for a messenger from the Governor. He's got the evidence of a woman . . . Anyway, we'll hear it later."

Now, I'm not much of a hand at describing mental states, so I can't tell you exactly what we felt then. Most of all was a fever and horror for fear they had already whisked Fred out and strung him up. But when we looked down into the yard from the Bridge of Sighs we saw Ed Nabors and the carpenter arguing over a crosscut saw on the trap itself, and the blessed morning light coming up in glory to show us we could knock that ugly contraption to pieces and burn it.

The corridor downstairs was deserted. Judge Hunt had got his wind back, and, being one of those stern elocutionists who like to make complimentary remarks about God, he was going on something powerful. He sobered up when he saw that the door to Fred Joliffe's cell was open.

"Even Joliffe," says the judge, "deserves to get this news first."

But Fred never did get the news, unless his ghost was listening. I told you he was very small and light. His heels were a good eighteen inches off the floor as he hung by the neck from an iron peg in the wall of the cell. He was hanging from a noose made in a child's skipping-rope; blackfaced dead already, with the whites of his eyes showing in slits, and his heels swinging over a kicked-away stool.

                    .   .   .

No, son, we didn't think it was suicide for long. For a little while we were stunned, half crazy, naturally. It was like thinking about your troubles at three o'clock in the morning.

But you see, Fred's hands were still tied behind him. There was a bump on the back of his head, from a hammer that lay beside the stool. Somebody had walked in there with the hammer concealed behind his back, had stunned Fred when he wasn't looking, had run a slip-knot in that skipping-rope, and jerked him up a-flapping to strangle there. It was the creepiest part of the business, when we'd got that through our heads, and we all began loudly to tell each other where we'd been during the confusion. Nobody had noticed much. I was scared green.

When we gathered round the table in Bob's office, Judge Hunt took hold of his nerve with both hands. He looked at Bob Moran, at Ed Nabors, at Doc Macdonald, and at me. One of us was the other hangman.

"This is a bad business, gentlemen," says he, clearing his throat a couple of times like a nervous orator before he starts. "What I want to know is, who under sanity would strangle a man when he thought we intended to do it anyway, on a gallows?"

Then Doc Macdonald turned nasty. "Well," says he, "if it comes to that, you might in-quire where that skipping-rope came from to begin with."

"I don't get you," says Bob Moran, bewildered-like.

"Oh, don't you," says Doc, and sticks out his whiskers. "Well, then, who was so dead set on this execution going through as scheduled that he wanted to use a gun when the trap wouldn't drop?"

Bob made a noise as though he'd been hit in the stomach. He stood looking at Doc for a minute, with his hands hanging down—and then he went for him. He had Doc back across the table, banging his head on the edge, when people began to crowd into the room at the yells. Funny, too; the first one in was the jail carpenter, who was pretty sore at not being told that the hanging had been called off.

"What do you want to start fighting for?" he says, fretful-like. He was bigger than Bob, and had him off Doc with a couple of heaves. "Why didn't you tell me what was going on? They say there ain't going to be any hanging. Is that right?"

Judge Hunt nodded, and the carpenter—Barney Hicks, that's

who it was; I remember now—Barney Hicks looked pretty peevish, and says:

"All right, all right, but you hadn't ought to go fighting all over the joint like that." Then he looks at Ed Nabors. "What I want is my hammer. Where's my hammer, Ed? I been looking all over the place for it. What did you do with it?"

Ed Nabors sits up, pours himself four fingers of rye, and swallows it.

"Beg pardon, Barney," says he in the coolest voice I ever heard. "I must have left it in the cell," he says, "when I hanged Fred Joliffe."

Talk about silences! It was like one of those silences when the magician at the Opera House fires a gun and six doves fly out of an empty box. I couldn't believe it. But I remember Ed Nabors sitting big in the corner by the barred window, and his shiny black coat and string tie. His hands were on his knees, and he was looking from one to the other of us, smiling a little. He looked as old as the prophets then, and he'd got enough liquor to keep the nerve from twitching beside his eye. So he just sat there, very quietly, shifting the plug of tobacco around in his cheek, and smiling.

"Judge," he says in a reflective way, "you got a call from the Governor at Harrisburg, didn't you? Uh-huh. I knew what it would be. A woman had come forward, hadn't she, to confess Fred Joliffe was innocent and she had killed Randall Fraser? Uh-huh. The woman was my daughter. Jessie couldn't face telling it here, you see. That was why she ran away from me and went to the Governor. She'd have kept quiet if you hadn't convicted Fred."

"But why? . . ." shouts the judge. "Why? . . ."

"It was like this," Ed goes on in that slow way of his. "She'd been on pretty intimate terms with Randall Fraser, Jessie had. And both Randall and Fred were having a whooping lot of fun threatening to tell the whole town about it. She was pretty near crazy, I think. And, you see, on the night of the murder Fred Joliffe was too drunk to remember anything that happened. He thought he had killed Randall, I suppose, when he woke up and found Randall dead and blood on his hands.

"It's all got to come out now, I suppose," says he, nodding. "What did happen was that the three of 'em were in that back room, which Fred didn't remember. He and Randall had a fight while they were baiting Jessie. Fred whacked him hard enough with that mallet to lay him out, but all the blood he got was from a big splash over Randall's eye. Jessie . . . Well, Jessie finished the job when Fred ran away, that's all."

"But, you damned fool," cries Bob Moran, and begins to pound the table, "why did you have to go and kill Fred when Jessie had confessed?"

"You fellows wouldn't have convicted Jessie, would you?" says Ed, blinking at us. "No. But, if Fred had lived after her confession, you'd have had to, boys. That was how I figured it out. Once Fred learned what did happen, that he wasn't guilty and she was, he'd never have let up until he'd carried that case to the Superior Court out of your hands. He'd have screamed all over the state until they either had to hang her or send her up for life. I couldn't stand that. As I say, that was how I figured it out, although my brain's not so clear these days. So," says he, nodding and leaning over to take aim at the cuspidor, "when I heard about that telephone call, I went into Fred's cell and finished my job."

"But don't you understand," says Judge Hunt, in the way you'd reason with a lunatic, "that Bob Moran will have to arrest you for murder, and . . ."

It was the peacefulness of Ed's expression that scared us then. He got up from his chair, and dusted his shiny black coat, and smiled at us.

"Oh no," says he very clearly. "That's what you don't under-stand. You can't do a single damned thing to me. You can't even arrest me."

"He's bughouse," says Bob Moran.

"Am I?" says Ed affably. "Listen to me. I've committed what you might call a perfect murder, because I've done it legally . . . Judge, what time did you talk to the Governor's office, and get the order for the execution to be called off? Be careful now."

And I said, with the whole idea of the business suddenly hitting me:

"It was maybe five minutes past nine, wasn't it, Judge? I remember the courthouse clock striking."

"I remember it too," says Ed Nabors. "And Doc Macdonald will tell you Fred Joliffe was dead before ever that clock struck nine. I have in my pocket," says he, unbuttoning his coat, "a court order which authorizes me to kill Fred Joliffe, by means of hanging by the neck—which I did—between the hours of eight and nine in the morning—which I also did. And I did it in full legal style before the order was countermanded. Well?"

Judge Hunt took off his stovepipe hat and wiped his face with a bandana. We all looked at him.

"You can't get away with this," says the judge, and grabs the sheriff's order off the table. "You can't trifle with the law in that way. And you can't execute sentence alone. Look here! 'In the presence of a qualified medical practitioner.' What do you say to that?"

"Well, I can produce my medical diploma," says Ed, nodding again. "I may be a booze hoister, and mighty unreliable, but they haven't struck me off the register yet . . . You lawyers are hell on the wording of the law," says he admiringly, "and it's the wording that's done for you this time. Until you get the law altered with some fancy words, there's nothing in that document to say that the doctor and the hangman can't be the same person."

After a while Bob Moran turned round to the judge with a funny expression on his face. It might have been a grin.

"This ain't according to morals," says he. "A fine citizen like Fred shouldn't get murdered like that. It's awful. Something's got to be done about it. As you said yourself this morning, Judge, he ought to have the law and nothing but law. Is Ed right, Judge?"

"Frankly, I don't know," says Judge Hunt, wiping his face again. "But, so far as I know, he is. What are you doing, Robert?"

"I'm writing him out a check for fifty dollars," says Bob Moran, surprised-like. "We got to have it all nice and legal, haven't we?"

FREDERIC BROWN

Don't Look Behind You

Just sit back and relax, now. Try to enjoy this; it's going to be the last story you ever read, or nearly the last. After you finish it you can it there and stall a while, you can find excuses to hang around your house, or your room, or your office, wherever you're reading this; but sooner or later you're going to have to get up and go out. That's where I'm waiting for you: outside. Or maybe closer than that. Maybe in this room.

You think that's a joke of course. You think this is just a story in a book, and that I don't really mean you. Keep right on thinking so. But be fair; admit that I'm giving you fair warning.

Harley bet me I couldn't do it. He bet me a diamond he's told me about, a diamond as big as his head. So you see why I've got to kill you. And why I've got to tell you how and why and all about it first. That's part of the bet. It's just the kind of idea Harley would have.

I'll tell you about Harley first. He's tall and handsome, and suave and cosmopolitan. He looks something like Ronald Coleman, only he's taller. He dresses like a million dollars, but it wouldn't matter if he didn't; I mean that he'd look distinguished in overalls. There's a sort of magic about Harley, a mocking magic in the way he looks at you; it makes you think of palaces and far-off countries and bright music.

It was in Springfield, Ohio, that he met Justin Dean. Justin was a funny-looking little runt who was just a printer. He worked for the Atlas Printing & Engraving Company. He was a very ordinary little guy, just about as different as possible from Harley; you couldn't pick two men more different. He was only thirty-five, but he was mostly bald already, and he had to wear thick glasses because he'd worn out his eyes doing fine printing and engraving. He was a good printer and engraver; I'll say that for him.

I never asked Harley how he happened to come to Springfield, but the day he got there, after he'd checked in at the Castle Hotel, he stopped in at Atlas to have some calling cards made. It happened that Justin Dean was alone in the shop at the time, and he took Harley's order for the cards; Harley wanted engraved ones, the best. Harley always wants the best of everything.

Harley probably didn't even notice Justin; there was no reason why he should have. But Justin noticed Harley all right, and in him he saw everything that he himself would like to be, and never would be, because most of the things Harley has, you have to be born with.

And Justin made the plates for the cards himself and printed them himself, and he did a wonderful job—something he thought would be worthy of a man like Harley Prentice. That was the name engraved on the card, just that and nothing else, as all really important people have their cards engraved.

He did fine-line work on it, freehand cursive style, and used all the skill he had. It wasn't wasted, because the next day when Harley called to get the cards he held one and stared at it for a while, and then he looked at Justin, seeing him for the first time. He asked, "Who did this?"

And little Justin told him proudly who had done it, and Harley smiled at him and told him it was the work of an artist, and he asked Justin to have dinner with him that evening after work, in the Blue Room of the Castle Hotel.

That's how Harley and Justin got together, but Harley was careful. He waited until he'd known Justin a while before he asked him whether or not he could make plates for five and ten dollar bills. Harley had the contacts; he could market the bills in quantity with men who specialized in passing them, and—most important—he knew where he could get paper with the silk threads in it, paper that wasn't quite the genuine thing, but was close enough to pass inspection by anyone but an expert.

So Justin quit his job at Atlas and he and Harley went to New York, and they set up a little printing shop as a blind, on Amsterdam Avenue south of Sherman Square, and they worked at the bills. Justin worked hard, harder than he had ever worked in his life, because besides working on the plates for the bills, he helped meet expenses by handling what legitimate printing work came into the shop.

He worked day and night for almost a year, making plate after plate, and each one was a little better than the last, and finally he had plates that Harley said were good enough. That night they had dinner at the Waldorf-Astoria to celebrate and after dinner they went the rounds of the best night clubs, and it cost Harley a small fortune, but that didn't matter because they were going to get rich.

They drank champagne, and it was the first time Justin ever drank champagne and he got disgustingly drunk and must have made quite a fool of himself. Harley told him about it afterwards, but Harley wasn't mad at him. He took him back to his room at the hotel and put him to bed, and Justin was pretty sick for a couple of days. But that didn't matter, either, because they were going to get rich.

Then Justin started printing bills from the plates, and they got rich. After that, Justin didn't have to work so hard, either, because he turned down most jobs that came into the print shop, told them he was behind schedule and couldn't handle any more. He took just a little work, to keep up a front. And behind the front, he made five and ten dollar bills, and he and Harley got rich.

He got to know other people whom Harley knew. He met Bull Mallon, who handled the distribution end. Bull Mallon was built like a bull, that was why they called him that. He had a face that never smiled or changed expression at all except when he was holding burning matches to the soles of Justin's bare feet. But that wasn't then; that was later, when he wanted Justin to tell him where the plates were.

And he got to know Captain John Willys of the Police Department, who was a friend of Harley's, to whom Harley gave quite a bit of the money they made, but that didn't matter either, because there was plenty left and they all got rich. He met a friend of Harley's who was a big star of the stage, and one who owned a big New York newspaper. He got to know other people equally important, but in less respectable ways.

Harley, Justin knew, had a hand in lots of other enterprises besides the little mint on Amsterdam Avenue. Some of these ventures took him out of town, usually over weekends. And the weekend that Harley was murdered Justin never found out what really happened, except that Harley went away and didn't come back. Oh, he knew that he was murdered, all right, because the police found his body—with three bullet holes in his chest—in the most expensive suite of the best hotel in Albany. Even for a place to be found dead in Harley Prentice had chosen the best.

All Justin ever knew about it was that a long distance call came to him at the hotel where he was staying, the night that Harley was murdered—it must have been a matter of minutes, in fact, before the time the newspapers said Harley was killed.

It was Harley's voice on the phone, and his voice was debonair and unexcited as ever. But he said, "Justin? Get to the shop and get rid of the plates, the paper, everything. Right away. I'll explain when I see you." He waited only until Justin said, "Sure, Harley," and then he said, "Attaboy," and hung up.

Justin hurried around to the printing shop and got the plates and the paper and a few thousand dollars' worth of counterfeit bills that were on hand. He made the paper and bills into one bundle and the copper plates into another, smaller one, and he left the shop with no evidence that it had ever been a mint in miniature.

He was very careful and very clever in disposing of both bundles. He got rid of the big one first by checking in at a big hotel, not one he or Harley ever stayed at, under a false name, just to have a chance to put the big bundle in the incinerator there. It was paper and it would burn. And he made sure there was a fire in the incinerator before he dropped it down the chute.

The plates were different. They wouldn't burn, he knew, so

he took a trip to Staten Island and back on the ferry and, somewhere out in the middle of the bay, he dropped the bundle over the side into the water.

Then, having done what Harley had told him to do, and having done it well and thoroughly, he went back to the hotel—his own hotel, not the one where he had dumped the paper and the bills—and went to sleep.

In the morning he read in the newspapers that Harley had been killed, and he was stunned. It didn't seem possible. He couldn't believe it; it was a joke someone was playing on him. Harley would come back to him, he knew. And he was right; Harley did, but that was later, in the swamp.

But anyway, Justin had to know, so he took the very next train for Albany. He must have been on the train when the police went to his hotel, and at the hotel they must have learned he'd asked at the desk about trains for Albany, because they were waiting for him when he got off the train there.

They took him to a station and they kept him there a long long time, days and days, asking him questions. They found out, after a while, that he couldn't have killed Harley because he'd been in New York City at the time Harley was killed in Albany but they knew also that he and Harley had been operating the little mint, and they thought that might be a lead to who killed Harley, and they were interested in the counterfeiting, too, maybe even more than in the murder. They asked Justin Dean questions, over and over and over, and he couldn't answer them, so he didn't. They kept him awake for days at a time, asking him questions over and over. Most of all they wanted to know where the plates were. He wished he could tell them that the plates were safe where nobody could ever get them again, but he couldn't tell them that without admitting that he and Harley had been counterfeiting, so he couldn't tell them.

They located the Amsterdam shop, but they didn't find any evidence there, and they really had no evidence to hold Justin on at all, but he didn't know that, and it never occurred to him to get a lawyer.

He kept wanting to see Harley, and they wouldn't let him; then, when they learned he really didn't believe Harley could be dead, they made him look at a dead man they said was Harley, and he guessed it was, although Harley looked different dead.

He didn't look magnificent, dead. And Justin believed, then, but still didn't believe. And after that he just went silent and wouldn't say a word, even when they kept him awake for days and days with a bright light in his eyes, and kept slapping him to keep him awake. They didn't use clubs or rubber hoses, but they slapped him a million times and wouldn't let him sleep. And after a while he lost track of things and couldn't have answered their questions even if he'd wanted to.

For a while after that, he was in a bed in a white room, and all he remembers about that are nightmares he had, and calling for Harley and an awful confusion as to whether Harley was dead or not, and then things came back to him gradually and he knew he didn't want to stay in the white room; he wanted to get out so he could hunt for Harley. And if Harley was dead, he wanted to kill whoever had killed Harley, because Harley would have done the same for him.

So he began pretending, and acting, very cleverly, the way the doctors and nurses seemed to want him to act, and after a while they gave him his clothes and let him go.

He was becoming cleverer now. He thought, What would Harley tell me to do? And he knew they'd try to follow him because they'd think he might lead them to the plates, which they didn't know were at the bottom of the bay, and he gave them the slip before he left Albany, and he went first to Boston, and from there by boat to New York, instead of going direct.

He went first to the print shop, and went in the back way after watching the alley for a long time to be sure the place wasn't guarded. It was a mess; they must have searched it very thoroughly for the plates.

Harley wasn't there, of course. Justin left and from a phone booth in a drugstore he telephoned their hotel and asked for Harley and was told Harley no longer lived there; and to be clever and not let them guess who he was, he asked for Justin Dean, and they said Justin Dean didn't live there any more either.

Then he moved to a different drugstore and from there he decided to call up some friends of Harley's, and he phoned Bull Mallon first and because Bull was a friend, he told him who he was and asked if he knew where Harley was.

Bull Mallon didn't pay any attention to that; he sounded excited, a little, and he asked, "Did the cops get the plates,

Dean?" and Justin said they didn't, that he wouldn't tell them, and he asked again about Harley.

Bull asked, "Are you nuts, or kidding?" And Justin just asked him again, and Bull's voice changed and he said, "Where are you?" and Justin told him. Bull said, "Harley's here. He's staying under cover, but it's all right if you know, Dean. You wait right there at the drugstore, and we'll come and get you."

They came and got Justin, Bull Mallon and two other men in a car, and they told him Harley was hiding out way deep in New Jersey and that they were going to drive there now. So he went along and sat in the back seat between two men he didn't know, while Bull Mallon drove.

It was late afternoon then, when they picked him up, and Bull drove all evening and most of the night and he drove fast, so he must have gone farther than New Jersey, at least into Virginia or maybe farther, into the Carolinas.

The sky was getting faintly gray with first dawn when they stopped at a rustic cabin that looked like it had been used as a hunting lodge. It was miles from anywhere, there wasn't even a road leading to it, just a trail that was level enough for the car to be able to make it.

They took Justin into the cabin and tied him to a chair, and they told him Harley wasn't there, but Harley had told them that Justin would tell them where the plates were, and he couldn't leave until he did tell.

Justin didn't believe them; he knew then that they'd tricked him about Harley, but it didn't matter, as far as the plates were concerned. It didn't matter if he told them what he'd done with the plates, because they couldn't get them again, and they wouldn't tell the police. So he told them, quite willingly.

But they didn't believe him. They said he'd hidden the plates and was lying. They tortured him to make him tell. They beat him, and they cut him with knives, and they held burning matches and lighted cigars to the soles of his feet, and they pushed needles under his fingernails. Then they'd rest and ask him questions and if he could talk, he'd tell them the truth, and after a while they'd start to torture him again.

It went on for days and weeks—Justin doesn't know how long, but it was a long time. Once they went away for several days and left him tied up with nothing to eat or drink. They came back and started in all over again. And all the time he hoped Harley would come to help him, but Harley didn't come, not then.

After a while what was happening in the cabin ended, or anyway he didn't know any more about it. They must have thought he was dead; maybe they were right, or anyway not far from wrong.

The next thing he knows was the swamp. He was lying in shallow water at the edge of deeper water. His face was out of the water; it woke him when he turned a little and his face went under. They must have thought him dead and thrown him into the water, but he had floated into the shallow part before he had drowned, and a last flicker of consciousness had turned him over on his back with his face out.

I don't remember much about Justin in the swamp; it was a long time, but I just remember flashes of it. I couldn't move at first; I just lay there in the shallow water with my face out. It got dark and it got cold, I remember, and finally my arms would move a little and I got farther out of the water, lying in the mud with only my feet in the water. I slept or was unconscious again and when I woke up it was getting gray dawn, and that was when Harley came. I think I'd been calling him, and he must have heard.

He stood there, dressed as immaculately and perfectly as ever, right in the swamp, and he was laughing at me for being so weak and lying there like a log, half in the dirty water and half in the mud, and I got up and nothing hurt any more.

We shook hands and he said, "Come on, Justin, let's get you out of here," and I was so glad he'd come that I cried a little. He laughed at me for that and said I should lean on him and he'd help me walk, but I wouldn't do that, because I was coated with mud and filth of the swamp and he was so clean and perfect in a white linen suit, like an ad in a magazine. And all the way out of that swamp, all the days and nights we spent there, he never even got mud on his trouser cuffs, nor his hair mussed.

I told him just to lead the way, and he did, walking just ahead of me, sometimes turning around, laughing and talking to me and cheering me up. Sometimes I'd fall but I wouldn't let him come back and help me. But he'd wait patiently until I could get up. Sometimes I'd crawl instead when I couldn't stand up any more. Sometimes I'd have to swim streams that he'd leap lightly across.

And it was day and night and day and night, and sometimes I'd sleep, and things would crawl across me. And some of them I caught and ate, or maybe I dreamed that. I remember other things, in that swamp, like an organ that played a lot of the time, and sometimes angels in the air and devils in the water, but those were delirium, I guess.

Harley would say, "A little farther, Justin; we'll make it. And we'll get back at them, at all of them."

And we made it. We came to dry fields, cultivated fields with waist-high corn, but there weren't ears on the corn for me to eat. And then there was a stream, a clear stream that wasn't stinking water like the swamp, and Harley told me to wash myself and my clothes and I did, although I wanted to hurry on to where I could get food.

I still looked pretty bad; my clothes were clean of mud and filth but they were mere rags and wet, because I couldn't wait for them to dry, and I had a ragged beard and I was barefoot.

But we went on and came to a little farm building, just a two-room shack, and there was a smell of fresh bread just out of an oven, and I ran the last few yards to knock on the door. A woman, an ugly woman, opened the door and when she saw me she slammed it again before I could say a word.

Strength came to me from somewhere, maybe from Harley, although I can't remember him being there just then. There was a pile of kindling logs beside the door. I picked one of them up as though it were no heavier than a broomstick, and I broke down the door and killed the woman. She screamed a lot, but I killed her. Then I ate the hot fresh bread.

I watched from the window as I ate, and saw a man running across the field toward the house. I found a knife, and I killed him as he came in at the door. It was much better, killing with the knife; I liked it that way.

I ate more bread, and kept watching from all the windows, but no one else came. Then my stomach hurt from the hot bread I'd eaten and I had to lie down, doubled up, and when the hurting quit, I slept.

Harley woke me up, and it was dark. He said, "Let's get going; you should be far away from here before it's daylight."

I knew he was right, but I didn't hurry away. I was becoming, as you see, very clever now. I knew there were things to do first. I found matches and a lamp, and lighted the lamp. Then I hunted through the shack for everything I could use. I found clothes of the man, and they fitted me not too badly except that I had to turn up the cuffs of the trousers and the shirt. His shoes were big, but that was good because my feet were so swollen.

I found a razor and shaved; it took a long time because my hand wasn't steady, but I was very careful and didn't cut myself much.

I had to hunt hardest for their money, but I found it finally. It was sixty dollars.

And I took the knife, after I had sharpened it. It isn't fancy; just a bone-handled carving knife, but it's good steel. I'll show it to you, pretty soon now. It's had a lot of use.

Then we left and it was Harley who told me to stay away from the roads, and find railroad tracks. That was easy because we heard a train whistle far off in the night and knew which direction the tracks lay. From then on, with Harley helping, it's been easy.

You won't need the details from here. I mean, about the brakeman, and about the tramp we found asleep in the empty reefer, and about the near thing I had with the police in Richmond. I learned from that; I learned I mustn't talk to Harley when anybody else was around to hear. He hides himself from them; he's got a trick and they don't know he's there, and they think I'm funny in the head if I talk to him. But in Richmond I bought better clothes and got a haircut and a man I killed in an alley had forty dollars on him, so I had money again. I've done a lot of traveling since then. If you stop to think you'll know where I am right now.

I'm looking for Bull Mallon and the two men who helped him. Their names are Harry and Carl. I'm going to kill them when I find them. Harley keeps telling me that those fellows are big time and that I'm not ready for them yet. But I can be looking while I'm getting ready so I keep moving around. Sometimes I stay in one place long enough to hold a job as a printer for a while. I've learned a lot of things. I can hold a job and people don't think I'm too strange; they don't get scared when I look at them like they sometimes did a few months ago. And I've learned not to talk to Harley except in our own room and then only very quietly so people in the next room won't think I'm talking to myself.

And I've kept in practice with the knife. I've killed lots of people with it, mostly on the streets at night. Sometimes because they look like they might have money on them, but mostly just for practice and because I've come to like doing it. I'm really good with the knife by now. You'll hardly feel it.

But Harley tells me that kind of killing is easy and that it's something else to kill a person who's on guard, as Bull and Harry and Carl will be.

And that's the conversation that led to the bet I mentioned. I told Harley that I'd bet him that, right now, I could warn a man I was going to use the knife on him and even tell him why and approximately when, and that I could still kill him. And he bet me that I couldn't and he's going to lose that bet.

He's going to lose it because I'm warning you right now and you're not going to believe me. I'm betting that you're going to believe that this is just another story in a book. That you won't believe that this is the *only* copy of this book that contains this story and that this story is true. Even when I tell you how it was done, I don't think you'll really believe me.

You see I'm putting it over on Harley, winning the bet, by putting it over on you. He never thought, and you won't realize how easy it is for a good printer, who's been a counterfeiter too, to counterfeit one story in a book. Nothing like as hard as counterfeiting a five dollar bill.

I had to pick a book of short stories and I picked this one because I happened to notice that the last story in the book was titled *Don't Look Behind You* and that was going to be a good title for this. You'll see what I mean in a few minutes.

I'm lucky that the printing shop I'm working for now does book work and had a type face that matches the rest of this book. I had a little trouble matching the paper exactly, but I finally did and I've got it ready while I'm writing this. I'm writing this directly on a linotype, late at night in the shop where I'm working days. I even have the boss' permission, told him I was going to set up and print a story that a friend of mine had written, as a surprise for him, and that I'd melt the type metal back as soon as I'd printed one good copy.

When I finish writing this I'll make up the type in pages to match the rest of the book and I'll print it on the matching paper I have ready. I'll cut the new pages to fit and bind them in; you won't be able to tell the difference, even if a faint suspicion may cause you to look at it. Don't forget I made five and ten dollar bills you couldn't have told from the original, and this is kindergarten stuff compared to that job. And I've done enough bookbinding that I'll be able to take the last story out of the book and bind this one in instead of it and you won't be able to tell the difference no matter how closely you look. I'm going to do a perfect job of it if it takes me all night.

And tomorrow I'll go to some bookstore, or maybe a newsstand or even a drugstore that sells books and has other copies of this book, ordinary copies, and I'll plant this one there. I'll find myself a good place to watch from, and I'll be watching when you buy it.

The rest I can't tell you yet because it depends a lot on circumstances, whether you went right home with the book or what you did. I won't know till I follow you and keep watch till you read it—and I see that you're reading the last story in the book.

If you're home while you're reading this, maybe I'm in the house with you right now. Maybe I'm in this very room, hidden, waiting for you to finish the story. Maybe I'm watching through a window. Or maybe I'm sitting near you on the streetcar or train, if you're reading it there. Maybe I'm on the fire escape outside your hotel room. But wherever you're reading it, I'm near you, watching and waiting for you to finish. You can count on that.

You're pretty near the end now. You'll be finished in seconds and you'll close the book, still not believing. Or, if you haven't read the stories in order, maybe you'll turn back to start another story. If you do, you'll never finish it.

But don't look around; you'll be happier if you don't know, if you don't see the knife coming. When I kill people from behind they don't seem to mind so much.

Go on, just a few seconds or minutes, thinking this is just another story. Don't look behind you. Don't believe this—*until you feel the knife.*

MARGOT BENNET

No Bath for the Browns

Before the real estate agent had time to shut
his eyes and stick a pin into the waiting list, he found he had
rented the house to Mrs. Brown. She took it, unseen, on a ten
years' lease, and on her way back to the basement room she
and her husband now lived in, she dropped a pound in a pavement artist's hat. The pound marked, for her, the end of a
year's exercise in concealing furious despair behind a façade
of untroubled, almost aristocratic, courtesy. Now, at last, she
had found a house.

When she unlocked the front door she felt like Robinson
Crusoe surveying, for the first time, what was to be his king-
dom. The grim mosaic of the hall floor would have been naked
to the sunshine if it had not been for the porch, a kind of sun
baffle-wall in coarsely stained glass. The floor of the porch was
also tiled, making it suitable for potted plants.

"A dear little house," Charles said to her, with just a hint of
a question in his voice.

Her mind was wandering on. "If we bought a carpet—second-hand, of course—we could cover those tiles."

"And how are we to conceal the railway line which passes under the bedroom window?" Charles asked.

She opened a buff-colored door and peered down the stairs. "Charles," she said in excitement. "There's a bath!"

They looked at the bath. "It isn't very handy," she admitted.

"No," Charles said. "But I suppose you can dive in from the top step and dry in the hall when you come out."

Greta ran upstairs. "Look!" she called. "Here's a room that isn't really good for anything. Don't you think we could move the bath up to this floor?"

"We'd never get anyone to do it inside of six months."

"Nonsense!" she said briskly. "We can do it ourselves. Cut off the water, move the bath, phone the water and the gas company and say our bath's not connected. Then we'd be priority. We can do it with ropes."

"I begin to see why this house was to let," Charles said.

Greta said she'd meant to tell him about that. It belonged, she said, to a man called Smith whose wife had left him for another man, at least that was what the neighbors said; anyway, she'd disappeared, and he was so heartbroken, the neighbors said, that he couldn't bear to live there any more.

"I'm surprised he ever bore it. Do you think it has a queerish smell?"

"It's probably only rats," Greta said, with a flash of her old spirit. "Now, I'll begin to scrub the floors tomorrow. We must buy some paint for those awful walls. You must get in touch with the storage people and the gas and electricity and water. There's the food office, and we must find a coal merchant who'll have us. Do you think we can get that broken window mended? Do try and eat well through the day—there'll be nothing but bread and margarine in the evenings. And buy some rat poison."

Their lives for the next month might have been planned by some lunatic master mind. One part of the day was spent in making pathetic appeals to gas, electricity, telephone, food, and fuel functionaries; the other in trying to buy things that could not be bought. In the evenings they scrubbed the floors, painted the walls, and ate bread and margarine. All their friends told them how lucky they were, and asked if they had any rooms to spare.

The faintly distressing smell they had rented with the house did not diminish. Charles said Mrs. Smith had run away, not to find romance, but to escape the smell.

Charles found it was impossible to turn on the bath faucets without taking off his shoes and standing in the bath. When he had done this he found that the pipes had been disconnected. He agreed that the bath must be moved.

It took them four hours to haul the bathtub upstairs: some of that time was spent in offering each other conflicting advice at the corners, but there was enough hard work to make Charles feel that his heart was affected. He sat trembling on the edge of the bathtub, while Greta went to make some tea.

She came upstairs without the tea and stood silent for so long that her husband began to feel nervous.

"I think you should have a look at the bathroom, not this bathroom, the other one," she said in a thin voice. His smothered thoughts leaped to the surface as he stared at her. She nodded.

"The tiles underneath the bath," she said. "I noticed they were loose, now that we'd moved it. I picked one out—you'd better come see."

He went downstairs. Greta led him to the spot where the bathtub had been. Yes, the tiles underneath it had been taken up and relaid. Clumsily.

"That's why the pipes were disconnected," Greta said behind him. "The bath had already been moved once before and put back. Lift up that loose tile and look."

He did so. His face was a bit green as he backed out and he and Greta went upstairs again. Neither of them spoke for some minutes. They were thinking of real estate agents, furniture stores, gas and electricity men, food and fuel offices, carpenters, builders, pots of paint, stacks of bread and margarine. They were thinking of the quiet and orderly lives they had once led, and of how they had never done anyone any harm. They were thinking of how impossible it would be to find another house in London as it was today.

Charles sat stiff and still. He hoped he would never be asked to get up, to speak, to act. Unpleasant as this moment was, he wanted it to last as long as his life and not be succeeded by any kind of future.

"Do you think the shops are shut?" Greta asked. "We could get some cement from the builder's," she said. "Or something airtight. I think jobs like that should be done properly." She smoothed her hair and hummed a little. "I'll make some tea while you go for the cement."

That night, when the rest of the work was over, they moved the bath downstairs again. The neighbors were curious about the noise, but they never learned what had caused it. This was just as well, for if any rumors had reached the ears of Mr. Smith, he would have been most upset.

Mrs. Smith was past caring.

MICHAEL GILBERT

The Uninvited

Mr. Calder was silent, solitary and generous with everything, from a basket of cherries or mushrooms, to efficient first aid to a child who had tumbled. The children liked him. But their admiration was reserved for his dog.

The great, solemn, sagacious Rasselas was a deerhound. He had been born in the sunlight. His coat was the color of dry sherry, his nose was blue-black and his eyes shone like worked amber. From the neat tufts at his heels to the top of his dome-shaped head, there was a royalty about him. He had lived in courts and consorted on his own terms with other princes.

Mr. Calder's cottage stood at the top of a fold in the Kentish Downs. The road curled up to it from Lamperdown, in the valley. First it climbed slowly between woods, then forked sharply left and rose steeply, coming out onto the plateau, rounded and clear as a bald pate. The road served only the cottage, and stopped in front of its gate.

Beyond the house, there were paths which led through the home fields and into the woods beyond, woods full of primroses, bluebells, pheasant's eggs, chestnuts, hollow trees and ghosts. The woods did not belong to Mr. Calder. They belonged, in theory, to a syndicate of businessmen from the Medway towns, who came at the week ends, in autumn and winter, to kill birds. When the sound of their shooting brakes announced their arrival, Mr. Calder would call Rasselas indoors. At all other times, the great dog roamed freely in the garden and in the three open fields which formed Mr. Calder's domain. But he never went out of sight of the house, nor beyond the sound of his master's voice.

The children said that the dog talked to the man, and this was perhaps not far from the truth. Before Mr. Calder came, the cottage had been inhabited by a bad-tempered oaf who had looked on himself as custodian for the Medway sportsmen, and had chased and harried the children who, in their turn, had become adept at avoiding him.

When Mr. Calder first came, they had spent a little time in trying him, before finding him harmless. Nor had it taken them long to find out something else. No one could cross the plateau unobserved, small though he might be and quietly though he might move. A pair of sensitive ears would have heard, a pair of amber eyes would have seen; and Rasselas would pad in at the open door and look enquiringly at Mr. Calder who would say, "Yes, it's the Lightfoot boys and their sister. I saw them, too." And Rasselas would stalk out and lie down again in his favorite day bed, on the sheltered side of the woodpile.

Apart from the children, visitors to the cottage were a rarity. The postman wheeled his bicycle up the hill once a day; delivery vans appeared at their appointed times; the fish man on Tuesdays, the grocer on Thursdays, the butcher on Fridays. In the summer, occasional hikers wandered past, unaware that their approach, their passing, and their withdrawal had all been reported to the owner of the cottage.

Mr. Calder's only regular visitor was Mr. Behrens, the retired schoolmaster, who lived in the neck of the valley, two hundred yards outside Lamperdown Village, in a house which had once been the Rectory. Mr. Behrens kept bees, and lived with his aunt. His forward-stooping head, his wrinkled, brown skin, blinking eyes and cross expression made him look like a tortoise which has been roused untimely from its winter sleep.

Once or twice a week, summer and winter, Mr. Behrens would get out his curious tweed hat and his iron-tipped walking stick, and would go tip-tapping up the hill to have tea with Mr. Calder. The dog knew and tolerated Mr. Behrens, who would scratch his ears and say, "Rasselas. Silly name. *You* came from Persia, not Abyssinia." It was believed that the two old gentlemen played backgammon.

There were other peculiarities about Mr. Calders's menage which were not quite so very apparent to the casual onlooker.

When he first took over the house, some of the alterations he had asked for had caused Mr. Benskin, the builder, to scratch his head. Why, for instance, had he wanted one perfectly good southern-facing window filled in, and two more opened, on the north side of the house?

Mr. Calder had been vague. He said that he liked an all-round view and plenty of fresh air. In which case, asked Mr. Benskin, why had he insisted on heavy shutters on all downstairs windows and a steel plate behind the woodwork of the front and back doors?

There had also been the curious matter of the telephone line. When Mr. Calder had mentioned that he was having the telephone installed, Mr. Benskin had laughed. The post office, overwhelmed as they were with post-war work, were hardly likely to carry their line of poles a full mile up the hill for one solitary cottage. But Mr. Benskin had been wrong, and on two counts. Not only had the post office installed a telephone, with surprising promptness, but they had actually dug a trench and brought it in underground.

When this was reported to him, Mr. Benskin had told the public ear of the Golden Lion that he had always known there was something odd about Mr. Calder.

"He's an inventor," he said. "To my mind, there's no doubt that's what he is. An inventor. He's got government support. Otherwise, how'd he get a telephone line laid like that?"

Had Mr. Benskin been able to observe Mr. Calder getting out of bed in the morning, he would have been fortified in his opinion. For it is a well-known fact that inventors are odd, and Mr. Calder's routine on rising was very odd indeed.

Summer and winter, he would wake half an hour before

dawn. He turned on no electric light. Instead, armed with a big torch, he would pad downstairs, the cold nose of Rasselas a few inches behind him, and make a minute inspection of the three ground-floor rooms. On the edges of the shutters were certain tiny, thread-like wires, almost invisible to the naked eye. When he had satisfied himself that these were in order, Mr. Calder would return upstairs and get dressed.

By this time, day was coming up. The darkness had withdrawn across the bare meadows and chased the ghosts back into the surrounding woods. Mr. Calder would take a pair of heavy naval binoculars from his dressing table, and, sitting back from the window, would study with care the edges of his domain. Nothing escaped his attention: a wattle hurdle blocking a path; a bent sapling at the edge of the glade; a scut of fresh earth in the hedge. The inspection was repeated from the window on the opposite side.

Then, whistling softly to himself, Mr. Calder would walk downstairs to cook breakfast for himself and for Rasselas.

The postman, who arrived at eleven o'clock, brought the newspapers with the letters. Perhaps because he lived alone and saw so few people, Mr. Calder seemed particularly fond of his letters and papers. He opened them with a loving care which an observer might have found ludicrous. His fingers caressed the envelope, or the wrapping paper, very gently, as a man will squeeze a cigar. Often he would hold an envelope up to the light as if he could read, through the outer covering, the message inside. Sometimes, he would even weigh an envelope in the delicate letter scales which he kept on top of his desk between a stuffed seagull and a night-scented jasmine in a pot.

On a fine morning in May, when the sun was fulfilling, in majesty, the promise of a misty dawn, Mr. Calder unfolded his copy of the *Times,* turned, as was his custom, to the foreign news pages, and started to read.

He had stretched his hand out toward his coffee cup when he stopped. It was a tiny check, a break in the natural sequence of his actions, but it was enough to make Rasselas look up. Mr. Calder smiled reassuringly at the dog. His hand resumed its movement, picked up the cup, carried it to his mouth. But the dog was not easy.

Mr. Calder read, once more, the five-line item which had

caught his attention. Then he glanced at his watch, went across to the telephone, dialed a Lamperdown number and spoke to Jack, at the garage, which also ran a taxi service.

"Just do it if we hurry," said Jack. "No time to spare. I'll come right up."

While he waited for the taxi, Mr. Calder first telephoned Mr. Behrens, to warn him that they might have to postpone their game of backgammon. Then he spent a little time telling Rasselas that he was leaving him in charge of the cottage, but that he would be back before dark. Rasselas swept the carpet with his feathery tail, and made no attempt to follow Mr. Calder when Jack's Austin came charging up the hill and reversed in front of the cottage gate.

In the end, the train was ten minutes late at the junction, and Mr. Calder caught it with ease.

He got out at Victoria, walked down Victoria Street, turned to the right, opposite the open space where the Colonial Office used to stand, and to the right again into the Square. In the southwest corner stands the Westminister branch of the London and Home Counties Bank.

Mr. Calder walked into the bank. The head cashier, Mr. Macleod, nodded gravely to him and said, "Mr. Fortescue is ready. You can go straight in."

"I'm afraid the train was late," said Mr. Calder. "We lost ten minutes at the junction, and never caught it up."

"Trains are not as reliable now as they used to be," agreed Mr. Macleod.

A young lady from a nearby office had just finished banking the previous day's takings. Mr. Macleod was watching her out of the corner of his eye until the door had shut behind her. Then he said, with exactly the same inflection, but more softly, "Will it be necessary to make any special arrangements for your departure?"

"Oh, no, thank you," said Mr. Calder. "I took all the necessary precautions."

"Fine," said Mr. Macleod.

He held open the heavy door, paneled in sham walnut in the style affected by pre-war bank designers, ushered Mr. Calder into the anteroom and left him there for a few moments, in contemplation of its only ornament, a reproduction, in a massive gilt frame, of Landseer's allegory "The Tug of War." Thrift and Industry appeared to be gaining a hard-fought victory over Luxury and Extravagance.

Then the head cashier reappeared and held open the door for Mr. Calder.

Mr. Fortescue, who came forward to greet him, would have been identified in any company as a bank manager. It was not only the conventional dress, the square, sagacious face, the suggestion that as soon as his office door closed behind him, he would extract an old pipe and push it into his discreet but friendly mouth. It was more than that. It was the bearing, the balance, the air of certainty and stability in a dubious and unstable world, which sits upon a man when he is the representative of a corporation with a hundred million pounds of disclosed assets.

"Nice to see you," he said. "Grab a chair. Any trouble on the way up?"

"No trouble," said Mr. Calder. "I don't think anything can start for another two or three weeks."

"They might have post-dated the item to put you off your guard." He picked up his own copy of the *Times* and re-read the four and a half lines of print which recorded that Colonel Josef Weinleben, the international expert on bacterial antibodies, had died in Klagenfurt as the result of an abdominal operation.

"No," said Calder. "He wanted me to read it, and sweat."

"It would be the established procedure to organize his own 'death' before setting on a serious mission," Mr. Fortescue agreed. He picked up a heavy paper knife and tapped thoughtfully with it on the desk. "But it could be true, this time. Weinleben must be nearly sixty."

"He's coming," said Mr. Calder. "I can feel it in my bones. It may even be true that he's ill. If he was dying, he'd like to take me along with him."

"What makes you so sure?"

"I tortured him," said Mr. Calder. "And broke him. He'd never forget."

"No," said Mr. Fortescue. He held the point of the paper knife toward the window, sighting down it as if it had been a pistol. "No. I think very likely you're right. We'll try to pick him up at the port, and tag him. But we can't guarantee to stop him getting in. If he tries to operate, of course, he'll have to show his hand. You've got your permanent cover. Do you want anything extra?"

He might, thought Mr. Calder, have been speaking to a customer. You've got your normal overdraft. Do you want any extra accommodation, Mr. Calder? The bank is here to serve you. There was something at the same time ridiculous and comforting in treating life and death as though they were entries in the same balance sheet.

"I'm not at all sure that I want you to stop him," he said. "We aren't at war. You could only deport him. It might be more satisfactory to let him through."

"Do you know," said Mr. Fortescue, "the same thought had occurred to me."

Mrs. Farmer, who kept the Seven Gables Guest House, between Aylesford and Bearsted, considered Mr. Wendon a perfect guest. His passport and the card which he had duly filled in on arrival showed him to be a Dutchman; but his English, though accented in odd places, was colloquial and fluent. An upright, red-faced, gray-haired man, he was particularly nice with Mrs. Farmer's two young children. Moreover, he gave no trouble. He was—and this was a sovereign virtue in Mrs. Farmer's eyes—methodical and predictable.

Every morning, in the endless succession of the fine days which heralded that summer, he would go out walking, clad in aged but respectable tweed, field glasses over one shoulder, a small knapsack on the other for camera, sandwiches, and thermos flask. And in the evenings, he would sit in the lounge, drinking a single glass of schnapps as an aperitif before dinner, and entertaining Tom and Rebecca with accounts of the birds he had observed that day. It was difficult to imagine, seeing him sitting there, gentle, placid, and upright, that he had killed men and women—and children, too—with his own well-kept hands. But then Mr. Wendon, or Weinleben, or Weber, was a remarkable man.

On the tenth day of his stay, he received a letter from Holland. Its contents seemed to cause him some satisfaction, and he read it twice before putting it away in his wallet. The stamps he tore off, giving them to Mrs. Farmer for Tom.

"I may be a little late this evening," he said. "I am meeting a friend at Maidstone. Don't keep dinner for me."

That morning, he packed his knapsack with particular care

and caught the Maidstone bus at Aylesford crossroads. He had
said that he was going to Maidstone and he never told unnecessary lies.

After that, his movements became somewhat complicated,
but by four o'clock, he was safely ensconced in a dry ditch to
the north of the old Rectory at Lamperdown. Here he consumed
a biscuit, and observed the front drive of the house.

At a quarter past four, Jack arrived with his taxi and Mr.
Behren's aunt came out, wearing, despite the heat of the day,
coat and gloves and a rather saucy scarf, and was installed in
the back seat. Mr. Behrens handed in her shopping basket,
waved goodbye, and retired into the house.

Five minutes later, Mr. Wendon was knocking at the front
door. Mr. Behrens opened it, and blinked when he saw the gun
in his visitor's hand.

"I must ask you to turn around and walk in front of me," said
Mr. Wendon.

"Why should I?" said Mr. Behrens. He sounded more irritated than alarmed.

"If you don't, I shall shoot you," said Mr. Wendon. He said it
exactly as if he meant it and pushed Mr. Behrens toward a
door.

After a moment, Mr. Behrens wheeled about, and asked,
"Where now?"

"That looks the sort of place I had in mind," said Mr.
Wendon. "Open the door and walk in. But quite slowly."

It was a small, dark room, devoted to hats, coats, sticks, old
tennis rackets, croquet mallets, bee veils, and such.

"Excellent," said Mr. Wendon. He helped himself to the old-
fashioned tweed hat and the iron-tipped walking stick which
Mr. Behrens carried abroad with him on all his perambula-
tions of the countryside. "A small window, and a stout, old
door. What could be better?"

Still watching Mr. Behrens closely, he laid the hat and stick
on the hall table, dipped his left hand into his own coat pocket
and brought out a curious-looking metal object.

"You have not, perhaps, seen one of these before? It works on
the same principle as a Mills grenade, but is six times as powerful and is incendiary as well as explosive. When I shut this door,
I shall bolt it and hang the grenade from the upturned bolt. The

least disturbance will dislodge it. It is powerful enough to blow the door down."

"All right," said Mr. Behrens. "But get on with it. My sister will be back soon."

"Not until eight o'clock, if she adheres to last week's arrangements," said Mr. Wendon quite knowingly.

He closed the door, shot the bolts, top and bottom, and suspended the grenade with artistic care from the top one.

Mr. Calder had finished his tea by five o'clock, and then shortly afterward strolled down to the end of the paddock, where he was repairing the fence. Rasselas lay quietly in the lee of the wood pile. The golden afternoon turned imperceptibly toward evening.

Rasselas wrinkled his velvet muzzle to dislodge a fly. On one side, he could hear Mr. Calder digging with his mattock into the hilltop chalk and grunting as he dug. Behind, some four fields away, a horse, fly-plagued, with kicking its heels and bucking. Then, away to his left, he located a familiar sound. The clink of an iron-tipped walking stick on stone.

Rasselas liked to greet the arrival of this particular friend of his master, but he waited, with dignity, until the familiar tweed had come into view. Then he unfolded himself and trotted gently out into the road.

So strong was the force of custom, so disarming were the familiar and expected sight and sound, that even Rasselas' five senses were lulled. But his instinct was awake. The figure was still a dozen paces off and advancing confidently, when Rasselas stopped. His eyes searched the figure. Right appearance, right hat, right noises. But wrong gait. Quicker, and more purposeful than their old friend. And, above all, wrong smell.

The dog hackled, then crouched as if to jump. But it was the man who jumped. He leaped straight at the dog, his hand came out from under his coat and the loaded stick hissed through the air with brutal force. Rasselas was still moving, and the blow missed his head, but struck him full on the back of the neck. He went down without a sound.

Mr. Calder finished digging the socket for the corner post he was planting, straightened his back and decided that he would fetch the brush and creosote from the house. As he came out of the paddock, he saw the great dog lying in the road.

He ran forward and knelt in the dust. There was no need to look twice.

He hardly troubled to raise his eyes when a voice which he recognized spoke from behind him.

"Keep your hands in sight," said Colonel Weinleben, "and try not to make any sudden or unexpected move."

Mr. Calder got up.

"I suggest we move back into the house," said the colonel. "We shall be more private there. I should like to devote at least as much attention to you as you did to me on the last occasion we met."

Mr. Calder seemed hardly to be listening. He was looking down at the crumpled, empty, tawny skin, incredibly changed by the triviality of life's departure. His eyes were full of tears.

"You killed him," he said.

"As I shall shortly kill you," said the colonel. And as he spoke, he spun round like a startled marionette, took a stiff pace forward and fell, face downward.

Mr. Calder looked at him incuriously. From the shattered hole in the side of his head, dark blood ran out and mixed with the white dust. Rasselas had not bled at all. He was glad of that tiny distinction between the two deaths.

It was Mr. Behrens who had killed Colonel Weinleben, with a single shot from a .312 rifle, fired from the edge of the wood. The rifle was fitted with a telescopic sight, but the shot was a fine one, even for an excellent marksman such as Mr. Behrens.

He'd run for nearly a quarter of a mile before firing it; he had to get into position very quickly, and he had only just been able to see the colonel's head over the top of an intervening hedge.

He burst through this hedge now, saw Rasselas, and started to curse.

"It wasn't your fault," said Mr. Calder. He was sitting in the road, the dog's head in his lap.

"If I'm meant to look after you, I ought to look after you properly," said Mr. Behrens. "Not let myself be jumped by an amateur like that. I hadn't reckoned on him blocking the door with a grenade. I had to break out of the window, and it took me nearly half an hour."

"We've a lot to do," said Mr. Calder. He got stiffly to his feet and went to fetch a spade.

Between them they dug a deep grave, behind the wood pile, and laid the dog in it, and filled it in, and patted the earth into a mound. It was a fine resting place, looking out southward over the feathery tops of the trees, across the Weald of Kent. A resting place for a prince.

Colonel Weinleben they buried later, with a good deal more haste and less ceremony, in the wood. He was the illegitimate son of a cobbler from Mainz and greatly inferior to the dog, both in birth and breeding.

Dune Roller

There were only two who saw the meteor
fall into Lake Michigan, long ago. One was a Pottawatomie
brave hunting rabbits among the dunes on the shore; he saw
the fire-streak arc down over the water and was afraid, because
it was an omen of ill favor when the stars left the heaven and
drowned themselves in the Great Water. The other who saw
was a sturgeon who snapped greedily at the meteor as it fell—
quite reduced in size by now—to the bottom of the fresh water
sea. The big fish took it into his mouth and then spat it out
again in disdain. It was not good to eat. The meteor drifted
down through the cold black water and disappeared. The
sturgeon swam away, and presently, he died. . . .

Dr. Ian Thorne squatted beside a shore pool and netted
things. Under the sun of late July, the lake waves were spark-
ling deep blue far out, and glass-clear as they broke over the
sandbar into Dr. Thorne's pool. A squadron of whirligig beetles

surfaced warily and came toward him, leading little v-shaped shadow wakes along the tan sand bottom. A back-swimmer rowed delicately out of a green cloud of algae and snooped around a centigrade thermometer which was suspended in the water from a driftwood twig.

3:00 P.M., wrote Dr. Thorne in a large, stained notebook. *Air temp 32, water temp*—he leaned over to get a better look at the thermometer and the back-swimmer fled—*28. Wind, light variable; wave action, diminishing. Absence of drifted specimens.* He dated a fresh sheet of paper, headed it *Fourteenth Day,* and began the bug count.

He scribbled earnestly in the sun, a pleasant-faced man of thirty or so. He wore a Hawaiian shirt and shorts of delicious magenta color, decorated with most unbotanical green hibiscus. An old baseball cap was on his head.

He skirted the four-by-six pool on the bar side and noted that the sand was continuing to pile up. It would not be long before the pool was stagnant, and each day brought new and fascinating changes in its population. *Gyrinidae, Hydrophilidae,* a *Corixa* hiding in the rubbish on the other end. Some kind of larvae beside a piece of water-logged board; he'd better take a specimen or two of that. *L. intacta* sunning itself smugly on the thermometer.

The back-swimmer, its confidence returned, worked its little oars and zig-zagged in and out of the trash. *N. undulata,* wrote Dr. Thorne.

When the count was finished, he took a collecting bottle from the fishing creel hanging over his shoulder and maneuvered a few of the larvae into it, using the handle of the net to herd them into position.

And then he noticed that in the clear, algae-free end of the pool, something flashed with a light more golden than that of mere sun on water. He reached out the net to stir the loose sand away.

It was not a pebble or a piece of chipped glass as he had supposed; instead, he fished out a small, droplike object shaped like a marble with a tail. It was a beautiful little thing of pellucid amber color, with tiny gold flecks and streaks running through it. Sunlight glanced off its smooth sides, which were surprisingly free of the surface scratches that are the inevitable patina of flotsam in the sand-scoured dunes.

He tapped the bottom of the net until the drop fell into an

empty collecting bottle and admired it for a minute. It would be a pretty addition to his collection of Useless Miscellanea. He might put it in a little bottle between the tooled brass yak bell and the six-inch copper sulfate crystal.

He was collecting his equipment and getting ready to leave when the boat came. It swept up out of the north and nosed in among the sand bars offshore, a dignified, forty-foot Matthews cruiser named *Carlin,* which belonged to his friend, Kirk MacInnes.

" 'Hoy, Mac!" Dr. Thorne yelled cordially. "Look out for the new bar the storm brought in!"

A figure on the flying bridge of the boat waved briefly and howled something unintelligible around a pipe clamped in its teeth. The cruiser swung about and the mutter of her motors died gently. She lay rocking in the little waves a few hundred feet offshore. After a short pause a yellow rubber raft dropped over the stern.

Good old Mac, thought Thorne. The little ex-engineer with that Skye terrier moustache and the magnificent boat visited him regularly, bringing the mail and his copy of the *Biological Review,* or bottled goods of a chemistry designed to prevent isolated scientists from catching cold. He was a frequent and welcome visitor, but he had always come alone.

Previous to this.

"Well, well," said Dr. Thorne, and then looked again.

The girl was sitting in the stern of the raft while MacInnes paddled deftly, and as they drew closer Thorne saw that her hair was dark and curly. She wore a spotless white playsuit, and a deep blue handkerchief was knotted loosely around her throat. She was looking at him, and for the first time he had qualms about the Hawaiian shorts.

The yellow flank of the raft grated on the stony beach. MacInnes, sixty and grizzled, a venerable briar between his teeth, climbed out and wrung Thorne's hand.

"Brought you a visitor this time, Ian. Real company. Jeanne, this gentleman in the shorts and fishing creel is Dr. Ian Thorne, the distinguished writer and lecturer. He writes books about dune ecology, whatever that is. Ian, my niece, Miss Wright."

Thorne murmured politely. Why, that old scoundrel. That sly old dog. But she was pretty, all right.

"How engaging," smiled the girl. "An ecologist with a leer."

Dr. Thorne's face abruptly attempted to adopt the protective coloration of his shorts. He said, "We're really not bad fellows at heart, Miss Wright. It's the fresh air that gives us the pointed ears."

"I see," she said, in a tone that made Thorne wonder just how much she saw. "Were you collecting specimens here today, Dr. Thorne?"

"Not exactly. You see, I'm preparing a chapter on the ecology of beach pool associations, and this little pool here is my guinea pig. The sand bar on the lake side will grow until the pool is completely cut off. As its stagnation increases, progressive forms of plant and animal life will inhabit it—algae, beetles, larvae, and so forth. If we have calm weather for the next few weeks, I can get an excellent cross section of the plant-animal societies which develop in this type of an environment. The chapter on the pool is one in a book I'm doing on ecological studies of the Michigan State dunes."

"All you have to do is charge him up," MacInnes remarked, yawning largely, "and he's on the air for the rest of the day." He pulled the raft up onto the sand and took out a flat package. "I brought you a present, if you're interested."

"What is it? The mail?"

"Something a heck of a lot more digestible. A brace of sirloins. I persuaded Jeanne to come along today to do them up for us. I've tasted your cooking."

"I can burn a chop as well as the next man," Thorne protested with dignity. "But I think I'll concede the point. I was finished here. Shall we go right down to the shack? I live just down the shore, Miss Wright, in a place perched on top of a sand dune. It's rugged but it's home."

MacInnes chuckled and led the way along the firm damp sand near the water's edge.

In some places the tree-crowned dunes seemed to come down almost to the beach level. Juniper and pines and heavy undergrowth were the only things holding the vast creeping monster which are the traveling dunes. Without their green chains, they swept over farms and forests, leaving dead trees and silver-scoured boards in their wake.

The three of them cut inland and circled a great narrow-necked valley which widened out among the high sand hills. It was a barren, eery place of sharp, wind-abraded stumps and silent white spaces.

"A sand blow," said Thorne. "The winds do it. Those dunes at the end of the valley in there are moving. See the dead trees? The hills buried them years ago and then moved on and left these skeletons. These were probably young oaks."

"Poor things," said the girl, as they moved on.

Then the dismal blow was gone, and green hills with scarcely a show of sand towered over them. At the top of the largest stood Throne's lodge, its rustic exterior blending inconspicuously into the conifers and maples which surrounded it on three sides. The front of the house was banked with yew and prostrate juniper for sand control.

A stairway of hewn logs came down the slope of the dune. At its foot stood a wooden bench, a bright green pump, and an old ship's bell on a pole.

"A dunes doorbell!" Jeanne exclaimed, seizing the rope.

"Nobody home yet," Thorne laughed, "but that's the shack up there."

"Yeah," said MacInnes sourly. "And a hundred and thirty-three steps to the top."

Later, they sat in comfortable rattan chairs on the porch while Thorne manipulated siphon and glasses.

"You really underestimate yourself, Dr. Thorne," the girl said. "This is no shack, it's a real home. A lodge in the pines."

"Be it ever so humble," he smiled. "I came up here to buy a two-by-four cabin to park my typewriter and microscopes in, and a guy wished this young chalet off on me."

"The view is magnificent. You can see for miles."

"But when the wind blows a gale off the lake, you think the house is going to be carried away! It's just the thing for my work, though. No neighbors, not many picnickers, not even a decent road. I have to drive my jeep down the beach for a couple of miles before I can hit the cow path leading to the county trunk. No telephones, either. And I have my own little generating plant out back, or there wouldn't be any electricity."

"No phone?" Jeanne frowned. "But Uncle Kirk says he talks to you every day. I don't understand."

"Come out here," he invited mysteriously. "I'll show you something."

He led the way to a tiny room with huge windows which lay

just off the living room. Radio equipment stood on a desk and lined the walls. A large plaster model of a grasshopper squatting on the transmitter rack wore a pair of headphones.

"Ham radio used to be my hobby when I was a kid," he said, "and now it keeps me in touch with the outside world. I met Mac over the air long before I ever saw him in the flesh. You must have seen his station at home. And I think he even has a little low power rig in the cruiser."

"I've seen that. Do you mean he can talk to you any time he wants to?"

"Well, it's not like the telephone," Thorne admitted, "the other fellow has to be listening for you on your frequency. But your uncle and I keep a regular schedule every evening and sometimes in the morning. And hams in other parts of the country are very obliging in letting me talk to my friends and colleagues. It works out nicely all the way around."

"Uncle Kirk had represented you as a sort of scientific anchorite," she said, lifting a microphone and running her fingers over the smooth chrome. "But I'm beginning to think he was wrong."

"Maybe," he said quietly. "Maybe not. I manage to get along. The station is a big help in overcoming the isolation, but— there are other things. Shall we be getting back to the drinks?"

She put down the microphone and looked at him oddly. "If you like. Thank you for showing me your station."

"Think nothing of it. If you're ever in a jam, just howl for W8-Dog-Zed-Victor on ten meters."

"All right," she said to him. "If I ever am." She turned and walked out of the door.

The casual remark he had been about to make died on his lips, and suddenly all the loneliness of his life in the dunes loomed up around him like the barren walls of the sand blow. And he was standing there with the dead trees all around and the living green forever out of reach. . . .

"This Scotch tastes like iodine," said MacInnes from the porch.

Thorne left the little room and closed the door behind him. "It's the only alcohol in the house, unless you want to try my specimen pickle," said Thorne, dropping back into his chair. "As for the flavor—you should know. You brought the bottle over yourself last week."

The girl took Thorne's creel and began to arrange the bottles

in a row on the table. Algae, beetles, and some horrid little
things that squirmed when she shook them. Ugh.

"What's this?" she asked curiously, holding up the bottle
with the amber drop.

"Something I found in my beach pool this afternoon. I don't
know what it is. Rock crystal, perhaps, or somebody's drowned
jewelry."

"I think it's rather pretty," she said admiringly. "It reminds
me of something, with that little tail. I know—Prince Rupert
drops. They look just like this, only they're a bit smaller and
have an air bubble in them. When you crack the little tail off
them, the whole drop flies to powder." She shrugged vaguely.
"Strain, or something. I never saw one that had color like this,
though. It's almost like a piece of Venetian glass."

"Keep it, if you like," Thorne offered.

MacInnes poured himself another finger and thumb of Scotch
and scrupulously added two drops of soda. In the center of the
table, the small amber eye winked faintly in the sunlight.

Tommy Dittberner liked to walk down the shore after dinner
and watch the sand toads play. There were hundreds of them
that came out to feed as soon as dusk fell—little silvery-gray
creatures with big jewel eyes, that swam in the mirror of the
water or sat quietly on his hand when he caught them. There
were all sizes, from big fellows over four inches long to tiny
ones that could perch comfortably on his thumbnail.

Tommy came to Port Grand every August, and lived in a
resort near the town. He knew he was not supposed to go too far
from the cottage, but it seemed to him that there were always
more and bigger toads just a little farther down the shore.

He would go just down to that sand spit, that was all. Well,
maybe to that piece of driftwood down there. He wasn't lost,
like his mother said he would be if he went too far. He knew
where he was; he was almost to the Bug Man's house.

He was funny. He lived by himself and never talked to anyone—at least that's what the kids said. But Tommy wasn't too
sure about that. Once last week the Bug Man and a pretty lady
with black hair had been hiking in the dunes near Tommy's
cottage and Tommy had seen him kiss her. Boy, that had been
something to tell the kids!

Here was the driftwood, and it was getting dark. He had

been gone since six o'clock, and if he didn't get home, Mom was going to give it to him, all right.

The toads were thicker than ever, and he had to walk carefully to avoid stepping on any of them. Suddenly he saw one lying in the sand down near the water's edge. It was on its back and kicked feebly. He knelt down and peered closely at it.

"Sick," he decided, prodding it with a finger. The animal winced from his touch, and its eyes were filmed with pain. But it wasn't dead yet.

He picked it up carefully in both hands and scrambled over the top of the low shore dune to the foot of the great hill where the Bug Man lived.

Thorne opened the door to stare astonished at the little boy, and wondered whether or not to laugh. Sweat from the exertion of climbing the one hundred and thirty-three steps had trickled down from his hair, making little stripes of cleanness on the side of his face. His T-shirt had parted company from the belt of his jeans. He held out the toad in front of him.

"There's this here toad I found," he gasped breathlessly. "I think it's sick."

Without a word, Thorne opened the door and motioned the boy in. They went into the workroom together.

"Can you fix it up, mister?" asked the boy.

"Now, I'll have to see what's wrong first. You go wash your face in the kitchen and take a Coke out of the icebox while I look it over."

He stretched it out on the table for examination. The abdomen was swollen and discolored, and even as he watched it the swelling movement of the floor of its mouth faltered and stopped, and the animal did not move again.

"It's dead, ain't it?" said a voice behind Thorne.

"I'm afraid so, sonny. It must have been nearly dead when you found it."

The boy nodded gravely. He looked at it silently for a moment, then said: "What was the matter with it, mister?"

"I could tell if I dissected it. You know what that is, don't you?" The boy shook his head. "Well, sometimes by looking inside of the sick thing that has died, you can find out what was wrong. Would you like to watch me do it?"

"I guess so."

Scalpel and dissecting needle flashed under the table light.

Thorne worked quickly, glancing at the boy now and then out of the corner of his eye. The instruments clicked within the redness of the incision and parted the oddly darkened and twisted organs.

Thorne stared. Then he arose and smiled kindly at the young face before him. "It died of cessation of cardiac activity, young fellow. I think you'd better be heading for home now. It's getting dark and your mother will be worried about you. You wouldn't want her to think anything had happened to you, would you? I didn't think so. A big boy like you doesn't worry his mother."

"What's a cardiac?" asked the boy, looking back over his shoulder at the toad as Thorne led him out.

"Means 'pertaining to the heart,'" said Thorne. "Say, I'll tell you what. We'll drive home in my jeep. Would you like that?"

"I guess so."

The screen door slammed behind them. The kid would forget the toad quickly enough, Thorne told himself. He couldn't have seen what was inside it anyway.

In the lodge later, under the single little light, Thorne preserved the body of the toad in alcohol. Beside him on the table gleamed two tiny amber drops with tails which he had removed from the seared and ruptured remains of the toad's stomach.

The marine chronometer on the wall of Thorne's amateur station read five-fifteen. His receiver said to him:

"I have to sign off now. The missus is hollering up that she wants me to see to the windows before supper. I'll look for you tomorrow. This is W8GB over to W8DVZ, and W8GB is out and clear. Good night, Thorne."

Thorne said, "Good night, Mac. W8DVZ out and clear," and let the power die in his tubes.

He lit a cigarette and stood looking out of the window. In the blue sky over the lake hung a single, giant white thunderhead; it was like a marble spray billow, ponderous and sullen. The rising wind slipped whistling through the stiff branches of the evergreen trees on the dune, and dimly, through the glass, he could hear the sound of the waves.

He moped around inadequately after supper and waited for something to happen. He typed up the day's notes, tidied the

workroom, tried to read a magazine, and then thought about
Jeanne. She was a sweet kid, but he didn't love her. She didn't
understand.

The sand walls seemed to be going up around him again. He
wasn't among the dead trees—he was one of them, rooted in the
sand with the living greenness stripped from his heart.

Oh, what the hell. The magazine flew across the room and
disappeared behind the couch in a flutter of white pages.

He stormed into the workroom, bumped the shelves, and set
the specimens in their bottles swaying sadly to and fro. In the
second bottle from the end, right-hand side, was a toad. In the
third were two small amber drops with tails, whose label said
only:

YOU TELL ME—8/5/57

Interest stirred. Now, there was a funny thing. He had almost
forgotten. The beads, it would seem, had been the cause of the
toad's death. They had evidently affected the stomach and the
surrounding tissues before they had had a chance to pass
through the digestive tract. Fast work. He picked up the
second bottle and moved it gently. The pale little thing inside
rotated until the incision, with all the twisted organs plainly
visible inside, faced him. Willy Seppel would have liked to
see this; too bad he was across the state in Ann Arbor.

Idly, Thorne toyed with the idea of sending the pair of drops
to his old friend. They were unusual looking—he could leave
the label on, write a cryptic note, and fix Seppel's clock for
putting the minnows in his larvae pail on their last field trip
together.

If he hurried, he could get the drops off tonight. There was a
train from Port Grand in forty-five minutes. As for the storm, it
was still a long way off; he doubted that it would break before
nightfall. And the activity would do him good.

He found a small box and prepared it for the mails. Where
was that book of stamps? The letter to Seppel: he slipped a
sheet of paper into the typewriter and tapped rapidly. String—
where was the string? Ah, here it was in the magazine rack.
Now a slicker, and be sure the windows and doors are locked.

His jeep was in a shed at the bottom of the dune, protected
by a thick scrub of cottonwood and cedar. Since there was no
door, Thorne had merely to reverse gears, shoot out, swing

around, and roar over the improvised stone drive to the hard, wet sand of the beach. Five miles down the shore was an overgrown but still usable wagon trail which led to the highway.

The clouds were closing ranks in the west as Dr. Thorne and his jeep disappeared over the crest of a tall dune.

Mr. Gimpy Zandbergen, gentleman of leisure, late of the high sea and presently of the open road, was going home. During a long and motley life, Mr. Zandbergen had wandered far from his native lakes to sail on more boisterous waters; but now his days as an oiler were over, and there came into his heart a nostalgic desire to see the fruit boats ship out of Port Grand once more. Since he possessed neither the money for a bus ticket home, nor the ambition to work to obtain it, he pursued his way via freight cars and such rides as he was able to hook from kindly disposed truck drivers.

His last ride had carried him to a point on the shore highway some miles south of his goal, at which he had regrettably disputed the intrinsic worth of the Detroit Tigers and had been invited to continue his journey on foot. But Mr. Zandbergen was a simple soul, so he merely shrugged his shoulders, fortified himself from the bottle in his picket, and trudged along.

It was hot, though, as only Michigan in August can be, and the sun baked the concrete and reflected off the sand hills at the side of the road. He paused, pulled a blue bandanna handkerchief from his pocket, and mopped his balding head under his cap. He thought longingly of the cool dune path which he knew lay on the other side of the forest, toward the lake.

It had been a long time, but he knew he remembered it. It would lead to Port Grand and the fruit boats, and would be refreshingly cool.

When the storm came, Mr. Zandbergen was distinctly put out. He had not seen the gathering storm through the thick branches, and when the sky darkened, he assumed that it was merely one of the common summer sun showers and hoped for a quick clearing.

He was disturbed when the big drops continued to pelt down among the oak trees. He was annoyed as his path led him out between the smaller and less sheltering evergreens. He swore as the path ended high on a scrubby hill.

Lightning cut the black clouds and Mr. Zandbergen broke

into a lope. He had taken the wrong turning, he knew that now. But he recognized this shore. He dimly remembered a driftwood shanty which lay near an old wagon road somewhere around here. If he made that, he might not get too wet after all.

He could see the lake now. The wind was raging and tearing at the waves, whipping the once placid waters of Michigan into black fury. Mr. Zandbergen shuddered in the driving rain and fled headlong down a dune. Great crashes of thunder deafened him and he could hardly see. Where was that road?

A huge sheet of lightning lit the sky as he struggled to the top of the next dune. There it was! The road was down there! And trees, and the shanty, too.

He went diagonally across the dune in gigantic leaps, dodging the storm-wracked trees and bushes. The wind lulled, then blasted the branches down ferociously, catching him a stinging blow across the face. He tripped, and with an agonized howl began to roll straight down the bare face of the sand hill. He landed in a prickly juniper hedge and lay, whimpering and cursing weakly, while the rain and wind pounded him.

The greenery ripped from the trees stung into him viciously as he tried to rise, gave up, and tried again. On the black beach several hundred feet away, waves leaped and stretched into the sky.

Then came another lull and a light appeared out in the lake. It rose and fell in the surf and in a few moments the flattened and horrified little man on the shore could see what it was. A solemn thunderclap drowned out his scream of terror.

Shouting wordless things, he stumbled swaying to his feet and clawed through the bushes to fall out onto the road. It saw him! He was sure it saw him! He struggled along on his knees in the sand for a short distance before he fell for the last time.

The wind shrilled again in the trees, but the fury of the storm had finally passed. The rain fell down steadily now on the sodden sand dunes, and dripped off the cottonwood branches onto the quiet form of Mr. Zandbergen, who would not see the fruit boats go out again after all.

The sheriff was a conversational man. "Now I've lived on the lake for forty years," he said to Thorne, "but never—*never* did I see a storm like today's. No sir!" He turned to his subordinate standing beside him. "Regular typhoon, eh, Sam? I guess we won't be forgetting that one in a hurry."

Dr. Thorne, at any rate, would not forget it. He could still hear in his mind the thunder as it had rolled away off over the dunes, and see the flaring white cones of his headlights cutting out his way through the rain. He had gone slowly over the sliding wet sand of the wagon road on the way home, but even at that he had almost missed seeing it. He remembered how he had thought it was a fallen branch at first, and how he got out of the car then and stood in the rain looking at it before he wrapped his slicker around it and drove back to town.

And now the rain had stopped at last, and the office of the Port Grand physician who was the county medical examiner was neat, dim, and stuffy with the smell of pharmaceuticals and wet raincoats. Over the other homely odors hung the stench of burnt flesh.

Snip, went the physician's bandage shears through charred cloth. Thorne lit a cigarette and inhaled, but the sharp, sickening other smell remained in his nostrils.

"According to his Seamen's International card, he was George Zandbergen of Port Grand," said the sheriff to Sam, who carefully transcribed this information in his notebook. To Thorne he said, "Did you know him, mister?"

Thorne shook his head.

"I remember him, Peter," said the physician, experimentally determining the stiffness of the dead fingers before him. "Appendicitis in 1946. Left town after that. I think he used to be an oiler on the *Josephine Temple* in the fruit fleet. I'll have a file on him around somewhere."

"Get that, Sam," said the sheriff. He turned to Thorne, standing awkwardly at the foot of the examination table. "We'll have to have your story for the record, of course. I hope this won't take too long. Start at the beginning, please."

Gulping down his nervousness and revulsion, Thorne told of returning from town about nine o'clock and finding the corpse of a man lying in the middle of a deserted side road. Dr. Thorne recalled puzzling at the condition of the body, for although it had been storming heavily at the time, portions of the body had been burned quite black. Thorne had found something at the scene also, but failing to see that it had any connection with the matters at hand, prudently kept his discovery to himself. The sheriff would hardly be interested in it, he told himself, but nevertheless he hoped that the bulge it made in his pocket wasn't too noticeable.

Officer Sam Stern made the last little tipped-v that stood for a period in his transcription and looked nervously about him. His chief peered approvingly—even if uncomprehendingly—at the notes and then said:

"How does it look, doctor?"

"Third degree burns on fifty percent of the body area, seared to the bone in some parts of the face and about the right scapula. How did you say he was lying when you found him, Mr. Thorne?"

"In an unnatural kind of sprawled position, on the right side."

The physician yawned, rummaged in a cabinet and produced a sheet with which he covered the charred body. "Pretty obvious, Peter, with these burns and all. Verdict is accidental death. The poor devil was struck by lightning. Time of death was about eight P.M." He tucked the sheet securely around the head. "That lightning's pretty odd stuff, now. Can blow the soles off a man's shoes without scratching him, or generate enough heat to melt metal. You never know what tricks it's going to play. Take this guy here: one side of him's broiled black and the other's not even singed. Well, you never know, do you?"

He picked up his phone and conversed briefly with the local undertaking parlor. When negotiations for the disposition of the unfortunate Mr. Zandbergen had been completed, he replaced the receiver and shuffled toward the door. Thorne could see that he had bedroom slippers on under his rubbers.

"You can finish up tomorrow, Peter," he resumed. "My wife was kinda peeved at me coming out this way. You know how women are, ha-ha. Good night to you, Mr. Thorne. I think there's an old overcoat in that closet I could let you take. You'll be wanting to send yours to the cleaners."

There was a genial guffaw from the sheriff. "We won't keep you any longer tonight, Mr. Thorne. Just let me know how I can get in touch with you."

"Through Kirk MacInnes on River Road," said Thorne. "He'll be glad to contact me through his amateur station." He edged through the door into the quiet night. The sheriff came close behind.

"So you're a ham, eh?" he said warmly. "Well, can you tie that! I used to have a ticket myself in the old days."

Polite noises. How about that? Kindred souls. Sorry about all this sloppy business, old man. Tough luck you had to be the one to find him. Really nothing, old man. *Why* didn't he stop talking? The weight in Thorne's pocket seemed to grow.

"You know, I'll be dropping in to see your rig some one of these days if you don't mind. I'll bet you could use a little company out there in the dunes, eh?"

No, why should he mind? Delighted, old man. Any time at all.

The thing in his pocket seemed to sag to his ankles. It would rip the pocket and fall out. And it had bits of charred cloth on it. Why didn't they go? They couldn't possibly suspect that he hadn't—

Oh, yes, he was on ten meters. Phone. Oh, the sheriff had done c.w. on 180? Well, wasn't that nice.

They walked to the cars under the big old elm trees that lined the comfortable street. A few stars came out and down where the street dead-ended into the river, they could see lights moving toward the deepwater channel that connected the river with the lake.

"Well, good night, Sheriff," Thorne said. "Good night, Mr. Stern. I hope next time we'll meet under more pleasant circumstances."

"Good night, Mr. Thorne," said Sam, who was thoroughly bored with talk he didn't understand, and anxious to get home to his wife and baby.

The police got into their car and drove off. Thorne sat quietly behind the wheel of the jeep until he was sure they were gone, then gingerly removed the weight from his pocket and unwrapped the handkerchief that covered it.

This one was the size of a closed fist and irregular in shape. He had found it flattened under the black char that had once been a man's shoulder, glowing with a bright yellow light in its heart. It looked the same as the three small drops he had previously seen, but he saw that what he had mistaken for golden flecks inside of it was really a fine network of metallic threads which formed a web apparently imbedded a few centimeters below the thing's surface.

The damn thing, he thought. There was something funny about it, all right.

Around him, the lights of the quiet houses were going out one by one. It was eleven o'clock. A few wet patches still glistened on the street under the lamps, and a boat motor on the river pulsed, then stilled.

Thorne looked around him quickly, then got out of the car and laid the thing on the curb. The wet leaves in the gutter below it reflected yellow faintly.

It was funny that a mere matter of shape could change his feeling toward it so radically. The smaller drops had been rather beautiful in their droplike mystery, but this one, although it was made of the same wonderful stuff, had none of the beauty. The irregular cavity in its side that would fit a human shoulder blade made it a thing sinister; the dried blood and ashes made it monstrous.

He took a tire iron out of the tool kit and tapped the glowing thing experimentally. It was certainly stronger than it looked, at any rate. When harder taps failed to crack it, he raised the iron and brought it down with all his strength. The tool bounced, skidded, and chipped the concrete curbstone, but the thing flew undamaged into the gutter.

Thorne bent down and poked it incredulously. And suddenly, with a cry of agony, he dropped the tire iron. It was hot! The tool arced down and lay sizzling sullenly among the little drops of water that still clung to the grass blades. His hand— He clenched his teeth to keep from crying out.

But the glowing thing in the gutter was not hot. Steam rose from the iron in the grass, but the little rivulets bathing the glowing thing were cool. He seemed to remember something, but then the shocked numbness coming over his hand took his attention and he forgot it again.

Down among the leaves and trash, the thing that was not shattered by the strength of Dr. Thorne grew, momentarily, more golden; and with a deliberate, liquid ripple the ugly bulges on its surface smoothed and it assumed the perfect drop shape of its predecessors.

200000 AU PLUS PLENTY WATTS. TELL ME PRETTY MAIDEN ARE THERE ANY MORE AT HOME LIKE YOU? ARRIVE NOON THURSDAY. LOVE. SEPPEL.

"You think you're pretty smart, don't you?" said Thorne.

"Yep," said Willy Seppel smugly, smirking around the edge

of his beer. He put down the glass and the smirk expanded to a grin. "Smart enough to see what those drops were that you sent me for a gag. That was a great little trick of yours, you know. I was all set to throw them out after reading that note of yours. The only thing that saved them was Archie Deck. He thought they might be Prince Rupert drops and tried to crack the tails off with a file."

"Aha," said Dr. Thorne.

Seppel looked at him with bright blue, innocent eyes. He was a large, pink-faced, elegantly dressed man with an eagle-beak nose and a crown of fine, blond hair.

"You don't have to look at me like that," said Thorne. "I've been able to find out a little bit more about them myself."

"Tell me," said the pink face complacently.

"They generate heat. And I found out the same way as Archie Deck probably did." He gestured with one bandaged hand. "Only I managed it the hard way." He swept up the empty glasses and beer bottles with a crash and disappeared into the kitchen. His voice continued distantly:

"I found those two I sent you inside the stomach of a toad. Or at least what was left of the stomach of a toad. Look in the lab room, the big shelf; second bottle from the end on the right-hand side."

Wiping his good hand on his trousers, he returned to Seppel, who stood looking thoughtfully into the toad's bottle. "It ate the drops," Thorne said shortly.

"Mm—yes," he mused. "The digestive juices might very possibly be able to—"

"Come on, Willy. What is it?"

"You were almost right when you said it generated heat," Willy said. "I brought one of them here to show you." He left the room and returned in a minute with a large cowhide briefcase.

"This thing's in a couple of pieces," Seppel apologized. "You'll have to wait until I set it up. Have you got a step-down transformer?"

Thorne nodded and fetched it from the bookcase.

"Now this little drop here may look like a bead, but it has some singular properties." He removed the thing from a box which had been heavily sealed and padded, and set it in a nest of gray, woolly stuff in the middle of the table.

"It gives off long infrared, mostly stacked up around 200,000 Angstroms. But their energy is way out of proportion from what you'd expect from the equation. This little gadget is something Deck and I rigged up to measure it crudely. Essentially, it's a TC130X couple hooked up to a spring gun. You put the drop in here, regulate the tension of the spring, and firing the gun releases this rod which delivers the drop an appropriate smack." His fingers with their immaculately groomed nails worked deftly. "We don't get a controlled measurement, of course, but it'll show you what I mean. . . . Where do you hide your outlets?"

"Behind the fish tank. Be careful not to disconnect the aerator."

"The screen on that end will show you the energy output. Watch now."

The horizontal green line on the little gray screen bucked at the firing of the spring, then exploded into an oscillating fence of spikes.

"Mad, isn't it?" remarked Dr. Thorne. "Hit it again, but lower the tension of the spring."

If anything, the spikes were even higher.

"The smack-energy ratio isn't proportional," said Seppel. "Sometimes a little nudge will set it off like a rocket. And again, after we tapped it for a week at Ann Arbor figuring out what it was, it showed a tendency to sulk and wouldn't perform at all after awhile."

"The energy output," Thorne said. "It's really quite small, isn't it?"

"Yes, but still surprising for an object this size." He removed the drop from the device and put it back into its little box. "We think that glowing heart has something to do with it. And those gold threads—they are gold, you know—come in there too. Old Camestres, the Medalist himself, was visiting the University, and he says that glow is something that'll have the physicists crawling the walls."

"Oh, come now," said Dr. Thorne broadly.

"You just wait," said Seppel. "We haven't done the analysis yet, but we expect great things. The glow," he added, "isn't hard radiation, if that's what you're thinking."

Willy was proud of it, Thorne thought. It was really his discovery after all, not Thorne's, and Seppel, who found challenge and stimulation in the oddest places, had hit the heights with the little golden drops.

But Thorne was remembering a larger drop, the size of a man's fist, and the charred body of a dead man.

"I found another specimen," he said, turning to a drawer in the worktable. "A larger one." He took out Mr. Zandbergen's drop.

"This is wonderful!" Seppel cried. "It's almost the size of a grapefruit! Now we can—"

Thorne cut him off gently. "I want to tell you about this one. Then I'll turn it over to you. When I first found it, it was irregularly shaped. Lumpy. Ugly. It's smooth now, just like the others, but it changed right before my eyes. It just seemed to run fluid, then coalesce again into the drop shape. And there's something else."

He told Seppel about the attempt to crack the thing and the abrupt heating of the tire iron.

"Yes, that could be," Seppel decided. "It's easily possible that a larger specimen such as this one could cause a metal object near it to become perceptibly warm. Infrared rays aren't hot in themselves, but when they penetrate a material their wave length is increased and the energy released heats the material. In the case of the tire iron, the conductivity of the metal was greater than that of your hand, and you felt the warm iron before the skin itself was affected."

"The iron wasn't warm, Willy. It was damn hot. And in a matter of seconds."

Seppel shook his head. "I don't know what to say. It's the funniest thing I've ever run across."

"The dead man who lay down on it didn't think it was funny," said Thorne.

"You don't think this little thing killed him, do you? He was charred to a cinder all along one side of him. Do you know what kind of infrared could do a thing like that? None."

"I didn't say I thought *this* one killed him," said Thorne, with a cue that Seppel chose to ignore. "I just said the body was right on top of it."

"Too wild for me," said Seppel. He got up, stretched leisurely, and glanced at the clock. "And anyhow, it's sack time. We can worry about it tomorrow, eh?"

Thorne had to smile. Good old Willy. No little glowing monster was going to keep *him* from his sleep.

"We'll put grapefruit back in the drawer," Seppel suggested, "have ourselves a snack, and go to bed."

"Wouldn't the big one be better off in a pail of ice?" asked Thorne, half laughingly.

"If it did decide to give out, it would probably melt the pail before it melted the ice. And besides," he added with dapper complacency, "they never radiate unless they're disturbed."

In the dream, there was sand all around him. He was in it, buried up to his neck. There was a sun overhead that was gold and transparent, and a wind that never seemed to reach his feverish face threw up little whirls of yellow sand.

Sometimes the familiar face of a woman was there. He cried her name and she was gone. And after that, he forgot her, for small shapeless things gamboled out on the sand into the sunlight, only to be burnt black as the rays struck them. . . .

For the fifth time that night, it seemed, Thorne awoke, his eyes staring widely into the darkness. He cursed at himself and turned the perspiration-soaked pillow over, pummeling it into a semblance of plumpness. Seppel lay beside him, snoring gently.

Somewhere in the lodge a timber creaked, and he felt the fear come back again, and saw the black, huddled heap lying before his headlights, and felt the pain renewed in his slowly healing hand. Of the dream, strangely enough, there was no memory at all.

Only the fear.

But why should he be afraid? There was nothing out there. Nothing out there at all.

But the heap in the road. Lightning. *But the little one had burned.* So what? *The little one was too small to burn a man seriously.* I know that. *He was burned.* Lightning, you silly fool! *He was burned!* Shut up. *One of them burned him.* Shut up! Shut up! *There's another one out there tonight.*

No. Nothing out there at all.

Nothing but the dunes and the lake. Nothing.

The wind squalls strummed the pine branches out there, and swirls of sand borne up the bluff from the beach below tickled faintly at the window. The waves of Michigan were roaring out there—but there was nothing else.

Finally, he was able to sleep.

It was nearly dawn when he woke again, but this time he

was on guard and alert as he lowered his bare feet softly to the floor. His hand closed over the barrel of a flashlight on the chest of drawers, and he moved noiselessly so that he would not wake the sleeper beside him.

He tiptoed slowly through the workroom and the living room. Something was on the porch.

As he came through the doors, he said sharply: "Who's there?"

An odor of burned wood hit his nostrils. He exclaimed shortly under his breath and shone the light down near the sill of the outside door. There was a round black hole in the door, smoking and glowing faintly around the edges.

He raced back into the workroom and pulled out the drawer that had held the grapefruit-sized drop. It was empty, and a hole gaped in the bottom of it. The hard wood was still burning slowly.

He yanked out the drawer, put it in the kitchen sink, and turned on the water. Then he filled a pan and soaked the hole in the door thoroughly.

They never radiate unless they're disturbed! That was a laugh. Not only had it radiated, but it had somehow focused the radiation. Dr. Thorne was no physicist, but he began to wonder whether the meter had told the whole story of the little glowing drop.

He unlocked the door and slid out into the night. Below the stair was a small, almost imperceptible track in the sand. He followed it down the ridge of the dune, lost it momentarily in a patch of scrub, then found it again in the undisturbed expanse of the sand blow.

He went down into the silent valley, the bobbling yellow light from his flash throwing the tiny track into high relief. When he reached the center of the bowl, he stopped among the long shadows of the gaunt spiky trees.

There was another track in the sand, meeting and merging with the little one. And the track was three feet wide.

He followed it as if in a dream to the crest of the first low shore dune and stood on its summit among the sharp grass and wild grape. The moon's crescent was low over the water and orange. He saw the track go down the slope and disappear into the waves which were swirling in a new depression in the sand.

The wind whipped his pajama shirt about his back as he stood there and knew that he was afraid of that track in the sand, and that no lightning had killed the little tramp.

It was not until he had locked the door of the lodge behind him that he realized he had run all of the way back.

Friday was a quiet day in the dunes country, but the police did receive three minor complaints. A farmer charged that someone had not only made off with and eaten three of his best laying hens, but had burned the feathers and bones and left them right in the chicken yard. The Ottawa County Highway Commission wanted to know who was building fires in the middle of their asphalt roads and plastering the landscape with hot tar. And a maiden lady complained that the artists in the local summer colony must be holding Wild Orgies again from the looks of the lights she had seen over there at three A.M.

Dr. Thorne bent down over the tracks in the sand. It certainly looked to him as though the big one had been waiting for Mr. Zandbergen's drop.

Seppel said, "Get out of the way there," and snapped his Graflex. "These sand tracks won't last long in the winds around here. And I frankly tell you that if I hadn't seen it with my own eyes, I would never have believed it." He circled the point of conjunction, laid his fountain pen beside it for size reference, and the Graflex flashed again.

"We'll want the door, too," he said, putting the camera aside and scrawling in his notebook.

Thorne howled.

"Well, just the part with the hole in it then," Seppel conceded. "Did you find out where the large track came from?"

"I tracked it to the woods. The ground there is too soft and boggy to hold a wide track like that, and I finally lost it."

Seppel struggled to his feet and retrieved his coat, which he had hung for safety's sake on the white peg branch of a skeleton tree. "Just imagine the size of an object which would make a three-foot track in soft sand!" he exclaimed. "And to think it's been in the lake for heaven knows how long and this is the first time it's come into evidence!"

"I wouldn't be too sure about that—about this being the first time, I mean. There have been some funny old stories told along these shores. I heard one myself from my grandmother when I was about twelve. About the dune roller that was bigger than a schooner and lived in the caves at the bottom of the lake. It came out every hundred years and rolled through the dune forest, leaving a strip of bare sand behind it where it had eaten the vegetation. They said it looked for a man, and when it found one, it would stop rolling and sink back into the lake."

"Great Caesar," said Seppel solemnly. "I can see it now—the great glowing globe lurking deep in the caverns where the sun never shines and there is no life except a few diatoms drifting in the motionless waters."

Thorne gaped at his friend for a minute, and then spied a suspicious twinkle in one blue eye.

"This is no laughing matter, you Sunday supplementist!" he said sharply.

"Hmp," said Willy Seppel, and brushed a few grains of sand from the sleeve of his handsome suit.

It was late when Miss Jeanne Wright got out of the movie in Muskegon—so late that she barely had time to do the shopping which had, ostensibly, been her reason for taking *Carlin* out. "You just can't buy decent dresses in Port Grand, Uncle Kirk," she had pleaded, and he really wouldn't mind if she took the boat, would he? MacInnes had growled indulgently from the depths of his new panadaptor and said he certainly did, confound it, and what was the matter with using the car? But he had tossed her the keys just the same.

The street lights of the city were going on when, laden with bundles, she finally hailed a cab and drove to the yacht basin. It was a beautiful evening, with soft-glowing stars in a sky that was still red-purple in the west. *Carlin* slipped majestically out among the anchored craft into Muskegon Lake.

A bonfire blazed cheerfully on the shore and singing voices from some beach party floated melodiously out over the water. They shouted a jocular greeting to *Carlin* and Jeanne blew a hail to them with the air horn. Her heart was light as she led the cruiser through the channel into the lake and headed for home.

A secretive smile danced on her lips, and she thought kindly about a certain stern-faced young biologist. He was a strange man, occasionally even rude in an unintentional sort of way, and preoccupied with such dreary things as plant cycles and environmental adaptations. But he had walked with her in the dunes one day and changed for a little while, and kissed her once, very gently, on the lips. And after that she had known what she wanted.

He would be sitting in his workroom now, looking over the day's bugs and not thinking of her at all. Or perhaps he would be talking to her uncle over the radio.

She hummed dreamily to herself. The cruiser's speed increased to twenty, and it rocked momentarily in a trough, setting the little good luck charm hung up over the wheel to bobbing like a pendulum. Ian had given that to her. She loved it because of that.

After a while she turned on the short wave receiver that sat on one of the lockers in the deckhouse and listened to Ian and her uncle.

"I have a colleague of mine out from Ann Arbor," Thorne was saying. "About that amber drop we found. Remember my telling you about it? I gave one to Jeanne for a souvenir. My friend is a biophysicist and thinks the drops are a great scientific discovery. His name is Willy Seppel. Say something, Willy."

"Gambusia," said Seppel, recalling the minnows in the larvae pail.

Jeanne listened absently. Ian was telling how the drops gave off hot light when they were disturbed. How he thought there might be bigger drops around that could really grind out the energy 40db. above S9. (What in the world did *that* mean?) Thorne and this Willy person would look for the bigger drops.

"Is it really hot?" Jeanne wondered, staring curiously at the pendant drop, swinging above the binnacle in its miniature silver basket. It didn't seem to be. But then Ian had said the little ones didn't radiate very much. Only enough to tickle a something-or-other.

Far out in the lake, the lights of an ore boat twinkled. She passed the little village of Lake Harbor and put out a bit farther from shore. There would be no more towns now until Port Grand.

Over the radio, her Uncle Kirk's voice, homely and kind, was describing the great things in store for the new panadaptor.

Ian would put in a comment here and there, but she noticed that he sounded tired, poor darling.

Cleanly, powerfully, *Carlin* sliced through the waves, pursuing the shadow of herself. The shadow was long, and very black. A boat with a searchlight, thought Jeanne, and looked astern.

It was there, riding high in the dark, choppy water: a great glowing globe of phosphorescence not twenty yards off the stern. It was coming after her, rapidly overtaking the cruiser.

She screamed then, and when the thing came on, she opened the throttle and attempted to outmaneuver it. But the great glowing monster would pause while she veered and spiraled, then overtake her easily when she tried to run away. The motors of the Matthews throbbed in the hull beneath her feet as she tried to urge them to a speed they were never meant for.

The thing was drawing closer. She could see trails of water streaming from it. What was it? What would it do if it caught her?

Bigger ones! Her eyes turned with horror to the tiny drop on its silver chain. Its glow was the perfect miniature of the monstrous thing in the water behind her. She sobbed as she wrenched *Carlin*'s wheel from side to side in hysterical frenzy. Across the cabin, the quiet voice of Ian was telling MacInnes how to rig the panadaptor as a frequency monitor.

Ian!

And if you're ever in a jam. . . .

With tears streaming down her cheeks she set the automatic pilot and fumbled with the little amateur transmitter that had been built into the locker. She had seen her uncle use it only once. That turned it on, she thought, but how did she know it was set right? Or did you set these things?

The little panel wore three switches, two knobs, a dial and a little red light. Naturally Kirk MacInnes had not labeled the controls of an instrument he had built himself. The panel was innocent of any such clutterment.

Carlin tore through the night. The glowing thing was less than fifteen yards behind.

Jeanne wept wildly and the placid voices over the receiver spoke sympathetically of the ruining of Thorne's beach pool by the storm.

Oh, those knobs and switches! This one, then this one, she

thought. No—that wouldn't be right. The transmitter might not even be on the air at all. Or she might be in some part of the band where Ian and her uncle would fail to hear her. But what was she supposed to do? And she couldn't read this funny tuning scale.

"I've got a swell mobile VFO in *Carlin*," said MacInnes.

"What's VFO?" said Seppel.

"In Mac's case, it means Very Frequently Offband."

Laughter.

Oh, what difference would it make? What could he do to help her? The brilliance of the huge thing was lighting up the water for yards around.

The calm voices floated from the receiver and the globe drew closer than it had ever been.

She clawed at the stand-by switch of the radio and suddenly her sobs and the beat of the engines were the only sounds in the deckhouse. She would try. That was all. She would try to reach Ian, and pray that her uncle had left the transmitter set to the correct frequency.

"Ian!" she cried, then remembered to press the button on the side of the little hand microphone. Forcing back her tears, she said, "Ian, Ian—can you hear me?"

Trembling, her hand touched the receiver.

"Jeanne!" the sound burst into the deckhouse. "Is that you? What are you doing?"

"It's after me, Ian!" she screamed. "A glowing sphere fifteen feet high! It's chasing the boat!"

"The boat," came MacInnes' voice numbly. "She took it to Muskegon."

"Jeanne! Listen to me. I don't know whether this will do any good, but you must try. You must do exactly as I say. Do you hear me?"

"I hear you. Ian! That thing is almost on top of the boat!"

"Listen. Listen to me, darling. You have that little amber drop somewhere in the boat. Do you remember? The little amber drop I gave you. Get it. Take it and throw it overboard. Throw it as far as you can. The amber drop! Now tell me if you heard me."

"Yes. I hear you. The drop. . . ."

The drop. It danced on its little silver chain and the light in its core was bright and pulsating and warm. She tore it from

its place over the wheel and groped back to the open cockpit of
the cruiser. She clung for a full minute to the canopy stanchion, blinded by the golden light.

And then the small drop arced brightly over the water, even
as a meteor had, many centuries past.

The light, reflecting off the walls painted a flat, clinical
white, was full of blurred, fuzzy forms. They might have been
almost anything, Thorne thought. And he shuddered as he
thought of what they might have been. A table, for instance,
with a burden that was sprawled and made black all along one
side.

Without moving his head or changing his expression he
squeezed his eyes shut very slowly and opened them again. But
it was not the medical examiner's office. It was the waiting
room of the little local hospital, and Willy Seppel was sitting
beside him on the leather couch. Through the open window
behind lowered blinds, a clovery night breeze stirred, parting
the smoke that filled the room and turning a page of the magazine that Seppel was staring at.

A young man of twenty-five or so sat across the room from
them and ate prodigious quantities of Lifesavers. "My wife,"
he had grinned nervously at them. "Our first."

The persons in the waiting room could see through the open
door to a room at the end of the hall. People in white would
periodically enter and leave this room, but another, grimmer
group which had entered nearly an hour ago had not come out.

"Willy, I'm going nuts," Thorne burst out at last. "What are
they doing in there? You'd think they'd at least let me know—
let me see her."

"Easy. It'll be any minute now." He proffered a gold cigarette
case, but Thorne shook his head. "Why don't you lie back and
try to relax?" Seppel said. "You've been crouching there staring
at the floor until your eyes look like a pair of burned-out bulbs.
What good do you think you're going to do her in that kind of
shape?"

Thorne sank back and lay with the back of his hand shading
his eyes. If he could have been there when they brought her in!
But it takes time to find where an unmanned boat has drifted.
Time while he sat before his receiver with nothing to do but
wait. The hands of the clock had wound around to one A.M.
before the call finally came and he knew she was saved.

It was three-thirty now. MacInnes and his wife were in there with her. He looked despairingly down the white corridor, and waited.

The sound of her voice, made broken and breathless with weeping, rose again in his mind. She had said the thing was fifteen feet high. The big one itself. And it could have—

This wouldn't do at all. The memory of his dream the previous night stood out in his mind with horrible clarity. The bright golden sun and the little burned things. But infrared doesn't burn. The bright golden sun.

"Sun," said Dr. Thorne to himself, very quietly.

"Mm'mm?" said Seppel.

"Sun," he repeated firmly. "Willy, do you always think the same way?"

"Nope."

"If I hit you, how do you think?"

"Mad," said Seppel, with a winning smile.

"But if you figure the best way to sneak out of here without being seen, how do you think?"

"Rationally."

"I've been thinking about the drops again. You know, we've got a pretty serious discrepancy in the so-called properties of the things. We've proved the infrared emission, but infrared doesn't sear flesh."

"That's what I've been trying to tell you," said Seppel, with patience.

"Nonetheless, I'm convinced that the big one Jeanne saw is the thing that did in the tramp. Now what if the energy emitted is not always infrared? What if the infrared is a sort of involuntary result of the blows we gave the drop, while ordinarily when it's aroused it gives off another wave length? Say something in the visible with a lot of energy, that that drop shape could focus into a beam."

Seppel didn't say a thing.

Silence precipitated heavily. The young man in the chair opposite them shifted his position and stared at them with gaping awe. Scientists!

There was a starchy swish and a nurse appeared in the doorway. Thorne started to his feet. "Can we—"

"Mr. De Angelo," she beckoned coolly. "It's a boy. Will you follow me, please?"

The young man gave a joyous, inarticulate cry and rushed out of the room.

Thorne dropped back. "Ye gods," he muttered.

"You've really got it bad, haven't you?" Seppel marveled.

"Oh, Willy, shut up. You know I'm only interested in her because of the thing that chased her. And wipe that look off your face. Between you and MacInnes a man doesn't have a chance."

Seppel looked slightly hurt.

"I'm sorry," Thorne apologized briefly. He walked around the room. The young man with the new son had been so anxious to leave that he had forgotten his Lifesavers. Thorne ate one. It was wintergreen. He hated wintergreen.

Seppel yawned delicately, then leaned forward and glanced out the door. "Someone's coming," he warned softly.

A tall man in a uniform of summer tans had left the room at the end of the corridor and walked purposefully toward the waiting room.

Seppel rose to his feet as the man entered the room. He said: "Good evening—or rather, good morning. Is there something I can do?"

"My name is Cunningham, commander of the Coast Guard cutter *Manistique*. Are you Mr. Ian Thorne?"

"My name is Seppel. This is Mr. Thorne. Won't you sit down?"

"Thanks, I will." To Thorne, who stood with his hands rudely clasped behind his back, he said briskly: "Mr. Thorne, at nine this evening your amateur station contacted our base with information that the cruiser *Carlin* was in difficulty off the mainland somewhere between Port Grand and Muskegon."

"It wasn't me, it was Kirk MacInnes." Thorne was not interested in brisk, nautical gentlemen.

"We found the cruiser drifting, out of gas, some seven miles off the Port Grand light. Miss Wright, the operator of the craft, was found lying unconscious on the cockpit floor. I've just seen her—"

"How is she?" Thorne cut in.

"The doctors say she is suffering from shock, but other than that, they can't find a thing wrong with her. Now what I'd like to know—"

"Is she conscious? Has she been able to talk?"

"She's very weak and what she says makes no sense. I thought perhaps you might be able to help us on that score."

Thorne looked at the Coast-Guardsman narrowly. "We were conversing with her over the radio, when she suddenly seemed to become disturbed and evidently fainted."

"Didn't MacInnes tell you anything?" asked Seppel.

"No."

"Quiet, Willy," Thorne said.

"She seemed to be trying to tell us that someone was chasing her," Cunningham persisted. "Are you sure she said nothing in her talk with you that could give us a hint of the trouble?"

"I knew there was something wrong from the sound of her voice. That's all. When she didn't answer, Mr. MacInnes radioed the Coast Guard."

"And we found her after a four-hour search. That young lady was very lucky that she ran out of gas. Her automatic pilot had the cruiser headed straight out into the middle of the lake."

"There was—nothing else on the water near her?"

"The lake was empty." Cunningham paused, then said casually, "Was there something you expected us to find, Dr. Thorne?"

"Certainly not. I was just wondering."

"I see." The officer got to his feet. "I don't mind telling you gentlemen that I think there's something you're not letting me know. My job is done, and it's true that legally I have no business questioning you at all. But my business *is* keeping the waterways safe. The young lady in the room down the hall didn't faint from nervous exhaustion or hunger. Something scared the hell out of her out there on the lake. If you know what it was, I wish you'd tell me!"

"Have you ever read any science fiction, Commander Cunningham?" Seppel asked, toying with his gold cigarette case. Rather belatedly, he said, "Cigarette?"

The Coast-Guardsman took one with suspicious thanks. "Are you trying to tell me that the little green Martians have put outboards on their rocket ships and are chasing the pleasure craft on our lake?"

Thorne said harshly: "What Dr. Seppel means is this. We have reason to believe that a highly unusual occurrence was responsible for tonight's unpleasantness. I don't like to mince words, Commander. I think I *do* know what was out there last

night, but I'm not going to tell you. I can't begin to prove my
suspicions, and I have a rather intense aversion to being
laughed at."

"I have no intention of laughing, Mr. Thorne. But if you
have information relative to marine safety, let me remind you
that you have an obligation to report it to the proper authorities."

"Proper authorities are not notorious for their sympathy.
They'd laugh in my face. No, thank you, Commander. Until I
have proof, I say nothing."

The door at the end of the corridor opened once more, and
closed softly. Kirk MacInnes and his wife came down toward
the waiting room. Thorne started up.

"She wants to see you, son," MacInnes said tiredly. "She's a
little stronger now, and she asked for you. I'm taking Ellen
back home. This has been pretty raw for her."

"I'm all right," his wife said stiffly. She clutched a damp,
tightly balled lace handkerchief, but her features were im-
mobile.

"Will Jeanne be all right?" Thorne asked brokenly.

"She'll be fine," said MacInnes, clapping him on the back.
"Now get down there and see her before those medics decide
she can't have any more visitors."

"I'm there now. And—thanks, Mac." He disappeared down
the corridor. The engineer and his wife left quietly.

"Thorne is a good man," Seppel said, "even if he is a trifle
mule-headed." His bright blue eyes looked humorously into the
half-angry face of the Coast Guard officer. He laughed, moved
over on the leather couch, and said: "Sit down here, Commander. Have another cigarette. Have a Lifesaver. I'm going to
tell you a singular story."

It was shortly before lunchtime in Thorne's dune lodge, but
the bubbling beaker on the range that Willy Seppel was stirring exuded a decidedly unappetizing aroma. Pungent, acidic
in an organic kind of way, with noisome and revolting over-
tones, the fumes finally brought indignant remarks from
Thorne.

"Look," he said, peering in the doorway, and holding his
nose. "I'm the last one to criticize another man's cooking, but
will you tell me what in heaven's name that is?"

"Oh, just a bit of digestive juice," said Seppel cheerily, turning off the gas and removing the beaker with a pair of pot holders. He carried his foul-steaming container into the workroom. Thorne fled before him.

"I suppose I'd better not ask where you got it," he said, from the sanctuary of the radio room.

"Don't be silly," said Seppel. "I merely raided your enzymes and warmed up a batch. Just an idea."

He took the little drop out of its container and set it on the table beside the beaker. "I thought since digestive juice provoked it into emitting once, it might do it again."

Thorne regarded him dubiously.

"I only wish," Seppel went on to say, "that the grapefruit-sized one hadn't escaped." He set the drop in a loop of plastic and dipped it into the brew.

"Take it easy with that one, Willy. It's the only link we have with the big one."

"So you think they can communicate, too," said Seppel without looking up.

"I don't know whether it's communication or sympathetic vibration or the call of the wild. But that thing did follow Jeanne because of the little drop in the boat, and it disappeared when it got what it wanted. The grapefruit heard mama, too, and got away. I'll bet if that little one had been strong enough to get through your fancy insulation, it would have disappeared along with the other one."

"And the two tracks merged into one," said Seppel, testing the soaked drop in the thermocouple. Nothing happened. "As the rustic detective was heard to remark, 'They was two sets o' footsteps leadin' to the scene of the crime, and only one set leadin' away.' I wonder what kind of a molecular bond that transparent envelope has?" He felt the drop with his finger, shrugged, and put it back into the juice.

"The big globe killed the tramp, if my idea is correct," said Thorne. "He must have seen the thing coming out of the lake, turned to beat it, and fell on his face. And I think he picked exactly the wrong place to fall."

"On grapefruit," Seppel agreed. "All mama wanted to do was to pick up her offspring. She couldn't help it if there was a body in the way."

"But she killed just the same," said Thorne. "Those old dune

roller stories hint that she may have done it before." He fished
the miniature drop out of the liquid and looked into its yellow
heart meditatively.

"And Willy," he said abstractedly, "unless something is done
soon, she'll do it again."

During the days that followed, Dr. Thorne went about his
work with quiet preoccupation; and this in itself was enough
to make Seppel more than a little suspicious. He rarely mentioned the drops, although he visited Jeanne every day, carrying sheaves of flowers and boxes of candy and fruit. Seppel
went along on these pilgrimages for the ride, but almost always
tactfully declined visiting the sickroom and hiked out instead
to the Coast Guard station for a parley with his new ally,
Commander Cunningham.

Anxiety furrowed Seppel's pink forehead as he paced up and
down the officer's quarters. "He's got something up his sleeve,"
he maintained. "He goes off in the jeep in the morning and
doesn't come back until noon. When I ask him where he's been,
he says he just went into town to see Jeanne. But visiting
hours are from two to four! If he doesn't go to the hospital,
where does he go?"

Cunningham shrugged, and picked up a folded newspaper
that lay on the table. "Have you seen this, Willy? It might
explain a few things."

Mystified, Seppel read aloud: "'We pay CASH for certain
unusual minerals. Highest prices, free pickup. Samples
wanted are round, semi-transparent, amber colored with metallic veining. HURRY! Write today, Box 236, Port Grand,
Michigan.'"

Seppel stared aghast.

"I take it you weren't acquainted with this," the officer said.
He walked to the window and looked down at a fruiter steam-
ing through the channel. "Do you know what he plans to do?"

"No, but I know what I'd do. There's some kind of an attraction between the big globe and the drops—a force that draws
the little ones home to mama when they get her call. We found
that out with a drop at Thorne's lodge. But that attraction is so
great that it works the other way too. Little Miss Wright told
you that. If the drops can't come, if we hold them back, mama
comes after her children. That's what Thorne will probably
count on."

It was Cunningham's turn to stare. "You mean he'll use the drops from the ad for *bait*?"

Seppel said gently: "What's a man to do, Rob? He can't let it go free. The fellow that finds the monster has three choices: he can run home and hide under the bed, and pretend he didn't see it at all, he can try to inform the proper authorities, or he can attempt to dispose of the monster himself. Thorne knows nobody will believe his dune roller story so he just doesn't waste time convincing people."

Cunningham turned abruptly from the window and said violently: "You aren't going to start on me too, are you, Willy? Sure. Here I am, one slightly used but still serviceable authority. I believe your damn dune roller yarn for some reason or other. But it doesn't do any good. I'd earn the biggest haw-haw from here to the Straits of Mackinac if I tried to initiate an official search for a round glowing thing fifteen feet high. The world won't unite simply because Michigan has itself a monster, you know. And what can I do, even if I take the *Manistique* out? Maybe Ian Thorne knows how to catch monsters, but I certainly don't."

"You want to let him go on, I suppose," Seppel said. He added a trifle wistfully, "I hate to see him get his hide fried off when he's just beginning to think about settling down."

"You watch him. That's all. And let me know when you think he's going to pull something. I'll do everything I can." He glanced at his watch. "I have to get out of here now, Willy. Keep your eyes open. All *we* can do is wait."

"And that," said Seppel, with dark doubt shading his pleasant voice, "seems to be all there is to say."

The drops glowed on the kitchen table. "Seven!" said Ian Thorne triumphantly. "How do they look to you, Willy? From the size of a pea to a tennis ball. Seven little devil eyes."

"What are you going to do with them?" asked Seppel. He wore an old lab apron over his trousers and wiped the breakfast dishes. It was very early in the morning.

"Just a little experiment. I got a bright idea the other day while I was visiting Jeanne. You can have the drops after I'm finished if you like, but I want to try this thing out first."

"I wish you'd let me help you."

"No, Willy."

"Cunningham believes you, too," Seppel went on recklessly.

"Why don't you tell us what you're going to do?"

"No." He scooped the drops into a bakelite box. "I'll be gone most of the day. I have some collecting to do out in the dunes."

He vanished into the bedroom and came out wearing hiking boots and a heavy leather jacket. An empty knapsack dangled over his arm. He put the bakelite box into the buckled pouch on the outside of the sack, and took a paper packet from the sink and stuffed it into his back pocket.

"Oops! Almost forgot my collecting bottles," he laughed, and went into the radio room.

Seppel put down the dish towel and stepped softly after him. There were no collecting bottles in the radio room. He was just in time to see Thorne drop a handful of little metal cylinders and a black six-inch gadget into the knapsack.

Thorne did not seem at all abashed to find Seppel standing there. He brushed past and went out the kitchen door.

"So long, Willy. Keep the home fires burning. Send out the posse if I'm not back before dark." The screen door slammed.

After waiting a minute, Seppel grabbed up the binoculars from the china shelf and glided silently through the sandy yard, past the generator building to the path that led down the side of the dune to the shed where the jeep was kept.

The early morning mist still curled around the trees and settled in the hollows, and a distant bird call echoed down on the forest floor. At a bend in the steep path, Seppel caught a glimpse of Thorne's broad back dappled by the pale sun rising through the fog.

The path turned sharply and cut off diagonally down the dune toward the shed. Instead of continuing, Seppel stepped off the path, and treading cautiously, circled across through the woods to arrive at a point on the slope directly above the garage. Then he removed his apron, spread it on the twiggy, dew-wet ground, and stretched out among the bushes, bringing his binoculars to bear on the man below.

Thorne removed a small wooden crate from the rear of the jeep. It bore the red-stenciled inscription:

G. B. VANDER VREES & SONS—HIGHWAY CONSTRUCTION

There were other words, too, but Thorne stood in the way of Seppel's vision. He quickly transferred the contents of the crate to his knapsack, and with a single look around him, set off down the dune trail that ran through the forest, parallel to the lake shore.

As soon as Thorne was out of sight, Willy Seppel scrambled heavily to his feet and went back up the path to the lodge. There he addressed some intense words to the microphone of the amateur station, an operation which would have been frowned upon by the FCC, which discourages the use of such equipment by unlicensed persons.

He would have maintained his disinterest and scientific detachment if he had been asked about it, but the truth was that Dr. Ian Thorne deeply loved the dunes. He had lived in them during his childhood, grown up and gone away, and come back to find them substantially the same. He recalled that had surprised him a little. You expected the dunes to change, they were like a person, though only one who has known the heights and swamps of them can explain the curious sleeping vitality of the sands under the forest. Things with a smaller life than the dunes would flutter and creep and stalk boldly through them until you might think of them as dead and tame. But Dr. Thorne had seen the traveling dunes shifting restlessly before the winds and felt a kinship with the great never-lasting hills.

The path he strolled along was an old friend. He had pursued the invertebrate citizens of the forest along its meandering length, waded in the marshy inter-dunal pools which it carefully skirted, and had itched from encounters with the poison ivy that festooned the trunks and shrubs beside it.

The path wound along the shore for a good five miles—horizontally, at least—and he did not hurry. The knapsack was too heavy, for one thing, and the still air was warming slowly as the sun rose up through the pines and oak trees. An insect chirred sleepily in a gorge on his right, and as if at some prearranged signal, an excursion of mosquitoes bobbed out to worry the back of his neck.

The path took him through a clearing in the sand covered with patches of dusty, green grass and scarlet Indian weed. On the lee side of a great bare dune at the edge of the clearing stood a single, short cottonwood, half buried in the sand. But the tree had grown upward to escape, modifying its lower branches into roots. The tree was one of the few forms of life that defied the dunes—by growing with them—and its branches were brave and green.

Thoughtfully, Thorne passed on again into the dimmer depths of the forest.

It was nearly noon when he reached the foot of a cluster of sand dunes, the principal peak of which rose some hundred and fifty feet above the floor of the woods. It was the highest point for many miles along the shore, and its name was Mount Scott. The path circled its eastern slope and then continued on, but Thorne stepped off onto the faintly defined, spider-web laced trail leading to the summit.

The going was rough. Thornapple branches probed after his eyes, and as the ascent grew steeper, sudden shifts in the dirty sand under his feet brought him to his knees. The tree roots across the path had partially blocked the sand, forming crude natural steps in the lower reaches of the dune; but as he climbed higher, the trees were left behind while the sand grew cleaner and hotter, and the wild grape, creeper and ubiquitous poison ivy became the prevalent greenery.

He was winded and perspiring when he finally stood on the peak of the dune. He glanced briefly about him and selected a spot partially shaded by a scrub juniper as his campsite. He sat down, shucked the knapsack and his heavy jacket, and lit a cigarette.

The hills below rolled away in gentle, green waves toward the farmlands and orchards in the east and the brilliant blue lake in the west. He could see the spires of the town of Port Grand poking out of the haze a few miles down the shore, and some white sails appeared off the promontory that hid the entrance to the river harbor.

He turned his attention to Mount Scott itself. The summit of the dune was really composed of two shallow humps, with a depression on the lakeward side in which Thorne had made his camp. Below this, a sheer, fairly clean slope of sand swept down to the low tangle of woods which lay between him and the shore.

He looked cautiously in the knapsack and removed the seven small drops, grouping them in a circle on the white sand of the lake slope. After that, he retreated to his hollow and settled down as comfortably as he could.

The paper packet in his pocket yielded three ham-and-pickle sandwiches, slightly soggy, which he consumed leisurely. A short foray around the peak brought dessert in the form of a handful of late blueberries. After his meal he employed himself at length with the contents of the knapsack. When the job was finally done, he sat down under the juniper tree and began to wait.

The shade of the tree diminished, disappeared as the sun climbed higher, and then reappeared on the other side of the tree, leaving Thorne with the sun in his face and a monumental thirst. The blueberries, unfortunately, were all gone.

At last, at four P.M., the largest drop began to move.

It rolled slowly out of the shallow hole in the sand that cupped it and moved down the hill. Thorne watched it roll *up* a small pile of sand that blocked its path and disappear into the woods at the foot of the hill.

At 4:57 one of the smaller drops followed in the track of the first. It had a little trouble when it came to the pile of sand— which was one of several strung across the face of the dune— but it negotiated the obstacle at last and disappeared.

Just as the sun was beginning to redden the water, a third drop began its descent. Quietly, Thorne rose and replaced it in its hole. The faint gleam within it might have grown a bit brighter when he interfered, but perhaps it was only the reflection of the sun.

The five remaining drops were grouped in a horseshoe, downward pointing, and the drop whose elopement had just been foiled reposed at the end of one prong. A few minutes later, the larger drop at the other prong attempted to roll down the hill. Thorne put it back and rapped sharply on each of the others with his cigarette lighter, tamping them down further into the sand. He was strained forward alertly now, with his eyes on the strip of forest below. The sun slipped grudgingly behind the flat lake, and a tang of pine washed up the slope. The drops did not move again.

With the departure of the sun, the glow in the heart of each alien thing leaped higher and higher, until the string of them was like a softly glowing corona in the sand—a strange earthbound constellation.

But their glow was not beauty, Thorne reminded himself. It was death. Death had dwelt in their great, glowing mother who

had already called two of her incredible children home. Death
that rolled seeking through the lake and the dune forest. . . .

His cigarette end made a dimmer eye in the dusk than the
glow of the drops. There was still enough light to see by—the
sky was red around him and the dune forest was silent.

He wondered idly what long forgotten power had strewn the
drops along the shore. They were not terrestrial, he was almost
sure of that. Perhaps they had been a meteor that had exploded
over the lake, and the life of the great thing—if it was life—
had been patiently gathering up its scattered substance ever
since, assimilating the fragments during its long rests at the
bottom of the lake.

From the size of it, it must have been growing for hundreds
of years, collecting a drop of itself here and there, from road-
beds and sand dunes and farmyards, responding to those who
imprudently hindered it with the only defense it knew.

And now he was to destroy it. It had killed a man. Perhaps
before this, even, men had found the drops attractive and care-
lessly put them in their pockets . . . and the dune roller
sought a man. It had killed the little tramp, and almost killed
Jeanne. He couldn't take a chance of letting it go again.

The image of Jeanne rose in his mind. The memory of the
time they had walked down the winding forest path, and of a
twig caught in her sandal. She had had grains of sand on her
tanned arms, and a bright yellow flower stuck crazily in one
dark curl. She had laughed when he plumped her down on the
moss-soft root of an old oak and took the twig out, but she had
not laughed when he kissed her.

Around him, the forest was still.

A cold breath whispered along his skin. The forest was still.
Not a bird, not an insect, not an animal noise. The forest was
still.

He felt like yelling at it: *Come on out, you!* Come out and
chase me like you chased her!

He fingered the stud of the little black instrument in his
hand. He would show it. Let it dare to come out.

Come out!

It came.

He had never dreamed it would be so big.

It had made no noise at all. In a fascination of horror he
watched it roll to the foot of the tall dune. It vanished among

the trees, but a warm yellow radiance lit the undersides of the fluttering leaves as it moved beneath them. The light blazed as it emerged from the brush and came straight toward him, rolling up the hill.

The small drops pulsed in their sandy snares and he gave each one a savage rap. As if it, too, shared the insult, the great globe flared, then subsided sullenly. But its ponderous ascent was alarmingly rapid.

He could not take his eyes away from it. The smaller drops were rocks, were mere bits of oddly glowing crystal; but this great thing before him seemed the most beautiful and the most terrible thing he had ever seen in his life. And it was alive. No man could have looked upon it and said that it was not alive. The brilliant golden heart in it swelled and blazed upon the golden veining that closed it in.

There were noises now from the winding path in the forest below, and the twinkling pinpoint lights of men. But Thorne did not hear them, nor see any light except the great one before him. He could not move. Sweat stood out on his face and the instinct to flee dissolved into terror that folded his legs like boneless things. He half-crouched on hands and knees and stared . . . and stared.

The thing was closer now, nearly up to the line of sand humps that Thorne had worked so hard on. He had to get away. There was no more time. He forced his paralyzed hands and feet to tear into the loose sand of the side of the depression and pull him up. He had to get on the other side of the hill.

In the last instant, his numbed fingers pressed the stud of the little transmitter that would activate the firing caps of the neonitro buried in the sand.

But the monster must have realized, somehow. Because he felt—when he flung himself out over the peak with the deep red sky around him—a searing, mounting pain that started on the inside and flooded outward. He rolled unconscious over the far side of the hill just as the five solemn detonations blasted the golden glowing globe to bits.

There were white, gauzy circles around the place where his eyes looked out. He was vaguely surprised to see six people with the eyes—three sets of two. He made the eyes blink and the six people changed into Seppel, MacInnes and Jeanne. He tried to raise an arm and was rewarded by a fierce jab of pain. The arm was thick and bandaged, like the rest of him.

The six—three—people had seen his eyes open and they moved closer to him. Jeanne sat down beside the bed and leaned her head close.

"I hope that's you in there," she said, and he was amazed to see there were tears in her eyes.

"How am I?" he mumbled through the bandages.

"Medium rare," said Seppel. "You doggone crazy fool."

"We almost got to the top, anyway," said MacInnes gruffly. "But you went and beat us to it."

"Had to," Thorne said painfully.

"You would," Jeanne said.

"Is it gone?" he asked. There were six people again and he felt very tired.

"Shivered to atoms," said Seppel with finality. "You should see the crater in the sand. But we'll still have small ones to study. Your ad brought in four more today. I was talking to Camestres on the phone, and he says he's sure he can swing a nice fat research grant for us as soon as you're able to get out of that bed—"

Thorne groaned.

"He says," Jeanne translated firmly, "that he's sticking to *Ecological Studies of the Michigan Dunes,* Chapter Eight. No more dune rollers, thank you."

MacInnes laughed and wagged his gray old head. "You'd better surrender, Dr. Seppel. Jeanne's got her mind made up. And one thing about her—whatever she says, she'll always be Wright."

"Don't be too sure about that," she said pertly, laying her two small hands gently on Thorne's bandaged arm. It didn't hurt a bit.

High on a dune above the lake, the moon rode high over a blackened crater in the sand. Two of the grains of sand, which gleamed in the moonlight a bit more golden than the rest, tumbled down together into a sheltered hollow to begin anew the work of three hundred years.

HENRY SLESAR

Something Short of Murder

Fran came out of Lila's apartment, shoving the green-printed racing sheets into her apron pocket. Lila, that lucky so-and-so! Three winners in a week! Fran shook her head as she went up the sagging stairs to her apartment on the next floor, displeased with her own luck and envying Lila's.

When the door slammed behind her, she hurried over to the kitchen table and shoved the remains of her husband's breakfast to one side. She took out the racing form, her eyes moving up and down the small print to find the listing of tomorrow's fourth race.

"Sonny Boy, County Judge, Chicago Flyer, Marzipan, Goldenrod . . ."

She read the names aloud, running her fingers through the dry brown hair on her forehead. Then she shut her eyes and looked upwards in a gesture. They had to mean something, or it was no good. That was her system. It wasn't much, but that was it.

"Sonny Boy," she whispered. Her husband, Ed, was an admirer of Jolson. "Sonny Boy," she said aloud.

She headed for the telephone and dialed quickly.

"Vito's," the man said.

"Hello, is Mr. Cooney there?"

"Hey, Phil," the man said. "For you."

"Hello?" Cooney said.

"Mr. Cooney? This is Fran Holland. Would you put five dollars for me on the fourth race tomorrow? I like—"

"Hold it, Mrs. Holland. I'm glad you called. You see, I was comin' to see you anyway, Mrs. Holland. After I got my hair cut."

"Coming to see me?" She looked at the instrument strangely.

"Yeah, Mrs. Holland. It's like this, Mrs. Holland. First of all, I ain't allowed to take no more bets from you, not until you settle up. Second of all, I'm supposed to come over and see maybe if I can collect the money you owe us. That's twenty-five dollars now."

"Twenty-five dollars? But that's not so much. I mean, is it?"

"Yeah, sure, Mrs. Holland. Only you don't understand, Mrs. Holland. This is front office. It wasn't my idea. Too much of this nickel-and-dime stuff around, you know what I mean."

"No! I don't know!" She was honestly indignant, as if the butcher had overcharged her.

"Well, I'll be over to explain it, Mrs. Holland. See you soon."

"No! Wait a minute—"

But the man named Cooney wasn't waiting. The click at his end of the wire was final.

She stared stupidly at the buzzing receiver before putting it back where it belonged. Then the thought of company—any company—sent her into a series of automatic actions. She cleared the breakfast dishes and piled them in the sink. She swept the crumbs from the table into the hollow of her palm and dropped them into the paper bag that was leaning against the stove. Then she untied her apron, and flung it into a closet.

In the bedroom, she stopped to see her face in the vanity mirror. It was a young face still, with all the marks of the years concentrated around her eyes. Her hair was jutting in too many directions, so she ran a comb through it with painful yanks.

She thought of calling Lila, but the idea of seeing that cheery gloating face again was too much. No, she'd talk this over some other time, when they were both commiserating over a tardy horse.

She sat at the kitchen table and smoked a cigarette. In another ten minutes, the doorbell sounded. She walked calmly to the door.

Cooney took his hat off. The band was tight, and left a circular dent in the shiny surface of his fresh-trimmed hair. He looked like an ageing insurance salesman, eager to make good.

"Morning, Mrs. Holland. All right to come in?"

"You know it's all right," Fran said.

He stepped inside, his small eyes probing the three rooms of the apartment. He sat down at the table, and began jiggling the small pile of ashes in the tray.

"Now what's this all about?" Fran said, like a scolding parent.

"It's nothing personal, Mrs. Holland. You know that. I like doin' business with you people. Only the management is gettin' a little edgy about the accounts receivable."

She almost smiled. "That's a laugh."

"No, seriously." He looked hurt. "How much dough you think we make with this kind of trade? Look, the two-dollar guy is the heart of the business. But when you start raidin' the cookie jar, Mrs. Holland—"

"I use my own money! You can't accuse me of—"

"Who's accusin'? Look, Mrs. Holland, you've owed us this twenty-five bucks since—" He dipped into his jacket and produced a little black ledger. "May 20th," he said. "This is almost two months. Now how do you suppose a big store or somebody would feel about that?"

"Listen, Mr. Cooney. You know I always pay you, sooner or later. Ever since I started—"

"You're a friend of Mrs. Shank, aren't you?" The question was sudden.

"You know I am. It was Lila who told me about—"

"Yeah. Well, she's not much better, Mrs. Holland. If it makes you feel any better."

"But she just won—"

"Very good for her. And when Mrs. Shank wins, we gotta ante up fast, or she's screamin' bloody murder. But when she's on the short end—" He scowled, and Fran no longer felt sure of herself.

"All right," she said bitingly. "If you're going to act that way, I'll just find somebody else."

"Sure. You do that, Mrs. Holland." He slipped the ledger back into his pocket. "Only there's still a matter of twenty-five bucks."

"I'll pay you next week."

"No, Mrs. Holland."

"What do you mean, no? I'll give you the money next week. My husband doesn't get paid until next week."

"Uh-uh, Mrs. Holland."

She stared at him, "What's the matter with you? I can't give you something I haven't got. What do you expect?"

"Twenty-five bucks, Mrs. Holland. That's my orders. You can borrow the money, can't you? From Mrs. Shank, maybe?"

"Not her," Fran said bitterly.

"You must have the dough in the house. Food money."

"No! I have a dollar and fifty cents That's all! I've been charging everything—"

The man stood up, and either the light in the room had changed, or he had. The meekness was out of his face, and he looked anything but harmless.

"I gotta have that money today, Mrs. Holland. If I don't get it today—"

"You'll what?" She couldn't believe his attitude; he'd always been a gentleman.

"I'll come back at six o'clock, Mrs. Holland."

"Come back?"

"To see your husband."

It was a word Cooney had never mentioned, not once. He'd been dropping by two mornings a week for the past three months. There were always evidences of Eddie's presence around. There were his breakfast dishes, scraped clean by his sizeable appetite. His crusty old pipe might be lying on the drainboard. There might be a shirt in need of mending, draped over a kitchen chair. But Cooney had never used the word before.

"Why?" Fran said. "Why do you have to do that? I told you I'd get the money. He doesn't have to know about this thing, does he?"

"Sure he don't, Mrs. Holland. All you gotta do is pay me what you owe—nothin' more. And he don't have to know a thing."

"It's not that I'm so ashamed of it!" she said loudly. "I haven't lost a fortune or anything!"

"Sure, Mrs. Holland."

"You can't do that to me, Mr. Cooney—"

The hat was being squeezed down over the oil-shiny hair. "I really gotta go, Mrs. Holland. You know where you can find me. At Vito's. If you come down any time before six, we can forget the whole thing."

"But I told you!" Fran's fingers were undoing the work of her comb. "I haven't got it! I can't get it! There isn't any way—"

"You know about hock shops?"

"I've already—" She stopped, and her fingers found their way to her mouth. If Eddie knew!

"So long, Mrs. Holland."

He went out, shutting the door quietly.

She listened to the man's retreating footsteps until the hall-way was silent again, and then she thought about Eddie. She looked across the kitchen table as if she could almost see her husband sitting at the opposite end, looking hurt and baffled as he had so many times before, shaking his head and saying: "Why do you do it, Fran? What for?"

How could she face that scene again? After all the promises, the tearful scenes of recrimination and forgiveness? The first time hadn't been so bad; they had been honeymooners still, and anything Eddie's bride did was cute and cockeyed and wonderful—even betting house money on the horses. They had laughed over it, then, and made up, before the argument had gone very far, in that special tender way reserved for newlyweds. But there had been a second time, and a third, and at each discovery, Eddie had looked more hurt and bewildered, until the bewilderment became anger. And then there had been the terrible scene last October, the day when he'd detected the white circle around her finger where Fran's engagement ring should have been . . .

She shivered at the memory. There had been no forgiveness in Eddie that time. She had sworn to him that the habit was broken; she had tried every way possible to convince him that she had learned her lesson. But still Eddie hadn't forgiven; he had merely warned.

"One more time, Fran, so help me. One more time and I walk outa here . . ."

She got up from the kitchen table and ran into the bedroom. She attacked the bureau drawers, scattering clothes and department store boxes filled with buttons and hatpins and scraps of fabric. She foraged through all her purses, her fingers digging into their linings in search of stray coins. She slapped at the pockets of her husband's two suits which hung in the closet, listening for the sound of jingling metal. She flipped open the plastic jewelry box Ed had given her the Christmas before, and was shocked at the scarcity of everything with more than dime-store value.

Even as Fran hurried into the living room, she had the feeling of having done all that she had just done before.

Beneath the pillows of the love seat she found a dime and a black penny. In a small porcelain vase on a bookshelf she found a folded dollar bill.

She brought all the money she had found to the kitchen table, and counted it.

"Two dollars and seventy-eight cents," she whispered.

She put her head between her elbows.

"Oh, God, God," she said.

Twenty-five dollars wasn't so much, she thought. But where would she get it? She had no friends, except Lila. Her family lived miles away. Where would she get it? And before six o'clock. She glanced at her wrist, but the watch she expected to see there she remembered was ticking in a pawnshop on Broadway. She glanced up at the electric clock on the kitchen wall, and gasped when she realized that it was almost eleven-thirty.

Less than seven hours! she thought. Twenty-five dollars! Nickels and dimes, Cooney had called it . . .

Then she had her idea. It was born of a painful memory, of an unpleasant scene on a windy street corner only two weeks before. She had just concluded a day of shopping, and there was an overpriced dress in a fancy striped box beneath her arm. She had been standing on the corner, her feet aching, praying that the Number Five bus would be empty. Then she had clicked open her purse, *this* purse, the one on the table, looking for nickels and dimes . . .

She stood up so fast that the chair scraped the linoleum. She went into the bedroom and did further repairs on her makeup. She put on her best pair of black suedes, and then took the silken thing she called her "evening stole" out of a drawer. The effect in the mirror didn't please her, so she changed her dress too.

When she was through, she looked a lot like the girl Ed used to show off at parties.

Then she went out.

The bus stop was four blocks from her apartment building. The good bus stop, that is, the one where Number Five, and Number Fifteen, and Number Twenty-Three nuzzled one another against the curb during the rush hours. Number Five was just lumbering off now, only half-filled at midday. But there were still people around, waiting for transportation to God-knows-what errand.

They were old people mostly. Old people weren't so good for what she had in mind. But Fran stepped determinedly up to the arrow-shaped stanchion and looked like a woman with a purpose.

Out of the corner of her eyes, she selected her first subject. She knew the first would be the hardest, so this one had to be good. He wasn't too old, really, maybe a little over fifty. His eyes were puffy, and his shoulders were hunched up as if the July sun, strangely enough, had made him cold. Both hands were in his pockets, and coins within them were making noises.

She sidled up to him, peering down the street for signs of the approaching bus. He looked at her with only mild interest.

Then she saw Number Fifteen heading in. She opened her purse and began to rummage inside it.

"Oh my God!" she said loudly.

The man's eyes widened at her exclamation.

She looked at him helplessly, and the half-humorous, half-worried expression on her face was a skilful blend.

"How do you like that!" she said. "I haven't got a *red cent*."

He smiled uncertainly, not knowing what to do. And his hands stopped jiggling the coins.

"What in the world should I *do*? I *must* get downtown—"

"I—uh—" The man cleared his throat. "Look, why don't I—uh—"

"Oh, would you? Could you lend me fifteen cents? I feel like such a fool—"

He was smiling now; this was anecdotal material for him. Fran didn't feel badly; she was the one doing the favor.

His hand came out of his pocket filled with silver. He plucked out a nickel and dime and handed them to her.

"Think nothing of it," he said. The bus braked to a halt in front of them. "You can mail it to me," he said. "Hah-hah. Well—here's the bus—"

"Not mine," she smiled. "I take the Number Five. Thank you *very* much."

"You're very welcome!" he said cheerfully, and clambered aboard his bus.

That makes your day, Pops, she thought.

A young man who had just stepped off the departing bus was folding a newspaper in front of her.

"Pardon me—"

"Huh?" He looked up, his pale eyes bewildered.

"I feel like such a fool, but—" She batted her lashes prettily. He was a very young man; he blushed. "But I left the house without a cent. And I simply must take the next bus downtown—"

"Gosh," he said, grinning with embarrassment. "I know just how you feel. Here—" He dug into his coat pocket. "Only got a quarter—"

"Oh, really—"

"No no. Keep the whole thing. Happens to me all the time." He looked at her face more closely, and seemed to realize she was older than her smile. He nodded and smiled and moved on.

"Pardon me," she said to the elderly lady who was peering myopically down the street. "I feel simply terrible about this, but an awful thing has happened to me—"

"Eyah?" the old lady said.

Fran smiled tightly. "Nothing," she said wryly.

A slim gentleman with glasses, carrying a book under his arm, was walking slowly toward the bus stop. He blinked at her as she approached.

"Pardon me," she said.

An hour later, she could have sworn that there was a blister on her right heel. Funny how simply standing at a bus stop could have done that to her foot. Why, she could walk for miles through a department store, and never . . .

Then she thought of the coins in her purse, and walked rapidly across the street. There was a drug store on the corner, and she entered one of the telephone booths and folded the doors closed.

She counted carefully.

The total was three dollars and fifteen cents. Added to the amount she had started out with, it made five-ninety-three. She sighed. She had a long way to go . . .

A man was standing outside the booth as she opened the doors.

"Pardon me," she said automatically. "I feel like such a fool, but I came out without a *penny*, and I have to get downto—I have to make a call."

The man grinned feebly. "Yeah?" he said. Then he realized what was expected of him, and his hand dove into his change pocket. "Oh, yeah, sure," he said. "I gotta dime."

"Thank you," she said. "Thank you very much."

She folded the doors again, and dialed a number without depositing the coin. She talked cheerfully into the dead instrument for a moment, hung up after a musical good-bye, and smiled winningly at the man who succeeded her in the booth.

Then she went back to the bus stop.

By three o'clock, she had collected almost ten dollars more. At a quarter of four, she returned to the telephone booth for another accounting.

"Fourteen dollars and nine cents," she said aloud.

Her finger poked into the coin-return aperture at the bottom of the telephone, and came out with a dime.

"This is my lucky day!" she laughed.

But four o'clock found her more discouraged. The crowd was growing thicker around the bus stanchion, but the increase in traffic didn't help her collect her nickels and dimes.

At four-thirty, she was still far short of her twenty-five dollar goal.

"Pardon me," she said to a fat man with a vacant face. "I feel like such a fool, but I seem to have left my house without any money at all. I wonder if I could impose on you to—"

"Go away," the fat man said, regarding her balefully.

"But you don't understand," she said. "I was simply going to ask if you had—"

"Madam, please go away," the fat man said.

It was her first refusal. She knew better than to argue; it wasn't worth it. But she suddenly felt stubborn.

"Look," Fran said hotly. "It's only fifteen cents. I mean, it's only *busfare*—"

She felt a hand on her arm and whirled angrily.

"Pardon me, lady—"

She looked indignantly at the man whose fingers were lying so firmly on the sleeve of her dress. He was in his early thirties, and his clothes were cut with angular accents. The fat man moved away from them, and that made her even angrier.

"What do *you* want?"

The man smiled. His teeth were long, and his narrow eyes had no part in the smile.

"I think you better come with me, lady."

"What?"

"Please. Do us both a favor and don't make a scene. What do you say?"

"I don't know what you're talking about!"

"Look, lady. I've been watching you for the past half hour. Does that make it any plainer? Now come quietly before I have to get nasty."

A whirlpool began to churn in her empty stomach.

"Why should I come with you? Who do you think you are?"

"If you want to see the badge, I'll flash it. Only we got enough people starin' at us already. So what do you say?"

She swallowed hard. "Yes. Of course."

They walked away from the bus stop, his hand still on her arm, smiling like an old friend who had made a chance meeting. He didn't speak until they reached a gray sedan, parked some thirty yards from the stanchion.

He opened the door for her.

"Inside, please."

"Look, mister, if you'll only let me explain—"

"You'll get your chance. Inside, lady."

She climbed in. He went around to the other door and slid in beside her. They drove off, making a left at the corner.

"You don't understand," she said pleadingly. "I wasn't doing anything wrong. I wasn't *stealing* or anything. I was just asking, you know what I mean? You see, I'm in trouble—"

"You're in trouble, all right." He sneaked through a changing traffic light, and made another left.

She put her face in her hands and started to cry. But the well was dry; the tears wouldn't come.

"No use pullin' that one," the man said. "I've seen your type lots of times, lady. But I'll have to admit—I never seen that particular dodge before. How much money did you think you could make?"

"But I don't *need* much. Only a few dollars! I have to have twenty-five dollars before six o'clock. I *have* to!"

"How much did you get?"

"Not much. Honest. Only a few dollars! You wouldn't arrest me for a few dollars?"

"How much, lady?"

She opened her purse, and stared at the mound of coins at the bottom.

"I don't know exactly," she said dully. "Fifteen or sixteen dollars maybe. But it's not enough . . ."

The car was wheeling down a side street now, away from the busy thoroughfare, toward the warehouse section near the river.

"Please!" Fran cried. "Don't turn me in! I'll never do it again! I was just desperate for that money—"

"How much more do you need, doll-face?"

"What?"

"To make the twenty-five?"

She looked down at her purse again. "I don't know for sure. Another ten would do it. Maybe not even that."

"Is that all?" he grinned.

His foot was pressing harder on the accelerator, as if he were suddenly more anxious to reach his destination. He whipped the car around corners, the wheels squealing in protest, and Fran became alarmed.

"Hey!" She looked out of the window at the strange deserted neighborhood. "What is this? Are you a cop or aren't you?"

"What do you think?"

She stared at him. "Why, you're no cop! You're not arresting me at all—" She edged over to the door, one hand on the handle.

"Uh-uh," he said. "Don't do anything foolish; you'll just hurt yourself. Besides, doll-face, I could still call a cop. I could still tell 'em about your racket—"

"They wouldn't believe you!"

"Maybe. But why take the chance?" He took his right hand off the wheel and reached to put it around her shoulders.

"Be careful!" Fran said shrilly.

"You're not being smart, honey. You gotta have the twenty-five before six. It's almost five now. Where do you think it'll come from?"

"Let me out of here!"

"Maybe I can help, doll-face." He pulled her to him, his eyes still on the road, his grin widening. "If you let me—"

"No," Fran said. "No!"

He slowed to turn another corner, and she saw her opportunity. Her hand hit the door handle upwards, and it swung open. The man cursed and grabbed for her arm.

"Leave me alone!" she screamed, swinging the heavy, coin-laden purse at his head. It thudded against his temple. He cried out in rage, and in grabbing for her, his hand caught the sleeve of her dress, ripping it. Then his other hand, heedlessly, left the steering wheel, and the car bucked like a wild horse suddenly untethered, throwing Fran against the open door and into the street.

She fell on all fours, sobbing but unhurt, and watched without horror or regret as the car hurtled over the sidewalk and plowed its nose into the stubborn red bricks of a warehouse building.

Her first thought was to run, for there was nobody on the street to see her flight. Then she remembered that her purse was still in the car, and she staggered to the wreckage to recover it.

The door was still open, and the purse was propped up against the side of the unconscious man. She didn't know if he was alive or dead, nor was the difference important to her at the moment. He was folded over the steering wheel, his arms dangling limply. Gasping, she reached for her purse.

Then, the idea occurred so naturally that she went about the business of locating the man's wallet without her fingers showing any sign of nervousness. She found the billfold in the inner breast pocket of his suit. There were many bills inside, but—with an odd sense of justice—she took only ten dollars.

Fran reached Vito's barber shop at ten minutes to six. Vito started a grin, but his face changed when he saw her drawn features and soiled clothing.

"Cooney, huh? Yeah, he's in the back. Hey, Phil! A lady!"

Cooney looked at her curiously when he came out of the back

room. He was in shirtsleeves, and holding a poor poker hand. He brightened when he saw her reach for the purse, and laughed at the sight of it full of coins.

"What'd you do, Mrs. Holland, rob a piggy bank?"

"Count it," she said distantly. "Count it for me, Mr. Cooney." They overturned the bag on the manicure table. Vito helped. When the addition was done, Cooney looked up.

"Thirty dollars and forty-six cents, Mrs. Holland," he said, smiling with satisfaction. "You got change comin'. I'm sorry I had to go lay down the law to you the way I did. But you see, you done okay."

She went up the apartment house stairs slowly. On the third floor, a door opened and a blonde woman, her hair heavy with curlers, looked out.

"Fran! For God's sake, where you been?"

"Shopping," she said wearily.

"You look beat. Buy somethin' nice?"

"No. Nothing much, Lila."

"Well, I got a hot scoop for you, kid. You won't have to make dinner tonight. You can come down and have pot luck with me if you don't feel like cookin' for yourself—"

"What do you mean?"

"You're on the town tonight, kiddo." The blonde woman laughed. "Ed musta called nine times this afternoon. Finally, he calls me up, thinkin' we were in here boozin' or something."

"Ed?" She blinked at the woman.

"Yeah. He called from the office. Wanted to tell you that he wouldn't be coming home, not 'til tomorrow. He had some kind of emergency with a client, or something. Said he had to fly out to Chicago on the five o'clock plane."

"Not coming home?" Fran said stupidly.

"Hey, snap out of it. You heard what I said. He went to Chicago. You can relax tonight, honey."

Fran sighed, and started up the next flight. "Thanks, Lila."

"That's okay," the blonde shrugged. "Hey, you sure you're okay?"

"Yeah, I'm all right. I'm just fine."

Upstairs, Fran unlocked her front door and went inside. The breakfast dishes in the sink looked gray in the fading light. She flung her purse on the table, and kicked off her shoes.

In the living room, she flopped heavily into a chair and lit a cigarette. She sat in an attitude of exhaustion, staring at the hazy light outside, smoking silently.

She pulled the evening stole around her shoulders, as if the room had grown cold.

"Chicago," she said bitterly.

Then the name meant something. It *meant* something. She stood up quickly. That was the whole secret of it, she thought. The name had to *mean* something.

She went over to the telephone and dialed the familiar number.

"Hello, is Mr. Cooney there?"

Her stockinged foot tapped impatiently on the linoleum.

"Hello, Mr. Cooney? Listen, this is Fran Holland. On that fourth race tomorrow. I'd like five dollars on Chicago Flyer. That's right. In the fourth race . . ."

ELLIS PETERS

The Golden Girl

"Shakespeare," said the purser moodily, over his second beer after the theater, "everything's Shakespeare this year, of course. He did his share of pinching, though. That 'my ducats and my daughter' stuff—there was another fellow did that better, I remember seeing the play once. *The Jew of Malta,* it was called, and Marlowe was the author's name. 'O gold, O girl! Oh, beauty! Oh, my bliss!' Seeing *The Merchant* tonight made me think of it again. And of a real-life case I once knew—only she wasn't his daughter. Not that one.

"I was a raw junior then, under old McLean on the *Aurea,* oh, ten years ago, it would be. I dream about it sometimes, but not so often, now. We were sailing from Liverpool for Bombay, my third trip, and this couple came aboard right in the rush before we sailed, and still you couldn't miss seeing them. It was this girl. She was so blindingly pretty, for one thing, corngold hair, smoky eyes. And then, so touchingly pregnant. You know, these loose smocks, and then the very slender arms on the ponderous body. And the careful, faintly clumsy gait, balancing the weight. She went slowly on the companionways, and held on fast to the rail. You could feel every male in sight holding himself back from rushing to help her.

"They were booked through to Bombay, probably going out to some expert advisory job. The husband, he was older, probably forty to the girl's twenty-two or so, but he had something, too. The women got their heads together over him before we were an hour out. Big, good-looking fellow, dark and quiet and experienced-looking, hovering round his missus with such solicitude all the other wives on board turned green with envy. A reformed rake, they had him down for. Don Juan after he met the one girl. Try and get him away from her! Plenty of them did try before we neared Bombay. But no, as far as he was concerned there was no woman aboard but his wife. He hung over her with that broody look, every day of the seventeen.

"Two days out we had a boat drill. We always did, though we never expected more than half of 'em to show up, not at that time of year, with the sea acting the way it so often does act. I was the officer on their boat, and I took care to show up near their cabin when the first siren sounded. He wasn't there, he'd gone to get her some library books. I had the pleasure of helping her on with her life-jacket. Like most women, she hadn't a clue how to put the thing on, instructions or no instructions.

"She didn't seem so big, under that loose tunic of hers. Just a bit of a thing she must have been, normal times, I thought. And the way she thanked me, I'd have jumped overboard for her. Yes, she felt fine, yes, she'd go up on deck and report properly, like the others. And she did, too. Like a kid playing a game, the gayest person around. Her husband soon came on the run, wild to snatch her away from the rest of us and look after her himself. There wasn't a man who didn't grudge him his rights.

"Like that, all the way. At our film-shows they held hands in a quiet corner. The women reckoned they hadn't been married all that long, and he hadn't got over the happy shock of getting her, and couldn't quite believe in his luck.

"We dropped about half our passengers off at Karachi, and made across for Bombay a bit subdued and quiet, as usual. And that night, round about midnight, the fire broke out.

"There was a ball going on at the time, we usually staged something gay to cushion the partings. So we never did find out how it started. All I know is, suddenly there were alarm sirens below decks, and unaccountably none up in the saloons and bars, and the music went on, and up on the boat-deck there were still people in the pool long after there was near-panic below. Communications went west because the whole loud-speaker system collapsed. And before you could say 'knife' there was smoke everywhere, and in ten minutes more, chaos. Nobody could give orders beyond the reach of his own voice. And once people got frightened, the range of a voice wasn't much.

"It wasn't a panic. They were a pretty decent lot, they'd have been all right if there'd been any way of telling 'em all just what to do. But there wasn't, except in small groups, and there weren't enough of us to go round the groups. And sometimes confusion and bewilderment can produce just the same results as panic. The best of 'em, the ones who're game and try to do something, do the wrong things for want of instructions. And the others get in their way and ours. What can you do? Thank God it was dead calm, and two or three ships had got our calls, and were moving in to pick up the pieces.

"It had to come to that. The fire spread like mad, and she began to list. We shoved everybody up on deck, got 'em into their life-jackets, and started getting the boats lowered. The din was something I'll never forget. Nobody was screaming, but everybody was shouting.

"I was clawing my way along B Deck in the smoke, opening cabin doors and fielding the stragglers, with one of the women on one arm, and a Goanese steward towing two more behind me. I shoved open the door of 56, and there was our golden girl, clinging to her husband, her eyes like big gray lakes of stupe-fied terror. They were fumbling her life-jacket awkwardly be-tween them. His lay on the lower berth. I bellowed at him furiously to get the thing on her, quick, and got hold of her with my free hand as soon as he'd bundled her into it. She toiled up the companionways after me, panting, her gait as labored and painful as an old woman's. I even had time to bleed a little, inwardly, at the thought of hustling her, but, man, we were in a hurry. The *Aurea* was lurching under us, shuddering on the dead-calm sea. She wasn't going to last all that much longer.

"Well, I got them up to their boat, into that pandemonium on deck. There was a westbound tanker standing off by then, with boats out for us, searchlights quivering along the black water. And then the deck heeled under us and started to stand erect, sliding us down toward the rail. The women screamed and clung to whatever was nearest. I thought we were going, so did we all, but she partly righted herself again. But the boat slid down by the stern, and jammed, and I knew we were never going to launch that one. Some of the others were safely away already, standing well off and waiting to salvage what they could when we foundered. Other boats were moving in from the tanker off in the dark there. One had come close, and was hailing us. I bellowed back at them, and they nosed in nearer. I grabbed hold of the golden girl. Two lives—you know how it is!

"Her husband yelled at me like a fury, and held on to her like grim death, screaming hoarsely something I couldn't even distinguish in the general hell. There wasn't time for convincing anybody of anything. I hooked my palm under his chin and shoved him off hard, and his grip of her broke. I picked her up in my arms and swung her over the rail, and dropped her gently and carefully into what I knew was the safest place for her, into the sea a few yards from the bows of the hovering boat. The officer I'd hailed was already leaning over to reach for her.

"And two things happened that I still dream about now and then, when I'm out of sorts. Her husband let out a shriek like a damned soul, a sound I'll never forget, and tore his way screaming to the rail, and hurled himself over it. And the girl, the golden girl—my God, she hit the water and she sank like a stone!

"Her face was turned up, mute, staring at me with those lost, terrified eyes, right to the second when the water closed over it. She vanished, and she didn't reappear.

"I was a whole minute grasping it. Can you imagine that? Then I dived after her, down and down, hunting for her, time after time after time, until they hauled me aboard the boat by force. I didn't find her. But once, I think, I glimpsed him, deep down there plunging as I was plunging. I seem to remember a face with hair torn erect, frantic eyes, mouth howling soundlessly. Her name? It would be nice to think I only imagined it. Better still to forget it. I can't do either.

"There was nothing left of him, either, by that time, except his life-jacket washing about aimlessly, where he'd torn it off and discarded it to dive for her. We never should have found either of them, if the vortex as the *Aurea* finally went under hadn't churned up everything from the depths and flung it to the rim of the area. The tanker still had boats out, and one of them fielded the girl's body, by a sheer fluke, as it showed for an instant before plunging again. We never did find him.

"It was finding her, and what we found on her, that brought Interpol into the story.

"She wasn't his wife, of course. She was a photographer's model and small-part actress he'd picked up at some club. She wasn't pregnant, either. Only the way he felt about her, I'll swear, was no fake. He'd never used her before. All his previous cargoes had been smuggled in by air, with other carriers, and this last one was to have been an easy stake, a pleasure cruise with a nice pay-off at the end of it. It was very profitable business. I think they weren't coming back.

"All the stuff she'd brought aboard in the padded bodice under her maternity smock they'd hidden, once the initial boat-drill was safely over, in that life-jacket of hers. A daft place? Well, look, I'll tell you something. Nobody ever believes they're going to need those damned life-jackets in earnest—nobody. It wasn't so daft a place. And she could make herself comfortable until she had to resume the burden at Bombay, and carry it tenderly ashore and through the Customs. Only they left the job of transferring it again until the last night, and the fire caught them unprepared.

"Of course, he could have worn the thing himself and given her the other. Maybe he would have, if I hadn't barged in on them and forced his hand. Or maybe he wouldn't. She was, after all, a professional doing a job for him. Once in the boat she'd have been safe enough. And whatever followed, it was she, with her disarming beauty and her interesting condition, who would have had the special V.I.P. treatment, and the best chance of retrieving their stake, and getting it safely into India.

"I still wonder which he was really diving for, the girl, or the thirty pounds' weight of thin bar gold that drowned her."

The Boy Who Predicted Earthquakes

"Naturally, you're skeptical," Wellman said. He poured water from a carafe, put a pill on his tongue, washed the pill down. "Naturally, understandably. I don't blame you, wouldn't dream of blaming you. A good many of us here at the studio had your attitude, I'm afraid, when we started programing this boy Herbert. I don't mind telling you, just between ourselves, that I myself was pretty doubtful that a show of that sort would be good television."

Wellman scratched behind an ear while Read looked on with scientific interest. "Well, I was wrong," Wellman said, putting the hand down again. "I'm pleased to say that I was 1,000 percent wrong. The kid's first, unannounced, unadvertised show brought nearly 1,400 pieces of mail. And his rating nowadays . . ." He leaned toward Read and whispered a figure.

"Oh," Read said.

"We haven't given it out yet, because those buzzards at

Purple simply wouldn't believe us. But it's the plain simple truth. There isn't another TV personality today who has the following the kid has. He's on short wave, too, and people tune him in all over the globe. Every time he has a show the post office has to send two special trucks with his mail. I can't tell you how happy I am, Read, that you scientists are thinking about making a study of him at last. I'm terrifically sincere about this."

"What's he like personally?" Read asked.

"The kid? Oh, very simple, very quiet, very very sincere. I like him tremendously. His father—well, he's a real character."

"How does the program work?"

"You mean, how does Herbert do it? Frankly, Read, that's something for you researchers to find out. We haven't the faintest idea what happens, really.

"I can tell you the program details, of course. The kid has a show twice a week, Mondays and Fridays. He won't use a script"—Wellman grimaced—"which is pretty much a head-ache for us. He says a script dries him up. He's on the air for twelve minutes. Most of that time he just talks, telling the viewers about what he's been doing in school, the books he's been reading, and so on. The kind of stuff you'd hear from any nice, quiet boy. But he always makes one or two predictions, always at least one, and never more than three. They are always things that will happen within forty-eight hours. Herbert says he can't see any farther ahead than that."

"And they do happen?" Read said. It was less a question than statement.

"They do," Wellman replied, somewhat heavily. He puffed out his lips. "Herbert predicted the stratosphere liner wreck off Guam last April, the Gulf States hurricane, the election results. He predicted the submarine disaster in the Tortugas. Do you realize that the FBI has an agent sitting in the studio with him during every show out of range of the scanners? That's so he can be taken off the air immediately if he says anything that might be contrary to public policy. They take him that seriously.

"I went over the kid's record yesterday when I heard the University was thinking of studying him. His show has been going out now for a year and a half, twice a week. He's made 106 predictions during that time. And every one of them, every single one of them, has come true. By now the general public has such confidence in him that"—Wellman licked his lips and hunted for a comparison—"that they'd believe him if he predicted the end of the world or the winner of the Irish Sweepstakes.

"I'm sincere about this, Read, terrifically sincere. Herbert is the biggest thing in TV since the invention of the selenium cell. You can't overestimate him or his importance. And now, shall we go take in his show? It's just about time for him to go on."

Wellman got up from his desk chair, smoothing the design of pink and purple penguins on his necktie into place. He led Read through the corridors of the station to the observation room of studio 8G, where Herbert Pinner was.

Herbert looked, Read thought, like a nice, quiet boy. He was about 15, tall for his age, with a pleasant, intelligent, somewhat careworn face. He went about the preparation for his show with perfect composure which might hide a touch of distaste.

". . . I have been reading a very interesting book," Herbert said to the TV audience. "Its name is *The Count of Monte Cristo*. I think almost anybody might enjoy it." He held up the book for the viewers to see. "I have also begun a book on astronomy by a man named Duncan. Reading that book has made me want a telescope. My father says that if I work hard and get good grades in school, I can have a small telescope at the end of the term. I will tell you what I can see with the telescope after we buy it.

"There will be an earthquake, not a bad one, in the north Atlantic States tonight. There will be considerable property damage, but no one will be killed. Tomorrow morning about ten o'clock they will find Gwendolyn Box, who has been lost in the Sierras since Thursday. Her leg is broken but she will still be alive.

"After I get the telescope I hope to become a member of the society of variable star observers. Variable stars are stars whose brightness varies either because of internal changes or because of external causes . . ."

At the end of the program Read was introduced to young Pinner. He found the boy polite and co-operative, but a little remote.

"I don't know just how I do do it, Mr. Read," Herbert said when a number of preliminary questions had been put. "It isn't pictures, the way you suggested, and it isn't words. It's just—it just comes into my mind.

"One thing I've noticed is that I can't predict anything unless I more or less know what it is. I could predict about the earthquake because everybody knows what a quake is, pretty much. But I couldn't have predicted about Gwendolyne Box if I hadn't known she was missing. I'd just have had a feeling that somebody or something was going to be found."

"You mean you can't make predictions about anything unless it's in your consciousness previously?" Read asked intently.

Herbert hesitated. "I guess so," he said. "It makes a . . . a spot in my mind, but I can't identify it. It's like looking at a light with your eyes shut. You know a light is there, but that's all you know about it. That's the reason why I read so many books. The more things I know about, the more things I can predict.

"Sometimes I miss important things, too. I don't know why that is. There was the time the atomic pile exploded and so many people were killed. All I had for that day was an increase in employment.

"I don't know how it works, really, Mr. Read. I just know it does."

Herbert's father came up. He was a small, bouncing man with the extrovert's persuasive personality. "So you're going to investigate Herbie, hum?" he said when the introductions had been performed. "Well, that's fine. It's time he was investigated."

"I believe we are," Read answered with a touch of caution. "I'll have to have the appropriation for the project approved first."

Mr. Pinner looked at him shrewdly. "You want to see whether there's an earthquake first, isn't that it? It's different when you hear him saying it himself. Well, there will be. It's a terrible thing, an earthquake." He clicked his tongue deprecatingly. "But nobody will be killed, that's one good thing. And they'll find that Miss Box the way Herbie says they will."

The earthquake arrived about 9:15, when Read was sitting under the bridge lamp reading a report from the Society for

Psychical Research. There was an ominous muttering rumble and then a long, swaying, seasick roll.

Next morning Read had his secretary put through a call to Haffner, a seismologist with whom he had a casual acquaintanceship. Haffner, over the phone, was definite and brusque.

"Certainly there's no way of foretelling a quake," he snapped. "Not even an hour in advance. If there were, we'd issue warnings and get people out in time. There'd never be any loss of life. We can tell in a general way where a quake is likely, yes. We've known for years that this area was in for one. But as for setting the exact time—you might as well ask an astronomer to predict a nova for you. He doesn't know, and neither do we. What brought this up, anyway? The prediction made by that Pinner kid?"

"Yes. We're thinking of observing him."

"Thinking of it? You mean you're only just now getting around to him? Lord, what ivory towers you research psychologists must live in!"

"You think he's genuine?"

"The answer is an unqualified yes."

Read hung up. When he went out to lunch he saw by the headlines that Miss Box had been found as Herbert had predicted on his radio program.

Still he hesitated. It was not until Thursday that he realized that he was hesitating not because he was afraid of wasting the university's money on a fake, but because he was all too sure that Herbert Pinner was genuine. He didn't at bottom want to start this study. He was afraid.

The realization shocked him. He got the dean on the phone at once, asked for his appropriation, and was told there would be no difficulty about it. Friday morning he selected his two assistants for the project, and by the time Herbert's program was nearly due to go out, they were at the station.

They found Herbert sitting tensely on a chair in studio 8G with Wellman and five or six other station executives clustered around him. His father was dancing about excitedly, wringing his hands. Even the FBI man had abandoned his usual detachment and impassivity, and was joining warmly in the argument. And Herbert, in the middle, was shaking his head and saying, "No, no, I can't," over and over again doggedly.

"But why not, Herbie?" his father wailed. "Please tell me why not. Why won't you give your show?"

"I can't," Herbert said. "Please don't ask me. I just can't." Read noticed how white the boy was around the mouth.

"But, Herbie, you can have anything you want, anything, if you only will! That telescope—I'll buy it for you tomorrow. I'll buy it tonight!"

"I don't want a telescope," young Pinner said wanly. "I don't want to look through it."

"I'll get you a pony, a motorboat, a swimming pool! Herbie, I'll get you anything!"

"No," Herbert said.

Mr. Pinner looked around him desperately. His eyes fell on Read, standing in the corner, and he hurried over to him. "See what you can do with him, Mr. Read," he panted.

Read chewed his lower lip. In a sense it was his business. He pushed his way through the crowd to Herbert, and put his hand on his shoulder. "What's this I hear about you not wanting to give your show today, Herbert?" he asked.

Herbert looked up at him. The harassed expression in his eyes made Read feel guilty and contrite. "I just can't," he said. "Don't you start asking me too, Mr. Read."

Once more Read chewed his lip. Part of the technique of parapsychology lies in getting subjects to co-operate. "If you don't go on the air, Herbert," he said, "a lot of people are going to be disappointed."

Herbert's face took on a tinge of sullenness. "I can't help it," he said.

"More than that, a lot of people are going to be frightened. They won't know why you aren't going on the air, and they'll imagine things. All sorts of things. If they don't view you an awful lot of people are going to be scared."

"I—" Herbert said. He rubbed his cheek. "Maybe that's right," he answered slowly. "Only . . ."

"You've got to go on with your show."

Herbert capitulated suddenly. "All right," he said, "I'll try."

Everyone in the studio sighed deeply. There was a general motion toward the door of the observation room. Voices were raised in high-pitched, rather nervous chatter. The crisis was over, the worst would not occur.

The first part of Herbert's show was much like the others had been. The boy's voice was a trifle unsteady and his hands had a tendency to shake, but these abnormalities would have passed the average viewer unnoticed. When perhaps five minutes of the show had gone, Herbert put aside the books and drawings (he had been discussing mechanical drawing) he had been showing his audience, and began to speak with great seriousness.

"I want to tell you about tomorrow," he said. "Tomorrow"— he stopped and swallowed—"tomorrow is going to be different from what anything in the past has been. Tomorrow is going to be the start of a new and better world for all of us."

Read, listening in the glass-enclosed room, felt an incredulous thrill race over him at the words. He glanced around at the faces of the others and saw that they were listening intently, their faces strained and rapt. Wellman's lower jaw dropped a little, and he absently fingered the unicorns on his tie.

"In the past," young Pinner said, "we've had a pretty bad time. We've had wars—so many wars—and famines and pestilences. We've had depressions and haven't known what caused them, we've had people starving when there was food and dying of diseases for which we knew the cure. We've seen the wealth of the world wasted shamelessly, the rivers running black with the washed-off soil, while hunger for all of us got surer and nearer every day. We've suffered, we've had a hard time.

"Beginning tomorrow"—his voice grew louder and more deep—"all that is going to be changed. There won't be any more wars. We're going to live side by side like brothers. We're going to forget about killing and breaking and bombs. From pole to pole the world will be one great garden, full of richness and fruit, and it will be for all of us to have and use and enjoy. People will live a long time and live happily, and when they die it will be from old age. Nobody will be afraid any more. For the first time since human beings lived on earth, we're going to live the way human beings should.

"The cities will be full of the richness of culture, full of art and music and books. And every race on earth will contribute to that culture, each in its degree. We're going to be wiser and happier and richer than any people have ever been. And pretty soon"—he hesitated for a moment, as if his thought had stumbled—"pretty soon we're going to send out rocket ships.

"We'll go to Mars and Venus and Jupiter. We'll go to the limits of our solar system to see what Uranus and Pluto are like. And maybe from there—it's possible—we'll go on and visit the stars.

"Tomorrow is going to be the beginning of all that. That's all for now. Good-by. Good night."

For a moment after he had ceased no one moved or spoke. Then voices began to babble deliriously. Read, glancing around, noticed how white their faces were and how dilated their eyes.

"Wonder what effect the new setup will have on TV?" Wellman said, as if to himself. His tie was flopping wildly about. "There'll be TV, that's certain—it's part of the good life." And then, to Pinner, who was blowing his nose and wiping his eyes, "Get him out of here, Pinner, right away. He'll be mobbed if he stays here."

Herbert's father nodded. He dashed into the studio after Herbert, who was already surrounded, and came back with him. With Read running interference, they fought their way through the corridor and down to the street level at the station's back.

Read got into the car uninvited and sat down opposite Herbert on one of the folding seats. The boy looked quite exhausted, but his lips wore a faint smile. "You'd better have the chauffeur take you to some quiet hotel," Read said to the senior Pinner. "You'd be besieged if you went to your usual place."

Pinner nodded. "Hotel Triller," he said to the driver of the car. "Go slow, cabby. We want to think."

He slipped his arm around his son and hugged him. His eyes were shining. "I'm proud of you, Herbie," he declared solemnly, "as proud as can be. What you said—those were wonderful, wonderful things."

The driver had made no move to start the car. Now he turned round and spoke. "It's young Mr. Pinner, isn't it? I was watching you just now. Could I shake your hand?"

After a moment Herbert leaned forward and extended it. The chauffeur accepted it almost reverently. "I just want to thank you—just want to thank you—Oh, hell! Excuse me, Mr. Herbert. But what you said meant a lot to me. I was in the last war."

The car slid away from the curb. As it moved downtown,

Read saw that Pinner's injunction to the driver to go slow had been unnecessary. People were thronging the streets already. The sidewalks were choked. People began to spill over onto the pavements. The car slowed to a walk, to a crawl, and still they poured out. Read snapped the blinds down for fear Herbert should be recognized.

Newsboys were screaming on the corners in raucous hysteria. As the car came to a halt Pinner opened the door and slipped out. He came scrambling back with an armload of papers he had bought.

"NEW WORLD COMING!" one read, another "MILLENNIUM TOMORROW!" and another quite simply, "JOY TO THE WORLD!" Read spread the papers out and began to read the story in one of them.

"A 15-year-old boy told the world that its troubles were over beginning tomorrow, and the world went wild with joy. The boy, Herbert Pinner, whose uncannily accurate predictions have won him a world-wide following, predicted an era of peace, abundance and prosperity such as the world has never known before . . ."

"Isn't it wonderful, Herbert?" Pinner panted. His eyes were blazing. He shook Herbert's arm. "Isn't it wonderful? Aren't you glad?"

"Yes," Herbert said.

They got to the hotel at last and registered. They were given a suite on the sixteenth floor. Even at this height they could faintly hear the excitement of the crowd below.

"Lie down and rest, Herbert," Mr. Pinner said. "You look worn out. Telling all that—it was hard on you." He bounced around the room for a moment and then turned to Herbert apologetically. "You'll excuse me if I go out, son, won't you? I'm too excited to be quiet. I want to see what's going on outside." His hand was on the knob of the door.

"Yes, go ahead," Herbert answered. He had sunk down in a chair.

Read and Herbert were alone in the room. There was silence for a moment. Herbert laced his fingers over his forehead and sighed.

"Herbert," Read said softly, "I thought you couldn't see into the future for more than forty-eight hours ahead."

"That's right," Herbert replied without looking up.

"Then how could you foresee all the things you predicted tonight?"

The question seemed to sink into the silence of the room like a stone dropped into a pond. Ripples spread out from it. Herbert said, "Do you really want to know?"

For a moment Read had to hunt for the name of the emotion he felt. It was fear. He answered, "Yes."

Herbert got up and went over to the window. He stood looking out, not at the crowded streets, but at the sky—where, thanks to daylight-saving time, a faint sunset glow yet lingered.

"I wouldn't have known if I hadn't read the book," he said, turning around, the words coming out in a rush. "I'd just have known something big—big—was going to happen. But now I know. I read about it in my astronomy book.

"Look over here." He pointed to the west, where the sun had been. "Tomorrow it won't be like this."

"What do you mean?" Read cried. His voice was sharp with anxiety. "What are you trying to say?"

"That . . . tomorrow the sun will be different. Maybe it's better this way. I wanted them to be happy. You mustn't hold it against me, Mr. Read, that I lied to them."

Read turned on him fiercely. "What is it? What's going to happen tomorrow? You've got to say!"

"Why, tomorrow the sun—I've forgotten the word. What is it they call it when a star flares up suddenly, when it becomes a billion times hotter than it was before?"

"A nova?" Read cried.

"That's it. Tomorrow . . . the sun is going to explode."

MIRIAM ALLEN deFORD

Walking Alone

John Larsen stood waiting for the bus to take him to work. It was only the middle of March, but spring had sent out a feeler; the air had a hint of warmth in it and the sky was a deeper blue than winter had known. Across the street little green spikes of leafbuds dotted the poplar trees flanking a billboard.

All at once he remembered sharply springlike mornings in his boyhood, forty years ago. He would wake and see a sky like this through the open window, and his heart would be filled with a strange, nameless emotion, made up of a yearning for something unknown, a longing for something not yet experienced.

The bus was not in sight. If it was late, he would be late too, and Sims would put on his sour face and say, "Busy day, Larsen. Can't you ever get here on time?" But it wouldn't be a busy day—it seldom was. People don't buy rugs and carpets the way they buy vegetables and paper napkins.

"Fed up," Larsen muttered to himself, waiting alone on the dreary corner. "Just fed up." His mind went back to the hour before, and Kate's peevish voice. "For heaven's sake, John, wake up! You want to be late for work? Next thing you know, they'll fire you, and then where'll we be? Hurry up! Think I like having to get up at all hours to cook your breakfast? Least you can do is eat it when I make it."

It was the same old monologue. When he'd left she would crawl back into bed, in her unappetizing curlers, and goodness knew when she'd crawl out again to dawdle through the day. He could fix breakfast himself in half the time she took, but then she wouldn't be a martyr to an inefficient, dreamy failure of a husband.

He shivered in his worn topcoat; it wasn't as springlike as he first thought, although the sun would warm things soon. His mind flitted to the woods and fields of his childhood, to the freedom and irresponsibility of those far-off years. He peered down the street; there was no sign of the bus.

Abruptly he crossed to the corner drug store, before common sense could change his mind. He fished for a dime in his pocket and went into the phone booth.

"Mr. Sims? This is Larsen. Look, I'm awfully sorry, but I just can't make it today. It's my back; I'm going to the doctor about it. I'll be there tomorrow, no matter how I feel. No, I couldn't hold out till lunchtime—my back's like a toothache. Yes, I know, but— Well, thanks, Mr. Sims. I'll do that, yes, sir. I'm sorry too."

Sims would wonder why he hadn't had Kate phone for him, if he felt so bad. Maybe he'd say it took a younger man to handle the job. Oh, to hell with it; it was too late now to reconsider.

He stayed on that side of the street, and the bus he took was one going in the other direction, away from the city. He rode to the end of the line.

Just to be alone—it was wonderful. Nobody nagging at him, no need to watch the time. He'd never been in the suburb where the bus landed him. For a while he just walked around, admiring houses and gardens—the sort of places he'd once dreamed of living in himself, when he and Kate were first married. Perhaps if they'd had any kids to be ambitious for, or if Kate hadn't turned into the slatternly shrew she'd become—

By noon he was tired of walking. He went back to the little business district and had a hamburger and coffee at a half-deserted lunch room. While he was there he asked about the bus schedule. Just so he got back home at the regular time, Kate would never know and have something new to yell at him about. No danger she'd phone him at the store; she knew they wouldn't call him off the floor except for an emergency. He bought a pack of cigarettes and a magazine and struck off along a promising road leading beyond the town.

It was more than an hour before he found what he wanted—a friendly little wood with a brook running through it and a sunny clearing by the side of an unfrequented road where he could sit on a fallen tree-stump and read and smoke and let the peace and silence seep into his nerves. Dotted around in the near distance were the tops of tree-hidden houses on the hill, but none of them was near enough to matter. Only an occasional car passed in either direction, and nobody noticed him in his snug sanctuary. It was very quiet; presently he dozed off.

He awoke with a start, and looked first at the sun and then at his watch. It was 4:40; he had plenty of time to catch the bus, He stood up and stretched, debating whether to walk on a bit farther or turn around and saunter slowly back to the bus stop.

Up the road, in the silence, he heard a shuffling in dry leaves. He peered out, and saw a girl in her early teens coming toward him on the opposite side of the road. He stood back, waiting till she had passed; it might scare the kid to see a strange man suddenly emerge from the woods. Leaning against a tree, he stood watching her.

She was a pretty girl, with long golden hair falling over the collar of her red sweater. She wore a dark blue skirt, red socks, and brown leather scuffs, and under her arm were a few school-books. She was singing to herself as she walked, in a clear, thin, childish voice. Pretty late for her to be coming home from school, but she might have stayed for some student get-together. Probably she lived in one of the houses whose roofs showed above the trees; there must be short cuts up to the hill to them.

She passed him now and he waited for her to go out of sight around a curve in the road. Then he heard a car coming, slowly, from behind them, in the same direction she was walking.

It was a rattletrap old black coupe, with only the driver in it.

Larsen caught a glimpse of him—a heavy-set man of about his own age, with a shock of dark hair, and no hat. The car passed him too, and Larsen stepped out onto the road and turned toward the town. Belatedly he thought he could have hailed the car and perhaps got a lift to the bus stop.

The girl was now about a hundred feet away, just nearing the curve. The car had caught up with her. It stopped.

Everything happened so suddenly Larsen could not collect his wits, which were dulled from his unaccustomed nap.

The driver jumped out, said something to the girl, and she shook her head. He grabbed her by the shoulder, hustled her toward the car. She struggled and started to scream; he clamped one hand over her mouth. He dragged her in, got in after, slammed the door. She jumped up—perhaps she saw Larsen now, where he stood paralyzed with bewilderment—reached for the door handle, tried again to scream. The man struck her twice, knocking her to the floor. Then he took the wheel and drove rapidly away. By the time Larsen, shaking himself from his stupor, had run to the curve, the car and its occupants were out of sight. He had not noticed the license number.

All the way back to the suburban town he pondered what he should do. It was his duty, he knew, to hunt out whatever police the town possessed and report what he had seen. But that would involve explaining why he himself was there, giving his name and address, appearing later as a witness if he had seen a crime committed and the man were caught. Then Sims would know he had lied about his absence from work. Kate would know too. Sims would probably fire him. Kate would make his life an even worse hell on earth. He might never get another job, even one as poor as this one, at his age. He had no money saved, and they were in debt for half the things in the house.

John Larsen had a clear, horrifying view of what he would be letting himself in for if he reported the incident.

He didn't really know the circumstances. The man might even be the girl's father. She might have been playing hooky, just as he had done, or have been disobeying some parental command. What he had witnessed might have been only severe but lawful punishment for some youthful misdemeanor.

Besides, what good could he do? He couldn't actually identify the man—he'd caught just a passing glimpse of him, could never pick him out in any assortment of heavy middle-aged men with thick dark hair. He would only be getting himself into a mess he'd never get out of, and for nothing at all.

He reached the town with time to spare, without catching sight or sound again of the black car; there were byroads all the way, any of which it could have taken. To pacify his conscience, he looked around for a policeman in the business district, but there was no sign of one. Stifling his uneasiness, he took the next bus, found it would land him in the city too early, got off about halfway, and waited for the following one. He reached home at the usual time, and, as usual, found that Kate didn't have dinner ready. He sat grumpily reading the evening paper, while she complained and scolded at him from the kitchen. They never asked each other for news of their day; there was never anything to tell that would interest either of them.

He had sense enough the next morning to tell Sims that the doctor had said it was merely a touch of lumbago, and that the rest had about fixed it. When he saw Sims' eyes on him he remembered occasionally to grimace and rub his back. By luck he sold a woman a big length of old-fashioned stair-carpeting they'd been trying to get rid of for months. Sims showed his gratification by saying good night and hoping Larsen's back would be better soon. He didn't, however, forget to dock him for the day off. That meant Larsen would have to skip lunches all next week; he couldn't let Kate know his pay was short.

When he stopped to get the paper, two evenings later, there was a picture on the first page. *Have You Seen This Girl?* the caption said. He recognized her instantly. The clothing they described was the same she had worn.

Her name was Diane Morrison, and she was the daughter of the principal of Belleville Consolidated Junior High School, where she was a first-year student. Usually her father drove her to and from school. On Tuesday she had waited for him till half-past four, then he found he would be tied up for another hour at least; so, as had sometimes happened in the past, the father told her she'd better walk the mile or so home and tell her mother he'd be late. When he got there about six she hadn't appeared. She was a reliable child who would have phoned if she had stopped off anywhere. Her parents had searched all the way back to the school and had called all her friends. But nobody had seen Diane. And nobody had seen her since.

Because there was a possibility of kidnaping, the F.B.I. had come into the case. They and the state and county police were combing the woods and hills around Belleville. So far they had found no trace or clue.

"For mercy's sake," Kate snapped, "can't you open your mouth except to eat? Never a word out of you, just woolgathering. Here I am, cooped up all day long, and you come home and act like I was a piece of furniture or something. How do you think I—"

He let her rave. He was trying to decide. Should he or shouldn't he? Would it help at all if he did? They might spot the man if he described him. But then where would John Larsen be? In the worst trouble of his life.

He glanced at Kate and almost considered telling her the truth and asking her advice. Then he reconsidered, quailing at how she would take it. And he knew what her advice would be—keep out of it and don't get us into an even deeper jam than you've risked getting us into already. Let the police do their work—that's what they're paid for.

He began buying a morning paper as well as an evening one, forcing himself, with a cold fear at the pit of his stomach, to search them for news.

A week later, under a covering of gravel in an abandoned quarry, they found her body. Her skull had been fractured in three places by some heavy instrument like a tire iron. She was covered with cuts and bruises, and she had been violated. Clutched in her right hand was a man's handkerchief, red-and-white checked.

John Larsen lay awake all night, with Kate breathing heavily beside him. By the time the window was turning gray, he had decided to let it go a while longer. He recalled crime stories he had read; there would be fragments of flesh under the girl's fingernails, the scientific cops would find minute threads and hairs on her clothing, they would go over the cars of all possible suspects for fingerprints. In a little place like Belleville they would soon get on to the dark-haired man, unless he was a stranger from some other place.

It was the purest chance that Larsen had witnessed the abduction. Suppose he *hadn't* been there—then they would have had to investigate just as they were doing now. He saw himself trying to explain to some incredulous F.B.I. man just what he was doing on a road near Belleville when he ought to have been at work in the city. Looking back now, his whole day of playing hooky seemed unbelievable childishness. Nobody would understand; they'd be sure he was lying. Why, they might think he'd made up the story just to protect himself. They might put him through a third degree. Lying there in bed, his flesh crawled. And he'd be ruined. The only thing to do was to pretend to himself that that day had never happened. They'd find the man soon, anyway—they always did. And then he'd be glad he'd had the sense to let bad enough alone.

When, three days later, he saw the headline, *Morrison Suspect Captured*, his relief was so great that tears came to his eyes. Standing in the bus, he read the story avidly.

The man arrested was an assistant janitor at the high school. His name was Joseph Kennelly. He had been under suspicion from the beginning, the story said. He knew the girl by sight, of course. He was unmarried, and lived alone in a two-room shack near the quarry where the body had been found. And he had a police record—not involving sex crimes, but a long series of arrests for disorderly conduct and for driving while drunk. He had spent part of his boyhood in a home for retarded children.

The police theory was that he had seen the girl leave school late, when his own hours of duty were over. There was no question that he had shown an unwholesome interest in her; now, when it was too late, boy students related how Joe had made vulgar cracks about Diane's golden hair and budding figure. He was a slipshod worker, on bad terms with the school principal, and had been in trouble more than once for drinking on the job; Mr. Morrison had threatened to have him fired. So the motives for the crime were clear—revenge and lust.

And the handkerchief was his—a laundry mark proved it. Moreover, he had a deep scratch, a week or two old, on the left side of his jaw.

He denied everything heatedly, of course. He had driven home that day as always, he said, and hadn't left his shack till he went to work the next morning. He hadn't even seen Diane—or anyone else. A nearly empty bottle of whiskey was found in the broom closet at the school, and Kennelly acknowledged he'd been feeling pretty high by the time he left. At home he'd gone on drinking, had passed out about ten o'clock, and hadn't wakened till dawn. Nobody could be found who had noticed him, at the school or elsewhere, between four o'clock Tuesday afternoon and nine Wednesday morning.

As for the handkerchief, he admitted it was his, but he claimed he had lost it somewhere, weeks before. The murderer must have been the one who found it. The scratch? Why, the morning after that big drunk he had been so shaky that he had done it himself while he was trying to shave.

So far, so good: John Larsen read the account with thankfulness that he had let things take their course. Then his heart plummeted like a cannon ball.

Joseph Kennelly was twenty-six years old. His picture showed a tall, skinny young man with lightish hair receding at the temples. And his car was a dark blue sedan.

Larsen reached his home, walking from the bus like an automaton. He threw the paper and his hat on the nearest chair, went into the bathroom, and locked the door: it was the only room in the house where he could be alone to think. "That you, John?" Kate called; then she saw where he had gone and returned to the kitchen. Dinner was just begun, as usual; he often wondered what on earth she did with herself all day. Sat glued to the TV set, probably, just as she used to sit glued to the radio.

Perched on the toilet seat, Larsen wrestled with his conscience. There was no use telling himself any more that his evidence didn't matter. He had seen Diane Morrison kidnaped, he had seen her kidnaper, and it was not Joseph Kennelly.

He couldn't phone from home—Kate would be on his neck at once. He must make some kind of excuse to call from outside. He played again with the idea of telling her. No, that was hopeless; he knew Kate.

She tried the doorknob.

"For gosh sake," she called, "what you got the door locked for? You sick or something?"

"I'm all right," he mumbled, and turned the key.

"I never saw such a man! Never a word out of you when you come home—you might think you didn't have a wife. I'm just a servant around here, to make your meals and look after you. Locking yourself in, like I was a stranger! Here I am, all day alone, working my fingers off—"

"What do you want me to talk about? I'm tired."

"And maybe *I'm* not, huh?"

"Let's not fight, Kate," he said wearily. An inspiration came to him. "I've got a fierce headache. If dinner isn't ready, I think I'll walk down to the drug store and get something for it."

"Wait till you've eaten," she said, placated. "That'll make you feel better." She made a conscious effort to achieve a friendly tone. "I was just looking at the paper. Gee, that's awful about that kid, isn't it? I'm glad they got the man. People like that ought to be fried in oil."

"How do you know he's the right one?" he couldn't keep himself from asking.

Kate flared up instantly.

"Well, so I guess you know more than the police, Mr. Smarty! If he wasn't the one did it, why'd they arrest him? They don't arrest anybody till they've got the goods on 'em—anybody can tell you that."

"I guess so," he said feebly, and started to set the table before she told him to.

He did have a headache, and no wonder. Kate's words started him thinking again. She was wrong; they *had* arrested an innocent man. But by that very token, they could never convict him. His mind flitted to the police laboratories he had read about. The hairs and fibers from the girl's clothing would belong to another man, a burly middle-aged man with thick dark hair, whoever he was. There were doubtless lots of other scientific findings he knew nothing about, and they'd all point away from Kennelly. The janitor might be indicted by the grand jury on what they got, but he'd never come to trial—they were sure to find the man who really did it.

And without John Larsen's sticking his fool neck out, to no end but his own ruin.

He didn't go out to phone.

The grand jury did indict Kennelly, and he was held without bail in the county jail. Larsen thought about him a good deal, though the sharp impact of that terrible day was growing dimmer. Tough luck for the guy, to be in prison all this time for something he didn't do. But from all accounts he was no good anyway, and a good scare might straighten him out. Any time now they would find they didn't have enough to try him on, or something would turn up that would lead them to the real criminal—though Larsen realized they wouldn't be looking very hard for any other suspect while they thought they had the guilty man.

Kennelly had a good lawyer—a prosperous uncle had turned up from somewhere and was paying the bill. Lawrence Prather, the lawyer's name was; he'd been defense attorney in a number of local murder cases and nearly always got his client off. Kennelly would be sure to be acquitted, if he was ever tried.

The date was set for the trial.

Larsen persuaded himself that if there had been the slightest doubt in his mind of the man's acquittal he would have sacrificed himself and gone to Prather with his story. But there wasn't any doubt. He heard the fellows talking about the case in the store, heard people sometimes in the bus; it was exciting a lot of interest. Everybody predicted Kennelly would go free, though everybody took it for granted he was guilty. Some of them were just cynical about justice; some of them thought you couldn't get a conviction on circumstantial evidence alone.

Sometimes, shivering, John Larsen imagined his interview with the defense lawyer. There would be no point in his going to him if he weren't willing to be a witness. And he could hear the prosecutor cross-examining him at the trial.

"And just how did you happen to be at that particular spot at that particular moment, Mr. Larsen?"

There'd be nobody to back him up; it would be just his word against everybody's. The prosecution might make it out that he was a friend of Kennelly's, or had been bribed to toss in this red herring; that he'd made the whole thing up. They might even suspect, or pretend to suspect, that he was covering up not for Kennelly but for himself. The people in that lunch room could identify him; he'd been in Belleville that afternoon. He'd be cleared, of course; but by that time, with all the notoriety, his goose would be cooked.

He stayed away from Prather's office. Kennelly's trial began in October.

Larsen couldn't go, naturally; he had to work. But he followed every word in print. He couldn't keep his mind on anything else. Sims caught him talking about it to a customer, and got angry. "We want people to think about rugs in here, not murders," he said. "If you can't attend your work, Larsen—" Larsen apologized humbly and watched his step.

He was amazed and frightened by the public excitement. It took almost a week to get a jury. Kennelly was booed and yelled at as he was taken to and from court. The sex murder of a young girl was the worst crime imaginable, and people wanted somebody punished for it. Larsen shuddered at the thought of daring to deprive them of their prey. It wasn't safe even to say aloud that he believed Joseph Kennelly might be innocent.

As the trial progressed, Larsen began having nightmares. He couldn't eat and was losing weight. Even Kate noticed and nagged him about it. Like everyone else, she was following the trial closely, and every night she wanted to talk it over. She *knew* Kennelly was guilty, and the electric chair was too good for him. If he went free, he ought to be lynched.

"Oh, shut up!" her husband finally shouted at her.

"I suppose you're sorry for him!" she retorted. "Maybe you wish *you* could do something like that and get away with it!"

Larsen went into the bathroom to keep from answering her.

He waited in vain, during the prosecution, for any mention of hairs or textile fibers; apparently either none had been found or they were being ignored because they did not implicate Kennelly. Nobody said anything about fingerprints or bloodstains in the car, either—doubtless for the same reason. An expert witness did prove that fragments of gravel taken from the seams of the defendant's shoes had come from the quarry, but then Kennelly had often visited the place, which was near his own home. If there were no witnesses to prove Kennelly's alibi, neither were there any to disprove it. The boys from the school who testified to his remarks about Diane had only vague generalities to offer. Larsen began to feel the load lifting from him.

But the defense was little more than a formality. Kennelly himself was his only witness, and he made a poor one—confessedly drunk all through the crucial period. No attempt was made to claim Kennelly was insane, as Larsen had hoped for. Prather gave a strong closing speech, pointing out the lack of direct evidence, pleading that no testimony had actually proved his client's guilt.

But then District Attorney Holcombe pulled out all the stops —denouncing the janitor, exposing his sorry record, calling him "a creature in human form, a vile, vicious rat." The most damning thing of all was that handkerchief. "I just don't believe in coincidences like that," said Holcombe sarcastically. "I'll tell you what I do believe—I believe that poor girl pulled the handkerchief out of Kennelly's pocket while she struggled with him for her honor and her life. And I believe she scratched his face in her feeble attempt to fight back, to escape from the monster who was attacking her."

The audience in the courtroom applauded, and had to be threatened with eviction.

In his charge to the jury Judge Stith tried to be neutral, but the jury could see which way he leaned. They leaned the same way; they remembered vividly the photographs of Diane's pitiful little corpse. Many of them had daughters of their own. Somebody had to be punished for the fiendish crime. They brought in a verdict of guilty on both counts, kidnaping and murder. It took only three ballots, the foreman told reporters afterward, to bring to their senses a couple of sentimental old fools holding out for a reasonable doubt.

But the judge *can't* condemn him to death, Larsen thought wildly. He can't, just on circumstantial evidence. The man will be given a life sentence at the most, and that means he'll be out on parole eventually. That much won't hurt him, a ne'er-do-well like him.

The judge sentenced Kennelly to the electric chair. He had daughters too.

But there's always an appeal, thought Larsen desperately. The appeal would be granted. Kennelly would have another trial, and by that time the truth would surely have come out.

"For heaven's sake, stop *fussing!*" Kate said a dozen times an evening. "What on earth's the matter with you lately? And you're smoking too much, John. I won't have it—you're spending a fortune on cigarettes!"

The appeal was denied.

The district attorney told the papers he was pleased. "Death is too good for a human snake like Kennelly," he said.

Prather did not carry the appeal to the state Supreme Court. "No grounds," he explained.

There *were* grounds. Larsen could furnish them.

Twice he got as far as starting to dial Prather's office. Then he realized all that it would mean, and hung up. Wait and see, he told himself. These things drag on for years, one reprieve after another.

"And why have you delayed so long in bringing me this information, Mr. Larsen?" he could hear the defense lawyer saying.

It would be useless to throw himself on the man's mercy, to

beg him to follow up the clue and leave John Larsen out of it. Without his testimony the new evidence would mean nothing. It might mean nothing now, anyway. At the very beginning, when Kennelly was first arrested—or before that—it would have been of use. Now he would only involve himself, he kept telling himself, with small chance of helping Kennelly.

If only there were somebody—anybody in the world—to whom he could tell everything, who would advise him and protect him and make things come out right!

Kennelly was in the death row at the state penitentiary. The date for his execution was set for three months away.

Then it was two months.

Then one.

Prather took Kennelly's uncle, his only relative, to the governor. The governor was running for re-election the next November. He wasn't reprieving a man convicted of the sex murder of a teen-age girl.

Then it was one week.

Then it was two days.

John Larsen had lost twenty pounds. He was afraid to sleep; once he screamed in a nightmare and woke Kate. He hardly noticed her nagging any more.

"If you're sick, go to a doctor."

"I'm not sick."

"You think I'm a fool? There's *something* wrong with you. What have you been doing, John?" She cast about for possibilities. "John, you tell me!" Suddenly she burst into tears. "I know what it is, and I ain't going to stand for it. You've got some other woman on your mind! If you think, after twenty-seven years, I'll let you—"

Larsen laughed. It wasn't a pretty sound.

Crazy plans flitted through his brain. He would go to Belleville, he would hunt until he found the dark-haired man, he would force the murderer to confess.

All nonsense.

There was no last-minute reprieve. In his heart Larsen knew he hadn't really expected one. Kennelly went to the chair on schedule, shouting his innocence with his last breath.

Reading every painful word of the newspaper story, John Larsen stood at last face to face with the bare truth.

Perhaps he could not have prevented the murder of the girl—though he might have if he had acted at once. But he had done enough.

He had let a man die, in order to hold on to a job he loathed and a wife he hated. He, John Larsen, had murdered Joseph Kennelly, whom he had never seen, as surely as that unknown man had murdered Diane Morrison.

He was a murderer, and murderers ought to die. But he hadn't had the courage to save Kennelly, and he didn't begin to have the courage to die himself. All he could do was to endure, to the last limit of endurance.

At the sight of his face that evening, Kate's words froze on her lips. He picked at his dinner in silence. Immediately after he went to bed. He slept the clock around in the heavy, dreamless sleep of an exhausted animal.

In the middle of the next morning he was displaying a rug to a customer. Suddenly he dropped it and stiffened.

He began to scream: "I did it! I did it! I did it!"

It took two men to subdue him until the ambulance came . . .

And near Belleville a heavy man with a shock of dark hair, a harmless "character" whom everybody knew and nobody ever noticed, prowled the lonely country roads in his old black car, his eyes alert for a good-looking girl walking alone . . .

JACK RITCHIE

For All the Rude People

"How old are you?" I asked!

His eyes were on the revolver I was holding. "Look, mister, there's not much in the cash register, but take it all. I won't make no trouble."

"I am not interested in your filthy money. How old are you?"

He was puzzled. "Forty-two."

I clicked my tongue. "What a pity. From your point of view, at least. You might have lived another twenty or thirty years if you had just taken the very slight pains to be polite."

He didn't understand.

"I am going to kill you," I said, "because of the four-cent stamp and because of the cherry candy."

He did not know what I meant by the cherry candy, but he did know about the stamp.

Panic raced into his face. "You must be crazy. You can't kill me just because of that."

"But I can."

And I did.

When Dr. Briller told me that I had but four months to live, I was, of course, perturbed. "Are you positive you haven't mixed up the X-rays? I've heard of such things."

"I'm afraid not, Mr. Turner."

I gave it more earnest thought. "The laboratory reports. Perhaps my name was accidentally attached to the wrong . . ."

He shook his head slowly. "I double-checked. I always do that in cases like these. Sound medical practice, you know."

It was late afternoon and the time when the sun is tired. I rather hoped that when my time came to actually die, it might be in the morning. Certainly more cheerful.

"In cases like this," Dr. Briller said, "a doctor is faced with a dilemma. Shall he or shall he not tell his patient? I always tell mine. That enables them to settle their affairs and to have a fling, so to speak." He pulled a pad of paper toward him. "Also I'm writing a book. What do you intend doing with your remaining time?"

"I really don't know. I've just been thinking about it for a minute or two, you know."

"Of course," Briller said. "No immediate rush. But when you do decide, you will let me know, won't you? My book concerns the things that people do with their remaining time when they know just when they're going to die."

He pushed aside the pad. "See me every two or three weeks. That way we'll be able to measure the progress of your decline."

Briller saw me to the door. "I already have written up twenty-two cases like yours." He seemed to gaze into the future. "Could be a best seller, you know."

I have always lived a bland life. Not an unintelligent one, but bland.

I have contributed nothing to the world—and in that I have much in common with almost every soul on earth—but on the other hand I have not taken away anything either. I have, in short, asked merely to be left alone. Life is difficult enough without undue association with people.

What can one do with the remaining four months of a bland life?

I have no idea how long I walked and thought on that subject, but eventually I found myself on the long curving bridge that sweeps down to join the lake drive. The sounds of mechanical music intruded themselves upon my mind and I looked down.

A circus, or very large carnival, lay below.

It was the world of shabby magic, where the gold is gilt, where the top-hatted ringmaster is as much a gentleman as the medals on his chest are authentic, and where the pink ladies on horseback are hard-faced and narrow-eyed. It was the domain of the harsh-voiced vendors and the short-change.

I have always felt that the demise of the big circus may be counted as one of the cultural advances of the twentieth century, yet I found myself descending the footbridge and in a few moments I was on the midway between the rows of stands where human mutations are exploited and exhibited for the entertainment of all children.

Eventually, I reached the big top and idly watched the bored ticket-taker in his elevated box at one side of the main entrance.

A pleasant-faced man leading two little girls approached him and presented several cardboard rectangles which appeared to be passes.

The ticket-taker ran his finger down a printed list at his side. His eyes hardened and he scowled down at the man and the children for a moment. Then slowly and deliberately he tore the passes to bits and let the fragments drift to the ground. "These are no damn good," he said.

The man below him flushed. "I don't understand."

"You didn't leave the posters up," the ticket-taker snapped. "Beat it, crumb!"

The children looked up at their father, their faces puzzled. Would he do something about this?

He stood there and the white of anger appeared on his face. He seemed about to say something, but then he looked down at the children. He closed his eyes for a moment as though to control his anger, and then he said, "Come on, kids. Let's go home."

He led them away, down the midway, and the children looked back, bewildered, but saying nothing.

I approached the ticket-taker. "Why did you do that?"

He glanced down. "What's it to you?"

"Perhaps a great deal."

He studied me irritably. "Because he didn't leave up the posters."

"I heard that before. Now explain it."

He exhaled as though it cost him money. "Our advance man goes through a town two weeks before we get there. He leaves posters advertising the show any place he can—grocery stores, shoe shops, meat markets—any place that will paste them in the window and keep them there until the show comes to town. He hands out two or three passes for that. But what some of these jokers don't know is that we check up. If the posters aren't still up when we hit town, the passes are no good."

"I see," I said dryly. "And so you tear up the passes in their faces and in front of their children. Evidently that man removed the posters from the window of his little shop too soon. Or perhaps he had those passes *given* to him by a man who removed the posters from his window."

"What's the difference? The passes are no good."

"Perhaps there is no difference in that respect. But do you realize what you have done?"

His eyes were narrow, trying to estimate me and any power I might have.

"You have committed one of the most cruel of human acts," I said stiffly. "You have humiliated a man before his children. You have inflicted a scar that will remain with him and them as long as they live. He will take those children home and it will be a long, long way. And what can he say to them?"

"Are you a cop?"

"I am not a cop. Children of that age regard their father as the finest man in the world. The kindest, the bravest. And now they will remember that a man had been bad to their father— and he had been unable to do anything about it."

"So I tore up his passes. Why didn't he buy tickets? Are you a city inspector?"

"I am not a city inspector. Did you expect him to *buy* tickets after that humiliation? You left the man with no recourse whatsoever. He could not *buy* tickets and he could not create a well-justified scene because the children were with him. He could do nothing. Nothing at all, but retreat with two children who wanted to see your miserable circus and now they cannot."

I looked down at the foot of his stand. There were the fragments of many more dreams—the debris of other men who had committed the capital crime of not leaving their posters up long enough. "You could at least have said, 'I'm sorry, sir. But your passes are not valid.' And then you could have explained politely and quietly why."

"I'm not paid to be polite." He showed yellow teeth. "And mister, I *like* tearing up passes. It gives me a kick."

And there it was. He was a little man who had been given a little power and he used it like a Caesar.

He half rose. "Now get the hell out of here, *mister*, before I come down there and chase you all over the lot."

Yes. He was a man of cruelty, a two-dimensional animal born without feeling and sensitivity and fated to do harm as long as he existed. He was a creature who should be eliminated from the face of the earth.

If only I had the power to . . .

I stared up at the twisted face for a moment more and then turned on my heel and left. At the top of the bridge I got a bus and rode to the sports shop at Thirty-seventh.

I purchased a .32 caliber revolver and a box of cartridges.

Why do we *not* murder? Is it because we do not feel the moral justification for such a final act? Or is it more because we fear the consequences if we are caught—the cost to us, to our families, to our children?

And so we suffer wrongs with meekness, we endure them because to eliminate them might cause us even more pain than we already have.

But I had no family, no close friends. And four months to live.

The sun had set and the carnival lights were bright when I got off the bus at the bridge. I looked down at the midway and he was still in his box.

How should I do it? I wondered. Just march up to him and shoot him as he sat on his little throne?

The problem was solved for me. I saw him replaced by another man—apparently his relief. He lit a cigarette and strolled off the midway toward the dark lake front.

I caught up with him around a bend concealed by bushes. It was a lonely place, but close enough to the carnival so that its sounds could still reach me.

He heard my footsteps and turned. A tight smile came to his

lips and he rubbed the knuckles of one hand. "You're asking for it, mister."

His eyes widened when he saw my revolver.

"How old are you?" I asked.

"Look, mister," he said swiftly. "I only got a couple of tens in my pocket."

"How old are you?" I repeated.

His eyes flicked nervously. "Thirty-two."

I shook my head sadly. "You could have lived into your seventies. Perhaps forty more years of life, if only you had taken the simple trouble to act like a human being."

His face whitened. "Are you off your rocker, or something?"

"A possibility."

I pulled the trigger.

The sound of the shot was not as loud as I had expected, or perhaps it was lost against the background of the carnival noises.

He staggered and dropped to the edge of the path and he was quite dead.

I sat down on a nearby park bench and waited.

Five minutes. Ten. Had no one heard the shot?

I became suddenly conscious of hunger. I hadn't eaten since noon. The thought of being taken to a police station and being questioned for any length of time seemed unbearable. And I had a headache, too.

I tore a page from my pocket notebook and began writing:

A careless word may be forgiven. But a lifetime of cruel rudeness cannot. This man deserves to die.

I was about to sign my name, but then I decided that my initials would be sufficient for the time being. I did not want to be apprehended before I had a good meal and some aspirins.

I folded the page and put it into the dead ticket-taker's breast pocket.

I met no one as I returned up the path and ascended the footbridge. I walked to Weschler's, probably the finest restaurant in the city. The prices are, under normal circumstances, beyond me, but I thought that this time I could indulge myself.

After dinner, I decided an evening bus ride might be in order. I rather enjoyed that form of city excursion and, after all, my freedom of movement would soon become restricted.

The driver of the bus was an impatient man and clearly his

passengers were his enemies. However, it was a beautiful night and the bus was not crowded.

At Sixty-eighth Street, a fragile white-haired woman with cameo features waited at the curb. The driver grudgingly brought his vehicle to a stop and opened the door.

She smiled and nodded to the passengers as she put her foot on the first step, and one could see that her life was one of gentle happiness and very few bus rides.

"Well!" the driver snapped. "Is it going to take you all day to get in?"

She flushed and stammered. "I'm sorry." She presented him with a five-dollar bill.

He glared. "Don't you have any change?"

The flush deepened. "I don't think so. But I'll look."

The driver was evidently ahead on his schedule and he waited.

And one other thing was clear. He was enjoying this.

She found a quarter and held it up timorously.

"In the box!" he snapped.

She dropped it into the box.

The driver moved his vehicle forward jerkily and she almost fell. Just in time, she managed to catch hold of a strap.

Her eyes went to the passengers, as though to apologize for herself—for not having moved faster, for not having immediate change, for almost falling. The smile trembled and she sat down.

At Eighty-second, she pulled the buzzer cord, rose, and made her way forward.

The driver scowled over his shoulder as he came to a stop. "Use the rear door. Don't you people ever learn to use the rear door?"

I am all in favor of using the rear door. Especially when a bus is crowded. But there were only a half a dozen passengers on this bus and they read their newspapers with frightened neutrality.

She turned, her face pale, and left by the rear door.

The evening she had had, or the evening she was going to have, had now been ruined. Perhaps many more evenings, with the thought of it.

I rode the bus to the end of the line.

I was the only passenger when the driver turned it around and parked.

It was a deserted, dimly lit corner, and there were no waiting passengers at the small shelter at the curb. The driver glanced at his watch, lit a cigarette, and then noticed me. "If you're taking the ride back, mister, put another quarter in the box. No free riders here."

I rose from my seat and walked slowly to the front of the bus. "How old are you?"

His eyes narrowed. "That's none of your business."

"About thirty-five, I'd imagine," I said. "You'd have had another thirty years or more ahead of you." I produced the revolver.

He dropped the cigarette. "Take the money," he said.

"I'm not interested in money. I'm thinking about a gentle lady and perhaps the hundreds of other gentle ladies and the kind harmless men and the smiling children. You are a criminal. There is no justification for what you do to them. There is no justification for your existence."

And I killed him.

I sat down and waited.

After ten minutes, I was still alone with the corpse.

I realized that I was sleepy. Incredibly sleepy. It might be better if I turned myself in to the police after a good night's sleep.

I wrote my justification for the driver's demise on a sheet of note paper, added my initials, and put the page in his pocket.

I walked four blocks before I found a taxi and took it to my apartment building.

I slept soundly and perhaps I dreamed. But if I did, my dreams were pleasant and innocuous, and it was almost nine before I woke.

After a shower and a leisurely breakfast, I selected my best suit. I remembered I had not yet paid that month's telephone bill. I made out a check and addressed an envelope. I discovered that I was out of stamps. But no matter, I would get one on the way to the police station.

I was almost there when I remembered the stamp. I stopped in at a corner drugstore. It was a place I had never entered before.

The proprietor, in a semi-medical jacket, sat behind the soda fountain reading a newspaper and a salesman was making notations in a large order book.

The proprietor did not look up when I entered and he spoke to the salesman. "They've got his fingerprints on the notes, they've got this handwriting, and they've got his initials. What's wrong with the police?"

The salesman shrugged. "What good are fingerprints if the murderer doesn't have his in the police files? The same goes for the handwriting if you got nothing to compare it with. And how many thousand people in the city got the initials L. T.?" He closed his book. "I'll be back next week."

When he was gone, the druggist continued reading the newspaper.

I cleared my throat.

He finished reading a long paragraph and then looked up. "Well?"

"I'd like a four-cent stamp, please."

It appeared almost as though I had struck him. He stared at me for fifteen seconds and then he left his stool and slowly made his way to the rear of the store toward a small barred window.

I was about to follow him, but a display of pipes at my elbow caught my attention.

After a while I felt eyes upon me and looked up.

The druggist stood at the far end of the store, one hand on his hip and the other disdainfully holding the single stamp. "Do you expect me to bring it to you?"

And now I remembered a small boy of six who had had five pennies. Not just one this time, but five, and this was in the days of penny candies.

He had been entranced by the display in the showcase—the fifty varieties of sweet things, and his mind had revolved in a pleasant indecision. The red whips? The licorice? The grab bags? But not the candy cherries. He didn't like those.

And then he had become conscious of the druggist standing beside the display case—tapping one foot. The druggist's eyes had smouldered with irritation—no, more than that—with anger. "Are you going to take all day for your lousy nickel?"

He had been a sensitive boy and he had felt as though he had received a blow. His precious five pennies were now nothing. This man despised them. And this man despised him.

He pointed numbly and blindly. "Five cents of that."

When he left the store he had found that he had the candy cherries.

But that didn't really matter. Whatever it had been, he couldn't have eaten it.

Now I stared at the druggist and the four-cent stamp and the narrow hatred for anyone who did not contribute directly to his profits. I had no doubt that he would fawn if I purchased one of his pipes.

But I thought of the four-cent stamp, and the bag of cherry candy I had thrown away so many years ago.

I moved toward the rear of the store and took the revolver out of my pocket. "How old are you?"

When he was dead, I did not wait longer than necessary to write a note. I had killed for myself this time and I felt the need of a drink.

I went several doors down the street and entered a small bar. I ordered a brandy and water.

After ten minutes, I heard the siren of a squad car.

The bartender went to the window. "It's just down the street." He took off his jacket. "Got to see what this is all about. If anybody comes in, tell them I'll be right back." He put the bottle of brandy on the bar. "Help yourself, but tell me how many."

I sipped the brandy slowly and watched the additional squad cars and finally the ambulance appear.

The bartender returned after ten minutes and a customer followed at his heels. "A short beer, Joe."

"This is my second brandy," I said.

Joe collected my change. "The druggist down the street got himself murdered. Looks like it was by the man who kills people because they're not polite."

The customer watched him draw a beer. "How do you figure that? Could have been just a holdup."

Joe shook his head. "No. Fred Masters—he's got the TV shop across the street—found the body and he read the note."

The customer put a dime on the bar. "I'm not going to cry about it. I always took my business someplace else. He acted as though he was doing you a favor every time he waited on you."

Joe nodded. "I don't think anybody in the neighborhood's going to miss him. He always made a lot of trouble."

I had been about to leave and return to the drugstore to give myself up, but now I ordered another brandy and took out my notebook. I began making a list of names.

It was surprising how one followed another. They were bitter memories, some large, some small, some I had experienced and many more that I had witnessed—and perhaps felt more than the victims.

Names. And that warehouseman. I didn't know his name, but I must include him.

I remembered the day and Miss Newman. We were her sixth-graders and she had taken us on another one of her excursions—this time to the warehouses along the river, where she was going to show us "how industry works."

She always planned her tours and she always asked permission of the places we visited, but this time she strayed or became lost and we arrived at the warehouse—she and the thirty children who adored her.

And the warehouseman had ordered her out. He had used language which we did not understand, but we sensed its intent, and he had directed it against us and Miss Newman.

She was small and she had been frightened and we retreated. And Miss Newman did not report to school the next day or any day after that and we learned that she had asked for a transfer.

And I, who loved her, too, knew why. She could not face us after that.

Was he still alive? He had been in his twenties then, I imagined.

When I left the bar a half an hour later, I realized I had a great deal of work to do.

The succeeding days were busy ones and, among others, I found the warehouseman. I told him why he was dying, because he did not even remember.

And when that was done, I dropped into a restaurant not far away.

The waitress eventually broke off her conversation with the cashier and strode to my table. "What do you want?"

I ordered a steak and tomatoes.

The steak proved to be just about what one could expect in such a neighborhood. As I reached for my coffee spoon, I accidentally dropped it to the floor. I picked it up. "Waitress, would you mind bringing me another spoon, please?"

She stalked angrily to my table and snatched the spoon from my hand. "You got the shakes, or something?"

She returned in a few moments and was about to deposit a spoon, with considerable emphasis, upon my table.

But then a sudden thought altered the harsh expression of her face. The descent of the arm diminuendoed, and when the spoon touched the tablecloth, it touched gently. Very gently.

She laughed nervously. "I'm sorry if I was sharp, mister."

It was an apology, and so I said, "That's quite all right."

"I mean that you can drop a spoon anytime you want to. I'll be glad to get you another."

"Thank you." I turned to my coffee.

"You're not offended, are you, mister?" she asked eagerly.

"No. Not at all."

She snatched a newspaper from an empty neighboring table. "Here, sir, you can read this while you eat. I mean, it's on the house. Free."

When she left me, the wide-eyed cashier stared at her. "What's with all that, Mable?"

Mable glanced back at me with a trace of uneasiness. "You can never tell who he might be. You better be polite these days."

As I ate I read, and an item caught my eye. A grown man had heated pennies in a frying pan and tossed them out to some children who were making trick-or-treat rounds before Halloween. He had been fined a miserable twenty dollars.

I made a note of his name and address.

Dr. Briller finished his examination. "You can get dressed now, Mr. Turner."

I picked up my shirt. "I don't suppose some new miracle drug has been developed since I was here last?"

He laughed with self-enjoyed good nature. "No, I'm afraid not." He watched me button the shirt. "By the way, have you decided what you're going to do with your remaining time?"

I had, but I thought I'd say, "Not yet."

He was faintly perturbed. "You really should, you know. Only about three months left. And be sure to let me know when you do."

While I finished dressing, he sat down at his desk and glanced at the newspaper lying there. "The killer seems to be rather busy, doesn't he?"

He turned a page. "But really the most surprising thing about the crimes seems to be the public's reaction. Have you read the Letters from the People column recently?"

"No."

"These murders appear to be meeting with almost universal

approval. Some of the letter writers even hint that they might be able to supply the murderer with a few choice names themselves."

I would have to get a paper.

"Not only that," Dr. Briller said, "but a wave of politeness has struck the city."

I put on my coat. "Shall I come back in two weeks?"

He put aside the paper. "Yes. And try to look at this whole thing as cheerfully as possible. We all have to go some day."

But his day was indeterminate and presumably in the distant future.

My appointment with Dr. Briller had been in the evening, and it was nearly ten by the time I left my bus and began the short walk to my apartment building.

As I approached the last corner, I heard a shot. I turned into Milding Lane and found a little man with a revolver standing over a newly dead body on the quiet and deserted sidewalk.

I looked down at the corpse. "Goodness. A policeman."

The little man nodded. "Yes, what I've done does seem a little extreme, but you see he was using a variety of language that was entirely unnecessary."

"Ah," I said.

The little man nodded. "I'd parked my car in front of this fire hydrant. Entirely inadvertently, I assure you. And this policeman was waiting when I returned to my car. And also he discovered that I'd forgotten my driver's license. I would not have acted as I did if he had simply written out a ticket—for I was guilty, sir, and I readily admit it—but he was not content with that. He made embarrassing observations concerning my intelligence, my eyesight, the possibility that I'd stolen the car, and finally on the legitimacy of my birth." He blinked at a fond memory. "And my mother was an angel, sir. An angel."

I remembered a time when I'd been apprehended while absentmindedly jaywalking. I would contritely have accepted the customary warning, or even a ticket, but the officer insisted upon a profane lecture before a grinning assemblage of interested pedestrians. Most humiliating.

The little man looked at the gun in his hand. "I bought this just today and actually I'd intended to use it on the superintendent of my apartment building. A bully."

I agreed. "Surly fellows."

He sighed. "But now I suppose I'll have to turn myself over to the police?"

I gave it thought. He watched me.

He cleared his throat. "Or perhaps I should just leave a note? You see I've been reading in the newspapers about . . ."

I lent him my notebook.

He wrote a few lines, signed his initials, and deposited the slip of paper between two buttons of the dead officer's jacket.

He handed the notebook back to me. "I must remember to get one of these."

He opened the door of his car. "Can I drop you off anywhere?"

"No, thank you," I said. "It's a nice evening. I'd rather walk."

Pleasant fellow, I reflected, as I left him.

Too bad there weren't more like him.

BRUNO FISCHER

The Dog Died First

Blood was on my mind that night, but it was blood of the French Revolution. I was correcting Modern European History papers while Dot was at a hen party at Marie Cannon's. At midnight I went to bed, knowing that between bridge and chitchat there was no telling when Dot would be home.

The sound of the car pulling into the driveway woke me. As we have no garage in our bungalow-type stucco house, we leave the car out in the open on the cinder driveway. I heard Dot enter the house through the back door, and then I was listening to water running in the kitchen.

It ran for a long time—too long for her to be getting a drink and she certainly wouldn't be washing herself at the kitchen sink. Drowsily I was wondering what she was up to now, and I wondered a lot more when she turned off the water and left the house again. The radium clock on the dresser said five minutes after one.

I turned on my side and looked through the window. Dot had left the car's headlights on and she was walking into their glare. The pail she carried in her right hand was evidently full of water. The weight of it made her neat hips sway. She opened the black sedan door, switched on the overhead light, dug a dripping scrubbing brush out of the pail and leaned inside the car.

So that explained her antics. No doubt somebody had spilled liquid on the upholstery and she was trying to scrub it off before it dried. I dug my head into the pillow to shut out the glow of the headlights coming in through the window.

I was almost asleep when the night lamp went on in the bedroom.

"Are you awake, darling?" Dot asked.

"Um,umph, um," I mumbled, turning my head to let her know I was too sleepy for conversation.

But as nothing ever stopped Dot from talking, my desire for slumber didn't. I'd trained myself to absorb her chatter without listening to it, and that was what I did then until a startling sentence jerked me fully awake.

"I couldn't get all the blood off," she had said.

"Blood?" I breathed, opening my eyes wide. "Did you say blood?"

Dot was taking a nightgown out of a drawer. "He died on the way to the doctor," she said complacently. "I feel like a murderer."

She straightened up with the nightgown in her hand. The soft, dim night light played over her tightly and precisely formed body, and her face was as guileless as a doll's.

"Who died?" I demanded hoarsely.

"The dog, of course," she said, dropping the nightgown over her head.

I sank back on the bed. A dog, of course. Well, what had I really expected?

"I wasn't going to tell you because you're always criticizing my driving," she explained. "Like when I smashed a fender last week. But I really couldn't help what happened tonight. The dog ran right under the wheel. Then when I got home I noticed the blood in the car and I tried to wash it off, but I couldn't quite because it had dried. I decided to tell you because you'll see it tomorrow."

I was drowsy again, but puzzled. "How does blood get inside a car when you run over a dog?"

"He was still breathing, so I took him to the vet, but he was dead when I got there. The dog, I mean. The poor little thing."

She put out the light and got into bed, but that didn't stop her voice. She told me about the dollar and seventeen cents she had lost at bridge and that Ida Walker looked dowdy and Marie Cannon stunning and Edith Bauer—

"How about some sleep?" I complained.

She was quiet—for about a minute, it seemed to me. Then she was shaking me.

"Bernie," she whispered, "there's somebody sneaking about outside with a flashlight."

The radium clock said ten minutes after three, which meant that I'd actually been asleep about two hours. Dot was sitting up, and past the vague outline of her shoulder and through the window I saw a splotch of light move along the side of the car.

"Maybe he's trying to steal the car," she whispered.

"Did you leave the key in the ignition?"

It didn't surprise me when she admitted that she thought she had. Snorting, I got out of bed and went to the window. Whoever held the flashlight seemed to have lost interest in the car and was walking toward the street.

"He's going away," I said hopefully. I was a man who liked to avoid trouble.

"I wonder what he wanted."

"I know what I want," I said. "Sleep."

I had one leg on the bed when the doorbell rang. I froze half on the bed, listening. There are few things more disturbing than a doorbell ringing at three in the morning.

"That must be the thief," Dot whispered.

I roused myself. "Thieves don't ring doorbells."

"Well, it's somebody," Dot pointed out.

It certainly was somebody. The doorbell kept on ringing. I fumbled into slippers and robe, went into the living room, turned on the light, opened the front door.

The man who entered held a flashlight in his hand, so he was the same one I had seen prowling outside. He had more paunch than chest and a lumpy face.

"Mr. Bernard Hall?" he said.

I nodded. "What is it?"

He didn't answer. He stepped past me into the living room, looked it over as if he were thinking of renting it, then fixed me with rather sad eyes.

"My boy Steve is in your History class. Stephan Ricardo."

"Ah, yes," I said, using my teacher-parent manner. But that was absurd. This man hadn't got me out of bed at three in the morning to discuss his son's scholastic problems. Then I remembered what Stephan Ricardo had told me his father did for a living, and I tensed.

"You're a detective," I said.

"That's right." Ricardo massaged his jowls. "Seems there's blood in your car."

"Is that what you were looking at with your flashlight?"

He nodded. "Uh-huh. There was an attempt made to wash it off, but it was soaked into the floor rug."

At that moment Dot came into the living room. She wore her flowered housecoat over the nightgown.

"I'm the one you want," she said. "I suppose I shouldn't have left the body in the bushes."

Ricardo pushed his hat back from his brow and blinked a couple of times. "You admit you did it, Mrs. Hall?"

"Should I have reported it to the police?" She handed him that disarming smile of hers. "The thing is, I didn't want any trouble."

"No," Ricardo said softly, "I guess you didn't want trouble." He kept looking at Dot as if he didn't quite believe she existed. "Why did you do it, Mrs. Hall?"

"It was an accident. He ran in front of the car."

Ricardo shook his head sorrowfully. "That won't get you anywhere, Mrs. Hall. His head was smashed in, but there were no other marks on his body."

"But that's impossible. I held him in my arms and his head looked all right. He seemed to be injured internally. He died before I could get him to the vet."

"The vet?" Ricardo said, blinking.

"Dr. Harrison, the veterinary on Mill Street," she explained patiently. "Where else would you take a dog?"

Ricardo opened his mouth, but he didn't say what he started to. Instead he drew in air. "Suppose, Mrs. Hall, you tell me about it."

Dot settled herself in the armchair and placidly crossed her fine legs. I stuck a cigarette between my lips and noticed that the match shook in my hand. I didn't for a moment believe that a detective would awaken and question her at three in the morning because a dog had been run over.

"I was driving to a bridge game at Marie Cannon's tonight," she said. "About two blocks from here a little black dog ran in front of the car and I couldn't stop in time. I got out and there was the poor creature in terrible agony. He was a little thing, all black with white paws and a white splotch on his face. I don't know what breed, though he had some spitz in him, because when I was a little girl I had a spitz that was the darlingest—"

"What time was this?" Ricardo broke in.

"Close to eight-thirty. Marie Cannon was anxious that we get to her house at eight-thirty, and it was just about that when I left here. I would be late, but I couldn't leave an injured dog lying in the road, so I put him in the car and drove to the vet."

"To Dr. Harrison on Mill Street," Ricardo said rather grimly. "A good seven miles away, though you were late."

"Do you know of a nearer veterinary?"

Ricardo admitted that he didn't.

"So I had no choice," Dot said. "But when I got there, I saw that the poor dog was dead, so there was no point to taking him in to Dr. Harrison. I drove back to East Billford and left the dog in some bushes beside the road."

"Just like that," Ricardo sighed.

Dot flushed guiltily. "I suppose it was a cruel thing to do, but by then it was about ten minutes after nine and the bridge game couldn't start until I got there because I made the fourth and Marie Cannon would be furious with me. And, after all, the dog was dead, wasn't he? And I did look to see if he had a license, but he didn't have even a collar. He was obviously a stray dog, and I didn't know what else to do with him."

After that gush of words there was a silence. I filled it by saying, "I suppose killing a dog should be reported to the police. That's the law, isn't it?"

"Uh-huh." He glanced at me and then returned his sad gaze to Dot. "Did you get blood on your dress when you picked him up?"

"I'm sure I didn't. One of the women at the bridge game would have noticed if I had." She frowned. "He didn't seem to bleed at all, but he must have, because I saw blood in the car when I got home hours later."

"Where did you leave the—ah—body?"

"On Pine Road, in a section where there are no houses. Just this side of that dirt road."

"Wilson Lane," he said.

"Yes, that's it. A short distance past Wilson Lane, coming toward town, there are thick bushes on the right side. That's where I left him."

Ricardo nodded and scratched his cheeks with the backs of his fingers. He was a plump man with too much waist and jowls, but the set of his lumpy face frightened me.

"You better get dressed, Mrs. Hall," he said, "and go there with me."

Her blue eyes widened. "You mean right now?"

"Right now."

"I'm going too," I said.

"Sure," Ricardo said.

We went into the bedroom to put on clothes.

"I don't understand why they make so much trouble about a dog being run over," Dot complained as she slipped her shoes on. "Of course I feel bad about it, but getting people out of bed in the middle of the night! Why doesn't he just give me a ticket and I'll pay the fine?"

I didn't say anything. My stomach was sickishly empty.

We drove in Ricardo's sedan, the three of us in the front seat.

On the way, Dot said, "I suppose Al Wilcox saw me carry the dog into the bushes. He lives down the street and knows me. I saw his white police car pass when I returned to my car."

"That's right, Mrs. Hall," Ricardo said grimly.

It was less than a mile to the spot. Three cars were parked along the side of the road, and by the light of a couple of powerful electric lanterns I saw five or six men gathered on the narrow grassy stretch between the shoulder of the road and the line of thick bushes. One of them was Al Wilcox in his policeman's uniform.

"All these men because a dog was killed!" Dot said. Even she was catching on that something bigger than that must be up.

Ricardo had no comment. He led us across the road and then I saw the long shape under the canvas. The men had become silent and were looking at Dot.

"Mrs. Hall, is this the spot?" Ricardo asked.

She nodded and slipped her hand through my arm. She frowned at the size of the thing under the canvas.

"Give her a look, Al," Ricardo said.

Wilcox bent over and gripped one end of the canvas and pulled it down. Dot uttered a shrill scream. I felt her sag against my side, clinging to my arm.

"Why that's—that's Emmett Walker!" she gasped. "I played bridge with his wife tonight."

It was Emmett Walker, all right, but no longer the handsome insurance agent Dot and I had known for years. His blond hair was matted with dried blood and some of it had run in ragged streaks over his face.

"Cover him up, Al," Ricardo said wearily. He turned to Dot, and there was controlled fury in his voice. "He was murdered, Mrs. Hall."

"But—but where's the dog?" Dot stammered.

"There is no dog, Mrs. Hall."

"But I left him right there in those bushes."

"No, Mrs. Hall," Ricardo said. "You struck Emmett Walker over the head with something and killed him. You dragged him into your car and drove here and dragged him into the bushes. That's how the blood got in your car."

"It's not true!" Dot had recovered from the shock and was now merely indignant.

At that point I should have said something. I should have come to my wife's defense. But even if I hadn't been too choked for words, I couldn't think of any that would do any good.

Al Wilcox spoke up. "I was passing here at a few minutes after nine, Mrs. Hall, when I saw you come out of these bushes and get into your car. At two o'clock I passed this way again and by my headlights I saw what looked like a man's leg sticking out of the bushes. I investigated and found him."

"Well, I didn't do it," Dot said angrily. "Why would I want to kill Emmett Walker?"

"Suppose you tell us, Mrs. Hall."

Dot turned to me in exasperation. "You try to make him understand, darling."

I gulped air into my lungs. I said, "Of course you didn't do it," but my voice quavered.

Ricardo moved away from us to consult with the other policemen in undertones. When he returned to us, he asked Dot if the dress she had on was the one she had worn at the bridge game. She said that it was. Then he asked me for the keys to my car and handed them to Wilcox.

"Okay, let's go," Ricardo snapped.

I didn't ask him where. I knew where.

This time there were four of us in the sedan. I sat beside Ricardo, who drove, and Dot sat in the back seat with another detective. Ricardo didn't waste time. He had questions for Dot as we drove.

"Where did you say that bridge game was?"

"At Marie Cannon's house."

"Is she the wife of George Cannon, the lawyer?"

"Yes."

"Who else was there?"

"There were only four of us. Besides Marie and myself, there were Edith Bauer and Ida Walker." Her voice broke a little. "Poor Ida! Who is going to break the news to her?"

"She knows already," Ricardo said. "She didn't take the news too hard."

"They haven't got along too well lately. There were rumors that Emmett wasn't—well, exactly faithful to her." Dot leaned forward toward the back of Ricardo's neck, and her voice was breathless. "Do you think that Ida killed him?"

"I know who killed him," Ricardo said crisply.

That ended all talk until we reached the County Building, which also contained police headquarters and the county jail. Dot was taken into an office on the second floor, but I got no farther than the door.

"You might as well go home," Ricardo told me. "Your wife is being held."

"What are you going to do to her—give her the third degree?"

His lumpy face smiled a little. "We're going to question her."

"She's entitled to have a lawyer present."

"Sure." He waved a pudgy hand. "You'll find a phone booth down the hall."

I went into the booth and dialed George Cannon's number. His voice was drowsy, but it got wide awake when I told him what was up.

"I'll be right there," he said.

I waited out in the hall. In ten minutes George Cannon arrived. His hair was mussed and his suit looked like a sack on his frail body, but that wasn't because he'd dressed in a hurry. He always managed to look seedy and disheveled, though he was the most prominent lawyer in East Billford.

Briefly I gave him the details. His thin mouth tightened as he listened.

"Emmett was supposed to call for Ida tonight," he told me. "She waited in my house until one o'clock and then I drove her home. I think she suspected that he was out with another woman. And all that time he was dead."

"Don't stand here talking," I said. "God knows what they're doing to Dot."

"Oh, they won't be rough with a woman. You wait here, Bernie."

He knocked at the door through which Dot had been taken and was admitted.

For a full hour I paced that lonely hall before George came out.

Glumly he shook his head. "They've taken her up to a cell through another door. She hasn't been charged yet. There are still loose ends."

"How does it look?"

"It's too soon to tell," he said, not meeting my eyes. "If the blood in the car is a dog's their circumstantial case will be shot." He patted my shoulder. "No use hanging around here. Go home and get some sleep."

He dropped me off at my house. Dawn was coming up, and in the grayness of it I saw that my car was gone. The police had taken it because it was evidence—evidence that might mean life or death.

The house was terribly empty. I went into the bedroom and there was her nightgown flung across the foot of the bed. I remembered how only a few hours ago I had watched her getting into that nightgown, and nobody could have looked less like a woman who had just murdered somebody.

She hadn't. She said so. She was flighty and talkative, but she had never before lied to me.

But she had never before had occasion to lie about murder. . . .

I tossed in bed for an hour and slept fitfully for another hour. Then the doorbell woke me. It was Herman Bauer, a fellow teacher at the high school. His wife Edith was an old friend of Dot's.

Herman, chubby and usually jolly, was now glum and embarrassed. He said that he had stopped off on his way to school to tell me that the police had questioned him and Edith.

"They got us out of bed at six-thirty this morning," Herman said. "They asked Edith about the bridge game last night. When Dot arrived, when she left, if she'd been in the house all that time, and so on. They also asked how well Dot and Emmett had known each other." He fumbled uneasily with the brim of his hat. "Neither Edith nor I mentioned that Dot used to go out with Emmett."

"That was years ago," I said. "Before Dot and I were engaged."

"Of course." Herman watched his fingers on his hat. "But the police mightn't understand." He turned to the door. "If there's anything I can do for you, let me know."

After Herman Bauer was gone, I stood in the same spot for a long time. He had it all figured out, the way everybody else figured it and the police certainly did. I couldn't know that they weren't right.

Rousing myself, I went to the phone to call the school and say that I wouldn't be in that day and maybe not for the rest of the week. Before I could start to dial the number, the phone rang.

It was George Cannon, and he said, "Bernie, can you come over to the district attorney's office right away?"

"Did anything new break?"

"Yes, but I'm afraid it's not good. The blood in your car has been analyzed." He paused and then added tonelessly, "It's human blood, and it matches Emmett Walker's blood type."

There went the last hope, I thought as I hung up. Police science had proved Dot's story about the dog a lie, and if that was false, everything else she had said was.

I dressed and left the house. The police had my car, so I had to walk to the County Building.

Detective Ricardo and George Cannon were in the district attorney's office. John Fair, the D. A., was one of those back-slapping politicians who never met a voter without heartily pumping his hand, but when I entered his office he merely nodded gravely and remained in his seat.

"The analysis of the blood in your car leaves no doubt of your wife's guilt," Fair began brutally. "It took her some forty minutes to arrive at the bridge game after she left home—a distance of little over a mile. We know now that her delay was not caused by killing a dog and driving out to Dr. Harrison and back. She told the far-fetched story about the dog to explain her delay and also the blood in her car. Obviously she met Emmett Walker and killed him with a blunt instrument, probably as he was sitting in the car with her."

"What time was Walker killed?" I asked, grasping at a straw. "I mean, if he died after she arrived at the bridge game—"

Ricardo shook his heavy head. "The medical examiner can't cut it that fine. Says he thinks Walker died between nine and ten-thirty last night, and he'll give or take half an hour at either end."

"What does my wife say?" I asked weakly.

Fair shrugged irritably. "In spite of virtually conclusive evidence, she sticks to her preposterous story about the dog. A very stubborn young woman and extremely foolish." He rose and came around his desk. "Hall, I'm not out for her neck. We have learned that she and Walker were sweethearts at one time. I'm sorry to have to say this to you, but it appears that she continued to be one of his women up until last night."

"No!" I heard myself shout.

"We haven't proved it yet," Fair admitted, "but that explains her motive for killing him. Let us say that she struck him in jealous rage. In that case, I would not insist on a first-degree murder indictment. I want you to talk to her, Hall. I want you to make her see that it will be to her advantage to make a full confession."

"Prison," I said bitterly. "Is that what you offer her, years and years in prison?"

"It's better than the electric chair," Fair said softly and returned to his desk.

George Cannon hadn't said a word since I entered the office. He was our legal mind. I asked him for his opinion.

"Bernie, I'm against any deal," he declared. "I believe I can get her off free."

He believed! I looked at him standing there, seedy and slight, and at his pinched face with that perpetually hungry expression. He was East Billford's top lawyer, but it was a small city and his reputation didn't extend beyond it. He didn't think her innocent—nobody did—but he was willing to risk her life to build up his reputation in a sensational murder trial.

"I'll talk to her," I told the district attorney.

Ricardo led me upstairs to a small bare room containing only a few chairs, and left me there. A few minutes later a matron brought Dot in.

There were tired lines about her eyes and mouth, but she looked beautiful. She felt wonderful in my arms and her tremulous mouth was unendurably sweet. The electric chair, I thought dully, or years in prison that would be a living death for her.

After a minute she slipped out of my embrace. "I'd like a cigarette, darling," she said.

I lit it for her, and she sat down and crossed her legs and drew smoke into her lungs. "Darling," she said then, "they're saying terrible things about me."

She sounded indignant. Not frightened, not broken up, but merely outraged that she should be accused of having done anything wrong.

"They're even saying that Emmett was my lover," she went on angrily.

"Was he?"

When the words were out of my mouth, I hated myself for saying them. But I had to know.

Her eyebrows arched. "Darling, you don't think that too?"

"Was he, Dot?"

"Certainly not." Again that vast indignation. "Emmett meant little to me, even when I went out a few times with him before I married you."

I bent over her and took her face between my hands and looked deeply in her blue eyes. They were grave and without deceit.

"Dot," I said, "did you kill him?"

"No."

"How did the blood get in the car?"

"From the dog I ran over."

But police science had proved that a man and not a dog had bled in the car. It didn't make sense that she would tell the truth about everything but that. It was all of one piece. Frantically I wanted to believe her, but deep inside of me I didn't know.

I straightened up. She was my wife and I loved her.

"We'll fight them," I said.

When I returned to the district attorney's office, the same three men were there waiting for me.

"Well, is it a deal?" Fair asked.

"No," I said.

Ricardo sighed. Fair pounded his desk. "Very well, it will be first-degree murder then."

I turned away. George followed me out of the office and put his hand on my shoulder.

"We've got a good chance to lick them," he said. "I don't think, at any rate, that Fair can get a jury to give her the chair. We may get away with temporary insanity if she'll cooperate. I'll tell her exactly what to say on the stand, and if she sticks to it—"

"She's innocent," I said and walked away.

I was running away from his legal logic, but I couldn't run away from my hellish doubts.

Emmett Walker had had an eye for pretty women, but he had married an unattractive one. He hadn't done well as an insurance agent. Financially, being the husband of a woman with a fat bank account had paid off better.

Ida Walker was dumpy, and she had a face to match. When she admitted me into the house, she didn't give the impression of a grieving widow. She was frank about it.

"I'm not a fool," she told me. "I was aware that Emmett was constantly betraying me."

"With Dot?" I asked, looking down at the carpet.

Ida's voice was gentle. "No, Bernie. I never suspected Dot." Then she added, "But a wife is the last to know."

Or a husband, I thought, and the silence that followed was more embarrassing for me than for her. After a minute I asked her what time Emmett had been supposed to call for her last night.

"He wasn't definite," Ida said. "He told me he had work to do at his office and at eight-thirty dropped me off at Marie's in the car. He said he would try to be back before ten to watch a prize fight on the Cannons' television set. At one o'clock I gave up waiting for him and George drove me home."

"Weren't you worried when Emmett didn't show up?"

"Worried?" Ida Walker's lips curled. "Not worried in the way you mean. I assumed that he was with another woman. Then the police got me out of bed and told me he was dead."

I stood up and Ida accompanied me to the door.

"I'm a lot sorrier for Dot than for Emmett," she said. "He deserved what he got. That devil had a way with women. Even I could forgive him a lot. I was willing to accept crumbs from him, but I don't regret that he's gone."

I wondered how much she had forgiven him in the end.

Edith Bauer was Dot's best friend. She was a highstrung, delicately formed woman whose figure would be a delight in porcelain. When I told her that Dot was being charged with first-degree murder, she burst into tears.

Her husband was there. Herman lived close enough to the high school, where he taught science, to walk home for lunch, and I found them seated at the dinette table.

After Edith dried her eyes, she asked me if I would care to have a bite with them. I shook my head. I'd had no desire that morning for anything but coffee. I sat at the table with them and asked Edith if any of the four women at the bridge game last night had left for any length of time.

"You mean left the house?" she said, frowning at the question.

"At least left the room."

"Not for more than a minute or two," Edith replied. "We four were playing bridge all the time, from about a quarter to nine until almost one o'clock, when we broke off. Of course we took time off for a snack, but we were all in the same room."

"Who served refreshments?"

"Marie, naturally, but she didn't have to leave the house to do that."

"How could you start playing at a quarter to nine when Dot didn't arrive until after nine?"

"George Cannon made the fourth," she said. "He wasn't anxious to play, and when Dot arrived he gave up his seat to her and went down to the basement to work with his tools. Cabinet-making is his hobby, and he showed us the record cabinet he's building out of bleached oak. It was one of the most attractive—"

She broke off. "How can I talk about furniture at a time like this?" she wailed and started to sniffle.

I turned my attention to Herman, whose chubby face was thoughtful as he chewed his food.

"Where were you last night, Herman?" I asked.

"Home alone, catching up on my reading." He scooped up a slice of tomato from his plate. "Why is that important?"

"Because," I said carefully, "Dot wasn't the only woman at the bridge game who used to go out with Emmett Walker."

"Meaning me," Edith said. "I had quite a crush on Emmett when I was a kid." She rose quickly—too quickly, it seemed to me—to go into the kitchen for the coffeepot.

Herman had his fork poised in midair, and he studied me over it. "What are you getting at, Bernie?"

"I'm not sure," I muttered.

And that was the truth. I was groping in the dark, trying to veer guilt away from Dot to somebody else. Anybody else.

I went to see Marie Cannon. Marie was a full-bodied, slow-moving woman who caught and held men's eyes when prettier women were ignored. The housecoat she wore had a tight, high waist and a wide, low neckline that accentuated her lushness. A handerchief was balled in her fist, and like Edith Bauer she wept at the sight of me, for she too was a close friend of Dot's.

"I can't imagine Dot killing anybody in cold blood," she said. "It must have been an accident, or temporary insanity."

I didn't argue. I had come to ask questions, and my first one was whether Dot had been greatly upset when she had arrived last night.

Marie thought that over. "She seemed somewhat out of breath, but that was all. George played out the hand before he gave up his seat to her, and as she waited she rather calmly told us that she had run over a dog." Marie unclasped her hand to stare at her moist handerchief. "George is afraid that the fact that she had a story about killing a dog all prepared before she got here will sound bad before a jury."

Somebody came down the stairs. Marie and I turned our heads as George entered the room. He wore a faded bathrobe and flapping slippers.

"I came home for a nap," he explained. "I had only a couple of hours' sleep last night when your phone call woke me." He looked at me. "You can use some sleep too, Bernie."

Sleep? Could there be any sleep for me while Dot was shut in by four walls?

"Why would Dot have said she left a dead dog in the spot where she left the body?" I said. "If she'd killed Emmett, she would have known that his body would be found there instead."

George shrugged. "She was aware that Wilcox had seen her come out of the bushes and that when the body was found Wilcox would put two and two together. She was frantic."

"Marie says she didn't seem very frantic when she arrived here a few minutes later."

"No, she didn't," George agreed, "but it's hard to tell with a woman like Dot. She's always breathless and bubbling and excited anyway. And she's—well, Bernie, she's lovely and charming, but her mind jumps about. I mean, that far-fetched story about a dog might have seemed like a valid explanation to her at the time, but she isn't exactly a logical person."

Not at all logical, I thought, and her flightiness used to annoy me. Now it might mean her death or imprisonment. Suddenly I was so tired that I could hardly stand. I leaned against the televison cabinet, and I remembered that it was on that screen Emmett Walker had intended to see a prize fight last night. Or so Ida had told me.

I said, "The one who had most reason to kill Emmett Walker was his wife."

Marie sat down abruptly. "Yes," she whispered. "You mean before she got here last night?"

"It's possible," I said. "By the way, where was Emmett's car found?"

"At his house," George replied. "The police believe that he returned home after driving Ida here and then Dot picked him up in her car." He shook his head. "I've considered every angle too, Bernie, but they all lead to Walker's blood in your car and Dot's preposterous story about a dog."

I wasn't being logical either. I looked at Marie, who was opening her handkerchief to blow her nose, and at George, who tightened his lips glumly.

"I'll do my best to save her," George said. "The odds are that she can be got off within the law."

Odds, like gambling odds. Gambling against whether she would die or spend long years in jail or be released with the stigma of blood on her hands.

There was pity in their eyes. Pity for me, as well as for Dot. I could not stand it and I said good-bye and got out of there.

Sometimes, when I was worn out from a day of teaching and wanted quiet to read my paper, Dot's incessant and meaningless chatter would irritate me. Now the absence of her voice made the house terribly empty. I had come back home, but I couldn't endure being there without Dot. I was about to leave when the doorbell rang.

A ten-year-old boy stood there—Larry Robbins, son of the druggist who lived in the next block.

"Mr. Hall," he said, "did you see a little black dog?"

I stared at him.

"He got lost," the boy said. "I let him out for a few minutes last night and he never came back. So I'm asking all the neighbors if they saw him. Did you, Mr. Hall?"

With an effort I kept my voice calm. "What did he look like?"

"A little thing about so big. All black except for a white spot over his nose, and white paws. I got him only last week—my uncle gave him to me—and we didn't get a collar for him yet or a license. Maybe somebody thought he was a stray dog, fed him and took him in."

"What time did you let him out last night?"

"It was after eight o'clock. You didn't see him, did you?"

"Thanks, Larry," I said and patted his head.

He blinked at me. "Thanks for what, Mr. Hall?"

"Never mind," I said, and then added, "No, I didn't see your dog, Larry."

A couple of hours later, the small bulldozer I had hired arrived near the intersection of Pine Road and Wilson Lane. I'd been waiting there for some time. When the bulldozer had trundled off the truck, I told the driver where to start digging. Then I drove to the nearest phone and called Detective Ricardo at police headquarters.

"Can you come right away to where Emmett Walker's body was found last night?" I said.

"You got something, Mr. Hall?"

"I don't know," I said. "But if I have, I want you there as a witness."

I hurried back to where the bulldozer was plowing up a fifty-foot-wide area that started at the bushes along the road. Though he'd dug some three feet deep and twenty feet into the field beyond, he had so far turned up nothing but boulders. I walked beside the bulldozer blade, my feet sinking into the loose, upturned dirt.

The scooped-out area doubled in size before Ricardo showed up. His fat hips waddled as he stumbled over the chewed-up ground. He brooded at the crawling, bucking bulldozer and sighed.

"Faith moves mountains, eh, Mr. Hall?" he commented dryly.

I told him about Larry Robbins' lost dog.

"So why didn't you come to the police and let them do the digging?" he demanded.

"Because there'd be too much red tape before I got them to move, if they moved at all."

Ricardo scratched his jowls reflectively. "This field belongs to Gridley. He wouldn't like what you're doing to it."

"I obtained his permission. I'm paying him and promised to have it leveled off after—"

The driver yelled. He was climbing off the seat. Ricardo and I ran toward him. There, on the ground, half covered by dirt, was a patch of black fur. It was some fifty feet back in an almost straight line from where Walker's body had been found.

Ricardo stooped, brushed dirt away from the fur, pulled the dead animal out into the clear by one of its legs. I had never before seen that little black dog, but I had heard it described by both Dot and Larry Robbins.

Dot hadn't had a logical mind. She had only told the truth. Suddenly I was feeling fine. I had never felt better in my life.

"Do you believe now that my wife ran over a dog?"

Ricardo straightened up and dusted his hands. "Why should I?"

"W-w-why?" I stammered from sheer incredulousness. "Don't you believe what you see?"

"I see a dead dog, all right, but there are at least two things this dog didn't do. He didn't bleed in your car and he didn't leave Walker's body in the bushes. I think I know how the dog got here."

"He was buried by the murderer."

Ricardo smiled thinly. "That's what you'd like us to think. Early this morning, after you left police headquarters, you decided to try to save your wife by making her cockeyed yarn seem true. You found a little black dog and killed it and buried it here. Then you pretended to find it."

The bulldozer driver was listening open-mouthed. As for me, bitter anger had replaced my elation.

"Are you going to have the dog examined?"

"Sure, Mr. Hall, though it probably won't be possible to tell if a car or a club killed it."

There was nothing to be said. The finding of the dead dog proved everything to me and nothing to the detective. I told the bulldozer driver to shove back the dirt he had scooped out and walked to my car. The car had been returned to me a few hours ago by the police—with the bloody floor rug missing.

Ricardo moved at my side. "I guess I'd do about the same thing for my wife," he said sympathetically, "but I'd be smarter."

I whirled at the edge of the road to face him. "So you're smart! But not smart enough to see that a story can sound so far-fetched that it has to be true. My wife isn't quite the fool all of you try to make her out."

Ricardo had no comment for long moments, and his sad black eyes were reflective. He wasn't a bad guy, I thought. Not one of those bullying, blustering cops. He was trying to do what seemed to him the right thing.

"You know," he mused, looking back at the splotch of black fur on the field, "There's another answer if your wife's story about the dog is true."

"It's about time you saw it."

Suddenly he grinned at me. "You wait here. I have to take the dog's body in. Might be evidence."

He waddled over the chewed-up field. It struck me that I could accomplish more than a policeman could, and by the time he caught up with me I could hand him something. I got into my car and drove off.

Marie Cannon came to the door. Those harsh, stricken lines at the corners of her eyes and mouth had deepened within a few hours.

"George isn't home," she said.

"I'm here to see you," I said.

She led me into the living room. She sat down, keeping her full-fleshed body stiff. I stood over her.

"Marie, you've been weeping all day for Emmett Walker."

She brought the handkerchief to her nose. "Of course I'm sorry he's dead. He was a friend."

"A friend and a lover," I said. "And maybe you're weeping a little for Dot too—or for your own conscience—because you know Dot is innocent. You know that Emmett was alive at around ten o'clock, which means that Dot couldn't have killed him."

I heard a car pull into the driveway at the side of the house. Ricardo, I thought, right at my heels. I hoped that he would have sense enough to let me handle Marie.

"No, no!" Marie was saying.

"We found the dog buried near where Emmett Walker's body was found," I told her. "That proves Dot's story, and it proves that one of the people who was in this house last night killed him. They were the only ones who knew where Dot had left the dead dog."

There was a whisper of feet on the porch. Then silence. That meant that Ricardo was playing along with me. He was letting me break down Marie while he listened through the open window.

Marie was sniffling into her handkerchief.

"This is what must have happened," I went on. "Last night, you went into the kitchen to prepare refreshments. Through the window you saw Emmett Walker arrive to watch the fight on your television. You slipped out through the kitchen door to talk to him."

"I didn't kill him!" she burst out. "Let me alone!"

"You didn't kill him!" I agreed. "None of you four women in the house could have, because none of you was out of the house long enough to drive the body away. But there was a fifth person in the house—your husband."

Now, beside the edge of the curtain on one of the two windows looking out on the porch, I could see a man's hip. Ricardo was taking it all in.

"No!" Marie was wailing. "No, no!"

"Yes," I said. "It's the only possible way it could have happened. George was in the basement making a record cabinet. I've been down there a number of times. There's a ground-level window looking out to the side of the house. George saw you run out to meet Emmett. Maybe you kissed Emmett. Maybe you arranged a meeting with him. Then you returned to the kitchen and took the refreshments out to your guests. Emmett lingered outside so as not to enter the house at the same time you did and give his wife ideas. And George came out of the basement through the garage door, and in his hand he held a hammer, or whatever heavy tool he'd snatched up from his work bench."

Marie wept. In a minute she would be talking for Ricardo to hear.

I glanced toward the window and saw that Ricardo had shifted his position and that considerably more than his hip was now visible.

Only it wasn't Ricardo. The detective had a fat paunch, a padded hip. The man out there was thin, frail. George Cannon, who had seen my car parked in front of his house and had come up on the porch quietly.

All right, let him hear. Maybe he would break down when

Marie did. Or he would flee and that would be as good as a confession.

I turned back to Marie. "So George killed Emmett Walker in blind, jealous fury. Then there he was with a murdered man on his hands. He had heard Dot tell that she had run over a dog and where she had left it. He saw how he could divert suspicion wholly from himself by shoving it all on Dot. He dragged the body into Dot's car, and the battered head bleeding on the floor rug fitted in with his scheme. He drove to where Dot had said she'd left the dog and found it and buried it in the fields behind the bushes and left Emmett's body there. He returned and drove Emmett's car to Emmett's house and walked back. The whole business had taken some time, but you women playing cards didn't know he was gone. Maybe he left one of his machine tools running so that you heard it upstairs and assumed he was in the basement."

"The disgrace!" Marie blubbered. "The scandal!"

And then I saw the gun. Outside the window George Cannon held it in his skinny hand against his hip. Rays from the sinking sun glinted on the barrel.

Breath clogged my throat. There was no chance in flight. Only in more words, and in not letting him realize that I knew he was there.

"So that's why you protected him," I said, "though he murdered the man you loved. You knew that George had killed him. Having seen Emmett alive and outside the house at ten, there was no other possibility. Yet you were ready to see Dot die for George's crime."

Her shoulders heaved. "George said he could get her off. And there would have been a frightful scandal if George had gone on trial. Everybody would have known that Emmett had been my—my—" Her voice went completely to pieces.

I looked at Marie as I spoke, but actually my words were directed to the man outside with the gun. "The police know the truth," I said. "When they found the dog's body, the pieces fell into place. With your evidence, there will be no doubt of his guilt. The police are on their way now to—"

Outside, somebody yelled. The man at the window jerked around, and all of George Cannon's slight body became visible. He held the muzzle of his gun against his temple.

The sound of the shot wasn't very loud. Then he crumpled out of sight below the window sill, and I saw Ricardo running up the porch steps.

I dashed out to the porch. Ricardo was looking down at the dead man.

"Shot himself when he saw me," Ricardo said. "Guess he thought I was coming to arrest him."

"Yes," I muttered. "I made him think so."

He raised angry black eyes to me. "Why didn't you wait for me?"

"Does it matter now?" I said, turning away from George Cannon's body.

Inside the house, Marie was sobbing brokenly.

"I guess not," Ricardo said softly. He went into the house.

I walked as far as the porch steps so that I would not be too near the dead man. In a little while, I thought, I would be bringing Dot home.

And I would buy Larry Robbins another dog.

HAL DRESNER

Room with a View

His frail body covered by blankets and cush-
ioned in six of the thickest pillows money could buy, Jacob
Bauman watched with disgust as his butler set the bed tray
before him and opened the curtains, drenching the room in
morning.

"Would you like the windows open, sir?" Charles asked.

"You want I should catch a cold?"

"No, sir. Will there be anything else, sir?"

Jacob shook his head, tucking the napkin into the space between his pajama top and his thin chest. He reached to un-
cover the breakfast plate, stopped and looked up at Charles, who
was standing like a sentinel by the window.

"You waiting for a tip?" Jacob inquired sourly.

"No, sir. I am waiting for Miss Nevins. Doctor Holmes said
you were not to be left alone at any time, sir."

"Get out, get out," Jacob said. "If I decide to die in the next
five minutes, I'll ring for you. You won't miss a thing."

He watched the butler leave, waited until the door closed and then lifted the silver plate cover, revealing a single poached egg, looking like a membrane-encased eye, resting on a slice of toast. A miserly pat of marmalade and a cup of pale tea completed the menu.

Ach! Jacob regarded the food with distaste and turned to the window. It was a glorious day outside. The great lawn of the Bauman mansion lay green and even as a billiard cloth, inlaid with the gleaming white gravel of the horseshoe driveway and dotted here and there with small bronze statuary, a flirtatious goddess cloistered in cherubs, a wing-footed messenger, a grim lioness in congress with her cubs; all very hideous but all very expensive. At the left end of the horseshoe, outside the small brick caretaker's cottage, Jacob saw his groundsman, Mr. Coveny, kneeling in examination of an azalea bed; to the right of the driveway, before the prohibitive iron spear gates, the doors of the two-story garage were open and Jacob could see his chauffeur polishing the chromium grill of Mrs. Bauman's blue convertible while talking to Miss Nevins, Jacob's young day nurse. Beyond the gate the outer lawn stretched unbroken to the road, a distance so great that not even Jacob's keen eyes could distinguish the passing cars.

Poor Jacob Bauman, Jacob thought. All the good things in life had come too late. Finally, he owned an impressive estate but he was too sick to enjoy it; finally, he was married to a young woman who was beautiful enough to turn any man's head but he was too old to take pleasure from her; and finally, he had gained a shrewd insight into the mysteries of human nature, but he was bedridden and limited to the company of his servants. Poor rich Jacob Bauman, he thought. With all his wealth, luck and wisdom, his world was bounded by the width of his mattress, the length of driveway he could see from his window and the depth of Miss Nevins' mind.

And where was she? He turned to the clock surrounded by bottles, pills, and vials on the night table. Six minutes after nine. Peering out the window again, he saw the girl in the white uniform look at her watch in dismay, blow a kiss to the chauffeur and start walking, hurriedly, toward the house. She was a robust blonde girl who walked with a gay bounce, arms swinging, an exuberance of energy that tired Jacob vicariously. Still, he watched until she disappeared beneath the porch roof and then turned back to his breakfast. She would stop to say good morning to the cook and the maid, he calculated, and that meant he would just be finishing his egg and toast when she knocked.

He was chewing the last dripping crust of toast when the knock came; he called "Go away" and the nurse entered, smiling.

"Good morning, Mr. Bee," she said cheerily. She put her paperbound novel on the dresser, glancing with no special interest at the chart left by the night nurse. "How are you feeling today?"

"Alive," Jacob said.

"Isn't it a terrific day?" the girl said, walking to the window. "I was standing outside talking to Vic before and it's just like spring out. You want me to open the windows for you?"

"I don't. Your doctor friend warned me about getting a chill."

"Oh, that's right . . . I forgot. I guess I'm really not a very good nurse, am I?" She smiled.

"You're a nurse," Jacob said. "Better you than the kind that never leaves me alone."

"You're just saying that. I know I'm really not dedicated enough."

"Dedicated? You're a pretty young girl, you've got other interests. I understand. You say to yourself, 'I'll be a nurse for a while, the work is easy, the food is good. So I'll save some money until I get married.'"

The girl looked surprised. "You know, that's just what I said to myself when Doctor Holmes offered me this job. You're very smart, you know that, Mr. Bee?"

"Thank you," Jacob said dryly. "You get old, you get smart." He took a sip of his tea and made a bitter face. "Ach. Terrible. Get this away." He kicked feebly under the covers.

"You really should finish it," the girl said.

"Get it away from me," Jacob said impatiently.

"Sometimes you're just like a little boy."

"So I'm a little boy and you're a little girl. But better we should talk about you." He began to re-arrange his pillows but stopped when the girl came to help him. "Tell me, Frances," he said, his face very close to her, "do you have your husband picked out yet?"

"Mr. Bee, that's a very personal question to ask a girl."

"So I'm asking a personal question. If you can't tell me, who can you tell? Am I going to tell anyone? Is there anyone I could tell? Your specialist-doctor won't even let me have a phone by my bed to call my broker once in a while. Too much strain it would be to hear that I lost a few thousand dollars. He doesn't know I can tell what I make and lose to the penny from the newspapers? . . . So tell me," he smiled confidentially, "what's your lover like?"

"Mr. Bee! A prospective husband is one thing but a lover . . . ?" She plumped the last pillow and crossed to the window chair. "I can't imagine what you must think of me."

Jacob shrugged. "I think you're a nice young girl. But nice girls today are a little different from nice girls fifty years ago. I'm not saying worse or better. I'm just saying different. I understand these things. After all, you're just a few years younger than my wife. I know men like to look at her, so I know they like to look at you, too."

"Oh, but your wife is beautiful. Really. I think she's the most stunning woman I've ever seen."

"Good for her," Jacob said. "So tell me about your lover."

"Well," the girl started, obviously pleased, "it's really not definite yet. I mean, we haven't set the date or anything."

"Yes, you have," Jacob said. "You don't want to tell me because you're afraid I'll fire you before you're ready to leave."

"No, really, Mr. Bauman . . ."

"So you haven't set the day of the week. But the month you've decided on, right?" He waited a moment for contradiction. "Right," he said. "Believe me when I tell you I understand these things. So what month? June?"

"July," the girl said, smiling.

"So shoot me, I'm a month off . . . I won't bother to ask you if he's handsome. I know he is . . . And strong too."

"Yes."

"But gentle."

The girl nodded, beaming.

"That's good," Jacob said. "It's very important to marry a gentle man . . . But not too gentle. The ones that are too gentle let themselves get stepped on. Believe me, I know. I used to be a very gentle man myself and you know where it got me? No place, that's where. So I learned to be different. Not that I still don't make the mistake now and then . . . but every time I do, I pay for it . . . A bad marriage can be a big mistake, maybe the biggest. You've got to know what kind of package you're getting. But you know, don't you?"

"Yes. He's wonderful. Really, he is. You can't tell, Mr. Bauman, because you don't really know him but if you ever sat down and—" she stopped and bit her lip. "Oh, I didn't mean—"

"So he's someone I know," Jacob said. "Now that's very interesting. I would never have guessed. A friend of mine, maybe?"

"No. No, really, I didn't mean to say that. It just came out wrong. It's not anyone—"

"Doctor Holmes?" Jacob guessed.

"Oh, no!"

"Maybe someone who works for me?" Jacob asked slyly, watching the girl's face. "Charles? . . . No, no. It couldn't be Charles. You don't like Charles very much, do you, Frances? You think he looks down on you, right?"

"Yes," said the girl, quite suddenly indignant. "He makes me feel that I'm some kind of a . . . oh, I don't know what. Just because he thinks he's so *elegant*. Well, if you ask me, he's just a *fish*."

Jacob chuckled. "You're absolutely right. Charles is a fish. A cold pike . . . But then who could it be? Mr. Coveny is much too old for you so that only leaves . . ." He paused, his eyes bright and teasing, his mouth open. Then he looked past her, out the window, and said, "No, I don't know. Give me a hint. Tell me what business he's in . . . Stocks and bonds, maybe? Oil? Textiles?" His voice rose. *"Transportation?"*

"Oh, you're just teasing me now," the girl said. "You know it's Vic. I bet you knew all the time. I hope you're not mad. Really, I would have told you before but—" A knock on the door interrupted her.

"Go away," Jacob called.

The door opened and Mrs. Bauman, a truly stunning red-haired woman, looking more like twenty than thirty in a daffodil-yellow sweater and provocatively tight tan slacks, came in.

"Good morning, all. No, sit down, dear," she said to Frances. "How's our patient this morning?"

"Terrible," Jacob said.

His wife laughed falsely and patted his cheek. "Did you sleep well?"

"No."

"Isn't he horrid?" Mrs. Bauman said to Frances. "I don't know why you put up with him."

"For the money," Jacob said. "Just like you."

Mrs. Bauman forced a laugh. "He's just like a baby, isn't he? Has he had his orange pill yet?"

"Yes," Jacob said.

"No," said Frances. "Is it nine-fifteen already? Oh, I'm—"

"I'm afraid it's almost nine-twenty," Mrs. Bauman said coolly. "Here, I'll do it." She uncapped a vial from the night table and poured a tumbler full of water from a silver pitcher. "Open wide now."

Jacob turned his head from her. "I can still hold a pill and a glass of water," he said. "You don't even *look* like a nurse." He popped the capsule in his mouth and swallowed a sip of water. "Where are you going, dressed up like a college girl?"

"Just into town to do a little shopping."

"Vic has your car all ready," Frances said. "He polished it this morning and it looks just like new."

"I'm sure it does, dear."

"If it's not shiny enough, buy a new one," Jacob said.

"I was thinking of doing just that," his wife countered. "But I thought I'd wait until you're up and around again. Then we'll get one of those little sport cars that only have room for two people and we'll go on long drives together, just the two of us."

"I can't wait," Jacob said.

"My!" said Mrs. Bauman. "Isn't it a marvelous day? Why don't you have Charles open the windows?"

"Because I don't want to get a chill and die," Jacob said. "But thank you for suggesting it."

Smiling tartly, Mrs. Bauman touched her fingers to her lips, then pressed them to her husband's forehead.

"You don't even deserve that much of a kiss today," she said coyly. "If he stays this grouchy," she said to Frances, "don't even talk to him. It'll serve him right." Her smile invited the girl into a woman's conspiracy. "I'll be back early," she said to Jacob.

"I'll be here," he said.

" 'Bye," Mrs. Bauman said cutely and left.

"Close the door," Jacob said to Frances.

"Didn't she look beautiful?" the girl said, crossing the room and then coming back. "I wish I could wear slacks like that."

"Do your husband a favor and wear them before you get married," Jacob said.

"Oh, Vic wouldn't mind. He hasn't got a jealous bone in his

body. He's told me a hundred times how much he likes it when other men look at me."

"And how do you feel about him looking at other women?"

"Oh, I don't mind. I mean, after all, it's only natural, isn't it? And Vic has had—" she colored slightly. "I don't know how we ever got talking about this again. You're really terrible, Mr. Bauman."

"Let an old man have a little pleasure by talking," Jacob said. "So Vic has had a lot of experience with women, has he?"

"Sometimes it's really embarrassing. I mean, some women will just throw themselves at a man. We were at a nightclub two weeks ago Wednesday. On Vic's night off."

Jacob nodded and again looked past the girl, who was starting to talk more rapidly. His wife had just become visible walking across the lawn toward the garage. She moved in a way quite different from Frances, much more slowly, almost lazily. Under the tan slacks her hips rocked, undulating, but just slightly, like a scale seeking its balance. Even the languid swing of her arms seemed to subtly reserve energy, not expend it profligately as Frances did, but rather save the strength, storing it, for the more important motions.

". . . she was really a frightening-looking girl," Frances was saying. "I mean, I was actually startled when I saw her come over to our table. Her hair was this jet black and looked like she hadn't combed it for weeks and she had so much lipstick on she must have used up a whole tube getting dressed . . ."

Jacob listened absently, his eyes still on his wife. She had reached the convertible now and stood leaning against the door, talking with Vic. Jacob could see her smile widen as she listened and then, tilting her head back, she laughed. He could not hear the laugh but he recalled it, from years before, as being sharp and light, a stimulating, flattering laugh. Vic, one foot contemptuously propped on the car bumper, thick arms crossed, smiled with her.

". . . really think she must have been drunk," Frances said, fully involved in her story. "I mean, I just can't imagine a woman having the nerve to just sit down in a strange man's lap and kiss him. I mean, right in front of his date and all. For all she knew, I could have been his wife."

"So what did Vic do?" Jacob asked, turning from the window.

"Well, nothing. I mean, what could he do? We were in a

public place and everything. He just tried to laugh and pretend it was a joke or something. But I couldn't. I mean, I tried to, but the girl didn't move and Vic couldn't just push her off. I mean, everyone was watching and I was getting madder and madder and—well, to tell you the truth, Mr. Bauman, sometimes I've got a terrible temper. I mean, when it comes to personal things like Vic, I just can't control myself."

"Like with Betty?" Jacob said.

Frances sucked in her lower lip. "I didn't think you knew about that," she said. "I'm really awfully sorry about it, Mr. Bauman, but I just walked into the kitchen to get my lunch and she had her arms around Vic and, well, I guess I saw red."

"So I heard," Jacob said smiling. "I didn't see Betty before she left but Charles told me she wasn't so pretty to look at any more."

"I guess I did scratch her up terribly," Frances said, lowering her eyes. "I'm really sorry about it. I tried to apologize to her but she wouldn't even listen to me. As if it were all *my* fault."

"And what did you do to the girl in the nightclub?"

"I pulled her off Vic by her hair," Frances admitted sheepishly. "And if he hadn't stopped me, I probably would have tried to scratch her eyes out, too. I mean, I really went crazy. It was worse than Betty, because she was actually *kissing* Vic. I think if there was a knife or something around, I would have tried to kill her."

"Really?" Jacob said. His look left the girl and returned to the window. Neither his wife nor Vic was in sight then. His eyes scanned the expanse of lawn, passed the statues glinting dully in the sun, to Mr. Coveny, who was still probing at the azaleas, and back again, resting on the blazing grill of the convertible. He saw an odd shadow on the car's hood and, squinting, defined it as the polishing cloth Vic had been using.

"And how do these little fights affect your feelings about Vic?" he asked casually.

"Oh, they don't. I mean, how could they? It's not his fault that women throw themselves at him. I mean, he certainly doesn't encourage them."

"Of course not," Jacob said. He narrowed his eyes, intently focusing on the dark window above the garage. He thought he had seen a flash of bright yellow there. Or was it just the sun reflecting off the lower pane? No, the window was open; it couldn't have been the sun. There it was again, among moving shadows, a very solid square of bright color, narrowing now and rising slowly, as if it were a piece of fabric, a bright cloth perhaps, being slowly removed from something, someone. And then it was gone and not even the shadows were visible within the frame of the window. Jacob smiled. "I'm sure Vic is very faithful," he said. "If there's anyone at fault, it's definitely the woman. Your jealousy is very understandable. It's only right to fight to hold on to what you have. Even if it means destroying some other part of your life."

Frances looked puzzled. "Do you think that Vic doesn't love me as much because of what happened? He said he understood."

"I'm sure he does," Jacob said. "In fact he probably loves you even more for showing your devotion. Men like things like that . . . No, I was just talking before. Just an old man's talk. After all, what else can I do besides talk?"

"Oh, you could probably do a lot of things," Frances said. "You're very intelligent. I mean, at least *I* think so. You should find a hobby. Crossword puzzles or something. I bet you'd be great at those."

"Maybe I'll try them sometime," Jacob said. "But right now, I think I'll try to sleep for a while."

"That's a good idea," Frances said. "I brought a new book to read today. I started it on the bus coming over. It's really terrific, all about this Frenchwoman who made a fool of a lot of kings."

"It sounds very good," Jacob said. "But before you start, I'd like you to do me a little favor." He turned and opened the single drawer of his night table. "Now don't be frightened," he cautioned as he withdrew a small gray revolver. "I keep this around in case of burglars. But it's been so long since it's been cleaned that I'm not sure it still works. Would you take it down to Vic and ask him to look it over?"

"Sure," the girl said, rising, taking the gun gingerly. "Hey, it's light. I always thought guns weighed about twenty pounds."

"I think that's a woman's gun," Jacob said. "For women and old men. Now be careful, it's loaded. I'd take out the bullets for you but I'm afraid I don't know very much about those things."

"I'll be careful," Frances said, holding the grip experimentally. "And you try to get some sleep in the meantime. Should I tell Charles to come up while I'm gone?"

"No, don't bother. I'll be fine. You take your time with your fiancé. I think I saw him go upstairs to his room a minute ago."

"He's sleeping," Frances said.

"Why don't you sneak up and surprise him then," Jacob said. "He'd probably like that."

"Well, if he doesn't, I'll tell him that it was your idea."

"Yes," Jacob said. "You tell him that it was all my idea."

He smiled, watching the girl leave, then nestled back in the pillows and closed his eyes. It was very quiet and he was so genuinely tired that he felt himself unwillingly starting to doze when the first shot, immediately followed by the second and then a third, sounded across the lawn. He considered sitting up to watch the activity from the window but it seemed like too great an effort. Also, he reasoned, there was nothing he could do, bedridden as he was.

RICHARD MATHIESON

Lemmings

"Where do they all come from?" Reordon asked.

"Everywhere," said Carmack.

They were standing on the coast highway. As far as they could see there was nothing but cars. Thousands of cars were jammed bumper to bumper and pressed side to side. The highway was solid with them.

"There come some more," said Carmack.

The two policemen looked at the crowd of people walking toward the beach. Many of them talked and laughed. Some of them were very quiet and serious. But they all walked toward the beach.

Reordon shook his head. "I don't get it," he said for the hundredth time that week. "I just don't get it."

Carmack shrugged.

"Don't think about it," he said. "It's happening. What else is there?"

"But it's *crazy*."

"Well, there they go," said Carmack.

As the two policemen watched, the crowd of people moved across the gray sands of the beach and walked into the water. Some of them started swimming. Most of them couldn't because of their clothes. Carmack saw a young woman flailing at the water and dragged down by the fur coat she was wearing.

In several minutes they were all gone. The two policemen stared at the place where the people had walked into the water.

"How long does it go on?" Reordon asked.

"Until they're gone, I guess," said Carmack.

"But *why*?"

"You ever read about the lemmings?" Carmack asked.

"No."

"They're rodents who live in the Scandinavian countries. They keep breeding until all their food supply is gone. Then they move across the country, ravaging everything in their way. When they reach the sea they keep going. They swim until their strength is gone. Millions of them."

"You think that's what *this* is?" asked Reordon.

"Maybe," said Carmack.

"People aren't rodents!" Reordon said angrily.

Carmack didn't answer.

They stood on the edge of the highway waiting but nobody appeared.

"Where are they?" asked Reordon.

"Maybe they've all gone in," Carmack said.

"*All* of them?"

"It's been going on for more than a week," Carmack said. "People could have gotten here from all over. Then there are the lakes."

Reordon shuddered. "All of them," he said.

"I don't know," said Carmack, "but they've been coming right along until now."

"Oh, God," said Reordon.

Carmack took out a cigarette and lit it. "Well," he said, "what now?"

Reordon sighed. "Us?" he said.

"You go," Carmack said. "I'll wait a while and see if there's anyone else."

"All right." Reordon put his hand out. "Good-by, Carmack," he said.

They shook hands. "Good-by, Reordon," Carmack said.

He stood smoking his cigarette and watching his friend walk across the gray sand of the beach and into the water until it was over his head. He saw Reordon swim a few dozen yards before he disappeared.

After a while he put out his cigarette and looked around. Then he walked into the water too.

A million cars stood empty along the beach.

IDRIS SEABRIGHT

White Goddess

                    "I don't for an instant suppose you really want my wretched teaspoons," Miss Smith said sharply.

Sharply, yes, but her voice held the rich, throaty, fruity tremulousness of a BBC actress playing an old woman, a young BBC actress; and Carson perceived, alongside of his indignation at being cheated out of his small booty—she must have eyes in the back of her head—the hope that she really was a young woman who for some personally cogent reason had elected to dress and act like a woman advanced in age. It was somehow less nerve-racking to think of her as a young woman in disguise than as an old woman who moved and spoke like somebody in her twenties.

Whoever she was, she was certainly not the gentle, woolly-headed, lovable victim he had intended. Mauve shoulderette and blue-veined hands to the contrary. He had met her on the boardwalk, which had always been one of his best hunting grounds for nice old ladies. He hadn't had to fish any more than usual for the invitation to tea. Now he saw that she was neither old nor a lady. And the name she had adopted was an insult. Miss Mary Smith—anonymity could go no further.

"What are you smirking about?" she demanded. "I want my spoons."

Silently he reached in his overcoat pocket and pulled out five teaspoons. She was right, he didn't need the money. He almost never could sell any of the things he took from people her age, and when he did the money was paid into a separate account and was never touched. It was a neurosis, less creditable than moral masochism, better than a lot of things he could think of. He enjoyed it a little too much to want to be rid of it.

He put the spoons down on the tea table in front of her, and sank back into his chair. She counted. Her foot—bunionless, but in a wide black oxford—began to tap. "That's only five. There were six. I mean to have the other one."

Reluctantly he gave her the last spoon. It was the best of the six, sterling and old, but so meager in all its proportions that it would never be worth much more than it had been at the time it was made. The bowl was full of fine, small dents, as if some infant, contemporary with Washington and Jefferson, had teethed on it. Wretched infant—the sharp, penurious edges must have finely lacerated his gums.

She snatched the spoon up and gave it a fierce rub on the folds of the tea cloth. She handed it back to him. "Look in the bowl."

Carson did as he was bidden. Miss . . . Smith obviously wasn't going to call the police, and while he was uncomfortable, he wasn't exactly afraid. "Well?" he said, putting the spoon down on the table again.

"Didn't you see anything?"

"Only myself, upside-down. The usual thing."

"Is that all!" She sounded jarred. "Give me back my water-color, while I'm thinking. It's worth even less than the spoons."

She *couldn't* have seen him pick up the watercolor. She had been making the tea, with her back to him, and there were no mirrors or shiny surfaces. She couldn't even have noticed the gap the watercolor had left, for it had been sitting behind three or four other tasteless pieces of bric-a-brac.

"We might as well have some tea," she said, pulling the restored watercolor over to her side of the table. Even framed, the picture was no bigger than a European postcard. It showed a palm tree, an island, water, all very runny and imitation-Winslow-Homery. No wonder Carson had thought it would be a good thing to steal. "Should you like a little gin in your tea? I find it helps."

"Yes, please."

She poured from the square bottle into the teapot and left the bottle sitting on the table. They drank. The tea was scalding hot, and Carson could only make its burden of spirits tolerable by loading his cup with sugar.

Miss Smith put her own cup down in the saucer. She coughed and then blew her nose into a man's cotton handkerchief. "You'd better get in," she said, tapping the surface of the watercolor with her middle finger, "and see how it fits."

Whooosh, whosh, thud. Carson was inside the watercolor, sitting on the island with the Winslow-Homery palms.

The grass was infernally stickery and the place was as noisy as pandemonium. The waves, blocks of granular blue frozen custard, landed against the beach with the rocky crash of pottery plates, the sea gulls skirled like bagpipes, the serrated palm fronds gave out the cry of sheets of tin.

Yet Carson was not too distracted to perceive that in the Smithian sense of the word the island did fit him rather well. The noise was an insulation; he didn't care whether any old lady's mantelpiece anywhere held bric-a-brac the right size to go into his pocket. He was as muzzy and comfortable as if Miss Smith had cuddled him up nicely in folds of her woolly shoulderette.

Heigh-ho. Must be the gin. He slept.

When he woke up everything was still going on. Gulls, waves and palms contributed their respective noises. Out beyond where the rigid blue freezer-product waves were forming there was a dark blue turbulence in the water. Had it been there before? Must have. He wasn't sure.

Could be caused by lots of things—a surfaced shark, a giant turtle, a Vernean octopus. Could be. Wasn't. *Wasn't.* Carson gave a feeble, frightened yip.

Pop. He was sitting opposite Miss Smith at the tea table again. She had put a cozy over the teapot, but it seemed to be still the same pot of tea.

She buttered a crumpet and put the whole thing in her mouth. "Did you like it on the island?" she asked, chewing.

"It was all right at first," he replied unwillingly. "Later there was something swimming around under the water I didn't like."

"Interesting." She grinned. "You didn't mind the noise, you didn't mind the isolation. It was something swimming around under the water you couldn't see that you . . . didn't like."

What was she up to? Was she trying to perform some sort of divine lay analysis on him? Trying, in approved psychiatric fashion, to find out what he was afraid of so she could rid him of the fear? Nah. More likely, she was mapping out the contours of his fear so she could embed him, fixate him, in it.

"Why are you so interested?" he asked. He tried to butter himself a crumpet, but his hands shook so he had to lay down the knife.

"It isn't often people try to steal things from me."

No. They wouldn't. It took Carson, with all the old ladies in the world to choose from, to get tangled up with somebody who was Isis, Rhea, Cybele—there were lots and lots of divine identities to pick from—Anatha, Dindymene, Astarte. Or Neith.

Carson licked his lips. "How about a little more tea?" he suggested. "And a little more gin in it? It makes a refreshing drink."

"There's plenty of gin in it already."

Nonetheless, she did not protest when he took off the cozy and picked up the square bottle. She didn't seem to be looking. He'd been fooled that way before, and she probably was watching. Yet it might be possible to get even a goddess drunk.

He set the bottle down with the label toward her, so she couldn't see how much was gone. "You pour."

Did the hand that held the teapot over his cup waver? He couldn't be sure. "Goodness, but you've made it strong," she said.

"Refreshing!" He managed a smile. "Do have a crumpet. Vitality is low, this time in the afternoon."

"Yes." She was shaken by a spell of coughing. A crumb seemed to have caught in her windpipe. He hoped she would choke to death.

She washed the crumpet down with the last of her cup of tea. "And now I'll have my paperweight."

It was the last of his booty. He had liked it the best of anything. Sadly he took the globe from his pocket and gave it to her.

She tapped it. Flakes of mimic snow floated up to the zenith of the sphere and then began to settle down on the snow scene at the bottom again.

"Pretty," she said admiringly. "Pretty snow."

"Yes. I admired it."

". . . getting late to try you on anything more. B'sides, I know pretty well what you're like. *You*'re the kind can't stand waiting for anything unpleasant." She upended the teapot over her cup.

Her voice was getting fuzzy. She had spilled a trail of drops over the tea cloth before she set the teapot down. Now was the moment, if there was to be a moment.

"Thank you for a pleasant afternoon," he said, pushing back his chair and rising. "Perhaps we can repeat the occasion at a later date."

Her mouth opened. A film of saliva glinted iridescently between her parted lips and then broke. "What rot. In with you, you stupid fool."

The paperweight received him. It was a little like pushing against a stiff wind, a little like swimming, but he could breathe well enough. He worked his way through the fluid—glycerine? —to the glass wall and peered out.

Miss Smith was snapping her fingers. Her lips moved. She started to get up. She collapsed on the floor. The teacup fell from her limp fingers and settled down beside her cozily.

Miss Smith had drunk herself out. As the moments passed, he began to wonder. He would have expected her to twitch. At last it was borne in on him that she wasn't out. She was dead.

About eight o'clock somebody came in and found her. There was a lot of rushing to and fro before the men with the stretcher came. The teacup stayed on the floor.

They hadn't thought to draw the blinds, either. Moonlight shone in on his glass prison and lit up the snow at the bottom brilliantly. If only it were real snow! He thought longingly of the exquisite little hole he could have scooped for himself in a snowdrift, the warm Steffanson-style slumber he could have enjoyed in his fluffy burrow. As it was, he floated vertically all night, aching with insomnia, as comfortless as an asparagus stalk in a sauce pan.

Day came at last. He didn't know whether he regretted Miss

Smith's death or not. Did an irrational belief in her *potential* benevolence still linger in him? After the island and this?

The morning was well advanced when a cleaning woman came in. She was young, her mouth was red, she had flamboyant yellow hair.

She plugged in the vacuum and went over the floor. Tardily she undressed the tea table and washed the tea things. She picked up his paperweight.

She shook it roughly. Snow began to fall around him. She pressed her nose up against the glass in a prodigy of short-focus accommodation. Her eyes were enormous. It seemed impossible that she should not see him.

She grinned. He recognized her. Miss Smith.

He might have known that Neith wouldn't stay dead.

She shook the glass once more. She set it down sharply on the mantel.

For a moment he had thought she was going to throw it against the tiles of the fireplace. But that would come later.

She might let him live on for days. She could set the globe in the sun, freeze it in the fridge, buffet it back and forth until he got as seasick as a resented fetus . . . the possibilities were many. In the end there would be the crash.

She drew her finger across her throat playfully. She unplugged the vacuum and went out.

WILLIAM SAMBROT

The Substance
of Martyrs

For centuries, the townspeople had held on
to their belief in the powers of their gold cross. What a sublime
ironic touch that the ravages of a war "to end all wars" brought
an answer to their prayers.

For reasons that will be apparent to you, I won't tell you the
name of the little German village in which I saw the miraculous
golden Christ on the cross. It's an obscure, somewhat poor hamlet, still not completely recovered from the ravages of World
War II.

It was Colonel Dumphrey who told me about the golden
Christ, and the strange history of miracles attributed to it. We
were motoring through southern Germany at the time, on our
way from Paris to Salzburg, where the colonel was to pass judgment on the authenticity of certain art treasures recently discovered in a salt mine near Salzburg.

Colonel Dumphrey (retired), D.S.O., O.B.E., was (and is) a

renowned scholar and linguist, an expert on Italian Renaissance
and Middle-European medieval art. During the war, Colonel
Dumphrey had been a major in Military Intelligence (British
Army), on special detached duty with the 45th Division (American).

Near the end of World War II, the 45th had captured a number of salt mines near Salzburg crammed with a vast quantity of
loot which the Nazis had stolen from Europe's finest museums
and private art collections.

To this day, not all the treasures known to have been stolen
by the Nazis have been recovered, so when the colonel was
contacted in Paris and asked to give his expert opinion on the
authenticity of the several pieces which had recently been found
in those same dismal salt mines, he readily agreed.

He decided to drive up from Paris to Salzburg, taking his time
and visiting some of the lesser-known but still interesting
German and Austrian towns, so rich in medieval art. He invited
me along.

We were well into southern Germany, meandering through
Christmas card villages, driving through a peaceful, sparsely-
inhabited mountainous country, when suddenly the colonel
slowed as we approached a road sign.

He hesitated, then abruptly swung the car off onto a bumpy
road. Ahead, there soon appeared the inevitable clump of stone-
and-timber houses. In their midst, the spire of a small cathedral
thrust up, peculiarly truncated.

As we approached, it was evident the church had been heavily
damaged during the war and still lacked complete repair. Several of the stained-glass Gothic apertures had been boarded up.
The slate roof showed evidence of frequent mismatched patch-
ing. All in all, a rather humble and shabby church and village,
tucked between the mountains. And yet . . .

Miraculous cures had taken place there, Dumphrey assured
me. People came from many hundreds of miles around to pray
before the little church's altar crucifix, a solid gold Christ on the
cross. To pray for—and occasionally to receive—miracles.

We got out of the car and immediately I was struck by the
feeling of peace and tranquility that flooded the square, the
town. People smiled at us, moved quietly in unhurried calm.
Most of them were going to or from the church.

We went in. It was very much like many other churches

throughout western Europe—a bit more brown and battered, perhaps. Many pews were scarred, a few were new. The floor showed patches of repaired tile, contrasting with ancient marble. To one side, a stained-glass window was oddly shattered; only two pieces remained suspended between the lead frames, each depicting an upraised, supplicating hand. The rest was opened to the sky.

Pigeons fluttered in and out between these suspended marvelously-colored stained-glass hands. Hands, Dumphrey whispered, which formerly belonged to a complete Mary, mother of Christ, but now were disembodied members, raised piteously to an uncomprehending stretch of blue, cold German sky.

The shattered stained-glass window was the people's monument to their bitter past—their penance, and their reminder. It was left exactly as it had been when the war swept over it.

Here the parishioners and visitors knelt on the marble floor, oblivious of the chill wind that swept through the broken window and caused the red sacristy lamp to flicker and sway ceaselessly.

Directly above the chipped altar was hung the magnificent crucifix. A great golden Christ, nailed to a mahogany cross. The outstretched arms seemed to steady and make firm the sagging church walls. It glowed in the flickering light of candles; the flaring shadows made the suffering features strangely alive. The closed eyes seemed to slowly open, to look down on the kneeling people, and gradually, to seek me out.

I had seen many excellent crucifixes. But I found myself staring piercingly at the golden Christ, hanging tautly, corded arms nailed with golden spikes to the dark wood. There flowed from that strained figure an unmistakable aura. It was palpable: I felt that the closed eyes were no longer closed, but were gazing at me—into me—with pity and love.

My heart began a slow, deep pound; I could have sworn I saw the golden ribs heave, the cruel deep spear marks gape wide. I continued to stare at the cross, barely conscious of the muted surf-sound of murmured prayers, the fluttering and cooing of pigeons. All was subordinate to that lonely, mysterious figure, hanging there, beckoning with a power that was indescribably real.

Dumphrey touched my arm and I started. We went outside and I took a deep breath.

"It—it's magnificent," I said slowly. "There *is* something—some presence there. Did you feel it?"

He nodded and I said, "I can rationalize it, I suppose. Mass hypnosis, that gleaming body concentrating the flickering light . . . But that . . . that feeling of utter peace, a profound sense of . . . of . . ."

"Love?" Dumphrey said.

"Yes. A deep, calm love. An acceptance." I glanced back. "I can readily understand why these people will come from miles away to kneel beneath that crucifix." I stopped. Dumphrey was lighting his pipe thoughtfully. "It must be beyond value to them. I have the feeling that it's very old."

"No," he said. "This one dates back to nineteen forty-five."

"*This* one?"

"There was another, exactly like this one," Dumphrey said. "And it was really old, dating back, I'm sure, to medieval times."

"What happened to it?" I said. "Was it solid gold, like this one?"

He looked at me, a rather odd look. "The villagers always thought so," he said.

They were proud of their crucifix, Dumphrey told me, standing there on the steps. Gleaming brilliantly in the candlelight, the great golden crucifix had always hung in their church—far beyond the memory of the oldest living inhabitant. It was the most precious object in their lives; not only because they believed it to be pure gold, but because it symbolized the complete unity of their faith. Even though the church doors were never locked and strangers never refused admittance, their crucifix had never been disturbed. Never.

But then no wars had ever really touched this hamlet. No wars, that is, until Hitler proclaimed his right to rule the world. Then war came to the village with a vengeance—and only after it was already lost for Germany and very bad for everyone.

With all the strong young men long since gone—killed or captured on the many fronts—there were only the *Herrenvolk* left to fight. The People's Army. The halt, the misfit, the old—the dregs of humanity. Poor fighting material, perhaps, but over them were placed the most brutal and fanatical of Hitler's officers: the dreaded Waffen S.S., Hitler's elite killer corps. Men sworn to defend the fatherland to the death.

Untersturmfuhrer Hohler, former assistant commandant at
the infamous Dachau concentration camp (then already over-
run) was given the job of fortifying the village and assuring
that the *Herrenvolk* would, if necessary, fight to the death in its
defense.

Hohler fortified the town. Ignoring the protests of the priest
and parishioners, he gave orders to use the belltower of the
church as a spotting post for their deadly .88 artillery. When the
first American light armor approached the town, they were
quickly knocked out by a hail of accurate artillery fire. They
withdrew, calling on their own artillery for support. There was
no choice but to reduce the belltower to rubble.

On a cold February morning, the American units of the 45th
whirled through the thin snow in a swift flanking movement
and the town was taken. Most of the *Herrenvolk* surrendered
immediately. *Untersturmfuhrer* Hohler was not among them.
He'd escaped.

The main body of troops moved on, but a few rendezvoused
before the church. A young infantry captain, his hands blue
with cold, brought an old priest to see then-Major Dumphrey.
Anguished, obviously in deep distress, the priest requested in a
halting whisper that Dumphrey go with him into the ruined
church.

Dumphrey went into the shattered building, past the broken
pews and the smashed windows, over bits of blasted stained
glass, littering the floor like sharded rainbows.

The priest pointed to the wall above the chipped altar. "We
have had a cross there for many centuries," he said in a choked
voice. "It was gold, pure gold. No one had ever touched it,
though the doors were never locked. And when the shelling
came, even though everything else fell, it was untouched. A
miracle," he whispered. "It made us humble, and sure that God
was protecting us. But now—" His finger trembled.

The wall above the altar was intact, but strangely bare-look-
ing. Against the dark smudge of centuries of candle smoke was
the pale outline of where the great gold crucifix had hung. The
crucifix was gone.

"*Untersturmfuhrer* Hohler has taken it," the priest cried
brokenly.

Hohler: *Untersturmfuhrer*, wearing the lapels of the dreaded
Schutzstaffeln; assistant commandant at Dachau, specialist in

death. The executioner of hundreds of thousands of Jews, a man with a dossier of crimes equaling in length the appalling list of names of his murdered victims. Even then, wanted by the Allies for trial (and subsequent hanging), even at the moment of his personal *Gotterdammerung*, Hohler could not resist adding the gold Christ to his already immense pile of loot.

"We'll get him," the young captain assured his priest. "Where can he run now?"

They got him, near Salzburg. Hohler readily admitted taking the crucifix, and when the indignant young captain brusquely ordered him to hand it over, Hohler laughed ironically, saying he no longer had it—that he'd thrown it away. However, a number of pure gold bars were found in his loot, at least equaling in weight the approximate mass that the melted-down Christ would have been. When questioned at length about this gold, Hohler, after some hesitation, admitted that the gold bars were, indeed, the melted-down remains of the stolen golden Christ.

Fortunately, the exact dimensions of the original Christ had been known and there were any number of skilled carvers in the village capable of making a mold. When the finished Christ was again ready to be hung for the Bishop's blessing, the worshipers more than filled the church. Children in the pews sniffled in the great cold that filled the shattered church. Shuffling and whispering, they stared in awe at the beautiful gleaming crucifix which hung once again above the chipped altar.

The adults knelt silently on the broken floor, enveloped in layers of clothing. Bitter drafts whistled through the empty windows. But it was a church again—their church.

Above the altar that strangely serene, that powerful golden figure enveloped them in a warmth they'd never known before.

And as if to prove that God was indeed among them, there occurred then the first of the miracles attributed to the golden Christ. A child, a victim of the shelling attack, had been brought to the service. The child had been buried alive in the ruins of his blasted home, pinned beneath the bodies of his parents. When they'd dug him out, he had shrieked once, then it was as though a light had been extinguished within him: his eyes went blank.

He became mute, an unresisting, unsmiling creature, with no spark of humanity.

But in the church he'd looked upon the golden Christ. A faint light leaped into his eyes. He stared. His eyes became brighter. Brighter. And suddenly he screamed, a terrible, piercing scream. He began to cry. The tears were real, genuine tears of emotion. He was alive again, a thinking, feeling human soul; in great anguish—but sane.

"He is a strong young man now, with children of his own," Dumphrey finished, as we walked down the worn stone steps and back to the car. "His was the first, but there have been similar . . . cures."

"I don't doubt it," I said. "Not any more."

We got into the car and Dumphrey looked reflectively at the people coming and going.

"But he lied, you know," Dumphrey said softly. "*Untersturm-fuhrer* Hohler, I mean."

"Lied? In what way?"

Dumphrey brought out his pipe, and stuffing it with tobacco he said slowly, "I don't need to tell you to be discreet about this, of course." He sighed. "Actually, even before Hohler was captured I'd already come into possession of the real stolen crucifix. It had been found by one of my team of specialists."

He made a wry face. "It had been mutilated so badly there was no thought of ever returning it to the church. The arms were twisted and bent, the torso battered, and the crown of thorns torn completely off the head."

"Hohler had actually thrown away the golden Christ?"

"Yes. After he discovered it wasn't gold at all," Dumphrey said. "Where the crown of thorns had been torn off showed dull gray. Where the arms had been twisted and bent, ugly black cracks showed through." He shook his head. "It was merely heavily-gilded lead."

"But—Hohler's gold bars—"

"Can't you guess where that gold came from?" Dumphrey said. "Hohler was one of the butchers of Dachau. Stripping the rings from his victims' fingers as they were led wailing into the gas chambers. Wrenching the gold teeth and fillings from their lifeless mouths as they were fed into the furnaces. Accumulating his pile of gold, melting it down into bars—"

"From the Jews . . ." I whispered.

"Yes, from the martyred Jews of Dachau," Dumphrey said. "Doubtless Hohler considered it a diabolical joke, saying the gold came from the stolen Christ. *But was he so far wrong?*"

He put the little car in gear and we moved slowly out of the village. "The pagan executioner stole from the Christians their Christ of gilded lead—only to replace it with one made of that most precious metal of all: the substance of martyrs."

ROBERT ARTHUR

Call for Help

For the tenth time that day, in a voice that
shook a little, Martha Halsey read aloud the item in the *Dellville
Weekly Call:*

The real estate firm of Boggs and Boggs today announced
that it is placing on the market the old Halsey house, directly
opposite the courthouse. The house, owned by the Misses
Martha and Louise Halsey, daughters of the late Judge Hiram
A. Halsey, has been ordered sold by their niece, Mrs. Ellen
Halsey Baldwin.

This time Louise, her blue-veined hands fluttering among the
scraps of quilt on which she was working in her wheelchair, said
nothing. Only the New England wind answered, giving a shrill
shriek of glee as it tore around the ivy-hung eaves of the old
house, so remote from the noise and bustle of the city.

All that day, since Ellen had brought in the paper from the
mailbox, just before breakfast, they had been rereading and
discussing the item from every angle. At first Louise had in-

sisted it must be a mistake. But Martha had snorted that to scorn. Then Louise had wanted to call Ellen and ask her about it. But some dormant current of caution deep in her mind had made Martha say no.

And now, after a day of talking, speculating, exhausting themselves with surmises, the answer suddenly dawned on her. It was the only possible answer, and with her unquestioning acceptance of that fact the reason for everything that had happened in these last six months—including poor Queenie's death the previous week—suddenly fitted into place.

Martha caught her breath before she spoke. Then quite slowly and calmly she revealed the truth to Louise.

"Louise, I'm convinced Roger and Ellen want us dead."

"Dead?" Louise stared at her from the wheelchair, a look of shocked disbelief on her face. "Oh, *no*, Martha!"

"There is no other answer," Martha said. Her features, like weathered New England granite, were stern. Despite her eighty years her blue eyes snapped.

"Now I understand why Roger and Ellen were so insistent we give up our house in town and come out here to live with them," she said. "Also why they persuaded us to give them our power of attorney so Ellen could handle what Roger called minor tiresome business details relating to our estate.

"The truth is quite simple when you examine the facts in the proper perspective. First Roger and Ellen isolated us from all our old friends and neighbors. Now they are bold enough to sell our house. Soon, very soon, they undoubtedly expect to inherit our stocks and bonds."

"But they can't do that until we're dead!" Louise gasped.

"That's exactly the point I'm making."

Martha rose and hobbled to the window of the bed-sitting room they shared, favoring her bad hip by refusing to move with too much haste. The New England autumn wind rattled the bare branches of the trees that surrounded the old Colonial house. Martha raised the window, bracing herself against the cold blast.

"Toby, Toby!" she called. "Here, Toby!"

There was no answering *miaow*, no tawny form leaping in. She slammed the window shut, and hobbled back to the circle of brightness cast by the big kerosene lamp on the center table, near her sister's wheelchair.

"First Queenie," she said despairingly, "now Toby! I tell you,

Louise, tomorrow or the next day Roger will be bringing Toby in all stiff and cold, and pretend to be grief-stricken—just as he did when he brought in Queenie last week. Poisoned, of course."

Martha stared fiercely at her sister, and Louise's eyes misted.

"Poor Queenie," she whispered. "Roger said she must have found some poisoned bait some farmer set out. It's true, Martha. Farmers do—"

"Would Queenie eat something like that, after being fed from your own hands for eight years?" Martha demanded. "Queenie was a very discriminating cat. I'll tell you who poisoned Queenie. Roger, and no one else!"

Louise stared at her as the wind whistled around their wing of the old house.

"But *why?*"

"Think back—all this last month. These spells you've been having. One day you feel weak and sick. The next day you're much better. Then, a couple of days later, you feel wretched again. What explanation do you have for that?"

"After one passes seventy-five—"

"Nonsense. You never had these spells when we were in our own house."

"No . . . That's true. I never did."

"Well then! I'm sure I don't have to remind you that as a pharmacist Roger has access to all kinds of drugs—including poisons."

"Oh, Martha, no!"

"Roger is very clever. He'd do it a little at a time, so that we would just get slowly sicker and one day die—*of natural causes.*" Martha almost hissed the last words. "All your symptoms, Louise, are of chronic poisoning, most likely arsenic. Queenie was fed from your plate. Being so much smaller, she died, while you only got sick. And Roger brought her in with a trumped-up story of eating some farmer's poisoned bait."

Martha breathed deeply, filled with scorn, "Then Roger realized the same thing could happen to Toby. Only Toby might get ill right here with us, and we'd suspect the truth. So he decided he'd have to get rid of Toby for good. And now poor, dear Toby is gone."

"Oh, how horrible," Louise breathed. "But how can you be *sure?*"

"On the basis of the evidence, including the new car Roger bought yesterday."

"But it isn't really a *new* car," Louise demurred. "It's second-hand. And Roger did need one, with winter right on top of us."

"That's the whole point. Need. Roger and Ellen need money badly. You know how little Roger makes in Mr. Jebway's drugstore. You just have to look at all the facts. Two years ago Roger came here out of nowhere—a stranger. He meets Ellen and nothing will do but she must marry him.

"But let's face it, Ellen is very plain. Why should Roger be attracted to her? I wondered at the time. Now I know. It's because she is our only heir, our niece. And we had the big house, and the stocks and bonds father left us. So Roger saw his chance. He married Ellen figuring someday soon he would get his hands on all of our property—by poisoning us both."

"It's true about Ellen," Louise said, doubt on her small, wrinkled features. "She is very plain. But she has a sweet nature, and men don't always marry a woman for her looks."

Martha pointed a bony finger at her sister. "You know as well as I do that Ellen has changed. Surely you've noticed how secretive she's become? How she avoids talking about the house when we mention it? How she and Roger exchange secret glances when they think we aren't looking? And especially how, when we talk money, they change the subject?"

Martha leaned forward, lowering her voice.

"I forgot. They could be listening outside the door. As I was saying, consider all the facts. We were happy in our home in town. Then last summer Ellen and Roger tried to make us believe they were worried about us. Because of my bad hip and your arthritis, they said we couldn't look after ourselves properly. Nonsense! We could have sold some of the bonds and hired a maid and a cook.

"But no. Like foolish old women we agreed to give Ellen our power of attorney and move out here with them. Now we're completely isolated. We never see anyone, and hardly ever leave the house. We never get any mail. Even Judge Beck hasn't been to see us, and I wrote him three days ago asking him—no, *imploring* him—to visit us. I said we wanted to talk over something important."

"You wrote Judge Beck?" Louise exclaimed. "You didn't tell me."

"Because I didn't want to worry you with my suspicions. But now I'm sure, and I'm going to tell everything to the judge. If we ever see him. I'm pretty sure now Roger never delivered my letter!"

Martha's lips tightened. "We may as well face it. Roger has become impatient. Quite obviously his plan is for you to go first. Then me. And no one will suspect a thing."

"Oh, Martha!" Louise's pale blue eyes blinked with agitation.

"I'm going to call them, and see what they say. Oh, I'm not going to accuse them. But we'll be able to tell by the way they answer my questions just how much they have to conceal."

Martha limped to the door, which led through a short hall to the main part of the house. Opening it she called, "Roger! Ellen!"

"Yes, Auntie?" a young woman's voice answered.

Martha returned to her seat and presently Ellen appeared, a young woman with popping eyes and a receding chin and a worried expression. She came in, wiping her hands on her apron, and smiled.

"Supper in a minute," she said. "Pot roast. Sound good?"

"Very nice, Ellen," Martha said. "But we wanted to speak to Roger."

"Did someone call me?" Heavy footsteps sounded in the hall and Roger appeared behind Ellen. Roger was short, with wiry hair and an appearance that would have been almost jolly if it had not been for the lines around his mouth and the heavy glasses he wore.

"Here I am, Aunties one and all." He laughed as if he had made a joke. "What can I do for you?"

He put his arm around his wife's waist and beamed at them. Over his smiling lips his magnified eyes seemed to be probing for their secret thoughts.

"My three favorite girls, all in the same house. My own secret little harem." He gave Ellen a squeeze.

"Roger, I was wondering why I hadn't heard from Judge Beck," Martha said. "Did you give him my letter?"

"Well, no." Roger seemed to hesitate. "I left it with his secretary, I was going to tell you tonight. Judge Beck is out of town."

"Out of town?" Louise exclaimed, staring at him.

Roger cleared his throat, and even Louise could not miss the look he and Ellen exchanged.

"He went to Boston on a case. His secretary said it was rather important."

"But the judge has no clients in Boston," Martha said firmly.

"He went for a local client," Roger said, his look of uneasiness becoming more pronounced.

"And when will he be back? The judge hates Boston."

"In a day or two," Roger said quickly. "As soon as he gets back he'll get your letter."

"Mmm." Martha shot Louise a look, and her sister gave a little nod, which said as plain as words that she too could see through Roger's evasions. "There's a story in this week's *Call*, Roger, that says that Ellen has turned our house over to Boggs to sell. Using, of course, the power of attorney we gave her. Surely that's a mistake."

Again they both saw the swift glance that passed between Roger and Ellen. Roger's air of drummed-up assurance faltered a bit.

"Well, no, Aunt Martha," he said. "The house needs so many repairs. We thought you were happy with us and—well, we felt it should be sold."

"Roger!" Martha rose and leaned on her cane, facing him. He was unable to meet her gaze. "You recall that we agreed to live out here with you and Ellen only if we could move back into our house any time we wished to do so. Isn't that so, Ellen?"

"Yes, of course, Martha," Ellen said, twisting her apron.

"Which means we have no intention of selling it while we live."

"We want to move back," Louise said, her voice tremulous.

"Oh, but Aunt Louise!" Ellen protested. "You can't!"

"And why not, pray?" Martha demanded.

"Why, winter is here," Roger said, regaining his composure. "The house needs a new heating system, and installing one would be a long, expensive job. Maybe next summer it could be done. But there's nothing worse than a cold house in the winter when you're not too well." His look was almost appealing, though the lines around his mouth seemed to deepen. "Besides, as Ellen says, we want you with us. We thought you were happy *not* living alone."

With a look Martha forestalled Louise from blurting out another protest. "We'll think about it and discuss it with Judge Beck," she said.

"That's my girl. Well, Ellen, let's have supper. I have to go back to the drugstore tonight. Mr. Jebway has a touch of the flu."

Roger and Ellen retreated to their part of the house.

Martha turned to Louise. "Well? Do you agree with me now?"

"Oh, yes," Louise breathed. "Oh dear, he told such lies. Why, the heating system in our house works perfectly. We've never had any trouble with it since Father put it in thirty-seven years ago."

"And what local client would Judge Beck go to Boston for?" Martha asked with fine scorn. She fixed her sister with her gaze. "You noticed how suddenly Roger decided he had to go back to the store this evening? As though his only thought was to get away before we could ask more questions. As likely as not he needs more poison from Mr. Jebway's stock."

"Martha!" Louise put her fingers to her tremulous lips.

That night the two sisters slept badly. Martha rose several times to put on her robe and hobble to the window to call for Toby. But still no answering *miaow* came.

"Toby is gone," she told Louise next morning. "We'll never see him again."

"Poor Toby." Tears misted Louise's faded blue eyes. "Why, they're monsters. And I used to think Ellen was so sweet."

"She was," Martha said. "Roger has changed her whole character. A woman naturally follows her husband's lead."

"But to be willing to help Roger murder us—"

"So far they have only murdered cats. We will find some way to keep them from murdering us. I have a plan." Martha's tone was grim. "I dislike resorting to it, but I will if I have to."

There were steps in the hall, and Ellen came in with a tray.

"Good morning," she said as she put dishes on the table. She looked as if she had not slept well. "Boiled eggs, hot cakes and tea. Nice and filling. Do you know there was ice on the chickens' pan this morning?"

"We didn't sleep at all well," Martha told her. "We were worrying about Toby."

"Oh, dear, isn't he back?" Ellen seemed genuinely distressed. "I do hope he hasn't been—I mean I hope he hasn't wandered away. But if he has, I'm sure he'll come back."

"I can't eat, really I can't," Louise said miserably after Ellen had gone. She poked listlessly at the hot cakes, golden brown.

"We must keep up our strength," Martha said. "Eat the boiled eggs. They're in the shell, so they're perfectly safe. And drink some tea."

"I'll try." Louise did manage a boiled egg and some tea, though it seemed rather strong. Martha ate all of the hot cakes and eggs on her plate. But she found the tea too strong.

"Do you think you could slip out to the telephone and call Judge Beck?" Louise asked when they had finished.

"You've forgotten!" Martha gave her a look full of meaning. "Last month Roger had the telephone taken out."

"Oh, goodness, yes," Louise exclaimed. "He said it cost too much."

"Even though we offered to pay for it. That was his first step in cutting us off from the world."

"Now we have absolutely no way to get help!" Louise's voice was panicky.

"Yes, we have. As I told you last night, I hate to resort to it, but I will if I have to. Now go on with your quilt. I'll finish reading the paper to you. We must pretend to keep busy. What shall I read first?"

"Oh, the obituaries," Louise said. "See if anyone we know has died." Her face became fretful. "We just don't get any news any more. Mary Thompson used to tell us everything, but she hasn't a car—" Martha's gasp stopped her. "What is it?"

"It's Mary Thompson!"

"She's not dead?" Louise asked, alarmed.

"No," Martha compressed her lips. "But she might as well be. The paper says she has entered the Haven Home."

"Oh, no!" Louise cried.

Martha nodded. "At her own request, the poor thing. Just imagine a woman her age being forced to live at that dreadful old place. It's drafty, decayed and full of rats. The Haven Home, indeed! Fancy names don't make fancy places. It's the county poorhouse, a disgrace to the community! It'll be the death of her."

"Poor Mary," Louise mourned. "Oh, I keep thinking about our teas, with the fire going and the cats sleeping in front of it, and Mary visiting with us."

Her expression became that of an eager child. "If we can get back into our own house Mary can come live with us! We'll hire some help and it'll be just lovely."

"We will," Martha promised. "Mary Thompson is not going to drag out her days at that horrible place as long as we have the means to help her."

The prospect of their own home again with their old friend sharing it brightened Louise's mood for several minutes. Then in the midst of stitching a piece of her woolen Sunday-best dress of twenty years before into the quilt, she paused.

"I—I don't feel well." She waited a moment, then turned stricken eyes to her sister. "I'm sick. I'd better go to bed."

Martha helped her into bed, and massaged her wrists. "Is it any better?" she asked presently.

"I feel so strange," Louise whispered. "Just weak and helpless and—and queer. As if—*as if I had been poisoned!*" The last words came out in a frightened, despairing whisper, and when they were uttered the two sisters stared at each other with realization naked in their eyes.

"The tea," Martha said. "Oh, he's clever, Roger is. But I didn't drink it and you only drank a little—" She gripped Louise's wrists tightly. "I'm sure you're not badly ill. You didn't take enough tea to seriously poison you. Anyway, I'm certain Roger plans to do it slowly, to make it seem like some wasting illness. But we'll insist on having Dr. Roberts. And he'll take a message back to Judge Beck for us!"

"You're so clever, Martha," Louise murmured admiringly.

"Until we see the judge, we mustn't let anyone know we suspect Roger and Ellen," Martha warned. "If Roger guesses that we suspect, he won't wait."

"No, of course not."

But Ellen, when she came in, did not wish to call the doctor. She fussed around Louise and suggested aspirin and bicarbonate and hot water bottles. Martha insisted, however, and at last, reluctantly, Ellen put on her coat and set out for the nearest neighbor, a quarter mile away, where there was a telephone. She returned to say Dr. Roberts was on a maternity case, but would come as soon as he could.

The hours dragged by. Louise did not get any worse. But she remained in bed, moaning from time to time, while Martha massaged her wrists and rubbed her temples with cologne. They both refused to eat lunch, to Ellen's obvious distress.

"But you *must* eat," she scolded. "To keep your strength up."

"I had a big breakfast," Martha said. "And I'm sure Louise will feel worse if she eats anything when she is suffering such distress. It's better to go without eating when your stomach is upset."

Seeming upset and worried, Ellen took the lunch away.

Dr. Roberts came in the afternoon, puffing and wheezing a little. He was a short, rotund man with fluffy white hair, only a little younger than the two sisters.

"What's this, what's this?" he asked, sitting down and feeling Louise's pulse. "Mmm. Nervous pulse. Let's see your tongue, young lady."

Martha hovered anxiously over them as Dr. Roberts progressed to his stethoscope and listened to Louise's heart.

"Something upset you, Louise?" he asked, stroking his chin. "Ellen tells me you lost your cat."

"She was poisoned," Martha said. "Now Toby is gone. We're afraid he was poisoned too."

"Mmm hmm. That's too bad. I'm afraid you're upset from worrying about your pets. I'm going to give you a prescription which Roger can fill for you. You're fortunate to have a pharmacist in the family. You'll save half the cost. Medicine is very expensive these days."

"Upset!" Louise exclaimed, as he reached for his prescription pad. "Doctor, I've been—"

Martha vigorously motioned her to silence. The doctor, busy with the prescription, paid no attention.

"Doctor," Martha asked as he packed away his stethoscope, "will you give Judge Beck a message for us?"

"Of course, of course, Martha. What message?" He stood up and gently massaged the bald spot on the top of his head.

"Ask him to come see us tonight! Tell him it's vitally important!"

"Vitally important. Hmmm. Hate to ask him to come out at night. He's got quite a cold."

"Then he isn't in Boston?" Louise exclaimed.

"Boston? Whatever gave you that idea? He was quite ill when I saw him last."

"Please ask him to come tonight," Martha begged. "Tell him it's a matter of life and death."

"Life and death? Hmmm." The doctor lifted bushy white eyebrows. "Well, all right, all right, if he's well enough. And don't fret about Toby and Queenie. Get a couple of lively kittens to take care of and you'll be new women."

"When we get back into our house in town, we will," Martha said in a tone of decision. "It will be nice to watch kittens play in front of the fire."

"Your house in town?" The doctor shot her a look. "Now why would you want to go back to that place? Too big for you— much too big. You couldn't take care of it. I'd advise you to stay here where you're well looked after."

After he had marched out, they heard Ellen intercept him in the hall. Martha hobbled to the door to listen. A minute later she limped back to Louise's side.

"He said you were just upset," she whispered. "He's prescribed tranquilizers."

"A tranquilizer! We should have told him it was poison!"

"He wouldn't have listened. Don't you see? Ellen and Roger have everyone on their side. Everyone thinks they are sweet, loving relatives taking good care of two helpless old women."

Martha wrung her hands in despair.

"Louise, even if Judge Beck comes tonight he'll think the same thing. I can see that now. We'll both be in our graves in a month and everyone will be sorry for Roger and Ellen."

"Couldn't we just give our stocks and bonds to Roger and Ellen?" Louise whispered. "Then they wouldn't have any reason to kill us."

"Certainly not." Martha's eyes snapped. "Then they'd just send us to the Haven Home. How would you like to end your days in that horrible place?"

"I'd rather die. But if no one will listen to us—"

"There's only one thing to do. We must escape."

"But Martha!" Louise half sat up. "You know we can't. Why, you couldn't possibly walk a quarter mile to the Lamb place, much less push me. We'd freeze to death. Just listen to that wind!"

The wind rattled the windows, as if for emphasis. But Martha was nodding mysteriously now.

"You'll see. I told you I had a plan all worked out. We'll escape, never fear."

"But suppose we do?" Louise asked. "They'll say we're foolish old women and bring us right back here."

"I've thought of that too. We'll escape and they'll let us go back to our old home. But we'll have to wait for Roger to come home first."

Despite Louise's curiosity, she refused to say anything more on the subject. The temperature dropped as the afternoon passed, and when the early darkness came they could feel the cold pressing in through the tall windows. Martha began assembling their personal knickknacks and jewelry into a pile, which she tied into an old shawl.

"We can't take much," she said. "We'll have to leave our clothes behind. But we can sell a bond, and buy more."

Louise was feeling better and sitting up now. "I wish I knew more about your plan. You certainly can't push me a quarter of a mile. We'll freeze."

"Help will come in time," Martha promised. "Now remember, we mustn't let Roger or Ellen suspect a thing, for they are murderers. They killed Queenie and Toby and they wish to kill us. Just let me do the talking."

"All right," Louise said in resignation. "But of course we don't dare eat any dinner."

"Of course not. Now *shhh*—Roger's here and I think I hear Ellen bringing supper."

There was a rattle of crockery and Ellen came in, bringing a tray laden with dishes and silver. Behind her Roger appeared, his thick glasses glinting in the light.

"Dr. Roberts had me bring some special medicine, Auntie Louise," Roger said. He managed a toothy smile as he took a bottle from his pocket, tossed it up and caught it. "Pure gold dust would be cheaper. But in a week you'll be feeling as skittish as a colt."

"Thank you very much, Roger. I'll take it later."

"Before meals, that's the prescription. Here you are now. Swallow it down."

He held out a red capsule and a glass of water. Louise gave an imploring glance at Martha, then swallowed the pill.

"That's my girl. You must take another one at bedtime."

"Have you seen Toby anywhere?" Martha asked. "He's still gone."

Roger wet his lips, and Ellen spoke quickly. "Toby? Why, no, but I'm sure he'll come back. He's just got wanderlust."

"I thought I heard him in the cellar. He sounded so pitifully weak." Martha looked anxious. "Please, Roger, would you go down right now and look?"

"In the cellar?" Ellen and Roger exchanged uneasy glances. "I can't see how he could be down there. We'd have heard him before this."

"Please, Roger. Look anyway. You heard him, didn't you, Louise?"

"Oh, yes, I'm sure he's in the cellar," Louise said.

"It will do no harm to look," Ellen suggested. "Perhaps he slipped in when I got the preserves two days ago."

"All right, I'll go." Roger squared his shoulders in an exaggerated gesture. "Off to the cellar to find old Toby."

He marched into the the hall and they heard him clump down the stairs. A moment later they heard his muffled voice from beneath them.

"No sign of a cat down here."

"Ellen, please go look too," Martha urged. "Toby may be hiding back in the coal bin where Roger can't see him."

"Well, all right," Ellen said, and went down into the cellar to join Roger. "Here, Toby," they could hear her calling. "Here, Toby, Toby."

Martha hobbled into the hall and quietly closed the cellar door. Then she slid the heavy bolt into place.

"There!" she said in triumph. "Now we can escape."

"But we'll freeze!" Louise wailed as Martha half pulled her out of bed and bundled her into her warm coat. "And they'll just send us back."

"No, they won't."

Martha got her own coat on, with a shawl over her head, and got Louise into the wheelchair. By now Roger and Ellen had discovered that the door had been bolted and were hammering on it.

"Aunt Martha!" Ellen called. "Open the door! Why did you lock it?"

"Hey, Auntie!" Roger cried out. "It's a good joke, but let us out now. Toby isn't down here. We've looked everywhere."

"He's not down there because they killed him," Martha said sternly to Louise.

She pushed her sister out into the hall, and out the front door onto the low stoop. The early evening was pitch dark, and filled with restless murmurings as a chill wind rattled the bare branches of the trees.

Louise cried out in dismay as Martha bumped her down the single step and continued on down the walk for a hundred feet. Then she turned the chair about, and locked the wheels.

"Now just wait," she said. "I'll be back in a minute."

Martha hobbled back into the house, ignoring the shouts and pleas of Roger and Ellen from beyond the bolted cellar door. Huddled in her shawl and coat, Louise waited in the outside dark, the wind tugging at her, nipping like little teeth, until Martha reappeared, bearing the shawl that held their jewelry.

"Martha!" Louise wailed. "I'm freezing already. What are you going to do?"

"You'll see." Martha stopped beside her, panting, and leaned on her cane. "You'll see, Louise. Just watch the house."

Louise watched. Behind the windows of the wing that had been their home a flicker of yellow light appeared. It wavered for a moment, then leaped up. Feeding on itself, it grew into a sheet of fire that thrust a finger through a partly opened window and still continued to grow, becoming brighter and stronger with every gust of wind that tore around the heavily-cluttered ivy-hung eaves.

"Fire!" Louise gasped. "The house is on fire!"

"I spread the kerosene from the lamp around the room," Martha said. "Just remember, Ellen and Roger planned to kill us. They did kill our cats. We have to protect ourselves. There was simply no other way."

Martha's voice rose urgently. "But remember. We must never tell anyone what they planned. They're our kin. No one would believe us. Let it be a tragic accident. Do you understand?"

"Oh yes, yes," Louise said, excited. "You're so clever. Now someone will see the flames and call the fire department, won't they?"

"Yes, a fire in the country always brings someone. It was the one way we could call for help, crippled as we are. After this, they'll have to let us go to our old home."

Then in silence they watched. The finger of flame shooting from the window became a tremendous torch. After a moment they heard in the distance the faint wail of the siren on the roof of the volunteer fire company in town.

"It's such a warm fire," Louise murmured, holding out her hands toward the blaze. "It does feel good."

The roof of their wing fell in with a great shower of sparks just as the fire engine with its helmeted volunteers came screaming up. But the rest of the house was engulfed in flame then, and there was nothing the fire company could do.

The fireplace in Judge Beck's living room crackled cheerily. Martha and Louise sat watching it, seeing happy pictures in the flames.

"Soon we'll be in our home again," Louise murmured. "With kittens playing on the rug and Mary Thompson keeping us company. Mrs. Rogers has a daughter who can sleep in for twenty-five dollars a week. We can easily afford that."

"Our money will certainly last as long as we do," Martha agreed. "I think I hear the judge coming now."

The door opened, but instead of a man, a big Siamese cat slipped through. It leaped into Martha's lap with a satisfied miaow.

"Toby!" Louise exclaimed.

"Toby!" Martha echoed. "Where on earth did you come from?"

"I thought he would be a welcome surprise," said Judge Beck's dry voice. The judge himself, a spare, tall, slightly stooped man of sixty had come into the room. "Something to make brighter a very sad occasion. One of the firemen spotted him last night not far from the ruins."

He gave each of them a firm handclasp, then blew his nose with a vigorous honk.

"Sorry," he said. "I caught a whopper of a cold down in Boston. Terrible city. Drafty, noisy."

"You—were in Boston?" Martha asked. Her mouth seemed suddenly to have become parched.

"Three days. They were wasted, too, I'm sorry to say."

He sat down, shaking his head.

"This is a very sad occasion. Those old houses are terrible firetraps. But we won't talk about that. It's better not to dwell on it. I want to talk about you, now that Roger and Ellen are—well, gone."

"Oh, we'll be all right," Louise said eagerly. "We'll move back into our old house. And we want Mary Thompson to stay with us. She mustn't stay another day in that terrible place."

Judge Beck blew his nose again. He looked unhappy as he fingered the Masonic emblem on his gold watch chain.

"Martha," he said. "Louise—" He paused. They stared at him, two pairs of bright eyes in ancient faces. "It's hard for me to tell you this, but my visit to Boston was about you."

"About us?" They echoed each other.

"About your father's estate, that is. As you know, it consisted of some money—which has been spent—and a number of New England and Toronto Railway bonds."

"Yes?" Martha asked, and they continued to stare at him.

"Well—railroads are having tough sledding these days, and the New England and Toronto went into bankruptcy last summer. That was why Ellen and Roger wanted you to move in with them, so they could look after you. Ellen wanted your power of attorney, to enable her and Roger to handle the remains of the estate without you learning what had happened. I wanted to tell you the truth, but they were afraid it would upset you. That's why we all played along and kept it a secret.

"Unfortunately, now you must know, dear Martha and Louise. I'm sorry, but the old house is uninhabitable. In fact, we can't even find a buyer for it. There's no money to fix it up. There's no money at all left in your father's estate."

Judge Beck paused, delicately. "You may have wondered why Roger and Ellen sometimes seemed so hard-pressed and harassed. Now you know. Believe me, they didn't mind. They loved you."

The two sisters looked at each other, in silent, stricken horror.

"The Haven Home." Louise's voice was a tremulous whisper. Martha's voice would not come at all.

LUCILLE FLETCHER and
ALLAN ULLMAN

Sorry, Wrong Number

She reached for the telephone on the night table once more, spinning the dial with unnecessary force. The light from the bed lamp—the only light glowing in the darkened room—caught in flashing pinpoints the jewels on her moving hand. On her face, softly beautiful in the flattering half-light beyond the lamp's white circle, a frown of annoyance matched her swift, over-energetic manipulation of the clicking dial.

The dialing completed, she sat tensely for a moment, feeling the uncomfortable strain on her back from sitting unsupported in the bed. Then the pulsing of the busy signal squawked in her ear and she slammed the phone back into place, saying aloud, "It can't be. It can't be."

She flounced back against the piled pillows, closing her eyes, shutting out the shadows of the room and the rectangle of hazy night she could have seen through the open window. As she lay there on top of the thin, summer coverlet, she could feel the evening breeze lightly fingering the folds of her nightgown. She could still hear the night sounds floating up from the river and from the streets three stories below.

In a fury of concentration she considered the aggravation that was making that hour one of torment. Where *was* the man? What was keeping him? Why had he picked this night of all nights to leave her alone, to vanish without a call, without word of any kind? That was not like him. Not like him at all. He knew only too well the effect such behavior might have on her. And on him, too. It was unbelievable that he'd deliberately provoke the kind of scene that had nearly done for her once or twice in the past. But if his absence now was not deliberate—what then? Had he been hurt? How unlikely that he'd been hurt without someone notifying her instantly!

There were other aggravations, all stemming from the larger aggravation of his unexplained absence. There was the matter of the telephone. In many ways that was the most infuriating thing of all—the telephone. She'd been ringing and ringing his office for more than a half hour. Or at least she'd tried to ring his office. Each time she'd dialed the number she'd got a busy signal. Not a "don't answer," which would have been a little more reassuring. But a busy signal. If he was there—and obviously someone was there—was it possible that he'd be on the telephone for a full half hour? Possible? Yes. Probable? No.

She ran over in her mind the things he might be doing, resolutely facing *all* the things he might be doing. Perhaps at last the impediments of illness—her illness—had cracked the reservoir of his patience. He had never seemed to mind the ever-lengthening periods in which she had been unable to respond to him. Although he was a man of intense passion—a vigorous, healthy animal—his self-control had always been inexhaustible. In other words, if she wanted to be plain about it, she'd never dreamed that there could be another woman—or women! But now . . . ?

Somehow that obvious possibility didn't seem to fit the circumstances. Not after she'd driven it out in the open and examined it thoroughly. He was a cautious man. Everything he did was carefully planned and neatly executed. He'd never in a million years be so stupid—or so careless—as to brand himself in so flagrant a manner.

And the milder prospects didn't fit either. He preferred everything on a large scale to match his own boldness, the boldness so perfectly reflected in his powerful, brooding good looks.

Thinking of him, she opened her eyes for a moment, glancing toward the wedding picture in its sleek frame on the night table. Dimly seen, except in the sharp clarity of her mind's eye, were her own ivory-satined magnificence and his towering, broad-shouldered, smiling presence. Nothing about him had changed, she thought. In ten years nothing had altered the clean, muscular lines of his body, or the rare, fleeting smile on his smooth, unlined face.

But she had changed. Only the utmost care controlled the little evidences that time and her now chronic invalidism left behind. Soon, unless she was able to regain her strength, to take advantage of the youth that still remained, even the utmost in art would no longer conceal the deepening network of wrinkles around her eyes, the puckering at the corners of her mouth, the sagging flesh under her chin. Had he perhaps noticed something more than illness in her aversion to daylight?

She returned to his likes—the things she knew he prized. After ten years of marriage—a marriage she'd planned with almost military thoroughness—she knew perfectly well that her father's fortune had been a mighty bulwark against any restlessness on his part. He had a profound respect for that mountain of money. It was hardly to be expected that he'd ever do anything to place himself out of reach of the Cotterell millions.

That was the way she wanted things, she reminded herself. Let there be no mistake about it. She had always wanted it that way. For the practical relationship with him that now flourished gave her what she wanted most—a man who above all gave force to the illusion she had created, the illusion of a happy marriage. She was envied by her friends, and to be envied was the most desirable state of affairs life had to offer.

The consideration of her tailor-made marriage palled, and once more the irritation of unwanted solitude boiled within her. That damned telephone! There was something fishy about that telephone—about that recurrent busy signal.

It occurred to her that there might be a mechanical defect of some kind in the dialing system. She sat up, reaching for the phone, impatient with herself for having failed to think of it before. She whipped the dial around to "Operator" and waited.

The intermittent purring in the phone was followed by a click and a pleasant voice saying, "Your call, please?"

"Operator," she said, "will you get me Murray Hill 3:0093?"

"You may make that call by dialing," the operator told her.

"But I can't," she said with annoyance. "That's why I called you."

"What is the trouble, madam?"

"Well, I've been dialing Murray Hill 3:0093 for the last half hour and the line is always busy. Which is too incredible."

"Murray Hill 3:0093?" the operator repeated. "I will try it for you. One moment, please."

"It's my husband's office," she said, listening to the operator dialing. "He should have been home hours ago. And I can't think what's keeping him—or why that ridiculous wire should be busy. His office is usually closed at six o'clock."

"Ringing Murray Hill 3:0093," the operator said mechanically.

Again the busy signal! The confounded, stupid, eternal busy signal. She was about to take the phone from her ear when, miraculously, the signal ended and a man said, "*Hullo?*"

"Hello!" she cried eagerly. "Mr. Stevenson, please."

Again the man said, stupidly, "*Hullo?*"

He had a deep, hoarse, thickly accented voice, a voice easily distinguished though but one word had been spoken.

She moved her mouth closer to the telephone, saying carefully, crisply, "I want to talk to Mr. Stevenson, please. This is Mrs. Stevenson calling."

And the hoarse voice said, "*Hullo, George?*"

Crazily, out of nowhere, a second voice—flat, nasal—answered, "*Speaking.*"

In desperation she cried, "Who's this? What number is this, please?"

"*I got your message, George,*" the deep voice rumbled. "*Is everything okay for tonight?*"

"*Yeah. Everything's okay. I am with our client now. He says the coast is clear.*"

It was fantastic. It was unbelievable and impossible. Icily she said, "Excuse me. What's going on here? *I'm* using this wire, if you please."

Even as she spoke she knew they could not hear her. Neither "George" nor the man with the deep voice could hear her. She'd blundered on a crossed wire. She'd have to hang up, dial the operator again, and go through the whole rigamarole once more. At least that was what she ought to do. But she couldn't. The strange men were talking, and what she heard froze her to the phone.

"Okay," the deep voice rumbled. *"Is it still at 11:15, George?"*
"Eleven-fifteen is right. You got it all straight now, I hope."
"Yeah, I think so."
"Well, run it down once more so I know you got it right."
"Okay, George. At 11:00 o'clock the private cop makes the bar on Second Avenue for a beer. I go in the kitchen window at the back. Then I wait for a train to go over the bridge—in case her window is open and she should scream."
"Right."
"Say, I forgot to ask you, George. Is a knife okay?"
"Okay," the nasal voice of George said flatly. *"But make it quick. Our client does not wish to make her suffer long."*
"I get it, George."
"And don't forget to take the rings and bracelets—and the jewelry out of the bureau drawer," George continued. *"Our client wishes it to look like simple robbery. Simple robbery. That's very important."*
"There won't be no slip-up, George. You know me."
"Yeah. Now once more. . . ."
"Okay. When the cop knocks off for a beer I go in the back window—the kitchen, that is. Then I wait for a train. After I'm through I take the jewelry."
"Right. Now you're sure you know the address?"
"Yeah," the hoarse voice grated. *"It's—"*
Rigid with fear and excitement she pressed the phone to her ear until it hurt her temple. But at that instant the line went dead, followed in a second or two by the steady monotony of the dial tone.

She gasped in horror, crying aloud, "How awful! How unspeakably awful!" Could there be any doubt about the meaning of those queer, unemotional, business-like remarks? A knife! A *knife!* He had said it as blandly as though it was the most ordinary thing in the world to talk of knives and open windows and women screaming.

9:35

She held the phone, staring at it, staring in horror at the cluttered night table. What had she just heard? It couldn't be— it just couldn't be. It was some trick of her imagination—a brief pause in time in which reality faded and a dream swept through the caverns of the mind. But the calm, impersonal tones of George and the man with the deep voice returned with unmistakable clarity the instant she tried to recall them. No dream ever had these sharp outlines. She *had* heard them. As sure as there was substance in that cool black instrument she held in her hand, she had heard those men. She had heard their different voices synopsizing the death of some poor woman—someone alone, unprotected, someone whose murder had been ordered as one might order the delivery of vegetables from the market.

But what could she do? For that matter, what *should* she do? She had heard all this accidentally, a mechanical slip in the telephone system. She had heard nothing that might lead directly to those awful men. Perhaps it might be best to force from her mind the remembrance of that curious conversation. But, no, there was that woman—perhaps a woman like herself, lonely and friendless—who might be warned if only there was a way. She could *not* stand idly by—she had to do something at once to ease her conscience. With shaking fingers she picked up the telephone and dialed the operator.

"Operator," she said nervously, "I've just been cut off."

"I'm sorry, madam. What number were you calling?"

"Why," she said, "it was supposed to be Murray Hill 3:0093. But it wasn't. Some wires must have been crossed, and I was cut into a wrong number and I—I've just heard the most dreadful thing—a murder—" She raised her voice imperiously. "And now I want you to get that number back for me."

"I'm sorry, madam, I do not understand."

"Oh!" she said impatiently. "I know it was a wrong number and I had no business listening, but these two men—cold-blooded fiends, they were—are going to murder somebody. Some poor innocent woman—who is all alone—in a house by a bridge. And we've got to stop them—we've got to."

"What number were you calling, madam?" the operator asked patiently.

"That doesn't matter," she snapped. "This was a wrong number. A number you dialed yourself. And we've got to find out what it was immediately."

"But—madam—"

"Why are you so stupid?" she raged. "Look. It was obviously

some little slip of the finger. I told you to try Murray Hill 3:0093 for me. You dialed it. But your finger must have slipped—and I was connected with some other number—and I could hear them but they couldn't hear me. Now, I simply fail to see why you couldn't make the same mistake again, on purpose. Couldn't you try to dial Murray Hill 3:0093 in the same sort of careless way?"

"Murray Hill 3:0093," the operator said quickly. "One moment, please."

As she waited, her free hand moved over the medicine bottles on the night table, picking up the tiny lace handkerchief that lay crumpled among them. She was dabbing at her forehead with it when the busy signal sounded, and the operator cut in to say, "That line is busy, madam."

In her anger she punched the side of the bed with her fist. "Operator!" she called. "Operator! You didn't try to get that wrong number at all. I asked you explicitly. And all you did was dial correctly. Now I want you to trace that call. It's your duty to trace that call!"

"One moment," said the operator pleasantly, if resignedly. "I will connect you with the Chief Operator."

"Please," she said, settling back indignantly against the pillows. Then another soothing, calmly efficient voice said, "Chief Operator," and once more she concentrated on the mouthpiece of the phone, talking with exaggerated care, her voice strained with annoyance.

"I'm an invalid, and I've just had a dreadful shock—over the telephone—and I'm very anxious to trace a call. It was about a murder—a terrible cold-blooded murder of some poor woman, tonight—at 11:15. You see, I was trying to reach my husband's office. I'm all alone—my maid is off and the other servants sleep out. My husband promised to be home at six—so when he didn't get home by nine I started to call him. I kept getting a busy signal. Then I thought something might be wrong with the dial and I asked the operator to try the number for me. And when she did I got on a crossed wire and heard this ghastly conversation between two killers. Then I was cut off again before I could find out who they were, and I thought if you could connect me again with that wrong number, or trace it, or something. . . ."

The Chief Operator was gentle and understanding—almost maddeningly so. She explained that only live calls could be traced. Calls that had been disconnected couldn't be, of course.

"I know they must have stopped talking by now," she said sharply. "They weren't exactly gossiping. That's why I asked your operator to try to get them back right away. You'd think a simple thing like that . . ."

The bitter criticism in her voice failed to ruffle the Chief Operator. "What is your reason for having this call traced, madam?"

"Reason!" she exclaimed. "Do I have to have any more reason than I've already given you? I overheard two *murderers*. The murder they were talking about is going to take place tonight—at 11:15. A woman's going to be killed—somewhere in this city. . . ."

The Chief Operator was sympathetic—and reasonable. "I quite understand, madam," she said. "I would suggest that you turn this information over to the police. If you will dial the operator and ask . . ."

She hung up for an instant, then picked up the receiver, waiting for the dial tone. Fury rose within her, flushing her pale cheeks, shutting her off from everything but the feverish twirling of the dial. She heard nothing of the whispering noises of ships cutting through the black river, or the rush, rush, rush of traffic slipping steadily along the express highway that skirted the river's edge. She heard nothing of the clanking and groaning of steel on steel, of the *cluckety-cluck, cluckety-cluck* of the train's approach to the bridge. She didn't notice the trembling of the window frames in her room—the vibrations transmitted molecularly from the shivering bridge. Not until the train had reached the roaring peak of its crescendo did she hear it, and by then the operator was saying, "Your call, please?"

"Give me the police," she said, wincing as the scream of tortured steel echoed in the night and then slowly died away.

While the phone purred she became once more aware of the oppressive warmth. She touched her forehead and the damp flesh under her eyes with her handkerchief. Then a tired voice said, "Police Station. Seventeenth Precinct. Sergeant Duffy speaking."

"This is Mrs. Stevenson—Mrs. Henry Stevenson—of 43 Sutton Place," she said. "I'm calling to report a murder . . ."

"*What* was that, ma'am?"

"I said I want to report a murder . . ."

"A *murder*, ma'am?"

"If you will only let me finish, please . . ."

"Yes, ma'am."

"It's a murder that hasn't been committed yet, but it's going to be. . . . I just overheard plans for it over the telephone."

"You say you heard this over the telephone, ma'am?"

"Yes. Over a wrong number the operator gave me. I've been trying to get them to trace that number myself—but everybody is so stupid. . . ."

"Suppose you tell me where this murder is supposed to happen, ma'am."

"It was a perfectly *definite* murder," she said witheringly, sensing the policeman's doubt. "I heard the plans distinctly. Two men were talking. They were going to murder some woman at 11:15 tonight. She lived in a house near a bridge."

"Yes, ma'am."

"And there was a private policeman on the street. He goes some place on Second Avenue for a glass of beer and then this killer is supposed to climb in a window and murder this woman with a knife."

"Yes, ma'am?"

"And there was some third man there—a client—that's what they called him—who was paying to have this—this terrible thing done. He wanted the woman's jewelry taken so it would look like a burglary."

"Yes, ma'am. Is that all, ma'am?"

"Well, it's unnerved me dreadfully—I'm not well . . ."

"I see. And when did all this take place, ma'am?"

"About eight minutes ago."

"And what is your name, ma'am?"

"Mrs. Henry Stevenson."

"And your address?"

"Forty-three Sutton Place. That's near a bridge. The Queensboro Bridge, you know. And we have a private patrolman on our street—and Second Avenue . . ."

"What was that number you were calling, ma'am?"

"Murray Hill 3:0093. But that wasn't the number I overheard. Murray Hill 3:0093 is my husband's number. I was trying to call him to find out why he hadn't come home—"

"Well," the policeman said dully, "we'll look into it, Mrs. Stevenson. We'll try to check it with the telephone company."

"But the telephone company said they couldn't check the call if the parties stopped talking. Personally I think you ought to do something far more immediate and drastic than just checking the call. By the time you track it down—they'll already have committed the murder."

"Well—we'll take care of it, lady," Duffy sighed. "Don't worry."

"But I *am* worried, officer," she complained. "You've got to do something to protect this person. I'd feel a lot safer myself—if you sent a radio car to this neighborhood."

Duffy sighed again. "Look, lady, do you know how long Second Avenue is?"

"Yes, but . . ."

"And do you know how many bridges there are in Manhattan?"

"Of course, but I . . ."

"Now what makes you think this murder is going to happen in your block, if it happens at all? Maybe it wasn't even a New York call you heard. Maybe you were cut into a long-distance line."

"I should think you'd want to try," she said bitterly. "You're supposed to be there for the protection of decent people. But when I tell you about a murder that's going to happen you talk as though I were playing some kind of prank."

"I'm sorry, lady," Duffy said calmly. "A lot of murders happen in this city. If we could stop 'em all, we would. But a clue like you've given me—well, it's vague, see? It isn't much more use than no clue at all. Now, look," he added brightly. "Maybe what you heard was one of them freak radio receptions. Maybe you somehow got hooked up with one of them crime programs. Maybe it was even coming in the window and you thought you heard it on the phone."

"No," she said coldly. "Not at all. I tell you I heard it on the telephone. Why must you be so perverse about this?"

"I want to help you if I can, lady," he assured her. "You don't think there could be something phony about this call—that maybe somebody's planning to murder you?"

She laughed, nervously. "Me? Why—of course not. That would be ridiculous. I mean—why should anybody? I don't know a soul in New York. I've only been here a few months and I see nobody except my servants and my husband."

"Well, ma'am, then there's nothing for you to worry about," he told her matter-of-factly. "And now—if you'll excuse me, ma'am, I've got some other things needing my attention. Good night, ma'am."

With an exclamation of disgust she dropped the phone back on its hook. From the night table she took a tiny vial of smelling salts, uncorked it and passed it under her nose. She inhaled the sharp fumes with relief, then replaced the stopper in the bottle, and put the bottle on the table. She returned to the pillows once more, wondering what next to do. Her anger at the casual attitude of the policeman subsided somewhat. After all, it was unlikely that those men could be traced directly. But still, they should do something—they could at least have offered to send out a radio alarm of some kind, to alert the police of the city to this danger that threatened someone—no matter where.

In a little while the urgency that was born of the murder call began to blur. Not that she could put completely out of her mind the memory of that shocking conversation—or the thought of that poor, doomed woman. But her own loneliness became again the most immediately disturbing fact. It was absolutely unforgivable for Henry to have left her this way. If only she had known, she could have insisted that the maid remain.

Now everything around her began to rasp her nerves. The dimly lit room, so richly, so splendidly furnished, became a hateful cocoon from which there was no escape. The expensive array of jars and bottles, boxes and atomizers, glowing dully on the vanity against the wall reminded her only of her ebbing beauty. The plumply upholstered chaise longue, the chairs and gayly covered little benches, the daintily painted boudoir tables—all planted in ankle-deep gray carpeting that matched the walls—looked as though they had been set there by an unimaginative stagehand. The room had no life. It was a cell. The bright chintz drapes and gently moving curtains that framed the windows might as well have been iron bars. She despised the place. She despised her inability to cope with loneliness. Again she snatched up the telephone and dialed the operator.

"Operator," she said, "will you for heaven's sake ring that Murray Hill 3:0093 number again? I can't think what's keeping him so long."

This time no busy signal! Instead the purring ring continued, until the operator broke in to say, "They do not answer."

"I know," she said tartly. "I know. You don't have to tell me. I can hear it for myself." And she hung up.

Now she lay back again, glancing at the half-open door to the room, listening with that intentness with which lonely people try to draw from the surrounding quiet some sound, some evidence of movement, some sign that the emptiness is at an end. But there was nothing. Her glance fell on the night table, with its clutter of medicine bottles, its clock, its crumpled handkerchief—all grouped around the telephone. Rather absently she reached out, opening the little drawer in the night table, taking out a jeweled comb and a small hand mirror. She began combing her hair, pulling the flashing comb swiftly through it, turning her head from side to side to study it in the mirror. Satisfied that she had restored the elegance of her hairdo, she took a lipstick from the drawer, carefully refreshing the crimson arcs that slashed across her face.

Henry had never failed to show his appreciation of her beauty, she thought. Lately, perhaps, his laconic comments had become a bit less spontaneous, a bit more mechanical. Or did they seem so now in the light of his present unexplained delay? Which reminded her that his whereabouts was still the problem of the moment, the annoying situation about which something had yet to be done.

From the same night-table drawer she took a small, black-covered loose-leaf notebook. She had opened it to the letter "J" when the telephone rang. Swiftly, eagerly she snatched it up, crying musically, "Hello-o-o."

Her gaiety collapsed when she heard, "This is Long Distance. I have a person-to-person call for Mrs. Henry Stevenson. Chicago is calling."

"Yes," she said. "This is Mrs. Stevenson." And a few seconds later, "Hello, Daddy, how are you?"

"Just fine," Jim Cotterell boomed. "Just fine, Leona. And—how's my girl tonight?"

All her life Leona Stevenson had heard and resented the modified bellow with which her bull-like father customarily conducted his customarily one-sided conversations. Usually he was telling someone what to do. And usually what was done had something to do with big Jim Cotterell's personal comfort or prodigious bank account, or both. His blustering energy and blistering tongue had rolled a pill formula into one of the world's largest pharmaceutical manufacturing businesses. No chemist himself, he'd spotted the vein of pure platinum that streaked the public's passion for self-medication. Chemists—as he liked to say whenever there were no chemists present, and sometimes when there were—chemists came a dime a dozen. But good salesmen were scarce and worth their weight in gold.

Thirty years ago Jim Cotterell had bullied a corner druggist into selling him for a song the formula for a harmless, and occasionally effective, headache remedy. Today his pills, powders and soothing syrups flowed from a dozen giant plants to every corner of the globe. He ruled this vast corporate network with an iron hand, the same hand that trembled with agitation whenever his daughter, Leona, chose to frown. It was strange about Jim and Leona, and no one knew it better than Jim and Leona.

Leona's mother, who had not survived her daughter's birth, had had a great beauty and a gentle pride. But she had been no match for the hustling demon who had swept her off her feet. Her death had been Jim Cotterell's first defeat, and a major one at that. It had left him empty of all tenderness, of all respect for the pleasanter, less acquisitive instincts. Except in those things that concerned Leona. Leona became not so much an object of love as a kind of souvenir of love. He tended her as a lost and shivering hunter would tend a flame. And as she grew he began to be afraid. Not that the flame would consume him, but that it would die.

Leona, inheriting beauty from her mother, had within her a queer mixture of her mother's pride and her father's stubbornness. As the years went by she developed no particular strength of character from this lopsided brew. Instead she became overly shrewd, overly calculating, determined to have her own way whatever the issue. And at whoever's expense.

Jim, for reasons carefully concealed in the depths of his aggressive nature, encouraged his daughter's excesses of temperament. In some twisted manner it pleased him—or satisfied some need in him—to have this one shrine before which he might abase himself. On the surface he had excused his indulgence by attributing to Leona a delicacy of health that threatened her life. His fears in this regard had been conveniently supported by the family physician who, frankly

puzzled by Leona's tantrums, had advised a policy of appease-
ment. The ease with which she had, in childhood, made both
sword and shield of an imaginary affliction had encouraged her,
until in later years a pattern of illness established itself with all
the manifestations of the real thing. The memories of childhood
sank below the surface of her consciousness—only the alarm-
ing physical symptoms appearing at moments of extreme stress
remained. So that now, in her thirties, she believed herself
hopelessly at the mercy of a weak heart. Her physician, still
puzzled, thought this might be so. There were certainly plenty of
indications to support his judgment. He had continued to treat
her accordingly. Only when she had determined to go to New
York did he suggest she consult another heart specialist.

"How's my little girl tonight?" Jim had asked.

"I'm terribly upset," she said, pouting.

"Upset?"

"Well, who wouldn't be upset?" she asked. "Wondering where
Henry is, and—hearing a murder being planned right over the
telephone!"

"For heaven's sake, honey, what in blue blazes are you talking
about?"

"I was trying to get Henry at the office. And somehow I got on
a crossed wire and I heard these two men talking about killing
some woman . . ."

"Now wait a minute," Jim said hoarsely. "Let me get this
straight. Why were you trying to get Henry at the office—at this
time of night?"

"Because he simply hasn't come home. I don't know what's
happened. I tried him at the office, and I kept getting a busy
signal. Until these two men got on, that is."

"Really, dear," her father roared, "this thing gets my cork.
This guy hasn't another responsibility in the world and he pulls
a trick like this. Even if he went to that meeting in Boston, he
should have . . ."

"Boston?" she cried. "What about Boston?"

"Didn't Henry say?" he asked. "There's a druggists' convention in Boston and in his last report Henry wrote that he was
thinking about running up there. But even if he made up his
mind at the last minute, he had no right to go without letting
you know."

"Maybe he's tried," she said doubtfully. "Maybe he's been

trying to get me at the same time I've tried to get him. If he had to catch a train he might . . ."

"He might, my eye! Nothing should have kept him from getting word to you."

"I know."

"Well, no need to worry, dear. I'll straighten Henry . . ."

"The trouble is," Leona broke in, "I can't help worrying. That phone call I heard . . ."

"Relax, honey. It was probably a gag—a couple of clowns. Who'd talk about a real murder over the phone?"

"It *was* real," she assured him sullenly. "And I don't feel at all right about it—alone in this house."

"Alone! You mean even your servants . . . ?"

"Of course," she said.

"Well, if that doesn't beat . . . Did you call the police?"

"Certainly. They weren't much interested. It's a crazy sort of thing."

"Well, you've done all you could under the circumstances. So don't let it bother you any more, honey. And tomorrow," he added, his voice heavy with the weight of his anger, "tomorrow we'll have a little talk with Henry—wherever he is."

"All right, Dad. Good night."

"Good night," he said, "and I wish you'd come home, dammit. The place is like a morgue. I don't know why I ever let Henry talk me into . . . Well, take care of yourself and don't worry. I'll call you tomorrow."

Leona hung up, the faintest trace of a wry smile on her face, thinking how Henry hated those calls to, or from, his father-in-law. Not that Henry ever said anything, but his hate was something you could feel rather than see, or hear.

9:51

She was somewhat appeased by her father's concern, and by the thought of scorching retribution awaiting Henry. Nevertheless she was unable to persuade herself to relax and permit time to answer her questions. Of the ominous talk between "George" and that other knife-wielding fiend, she had done everything she could to bring it to the attention of the police.

There was no reason why in all honesty she could blame herself if some tragedy occurred. Tomorrow's papers would probably reveal the end of that story—if end there was. And if some innocent soul *was* found stabbed to death, and robbed, she'd have Henry write to the newspapers, and to the Police Commissioner, and perhaps to the Mayor, disclosing the casual, disinterested manner in which the Police Department treated information of so vital a nature. Then, too, she thought, they would have to investigate a real mystery, since her testimony would prove the robbery was only a fake and that someone had hired the poor woman's murderer. Such a thing would be a sensation in the press, and her unselfish attempt to forestall the crime would certainly make headlines. Her friends in Chicago would be amazed at her daring. And she an invalid—or very nearly one.

But where was Henry? She had interrupted her thoughts several times to listen again to the tiny sounds—amplified by the raptness of her attention—that might mean someone's presence in the house. A board creaked, or a bit of paper fluttered in the gentle breeze, and for a moment she'd fancy she'd heard a step, or a human breath. Each time her heart would beat faster in anticipation; each time disappointment fed the flame of her resentment. She couldn't lie there just *waiting*. She could, at least, make some effort to get news of Henry.

She remembered the little black notebook and fished it out of the night-table drawer, turning again to the J's. There was an entry for a "Miss Jennings," and next to it the number: Main 4:4500.

This she dialed.

The birdlike ladies who nested in the Elizabeth Pratt Hotel for Women were twittering madly in the main lounge. It was Bingo night, and perched around a score of tables—bridge tables, library tables and just plain tables borrowed from the dining room—the ladies concentrated their attention on the cards in front of them, clucking, chirruping, occasionally crowing as the numbers were called.

It was a fusty room, ancient, threadbare, smelling of old velvet and respectability. Dim and dusty paintings in enormous gilt frames hung on the fading brown walls. Over-stuffed settees and chairs, separated by tables holding an assortment of pottery lamps with fringed shades, stood against the walls in stiff array.

Overhead a tortured brass chandelier, on which the substitute illuminating gas cocks spoke the age of skepticism in which it had been manufactured, shed a kind of light from clusters of shaded electric bulbs. There was nothing in or about the room to disturb the illusion of the past in which most of the hotel's guests lived.

At one end of the room a large bony woman in rusty black peered through her pince-nez at the numbers she was drawing from the drum before her. As each number revealed itself to her close inspection she would cock her head on one side, look out across the lounge, and call the number in a loud, high, piercing voice. Then her thin face would crack in a smile, and she'd prepare to draw another number. The process had been going on for some time with monotonous regularity, when an unprecedented interruption threw the lady with the pince-nez completely off balance.

A wispy little woman in gray, with starched collar and cuffs, had crept into the lounge and raised a hesitant hand toward the number-caller. "H-s-s-s-t!" she said. "Miss Jennings—!"

The lady addressed, startled and outraged, glared at the intruder. "Please!" she said sharply, and began once more to select a number from the drum. But the intruder, although visibly intimidated, was not to be put off. "It's the phone," she murmured apologetically. "For you . . . Miss Jennings . . . a Mrs. Stevenson . . ."

Miss Jennings, holding the cardboard slip in midair, looked sharply at the nervous little woman. "Who?" she asked, startled.

"A Mrs. Stevenson . . . If she's still holding on . . ."

Miss Jennings' eyes widened, and the pince-nez on her beak trembled. "Oh!" she cried. "Tell her I'll be right there." Then, rotating her head with its dyed black topknot toward her audience, she said excitedly, "I'm terribly sorry, ladies. I hope you won't mind. It's an urgent call from Mrs. Stevenson . . . You know—Mr. Cotterell's daughter . . . Mr. Cotterell who owns the Cotterell Company . . . My company . . ." And off she flew.

Sailing out of the lobby, past the desk behind which the switchboard was located, she called out to have Mrs. Stevenson put through to her room. This was at the end of a long, narrow corridor on the first floor—a distance she seemed to negotiate without once setting foot on the carpeted stairs or the corridor's bare boards. She unlocked her door, flung herself into the mon-

strous green velour chair next to her brass bedstead and
swooped up the telephone—all in one continuous motion.
"Hel—hello. Hello, Mrs. Stevenson," she puffed, her beady eyes
more birdlike than ever now that the pince-nez lay at the end of
its silken cord in her lap. "So nice of you to call."

"I'm sorry if I disturbed you," Leona said.

"Why, not at all," Mrs. Jennings cried. "I was just participat-
ing in a bit of entertainment here at the hotel. I hope I haven't
kept you waiting.

"No," Leona told her, "you haven't. I only wanted to ask you if
you knew where Mr. Stevenson might be. My phone—has been
busy so much this evening that I—I'm afraid he may not have
been able to call me. And I'm most anxious. . . ."

Miss Jennings clutched the phone tighter to her bony bosom.
A gleam of unholy interest awoke in her eyes. This *was* exciting.

"Why, no," she said breathlessly, "I haven't any idea. It's odd
that he hasn't reached home yet."

"Would he have had some reason for working late?" Leona
asked.

"N-no. I don't think so. He wasn't there when I left at six."

"He wasn't?"

"No. As a matter of fact he was only there for a few minutes
during the day. That was around noon. He went out with that
woman then and that was the last I saw of him."

"Woman—?"

"Why, yes," Miss Jennings said, the gleam brighter than ever.
"There was a woman who waited more than an hour for Mr.
Stevenson to come in. Very anxious, she was."

Leona hesitated a moment. Then she asked, tremulously,
"Was—was it—someone Mr. Stevenson knew? Someone who'd
been there before?"

"N-n-n-no. She'd never been there before. I don't believe. And
Mr. Stevenson didn't seem to—to want to recognize her. At first,
that is."

"Do you remember her name, Miss Jennings?"

"It was Lord—L-O-R-D, *Mrs.* Lord. I believe her first name
was Sally.

"Well, what did they do?" Leona demanded.

Miss Jennings cast her glance at the ceiling, recalling just
what had happened that day.

"Mr. Stevenson seemed a bit embarrassed. I could tell he was
trying to make the best of the situation, though. He told Mrs.

Lord he had an appointment, and asked her if she would care to see him another day. She said, no, it was important. So Mr. Stevenson suggested that she have a bite to eat with him before his appointment. Then they went out."

"And he didn't come back at all?"

"No, Mrs. Stevenson. I left at six, as I told you, and he hadn't come back. There was only one message for him during the afternoon."

"A message? From whom?"

"Oh, it was from that Mr. Evans—the man who calls Mr. Stevenson every week. A regular pest he is, too."

"Well," Leona said falteringly, "this is all very strange. But I'm sure if it were anything important Mr. Stevenson would have told me. He's always telling me the things that happen at the office."

"Yes, Mrs. Stevenson." There was a faint, mocking smile on her face as she said it.

"Tell me," Leona continued, "did Mr. Stevenson say anything about a trip to Boston? He—he mentioned something to me . . ."

"Oh, that!" Miss Jennings said. "He did report to Mr. Cotterell that he might go to the convention in Boston. But if he went today—I wouldn't know."

"Well, thank you," Leona said as brightly as she could. "Thank you very much, Miss Jennings. I won't keep you any longer."

"Thank *you*, Mrs. Stevenson. It's been a pleasure. I hope I've been helpful. Most of us in the office—well—we sort of envy you, Mrs. Stevenson. Mr. Stevenson is so devoted to you."

"Yes," Leona said, "he is—"

"I hope you liked the flowers today," Miss Jennings went on. "I thought camellias would be nice, for a change. . . ."

"Very nice," Leona said. "Good-bye, Miss Jennings."

Miss Jennings said "Good-bye" and hung up. She leaned back, staring contentedly at the brass ceiling fixture from which three naked bulbs sprayed light. She saw neither the harsh light nor anything else. Her eyes were turned inward, inspecting what promised to be a startling, juicy secret. She had no doubt that it was a secret, or something that had been a secret. Any simple explanation of Mr. Stevenson's strange actions she rejected at once. There had always been something a little odd about Mr.

Stevenson. An atmosphere of conflict that his rugged, handsome face and reserved bearing did not dispel. He certainly spent little enough time in the office, when you came to think of it. And Miss Jennings, with her devious mind spinning along in high, was coming to think of everything.

Pale and shaken, Leona fell back against the pillows. So that *was* it! What could not happen had happened! The fool! The utter damned fool! To get himself trapped in a shoddy affair with a wench he'd known years ago. To get caught at it almost instantly. To expose the casual way he'd treated his duty to her father's company. To force upon her a choice that in one direction meant public disgrace—the shattering of her life's pleasant illusion—or in the other to live a life of private shame, forever defeated by Henry's knowledge that she no longer could destroy him. It was unthinkable! Why had all this happened tonight? Was someone trying to drive her out of her mind? Was someone —Henry perhaps—trying to bring on another heart attack?

Something caught in her memory . . . That woman's name —Lord. She'd heard that before. Or seen it. Today. Some time today she'd come across that name. It was difficult, in her anxiety, to recall where she's seen it. She *had* seen it, she was certain. And in an instant she remembered where. Swinging her feet off the bed she stood up, shakily at first. She walked toward her vanity table, switching on one of the lamps that stood at either end of it. Her eye fell upon the white card by the flower bowl—the card that had come with the camellias Henry had sent today. "All my love, Henry," he had written. She snatched it up, tearing it to shreds, strewing them on the floor. She began to rummage among the litter on the vanity, until behind a row of perfume bottles she saw it—a slip of paper with a few lines on it in the maid's heavy scawl. As she picked it up the telephone rang.

She scuttled back to the bed, the paper clutched in her hand, and picked up the phone. A man's voice—hollow, tired, elderly, with an unmistakable British accent, said, "Mr. Stevenson, please."

"He's not in," she snapped. "Who's calling?"

"This is Mr. Evans. When do you expect him? It's very urgent. I've been telephoning his office, and he doesn't seem to be there."

"I'm sure I don't know where Mr. Stevenson is," she replied. "You'd better call back later."

"In about fifteen minutes?" the man asked. "I haven't much time. I'm leaving the city at midnight."

"All right," she said. "In about fifteen minutes."

"Thank you," he murmured, "I will. And—you'll tell him that I called, please? In case he does come in? The name is Evans— E-V-A-N-S. It's very important."

Evans and his call drifted out of her mind the moment she had hung up. She moved the slip of paper she'd taken from the vanity under the light. It was headed: "Calls for Mr. Stevenson." Underneath were three brief entries:

3:10 P.M. Mr. Evans. Richmond 8:1112.

4:35 P.M. Mr. Evans. Richmond 8:1112.

4:50 P.M. Mrs. Lord. Jackson Heights 5:9964.

There it was. Mrs. Lord! Calling Henry right in his own home—in *her* home. It was ridiculous. There were limits to that sort of thing, and one had been reached now. She reached for the telephone, dialing the Jackson Heights number, her face frozen, jealous, hard as flint. The fingers of her free hand flickered in a nervous, silent tattoo on the edge of the bed as she waited. Then the call signal clicked off and, incongruously, a child's reedy voice said, "Hello, this is the Lord residence."

Puzzled, Leona said, "I'd like to speak to Mrs. Lord, please."

"One moment," the child said. "I'll see if she's in."

She could hear the jar as the phone was set down. Faintly a man's voice said, "Is that for me, son?" She heard the child say, "Mommy," and then there was a confused murmur of male voices, not quite near enough to the telephone to be distinguishable. She strained to listen, to recognize, if possible, the men speaking. But there was nothing familiar about either of their voices. Suddenly she tensed, grinding the phone into her ear in her desire to strengthen the sounds she heard. For distinctly she had heard the name "Stevenson" emerge from the blur of talk. And "Cotterell Corporation"! And "Staten Island." After that someone—a woman—moved close to the phone, cautioning the child to get back into bed, saying to one of the men, "Fred—how could you? He was out on the sidewalk in his bare feet." Then there was a grating sound as the phone was picked up, and the woman said, "Hello?"

Leona's mouth had suddenly filled with cotton. She paused

for a second to swallow. "Hello," she managed to say. "Mrs. Lord?"

"This is she."

"This is Mrs. Henry Stevenson, Mrs. Lord. I—I don't believe we have met—but I understand you saw my husband this afternoon?"

"Oh—why—yes," the other replied with some hesitancy.

The woman's obvious nervousness released Leona's tongue.

"Ordinarily, of course, I wouldn't dream of bothering you, Mrs. Lord," she said with heavy sarcasm. "But—as it happens— my husband hasn't come home this evening. I can't seem to locate him at all. And I thought perhaps you might give me some idea . . ."

"Oh—why—yes," the woman said again, faintly.

"I can't hear you, Mrs. Lord. Will you please speak up a little?"

"Certainly—I—"

"Is there anything wrong?" Leona asked icily. "You're not keeping something from me, I hope."

"Oh, no . . . Could I call you back?"

"Call me back? Why?"

"Because I . . ." The woman's voice suddenly changed from quiet desperation to an odd, strained gaiety. "It's my bridge day, you know."

"What's that?" Leona demanded. "What has bridge got to do with it? Excuse me, but I don't understand you at all, Mrs. Lord!"

"And then there's that trip to Roton Point," the woman went on idiotically.

"Look here," Leona said harshly, "are you trying to make fun of me, Mrs. Lord? Just in case you don't happen to know, I'm an invalid. I can't stand very much aggravation. Now tell me: Is my husband there with you? Is he? Tell me the truth!"

"It's three eggs separated," the woman babbled, "two measuring cups of milk, a third of a cup of shortening. Cream the shortening with a little sugar, then add a level tablespoon of flour . . ." For a second there was silence, than the woman whispered into the phone, "Leona . . . Leona . . . it's Sally Hunt, Leona. Remember? I'm sorry to be so ridiculous, but my husband was standing so near. I can't talk here. I'll call you back as soon as I can. Wait for me . . ." And she was gone.

Leona lay back in the bed, relaxing a little. She was completely bewildered by this latest revelation. How strange that
Sally should re-enter her life at this time!

Sally Hunt!

Sally had been in love with Henry, probably was still, although she seemed to be married and a mother. She'd been in
love with him when she'd invited him to that dance at college.
That was the night Leona had picked him out of the crowd. It
was so long ago. But she found it easy to remember that night.

Dance music had been blasting from the phonograph perched
on the Assembly Hall stage. Below, in the large room hung with
banners and paper streamers, couples danced, or stood and
talked, or wandered off to the refreshment table. Most of the
boys looked alike—crew haircuts, baggy slacks, tweed jackets.
And the girls had their own uniform—sloppy sweaters and
skirts, hair worn long and knotted at the nape of the neck.

But there were two who were different.

The man dancing with Sally was certainly no college lad. His
clothes matched, his hair was cut conventionally and carefully
groomed, his dancing was definitely on the unimaginative, non-
violent side. He was tall, solidly knit, darkly handsome. It was
easy to see from the adoring way Sally looked up at him that
something more than festival spirit had brightened her glance.

There was nothing particularly revealing in the young man's
face. He looked over Sally's head at the rest of the dancers with
an air of indifference that came close to being patronizing.

Leona, a sophisticated, pallid beauty in black faille with her
shining hair in a shoulder bob, was as noticeable in that crowd
of youngsters as an ocean liner in a fleet of tugs. Everything
about her was almost too obviously different. That her difference had been achieved at no small cost was plain. Girls didn't
dress that way on pin money.

She watched Sally dancing for a few moments, then marched
across the floor, making for Sally's partner's broad back. She
tapped him on the shoulders and said, smiling, "May I cut?"

They had been startled, had stood apart, Sally bewildered, the
man looking at Leona with unabashed curiosity.

"You don't mind, do you, Sally?" Leona said.

Sally recovered quickly, saying, "You've made a conquest,
Henry. Congratulations."

Leona turned her languid gaze full on Sally's partner. "I'm Leona Cotterell. What's your name?"

Before he could answer, Sally swiftly introduced him. "This is Henry Stevenson, Leona."

Leona smiled, tossed her shining head gaily, and moved toward him. "Shall we dance?" she said. That was all there was to it.

They danced, and Leona had been dazzling. There had been no indifference in Henry's expression after that. He had been frankly enchanted, and though there had been nothing flashing in his talk, he had managed to convey a sense of appreciation of her charm, of the gulf that separated her from her schoolmates, that separated her, for example, from girls like Sally.

He guessed right away that her father was Jim Cotterell. "That's the kind of man I admire," he said, "knows what he wants. Has the brains to go out and get it. Money. You can do anything with money. Some day . . ." And he stopped, smiling boyishly.

Leona liked his smile. It did not sprawl all over his face like the toothy contortions of some of the other boys. Rather it seemed as though candles lit in his eyes, and attractive arcs deepened at the upturned corners of his mouth. It added strength to his expression. It was a candid smile, neither naïve nor superior.

As they continued to move slowly about the floor Leona found that there were other things about this self-possessed young man that appealed to her. He made no bones about not being a college man himself.

"Too poor," he said, not smiling now. "My family's too poor. I have to help out as much as I can."

Leona picked that up smoothly. "Some of the most interesting men I know don't go to college. My father isn't a college man."

"Oh?" Henry said in amusement. "Then there's hope for me. To be successful, I mean."

"My father always says," she replied, "if a man hasn't any talent for making money, college won't knock it into him. And if he has a talent for making money, why waste time in college?"

That had pleased Henry. "Hurrah for Father!" he said.

The music stopped and Henry took his arm from her waist, dropped the hand he had been holding. "Thanks," he said, "many thanks."

Leona smiled at him, almost mischievously. "Let's sit the next one out?"

"Now wait a minute," he said in mock horror. "What about Sally? After all, Sally's my—my escort—if she hadn't invited me . . ."

Leona pointed across the floor to Sally talking animatedly to a crew haircut. "Sally's taken care of, and we'll only be a few minutes. Come on out and I'll show you my car—it's a honey."

She took his hand and led him out of the hall. They crossed the moonlit lawn to the road that ran past it. Dozens of cars were parked along the curb, but one was lower and longer and twice as rakish as any of those near it.

"Isn't it *beautiful?*" she crowed. "No one's got one like it. It'll do a hundred and ten, the man said who sold it to Daddy. Daddy thought it was too much car for me, but after I saw it there just weren't any other cars."

"It's something, all right," Henry said. "A Bugatti! Not bad! Not bad at all!"

Leona took his arm. "How'd you like to drive it?" she urged. "Just down the road a bit. No one will miss us."

He'd agreed quickly enough, and she could clearly remember now how he had loped back across the lawn to get her fur jacket and his own overcoat. In a matter of minutes they had been roaring down the road, top down, the Bugatti trembling with impatient power. The sharp winter air sliced at their faces, stirring them with tingling exhilaration. She knew now—as she thought about it—that it wasn't herself, or the outlandish car, that accounted for Henry's almost frenzied pleasure in that drive. It was what she and the throbbing car represented—not seen always from afar, not dreamed about, but here under his hand. That was why his face, as he drove, was alight. That was why he had cast aside the reserve of the dance floor.

She had sensed most of what later she knew for fact, and her mind had begun even then to scheme, to plan, to fix a pattern for the future. There was already in this brief encounter an element of certainty growing within her. She directed him to make a turn which brought them shortly to a dead-end.

"Some car," he said, slowing reluctantly to a halt. "This baby can really roll. I'd like to take it out some day and turn it loose."

"You will," she answered slowly. She reached out and turned

off the ignition. "Let's sit for a minute. I want to talk."

"Say," he said laughing, "I hardly know you. I'm afraid you'll have to take me home. Or must I get out and walk?"

Leona leaned back against the roadster's cushion to look at the night sky, black velvet strewn with stars, torn in one place by a cold blade of moon.

"Sally Hunt," she said, dreamily. "I'd never put the two of you together in a million years."

He turned from the wheel to face her, his arm across the back of the seat. "Why not?"

"Oh—just a feeling. I've been around a good deal. My father's taken me everywhere—abroad and so forth—and I've met a lot of people. You begin to classify people after a while—after you've traveled like that. You and Sally just aren't in the same class. You're worlds apart."

"You mean money," he said bitterly. "You mean her family's got money and I oughtn't to try to cut in on that kind of setup?"

"You're completely wrong," she said hastily. "I wasn't thinking of that at all."

"No? What then?"

"I was thinking that Sally's right for that small town you both come from. But you're different."

"I'm different, am I? You can tell all that—now?" His little laugh was derisive.

"Why not?" she asked. "Look at those kids back at the dance. College boys from nice, rich, respectable families. But you made them look like babies. And most of them will be babies all their lives."

"And me?"

"You're not a baby, Henry. Maybe you've never been a baby."

That was when he had leaned over and kissed her—roughly, expertly, long enough to start little shivers of ecstasy racing along every nerve in her body.

Then he'd settled back, looking at her like a craftsman inspecting the product of his art. "I've always wanted to kiss a million dollars," he said.

She smiled slyly. "Would you like to try for two million?"

She'd caught him off balance, forcing him to grin in spite of himself. She'd drawn his claws—for a moment, anyway—and his eyes had sparkled with amusement.

"Ouch!" he'd said, and then, "Maybe I am a little dryer behind the ears than those punks back at the dance. But it's only because I've had to make my own way so far—and not so far at that."

"You'll go far. I know you will. It's in the way you look. The way you affect other people. People like me."

His expression had grown cold and cynical again. "This is really funny," he said. "Me sitting here soaking up flattery from a girl whose millions of dollars and fur coats and Bugatti roadsters I'll never see again."

"You don't know," she said. "You don't know—anything."

"I don't get it."

"You will," she said softly, "by-and-by. Tell me about yourself, Henry. Where do you come from? Who're your people?"

He laughed cynically. "That's an easy story to tell. I come from what is usually referred to as 'the wrong side of the tracks.' My old man delivers coal when he's sober, and speeches about poverty when he's drunk. My mother would have been all right if she hadn't fallen for Father. She had some education, and wanted more. Instead she's worn herself out raising six kids, keeping them alive and out of trouble, with a roof—a leaky roof—over their heads and something or other to go in their stomachs. That's all. The American dream."

"But what about you?" she asked. "You don't look exactly as though—as though—"

"As though the seat was out of my pants? As though I broke cigarettes in half to make them last longer? No," he said, "it isn't that bad. My mother made me go to high school, instead of going to work after I'd finished the eighth grade. In high school they found out I could run fast with a football under my arm. I was big stuff. Sally Hunt took me around to meet her family—in our town the Hunts are considered pretty fancy—and her old man took a liking to me. He got me a job in the town's biggest drugstore."

"A drugstore!" she exclaimed. "Why, Henry, it's fate!"

"Sure," he grinned, accepting her sarcasm, "I thought you'd feel that way."

"Tell me more," she cried gaily. "Are we still in the same business?"

"Of course," he said. "I'm now the manager of everything except the prescription department. Local boy makes good. Good sodas, good sandwiches . . ."

"What about Sally?" she asked.

The brief, silly moment was gone. He hesitated, the brooding look that seemed most natural to him returning to his face.

"Sally's a good kid," he said. "We're good friends. Nothing more. Her family's been swell to me. Helped me out when things got too tough at home. But I don't know. Sometimes I feel as though . . ."

He wasn't looking at her now. His eyes were fixed on something distant, something as far away as the black woods beyond the fields at the far side of the road, something much farther than either of them could see.

"Yes?" she prompted gently. "As though . . . ?"

"As though I'm trapped. As though no matter what I do—how hard I work—I'll never get what I want because I want too much."

They sat in silence. Henry offered her a cigarette, took one himself and lit them both. His outburst seemed to have left him charged with unspoken anger. Finally he exhaled a huge plume of smoke, turned toward her with a grin on his face and said, "You and your damned Bugatti! Let's get back to the dance."

They drove back swiftly, saying nothing until he'd parked the car and opened the door for her to step out. Then she caught his sleeve. "How'd you like to meet my father, Henry?"

"Sure," he said. "That would be fine. We have a lot in common. We're both in the drug business." He laughed, not bitterly this time, but to show her that he thought the situation quite funny.

"I mean it," she said. "I think he'd like you. Especially if I told him to. He's coming to New York next week-end and I'm going to cut classes next Saturday. Why not meet us?"

"You know," he said slowly. "Why not? What've I got to lose?"

That had been the beginning. Henry, like a restive colt, hadn't been too easy to handle at first. Pride, his independence, his knowledge that one of the richest girls in America took a special interest in him, a very special interest in him, made him suspicious. But she could wait. Henry had said that maybe he wanted too much. That was the key with which she'd unlock his heart. With the world in his grasp, his pride couldn't hold out. And when that had crumbled she'd have what she wanted.

She remembered that almost comical scene with Sally Hunt, not long after the dance. Sally had come to her room one afternoon, somewhat hesitant, but with determination clouding her pretty, usually cheerful face.

"Leona, there's something I've got to talk to you about."

Leona was bending over a couple of suitcases on her bed. She looked up at Sally, saying peevishly, "Well—say it, for goodness' sake, and get it over with. I'm leaving for Chicago in a few minutes."

Sally had stared at the floor for a moment, then abruptly lifted her eyes and leveled them at Leona. "You've been seeing a lot of Henry these past few weeks, Leona, and there's something . . ." She hesitated.

"Yes?" Leona was obviously scornful.

"There's something I felt—I thought—I ought to tell you."

"You said that before. And I say, out with it."

"He's not the type—to play around with, Leona. Don't play around with him any more—please."

"And who says I'm playing around with him?" Leona wanted to know, stalking to her closet for another armful of clothes.

"Oh—Leona—he's not your kind—any more than the others . . ."

Leona stopped dead in her tracks. "I like your nerve . . ."

But Sally went on earnestly, "If you don't stop now, you'll regret it, Leona. Henry's not right for you. I've known him almost all my life. My father's helped him. My whole family has treated him almost as though he were one of us. And he's all right when one of us is near him—to sort of look after him. But he's—he's all sort of twisted up inside. He's sweet and kind and gentle—for a while, and then he has—moods. He wants things he can't get. And deep down inside of him it drives him wild. That's when he needs—us. Oh, I suppose I do love him. But the understanding is more important than the love. He isn't safe with someone who doesn't understand him. He's done things that—that would get him into all kinds of trouble if people didn't know about him."

Leona laughed recklessly. "It's a nice trick, but it'll get you nowhere, Sally. You just can't stand the competition. As a matter of fact, I think a great deal of Henry Stevenson. And I understand him. And I happen to think he's much too good for that town of yours. If I want to show him a good time, introduce him to certain people, that's my business. If I want to marry him—that's my business, too."

"Marry him!" Sally gasped. "You don't mean that. You're kidding."

Leona smiled complacently. "Is there any good reason why I shouldn't?"

Sally had folded up after that, she remembered as she stirred restlessly on the bed. There hadn't been much fight in Sally. And a lot of good it would have done her if there had been.

Fight hadn't done Jim Cotterell much good, either, although he'd struggled like a steer at branding time.

"But the fellow has nothing," Jim had said a year later, a hint of pleading in his rumbling voice. "Sure, he's a well set-up lad. But he's an ordinary kid—common as rocks—a dime a dozen. After all the money I've spent on your education—taken you abroad—given you everything you've ever wanted—why do you want to throw yourself away?"

"I love him," Leona said clearly, staring her father in the eye.

"Rubbish!" Jim bellowed. "You're just being stubborn."

She argued with him stubbornly to establish once and for all that she wasn't being stubborn. She loved Henry. She said it repeatedly. But Jim knew better. She loved Henry the same way she'd loved that Bugatti roadster, he'd roared.

"The trouble with you," Leona blazed, "is that you don't want me to marry anybody. You only want me to say here, and stay home—with you."

Defiance stiffened her whole body as she stood there. Jim, looking miserable, walked up and down the length of his den, his beefy face almost purple with dismay and displeasure.

"It's not true—not at all," he said, halting before her. "You know I'd give you anything in this world. I've always given you what you wanted—let you do what you wanted to do, without any thought of my own feelings. But this time it's different. Marriage is a big thing for a girl in your position. I've worked hard. I've built a big business. For me? No! First for your mother, now for you. When I die, you'll get it all. And I wouldn't want to see some dumb cluck get his hands on it just because you'd saddled yourself with him. At a time when you were too wrought up to think properly, too.

"Listen to me, honey," he went on. "You must think about this some more. Give yourself a year—say—to see if this lad wears well. See him as much as you want. And then, if you still want him . . ."

His reasonableness only fueled her impatience.

"You're hateful!" she cried. "Selfish and hateful. You don't care about me. You're thinking only of yourself and that hateful old business. You've taken a dislike to Henry simply because you think he'll interfere with your selfish plans. Suppose he *is* a country boy. What were you when you started—down there in Texas?"

She was trembling with rage. She gloated at the immediate concern that spread swiftly over Jim's face.

"Take it easy, honey," he begged. "You'll make yourself sick."

"Sick!" she shouted. "Make myself sick! You're the only one who's making me sick. You and your wonderful business and your wonderful money. You don't care if they drive me into my grave, just so they're safe and nobody takes them away from you."

She began to sob, and Jim tried to put his arm around her. She moved away from him, sinking dejectedly into a chair. "I—I don't want to talk about it any more," she said sadly through the tears. "I don't feel very well . . ." And then, with furious concentration, she had managed to faint, hearing, as she approached the welcome dark, her father frantically summoning the butler.

The wedding had been a well-oiled, richly caparisoned triumph. She recalled readily the exultant, passionately possessive vibrance with which she had uttered, "I—Leona—take thee—Henry—"

And Henry's bearing had measured up to her hopes. Neither nervous—nor overly relaxed—his manner had charmed the wedding guests. Already he had begun to absorb the soothing, emollient effects of contact with endless luxury. If within himself there were any lingering doubts, any reservations, she'd quickly disperse them. For the present he carried himself perfectly, and she was proud.

Even Jim had seemed, for a few moments at least, to warm to the scene. But she knew his smiling, tired face hid much misery. Jim would never completely accept Henry. Never. No matter how hard he tried.

All of this had occupied her thoughts during the wedding and after at the breakfast in Jim's great house. To her Henry was a project undertaken, an equation to be solved. She intended to solve the equation, complete the project at any cost. In the end Jim would have to admit his mistake. The pleasure of that victory not yet won bubbled merrily in her brain as she deftly— unseen by anyone—guided Henry's hand through the maze of silverware that gleamed on the breakfast table.

During the long European honeymoon that followed she had been pleased by the unembarrassed ease with which Henry submitted to her teaching. There was no doubt that the limitless offering of luxury she made to him, coupled with her lacquered good looks and the exceptional willingness of her body, had disarmed him. He accepted her teaching with good grace, even with appreciation. If she insisted upon choosing his clothes, and the way in which he was to wear them, it was a matter for delight rather than annoyance or indifference. He seemed quick to realize how important these things really were in her world, how much more comfortable he could feel if his appearance was correct, his manner beyond reproach. And he was not unaware of the way his rugged, husky handsomeness was set off by all this careful grooming.

Leona watched him settle into a life in which the past—whatever it had been—vanished, or so she thought. It didn't really matter. The important thing was that he would in time become so entranced with the life she sketched for him that no power would ever be strong enough to challenge its values. Which was the way she wanted things to be.

A look of triumph—a smile of smug satisfaction—played over her worn and fretful features as she lay there thinking of what had happened since the night Sally Hunt introduced her to Henry.

Just then she heard a throaty blast from one of the ships in the river. The smile faded as she started up, glancing at the medicine bottles on the night table, at the clock next to them. As she did so the telephone came to life, startling her.

9:55

It was Sally.

"I'm sorry I had to be so silly and mysterious just now," she said. "I couldn't talk. I was afraid my husband would overhear me. So I found an excuse to slip out to this phone booth."

"Well," Leona said, "it certainly was odd, to say the least."

"You'll probably think the whole thing is peculiar, Leona— hearing from me after all these years. But I had to see Henry again today. I've been so terribly worried about him."

"Worried? Why, may I ask, should you be worried about Henry? I hope you'll remember, Sally, it never was much use trying to pull the wool over my eyes."

"I'm not trying to do anything—but help. This may be very serious—deadly serious for Henry. It's a little difficult to explain. I 'll try to tell you as quickly as I can."

"Please do," Leona said brusquely.

"Well—Fred, my husband, is an investigator for the District Attorney's office . . ."

"How cozy!" Leona murmured.

"About three weeks ago he showed me a newspaper clipping about you and Henry. It was something or other from the Society page . . ."

"I remember."

". . . and he wanted to know if that wasn't the Henry Stevenson who'd once been my beau."

"Your beau?" Leona said. "How quaint!"

"I told him it was, and Fred laughed and said, 'Well, what d'y' know.' Then he stuffed the clipping in his pocket. I asked him what was so unusual about seeing Henry's name in the paper. He just smiled and said it was a coincidence—something to do with a case he was on."

"A case!"

"Yes. He said it wasn't anything he could talk about—just a hunch. I tried to worm some more out of him. But he started kidding me about still being in love with Henry . . ."

"Which, of course, you denied," Leona said sarcastically.

"Why, of course—" Sally sputtered. "What a ridiculous thing to say after all these years!"

"Do go on—"

"We were almost finished breakfast by that time. The phone rang. It was one of Fred's men—one of the men from the D.A.'s office. I heard Fred say something about 'Stevenson' and someone who sounded like 'Harpootlian.' Fred said, 'Well, sure we'll go. Tell Harpootlian to set it up. Make it Thursday, around 10:30, at the South Ferry change booth.' "

Sally paused for a moment, and Leona blurted angrily, "Look, Sally. This is all very interesting. But can't you get to the point?

Henry may be trying to call me at this very moment. Anyway, what possible connection can there be between Henry and all this rubbish about your husband?"

"I'm telling you as quickly as I can," Sally wailed. "But it's sort of complicated and I've got to tell you the whole story. I wouldn't bother you, Leona, if it wasn't important."

"Well—" Leona sighed in resignation, "what next?"

"I—I followed them—"

"You what—?"

"I followed them. That Thursday morning. I know it's hard to believe—it sounds so crazy—but I was frightened. I wanted to know what was going on. After all, I'd known Henry almost all his life. I—well—there are things about him that are rather strange. I tried to tell you once, years ago."

Leona made impatient little noises. "Really," she said. "But really—is all this necessary? If you're trying to alarm me, Sally, you might as well stop right now."

Sally's reply was even more forlorn. "Please don't be so suspicious of me," she pleaded. "I'm only telling you what happened because it may have something to do with Henry's absence tonight. I don't know for sure. But let me finish . . ."

"By all means," Leona said. "As quickly as you can."

"It was drizzling that morning. I was carrying an umbrella, so that it shielded my face most of the time, although I don't think that made much difference. It's not hard to follow people— especially in the rain.

"I saw Fred meet two men—one of them was Joe Harris who works with Fred most of the time, the other was a dark, heavy-set fellow with wavy white hair. I suppose he was this man, Harpootlian, Fred had mentioned.

"I waited in the distance until they had moved with the crowd toward the ferry. Then I bought a ticket and followed. It wasn't hard to keep out of sight on the ferry. I spent most of the trip in the john, anyway."

"How lovely!" Leona sneered.

"Well, it was the best place . . . Oh, well," Sally continued doggedly, "after they left the ferry at Staten Island they got on the train. I was right behind them. Not in the same car, of course . . ."

"Of course!" Leona echoed.

". . . but a couple of cars away. I watched for them to get

off, and when they did I did too. It was still drizzling and nobody paid any attention to me. Most people were hurrying along, anxious to get out of the rain, I imagine."

"Very observant—" Leona said.

"This place was a sort of beach colony, Leona. It looked terribly run down and empty. The streets were all crooked and badly paved. They were covered in spots with drifts of sand. The houses were mostly shacks and right in the center of them was a boarded-up casino. After Fred and the two men had walked off toward the beach I went over to the casino and watched from a corner of the porch. I had a good view from there. And nobody was likely to notice me in the shadows."

"Really!" Leona said, "am I really expected to . . . ?"

"It's true! It's true!" Sally exclaimed. "I told you it would sound crazy . . ."

"Crazy is hardly the word . . ."

"There was only one person besides Fred and the two men in sight—a boy digging clams by the water's edge. The man with the white hair seemed to stop for a moment and stare at the boy, and the boy moved his head just a trifle toward something in the distance. Then he went on digging, and the men walked over to a luncheonette and went inside."

Leona, fuming with indignation, interrupted, crying, "For heaven's sake, Sally, must you go on like this? Can't you tell me what it's all about without dragging me all over Staten Island? Or are you deliberately keeping me on the phone for some other reason?"

Sally reassured her. "You've got to hear it all. Do you think I like being cooped up in this stuffy booth? The man who owns the store keeps looking over here all the time. He's angry because he wants to close up.

"Anyway," she continued, "I waited there in the drizzle for about an hour and nothing happened. Then, just as I was thinking I'd been a terrible fool for taking that awful trip, I saw something very strange. The boy who'd been digging clams stood up and stretched his arms as though he were yawning. A little while after that I heard a motor boat roaring off the shore, and soon I could see the boat speeding toward the land. When it got near it slowed down and headed for a broken-down wharf next to one of the weirdest houses in the whole place.

"I wish you could have seen that house, Leona. Old as the

hills, and slightly lopsided. I suppose its foundation has been sinking for years. It's a scary-looking, scroll-work sort of place, like one of those Charles Addams houses—in the *New Yorker*, you know."

"Please," Leona said, *"will* you get to the point!"

"Well, the boat went to this wharf and a little hunchbacked man hopped out and tied it up. Then a tall, heavy, middle-aged man climbed out of the boat. He was dressed all in black except for a Panama hat, and he was carrying a brief case under his arm. The minute he was safely off the boat the little hunchback started up the motor and raced away.

"The man in black walked down the wharf and into the old house. A moment later the clam-digger picked up his pail and shovel and started toward the luncheonette. I noticed that when he passed there he stumbled, knocking the pail of clams against the luncheonette door. It must have been a signal. He went on down the beach, and Fred and the others slipped out of the luncheonette and walked up to the old house. The man with the white hair knocked, the door opened, and in they went.

"I still don't understand any of it, Leona—who those people were, or what was happening in that house . . ."

"A brothel, no doubt," Leona suggested sarcastically.

". . . but I know they were in there for a good half hour. When they came out, Fred was carrying that brief case—the one the man in black had brought!"

"All right," Leona said, "Fred was carrying a brief case. What next?"

"I don't know," Sally said feebly. "After that I had to hurry to get home—ahead of Fred, of course. But I know," she added vigorously, "that we've got to do something . . . before it's too late!"

Before Leona could reply, a coin clunked to the bottom of the box and the operator interrupted. Sally's five minutes were up. Leona could hear her muttering as she ransacked her purse. Finally she said, "Here it is, operator." And then, "Leona, Leona—are you still there?"

"Yes, I'm here," Leona said suspiciously. "This is all very strange, I must say."

"I know," Sally agreed. "It's very strange to me. I couldn't believe it. I couldn't connect Henry with—with the kinds of crimes Fred investigates. That's why I went to see him today— to find out the truth from him."

"And did you?" Leona asked grimly.

"I saw him—you know that—but I couldn't find out anything. I didn't have a chance."

"But you went out with him," Leona said. "His secretary saw you."

"Yes, I went out with him. He wasn't very enthused about it either. Of course I didn't exactly expect him to jump for joy. But he was—hardly civil. He seemed terribly preoccupied. I'd known him to be that way as a boy, and it was usually when he was—well—going through some sort of conflict with himself.

"He asked me if I'd like a bite of lunch with him, and we went to the Georgian Room at the Metropolis. Almost as soon as we sat down a man named Freeman—Bill Freeman—a prosperous-looking elderly man—came over and started to talk stock market with Henry."

"Freeman?" Leona said. "I'm sure we don't know any Mr. Freeman—"

"Henry didn't seem to want to talk about it. But Mr. Freeman kept right on. I got the idea that something very serious had occurred in some stock or other that morning. Henry said, 'You've got to be wrong some time,' and Freeman laughed and said, '*Some time*, Stevenson? You've had more than a little tough luck, I'd say. But a man in your position can take plenty of punishment. Now me, I've got to be careful. I'm just a small potato.'

"Henry didn't eat much, and neither did I. What bothered me was that with Mr. Freeman there, talking about his troubles, I couldn't say a word. Finally we got up to go, and Freeman left. Henry and I walked into the lobby of the hotel. Henry said he was sorry, he had an appointment in a few minutes, and why didn't I call *you*, Leona, some time and perhaps we could all get together. He didn't seem to mean it, though. Not really. We were standing near the entrance of a broker's branch office in the hotel, and a dried-up little man came out and called to Henry, 'Oh, Mr. Stevenson, I'd like to see you as soon as possible.' Henry turned very pale, it seemed to me, and he said to the little man, 'All right, Mr. Hanshaw, I'll be with you directly.' He said good-bye to me rather hurriedly and I watched him walk into the broker's office. On the door it said, T. F. Hanshaw, Manager."

"Well—he must—he must have said *something* to you," Leona sputtered. "I'm sure he didn't sit there and talk stocks and bonds—about which he knows nothing—every single solitary minute."

"Oh," Sally said, "I *did* ask him if he was happy, and how he enjoyed his work. He said, 'Fine—fine. I'm a big vice-president now. I push more buttons than anybody—except all the other vice-presidents.' He was trying to be funny, but I could tell the bitterness that he really felt. I started to ask him something about it, and that was when Mr. Freeman came over."

"I don't understand this at all." Leona's sneering skepticism was plain. "When Henry left me this morning he was quite his usual self, I assure you. We've been awfully happy for more than ten years—awfully happy. Henry hasn't had a care in the world. Daddy saw to that. And as far as his business association is concerned, I'm quite sure it's most suitable for Henry. You must have mistaken his remarks—if he made them at all. I'm still not so certain this isn't some kind of game you're trying to play with me, Sally."

Again, before Sally could reply, the operator said, brightly, "Your five minutes are up, madam. Please deposit five cents for the next five minutes."

Sally fished in her bag, saying at last, despairingly, "I haven't another nickel. I'll have to call you back when I get change." Then she added in a rush, "I only want to say—I know now— that Henry *is* in trouble. Fred's working on some kind of report tonight. The case, whatever it is, seems to be coming to a head. He's been telephoning. I've heard Henry's name over and over again. And there's somebody else in it, too—somebody named Evans."

"Your five minutes are up, madam," said the operator.

"Waldo Evans," Sally hurried on breathlessly. "I think that's the name I saw on that Staten Island house . . ."

"Your five minutes are *up*, madam."

10:05

As soon as Sally had hung up, Leona reached for the crumpled bit of paper on which she'd found Sally's phone number. There it was. "Mr. Evans. Richmond 8:1112." She carefully dialed the number, surprised when the operator interrupted after a brief interval to ask, "Are you calling W. Evans, Richmond 8 : 1112?"

"Why, yes," Leona said apprehensively. "That's right."

"That number . . . has been disconnected."

She sat bolt upright in bed, laying the phone down on its cradle, staring into space—her eyes wide and bewildered. The events of this strange evening chased each other madly through her brain. Henry's absence, the killers on the telephone, Miss Jennings, Sally's crazy tale—none of it made sense. And yet, somehow, there was disaster, danger in the air. Perhaps Henry *was* in trouble. Perhaps there *were* things she'd never suspected going on. The thought that she should be alone in this nerve-racking quandary encouraged a rising tide of self-pity. Why had all this to happen tonight—the one night when she had no one—not even a servant—near her? It was too much. Entirely too much for an invalid to bear. Her lips quivering, she dialed the Long Distance Operator and placed a call for Jim Cotterell in Chicago.

The Chicago operator repeated the number, and soon Leona could hear the phone in Jim Cotterell's house ringing. Someone picked it up, and Leona called, "Hello," but she was instantly cut off. The silence angered her and she made little sounds of exasperation. Seconds went by and then the operator said smoothly, "Mr. Cotterell is not at the Lake Forest number, madam. I will try to locate him for you."

"What?" Leona asked irritably.

"I will call you back, madam," the operator replied, and rang off.

Defeated by her father's habit of running off to night clubs, or all-night card games, she cast about again for someone in whom she could confide her anxiety. It was difficult—being almost a total stranger in New York—to select someone close at hand. The paucity of choice was maddening.

At last she thought of the doctor—Doctor Alexander. Just the person. He'd examined her several times. He'd made several tests, the results of which she still didn't know. She could send for him, and he'd have to come. At least she'd have someone near her for a while.

She groped for the phone, halting the action while another train rolled noisily over the bridge. It was awful—that confounded racket. How foolish, she thought, to live in a city where no one, no matter who he might be, could find peace and quiet. She thought, too, of the train the killer had mentioned (How like this one it must be!) and she shuddered. It was best not to remind herself of that horrible thing.

The noise of the train died away and she made another movement toward the telephone. It chose that moment to ring and she picked it up.

It was the man Evans. She had no difficulty in recognizing immediately the weary, hollow, cultured voice.

"Is Mr. Stevenson there?" he asked.

"No," she said. "Is this Mr. Evans?"

"Yes, Mrs. Stevenson."

She said crisply, "First of all—I want to know the truth about this Staten Island business. I've just heard about it tonight— and I'm nervous enough as it is—what with Mr. Stevenson not being here—and then getting all sorts of strange calls—including two murderers—" She broke off, mystified.

As she talked, she had become increasingly aware of a far-off, whining sound in the telephone. It came from wherever Mr. Evans was. As she listened its volume grew. It sounded like something she had heard many times before—whenever fire apparatus or police cars careened along the city streets. Nervously she called, "Are you still there, Mr. Evans?"

The sound grew louder and again she cried, "Mr. Evans—? Are you still there?"

There was no reply save the whining sound, and in despair she hung up. Immediately the phone rang.

"Hello? Mr. Evans?" she asked quickly. There was no answer. Instead she heard a rushing, grinding roar more frightening than before.

"Mr. Evans—" she called again, loudly, to be answered only by rolling thunder.

Almost hysterically she cried, "Hello! Who's there? Who's calling?" She paused a moment, then cried, "Why don't you answer me?" Again she paused. Then, as no voice arose over the mysterious din, the floodgates of hysteria broke and she screamed, "ANSWER ME!"

From far off, almost buried by the continuous roar, she heard a faint voice say, "Leona—?"

Frightened, Leona asked, "Who's *that*?"

The noise seemed to retreat now and, more distinctly, the

voice said, "It's Sally. I'm phoning from a subway station. All the stores close in this neighborhood at ten o'clock. I had to speak to you, so I came down here. I've been home, Leona—since I spoke to you—and *more* has happened."

Leona, her face strained and tense, said, "This time, Sally, please get it all out, or don't bother me any more. I've listened to just about enough tonight."

"There was a police car standing in front of the house when I got home," Sally told her in a rush. "That house on Staten Island burned down this afternoon. The police surrounded it. They captured three men. But this Evans man escaped."

"But who is Evans? What's his connection with Henry?" Leona asked.

"I still haven't found out, Leona. But I do know the whole thing has something to do with your father's company . . ."

"My father's company? But—that's absurd. My father called me from Chicago tonight and he never mentioned a thing."

She stopped, waiting for the noise of another train to subside. Then she continued, "Now look, let's get this thing straight. Who's been arrested? And why?"

"Three men," Sally answered. "I don't know why."

"And why do you think Henry's one of them?"

"I didn't say he was," Sally said. "I only know he's terribly involved."

Leona's exasperation grew. "Did they say he'd been arrested —or was going to be?"

"No, not exactly."

"Then—what are you talking about?" Leona asked furiously. "Why are you calling me like this? Don't you realize you're frightening me to death?"

"I know, but—"

". . . first I picked up my phone and overheard two horrible murderers . . ."

"Murderers—!"

". . . planning to kill a woman . . . then this creature, Evans, calls me, sounding as though he was talking from the grave . . . then everybody else is either busy or disconnected . . . and now you—for no good reason at all . . ."

"I'm sorry—"

". . . for no good reason at all . . ." She paused for breath.

"Are you jealous that I took him away from you? Can't you bear to see me happy?"

"Really, Leona . . ."

"Can't you stop telling lies and making trouble even now? I don't believe a word of it—do you hear?—not a word of it. He's innocent. He's on his way home to me—right now!"

Before she could say any more, Sally hung up.

She lay there fluttering her fingers, wondering if she had been right in allowing herself the luxury of that screaming moment. Despite everything, Sally might really know something that involved danger for Henry. But what? Money? All that talk about the stock market? It was hard to understand. She knew that no one dabbled in the market without money. Henry had no money. His salary as a vice-president of the Cotterell Company was not large, and most of it went into the household expenses which he insisted on paying. His pride made him do that, just as his pride had been responsible for that silly episode of the apartment—the apartment he had wanted to rent for her when they were living with her father in Chicago. No, Henry really had nothing. It was all right for him to keep the house going. But the heavy expenses were still borne by Jim Cotterell.

She couldn't see any opportunity Henry might have had to play the financier. Even the investments Jim kept turning over to her—to reduce the death taxes that some day would be levied against his estate—were registered in her name, untouchable as far as Henry was concerned. Unless, of course, she died. If she died they'd be Henry's. Her will took care of that—and she was glad for Henry's sake. But what a morbid thought—at this time! She'd put that out of her mind at once. It was too frightening.

But there must be some reason behind Sally's outlandish tale. Unless it was pure fantasy on Sally's part. Unless Sally had some obscure, demented idea of hurting her because of the past. Suppose she had. Was she capable of concocting the story she'd just told? And if she was, why tell it on this particular night?

The mystery grew in her mind, swirling about in clouds of conjecture. Tiny, frightful suspicions blossomed and refused to die. Each hideous thought bred another, and her imagination became a screen across which flashed a succession of fiendishly logical possibilities. Suppose! Suppose! Like nightmares, their overpowering terror brought about sharp physical reaction. Her heart began to beat faster, painfully faster. In breathing she found it was only with effort that she could force the air from her lungs. Trembling, she found her handkerchief and mopped hurriedly at the clammy evidences of fright on her face. She no longer tried to understand what had happened to Henry—or what might have happened. Her concern for herself outweighed all else. The thought of chaos to come, of the toppling of her little edifice of deceit, was unbearable. She had started to rock in agony on the bed when the telephone again shrilled into action.

"Is this Plaza 9:2265?" a man asked.

"Yes, what is it?" she said shakily, almost in a whisper.

"This is Western Union. I have a message for Mrs. Henry Stevenson. Is there any one there to receive the message?"

"This is Mrs. Stevenson."

"The telegram is as follows: 'Mrs. Henry Stevenson, 43 Sutton Place, New York, New York. Darling, terribly sorry, but decided attend Boston meeting at last minute. Stop. Taking train out. Stop. Back Sunday morning. Stop. Tried to call you but line always busy. Stop. Keep well, happy. Love. Henry.'"

10:15

Dumbfounded, she sat there, her hand moving toward her mouth in a gesture of despair. The Western Union operator wanted to know if a copy of the message was to be delivered and she said, "No, it's—not—necessary," in a faint voice and mechanically replaced the phone. Now she could hear another grinding roar from the bridge and, as in a dream, she slipped from the bed and tottered to the window. One hand on the casement, she looked out at the great Gothic outlines of the bridge silhouetted against the night. Now she could see the train, a long column of segmented light, moving wormlike on to the bridge, its clatter growing louder as it swung toward her, louder and louder and louder, then diminishing as it swung back and away. She could feel the window casement tremble under her hand. She stood there as though hypnotized. Shreds of talk drifted through her mind, *"Then I wait . . . until the train goes over the bridge . . . our client says the coast is clear*

*. . . got your message, George, everything okay for tonight?
. . . Where's Henry? Business. What business? . . . sometimes days have gone by when Mr. Stevenson hasn't come in
. . . Henry is in trouble . . . desperate trouble . . . darling,
terribly sorry, taking next train out . . . then I wait until a
train goes over the bridge . . . then I wait until a train goes
over the bridge . . .*

With a moan she wrenched herself back to reality, weaving
back to the bed, clutching at the impersonal coolness of the
telephone. The depth of her urgency was translated into the
nervous force with which she spun the dial.

Over the babble of voices in the apartment's small, bare living
room a fan droned steadily, its blast directed at the telephone
switchboard that lined one wall. It offered comfort to the four
girls seated at the board busily working telephone plugs, pressing keys, swiftly writing down the messages that later would be
relayed to the Answering Service's customers. On a couch near
the open windows a fifth operator was resting. If she turned her
head toward the windows she could look out on the stark fire
escape, with one bedraggled geranium tilting crazily in a pot in
one corner. Not being a nature-lover, however, the girl lay and
watched the others working out their tours of duty. At a signal,
she stood up and slid into a seat at the switchboard as the other
operator slid out. She slipped the tape of a suspension mouthpiece around her neck and adjusted the receiver over her hair.
Her eye caught the first winking light, and she went to work,
saying, "No, madam, Doctor Alexander is not in. May I take the
message?"

She listened for a moment, her face a picture of alarm. "What
is that, madam? No—I couldn't say . . . If you'll give me your
name and telephone number? Yes, madam. Yes—Mrs. Stevenson. Mrs. Henry Stevenson. Plaza 9:2265. I'll certainly try to
reach him."

Dr. Alexander laid his cards down, arranging them in long,
neat rows with his long, neat hands.

"There you are, partner," he said, smiling across the table.
"See what you can do with that."

"Perfect!"

"I thought it would be—if I understood your bidding." He
turned to his hostess, who sat at his left. "Excuse me for a

couple of minutes, will you, Mona? I'd like to call—"

"Of course, Philip," she said. "You know where the phone is—?"

"I'm afraid . . ." he said, rising.

"Right across the hall in the den. You'll see the phone on Harry's desk. Can't miss it."

"Now I remember," he said, "how stupid of me . . ."

Long strides took his erect figure swiftly out of the room. The two women at the bridge table involuntarily turned to watch him go. He commanded much attention from women. As a consequence he also commanded fat fees—deservedly fat, for his skill was at least the equal of his imposing personality.

As he sat now at the desk, the telephone in front of him, the lamplight cut attractive shadows under the lean planes of his face. It was a hawklike face, vigorous, healthy, with lines deepened by time and humor at the corners of his gray eyes and around his thin lips. His hair was a thick dark shock neatly graying at the temples. He was, as so many prosaic husbands had remarked when prosaically footing the bills, an Arrow Collar medico—a screen character armed with a scalpel instead of a script. But they had to admit he was good—even though their wives often acquired a dreamy, beyond-the-horizon kind of look along with the look of health.

Mechanically he dialed the Answering Service, thinking how pleasant it would be if nothing were to disturb his evening. He was enjoying himself—a rare thing for even successful medical men.

"Doctor Alexander," he said to the girl who answered. "Anything for me—and I hope there isn't?"

"Oh—there *is*, Doctor," she told him. "A Mrs. Stevenson. Mrs. Henry Stevenson. Very ill and worried, she said. One of your heart patients, she said. She sounded kind of frantic to me."

"Anything else?" he asked.

"No, Doctor, just Mrs. Stevenson."

"Fine," he said. "I'll call Mrs. Stevenson right away."

He took a small, beautifully bound notebook from a pocket of his dinner jacket and picked out Leona's telephone number. He hesitated before dialing, thinking despairingly that this might be a bothersome call. Mrs. Stevenson was inclined to be imperious. She was also inclined to be imperious at great length, and he had no desire now to listen to her interminable elaborations of her condition. Evidently she had frightened the girl at the Answering Service, although there was little chance— Well, grin and bear it, he thought. It can't be too bad, since by this time she must know the real state of affairs.

He dialed the number.

Leona answered the phone in the instant of its first ring. Whimpering one moment, belligerent the next, she flooded his ear with her troubles.

"I'm terribly, terribly frightened," she said weakly. "My heart feels as though it had a clamp around it. The palpitation is so painful—I—I can't bear it. My lungs feel as though they'll burst if I take a deep breath. And I can't stop trembling. I can hardly hold this phone, it's so bad."

"Oh—come—come, Mrs. Stevenson," he said soothingly. "I'm sure it's not that bad. Where's your maid tonight? Can't she sit with you? I'm sure that if someone were there with you you wouldn't be suffering."

"There's no one here—no one," Leona cried. "And I'm not well. I know I'm not well. I want you to come here tonight. You're my doctor and I need you now—tonight."

"Why—I'm afraid I can't," he told her, still professionally silken. "I'd come if I thought it was necessary—but I know that it isn't. You're just having a bad case of nerves, that's all. If you'll force yourself to relax and sit quietly for a few minutes you'll see how much better you'll feel. If you wish, take a couple of bromides. They'll help quiet your nerves."

Leona cried, "But you know I'm a sick woman. What have I been coming to you for all these months? How can you refuse to see me now, when I need you? What kind of a doctor are you, anyway?"

His jaw set grimly. This was going a bit too far, even for the rich Mrs. Stevenson. "Look here, Mrs. Stevenson," he said briskly. "Don't you think it's about time you faced this thing squarely and began to co-operate with your husband and me?"

"What are you talking about?" she asked. "What do you mean—co-operate?"

Her question took him aback. "What am I talking about? Why, Mrs. Stevenson, you know as well as I do. I explained it all to your husband—a week ago."

"My husband? You must be trying to aggravate me like all the rest of them. I assure you my husband hasn't said a word to me . . ."

Doctor Alexander was becoming more and more puzzled. "Surely your husband . . . I told him the whole story . . . He promised . . . And he hasn't said a *thing?*"

"What whole story?" Leona demanded. "What story? What is all this mystery?"

Doctor Alexander paused. This was rather confusing.

"Well, that's very, very strange indeed, Mrs. Stevenson. I discussed your case with him—completely—about ten days ago. He came to my office."

"And what did you tell him, Doctor?"

"Really, dear lady, there's hardly time to go into all that now. If you will compose yourself—get some sleep—perhaps we can discuss it tomorrow."

"You'll discuss it now—NOW! Do you hear me!" Leona shrieked. "How do you suppose I could get through this night not knowing—wondering what kind of terrible thing is going to happen to me next? I won't hear of you . . ."

Doctor Alexander shrugged his shoulders, and arched a cynical eyebrow at the telephone.

"All right, Mrs. Stevenson. If you will hold the phone for one moment . . ."

He laid the phone on the desk and walked out of the den back to the living room. In the doorway he stopped. The hand had been played and they were waiting for him.

"I'm sorry," he told them. "I'm going to be a few minutes longer . . ."

"Another of your conquests, Philip?" his partner said with a shade too much gaiety in her voice.

"Of course. But I'll only be a little while. Hate to hold up the rubber this way, though."

He returned to the den. "Thank you for waiting, Mrs. Stevenson," he said.

"I hope you'll clear up this mystery at once," she demanded, sulkily. "I had no idea that my husband had been consulting you."

"He came to my office to hear my diagnosis of your condition. He told me that he had been warned by your father about your heart—that you were subject to attacks, had been since childhood. He said, in response to my questions, that you had long periods of good health, that he didn't know anything about a heart condition before he married you. Your father told him on your wedding day. It was quite a shock."

"My father is inclined to be—rather blunt."

"Your husband said that you hadn't had any attack until about a month after your return from the honeymoon. Is that right, Mrs. Stevenson?"

"Yes," she said. "I remember that. I was sorry it happened."

"Your husband told me that it had happened because he wanted to break away from your father's firm, and you wouldn't hear of it."

"I—I suppose it was that," Leona agreed. "Henry wanted—quite foolishly, of course—to get out on his own. He's impetuous that way—at times."

"According to him it was more than that, Mrs. Stevenson."

"Oh? More?"

"Yes, I believe there had been some friction with your father —hadn't there?"

"Well, yes . . ." she admitted grudgingly. "Henry had the idea that Dad was not giving him sufficient responsibility. A ridiculous notion."

"Your husband didn't seem to think so."

"Just the same, it was ridiculous. Why, Dad even made Henry a vice-president and gave him one of the most beautiful offices . . ."

"At any rate, he quarreled with your father and then with you. And you became gravely ill."

"Yes," she said. "I can't stand quarrels."

"Your husband apparently guessed that," the doctor said dryly. "He didn't care for them either—after that. He seems to be a pretty strong man—and shrewd, if I may say so. At any rate he said there were no further attacks until he surprised you with that apartment—the one he wanted you to live in."

"Oh—yes," she said. "He was very foolish. He wanted to take me away from my father's home and live in a place he had rented. Poor Henry. He knew nothing about such things. He hadn't begun to appreciate how wonderful it was living with my father, with no problems of making a home. Dad never bothered us. It was just that Henry had some silly idea about being the man of the house—like some ordinary bookkeeper or salesman in the suburbs."

"You quarreled about that too, didn't you?"

"Yes," she said. "And, although I tried not to be, I was terribly sick."

"That coincides with your husband's story," Doctor Alexander said. "It made him determined not to cross you again. But you went into a decline after that, and you've got worse—he says—until now you're almost a permanent invalid. Naturally he wanted to know what to expect in the future."

"I'm sure he was upset," Leona said. "He's always watched over me. He's very much in love with me."

Doctor Alexander coughed. "I agreed with him that he hadn't any picnic. I asked him if he had ever thought of leaving you." He heard Leona gasp, and hurried on. "He looked up as though shocked. Said he hadn't considered it. I told him that in my view that was what you needed, Mrs. Stevenson. Obviously he'd been the cause of all your emotional disturbances for these past ten years. If he dropped out of the picture you might improve at once."

"That's—that's horrible of you—just horrible," she whispered tearfully.

"He thought it might kill you," the doctor went on calmly. "But of course I reassured him on that point. I told him you'd probably make a pretty frightening scene, but in the long run you'd pull out of it—as you would, I'm sure. In other words, I told him the truth, dear lady. There's nothing wrong with your heart . . ."

"What!"

"That's right, Mrs. Stevenson. Organically your heart is as sound as a bell."

"How can you say such a thing?" she raged. "You know I'm a sick woman . . ."

"It's not the kind of sickness you thought," he said. "It's in your mind . . ."

"My *mind!* I think you're in league with—with those others to *wreck* my mind."

"Please, Mrs. Stevenson, you must be reasonable. Nobody is trying to harm you."

"They are!" she cried. "They are!"

"I'm sure I don't know what you're talking about," he said easily. "May I suggest that you discuss this whole thing with Mr. Stevenson . . . ?"

"Discuss it? How can I discuss it? He isn't here. I don't know where he is."

"Perhaps tomorrow will be time. . . ."

"Oh, you . . ."

He could almost feel the shock as she banged the receiver back in place. The dial tone hummed in his ear for an instant. He lowered the phone part way, his hand poised over the dial on the desk. Call her back? No. He smiled cynically, shrugged his shoulders, gently replaced the phone in its cradle. As he started for the door a voice floated in from the other room. "Philip! You've been long enough, darling."

Leona—stunned, incredulous—stared at the telephone instrument, an infernal machine especially designed to torture her beyond endurance. Anger, hurt pride, doubt fought within her. It couldn't be so! Perhaps in her childhood she had exaggerated the seriousness of her illness. But now she was sick! She wasn't pretending! She was sick! She was sick! Her hand went to her heart, pressing it close where the hurt was. She took a deep breath, feeling the sharp, stabbing pain. Alexander was a fool. A brutal fool. The idea of telling her all those terrible things, suggesting that she had caused Henry any real unhappiness. Was he deliberately trying to upset her, to bring on some kind of a crisis? She'd see that he was reported to the Medical Association.

And his lies about Henry! They were lies, all right, and she'd make Henry face the doctor with them. They *were* lies. She was a sick woman. And Henry loved her and wanted to help her. It *must* be that way. It couldn't be any other way. It couldn't.

Suddenly her eyes blazed defiantly. She tossed aside the coverlet, swinging one foot to the floor, then the other. She rose to her feet, holding her breath, taking a shaky step toward the window. Her heart was beating crazily. She clutched at her breast as if she could still its fluttering with the pressure of her fingers. And once more the telephone rang!

It was too much! She toppled back upon the bed, gasping for breath, racked with the intensity of her anguish. "Liars!" she sobbed. "Liars . . . liars . . . liars!"

The phone continued to ring, and she turned her stricken face toward it, crying, "I won't talk to anybody. I hate you all!"

But the measured rings mocked her anger. Then, above the ringing she heard a familiar sound. She could feel the faint trembling of the building as another train crossed the bridge. Its closeness restored her to her senses, choked off the feverish impulses that sprang from jangled nerves. Meanwhile the phone rang and rang. She picked it up.

10:30

"Hello," she said, her voice emerging weakly, tearfully.

"Mrs. Stevenson?"

She had no difficulty this time in recognizing his voice. "Yes, Mr. Evans," she said, "this is Mrs. Stevenson."

"Has Mr. Stevenson come in yet?"

"No," she said tautly, "he hasn't. He won't be home until tomorrow." Then explosively she added, "Will you please— please, for goodness' sake, Mr. Evans, tell me what this is all about? Why are you calling him every five minutes?"

Evans said apologetically, "I'm very sorry. I haven't meant to annoy you."

"Well, you are annoying me," she cried. "I insist that you—"

"It's rather a precarious moment—for Mr. Stevenson, that is," Evans said mournfully. "I thought that if you could tell him . . ."

"I can't take any messages now," Leona broke in wildly. "I'm too upset . . ."

"I'm afraid you must try, Mrs. Stevenson. It's very important."

"What right have you . . . ?" she started to ask.

But Evans went on imperturbably, "Please tell Mr. Stevenson that the house at 20 Dunham Terrace—that's D-U-N-H-A-M— 20 Dunham Terrace—has been burned down. I burned it down this afternoon."

"*What?* What's that?" she cried, startled.

"Also—please tell Mr. Stevenson," he continued calmly, "that I do not believe Mr. Morano—the name is spelled M-O-R-A-N-O —betrayed us to the police, as Mr. Morano has already been arrested. And so it is no use trying to raise the money now."

"And—who's Morano?" Leona asked shakily.

Evans ignored her question as he had the others. "Thirdly," he said, "will you please tell Mr. Stevenson that I escaped and am now at the Manhattan address? However I do not expect to be here after midnight—and if he wishes to find me—he may call

Caledonia 5:1133. Will you write that down correctly, please? Caledonia 5:1133."

"But—what is this all about?" she protested.

"And now I believe that is all," Evans said smoothly. "If you will be so good as to repeat it to me—"

"Repeat it to you! I'll do no such thing," she shrilled. "Do you realize that I'm an invalid, Mr. Evans? Dangerously ill? I—I can't stand much more of this . . ."

There was a touch of pity, a quality of understanding in Evans' weary voice as he said, "I am well aware of your unfortunate position, Mrs. Stevenson. In fact I've known all about you for some time."

"You know all about *me*?" Leona said furiously. "Well—I've never in my life heard of *you* before—never!"

With some deference Evans said, "I am very sorry for you, Mrs. Stevenson. But I can assure you the whole affair has not been—ah—entirely Mr. Stevenson's fault."

"For heaven's sake will you stop talking in riddles, please? What has happened?" she demanded.

"Perhaps it *would* be better to tell you," Evans said thoughtfully, "before the true facts are garbled by the—ah—police."

"The—*police* . . . !"

Evans paused for an instant, then said slowly, "Do you have a pencil, Mrs. Stevenson? There are names and places in what I am about to tell you that might prove helpful—if you—ah—were to write them down . . ."

I shall begin with the night when I first became acquainted with Mr. Stevenson (said Evans). I believe the exact date of the meeting was October 2, 1946. The place was your father's factory at Cicero, Illinois. Things had been rather busy, and I was working late in my laboratory—checking through some of the formulae records. A slight sound behind me attracted my attention and I turned to see someone staring at me through the glass pane in the door to my room. A moment later the door opened and a young man came in.

"Good evening," he said. "Late for you, isn't it?"

"Yes, Mr. Stevenson," I replied. "Necessarily so."

I explained that it was my custom to work late at night.

"I've wondered about this place," he told me, roaming about the laboratory. "First time I've had a chance to look it over."

I was pleased at this. I seldom had visitors who were interested in my work, and the opportunity to show off was, I must confess, most welcome. Since Mr. Stevenson was Mr. Cotterell's son-in-law, the visit was doubly interesting.

The laboratory was a pleasant place. I had the very best equipment with which to work, and all of it had been placed in the best possible arrangement under the batteries of fluorescent lights that gleamed from the ceilings and reflected off the softly colored wall tiles.

"Is there anything in particular I can show you?" I asked.

"No—no—just curious," he said. "Always been curious about this department. What do you do here?"

"Our work here," I said, "involves the chemistry of narcotics. Narcotics are not always the harmful things we read about. Many of them are boons to mankind when taken in the proper dosage—such as in some of the Cotterell products."

I suppose my somewhat pedantic manner amused him. He smiled at me. "Look, Evans," he said, "I've been around drugs most of my life. Now, tell me, just what goes on here?"

"Well," I replied, "in this laboratory we break down raw opium into its various alkaloids. I suppose you know that opium has twenty-four alkaloids—morphine, codeine . . ."

"Fine," he said, interrupting me. "Dope. Must be a lot of it in here."

"There certainly is," I agreed. "It's quite a responsibility, if I may so so, sir."

"What do you do with the various alkaloids?" he asked.

"Why, they're used in Cotterell products, of course."

"No, no," he said. "I mean, what do you do with them before they're needed by the factory? You don't just keep them around in jars on a shelf."

"Well—that's rather a secret," I told him.

"As it should be," he said. "I suppose I could ask Mr. Cotterell . . ."

"Nonsense," I assured him. "I was only impressing upon you how carefully we guard this information. Of course there's no reason why Mr. Cotterell's son-in-law should not know about it."

I walked over to the tiled wall facing the door and inserted a key into a small aperture just above the light switch. Part of the wall slid aside, revealing the huge safe in which our narcotic supply was kept. Mr. Stevenson seemed much impressed.

"Worry you?" he wanted to know. "Having all that human dynamite around?"

"As I said before," I assured him, "it's a responsibility, but that vault is not likely to yield to anything except the right combination."

"What I mean," he continued, "is: what about mistakes? Suppose you made a mistake in the amount that you released for one of the products. Couldn't it do a lot of harm?"

"It's most unlikely that such a thing could happen," I assured him. "Our measures are exact, and conform to the formulae involved. I've been here fifteen years, and nothing untoward has happened."

"Of course," he said with a smile, "I was just curious."

He dropped into the laboratory a few times after that—always very friendly and decent to me. I showed him the various processes in action, and he seemed to have from his years of drugstore experience a basic grasp of what was fairly complicated terminology. I was flattered that so important a figure in the company was so cordial to me.

You haven't told me anything I don't know, she thought. *Henry is like that. Curious. Thorough. Makes it his business to know everything about the company. What Dad calls snooping. That's one of the things they argue about. Henry thinks Dad resents him, is trying to hold him down. He even told Doctor Alexander about it. Maybe Dad's too severe.*

About a month after my first meeting with Mr. Stevenson I was outside the plant waiting for a bus to take me to my home. It was a bitter evening, with a high wind driving a cold rain almost horizontally across the city streets. My umbrella was not very much protection, as you can imagine. I was utterly miserable, waiting on that corner. But not for long. A most magnificent black sedan stopped directly in front of me, and someone called, "Evans!"

I peered through the rain and saw it was Mr. Stevenson. "Hop in," he said. "Give you a lift."

"Very kind of you," I said. "But I'd not like to trouble you. Perhaps you could help me pick up a bus farther down. I own I've no wish to stand in the rain any more."

"Forget it," he said. "Glad to take you home. As a matter of fact, I hate driving alone."

We rolled smoothly along, and I couldn't help admiring the beauty of that automobile.

"My wife's," Mr. Stevenson said, when I mentioned it.

"I've never owned a car," I told him. "They've always seemed a bit too—well—mechanical. Personally I'd rather have a brace of spanking horses and a good carriage."

Mr. Stevenson didn't stop me, so I suppose I rattled on for quite some time about—horses. You see, I was brought up around horses. In Surrey, that is. And I suppose no one ever gets it out of his blood.

"Horses are fine creatures," I said, "so powerful—and at the same time, so gentle. I've often wished I owned hundreds of them."

At this Mr. Stevenson looked at me rather oddly. "You don't say . . . ?"

"Yes," I assured him. "Nothing I'd like better. Like to have my own little place. Good clean stables. Plenty of pasture. And the best stock in all England."

"England?" asked Mr. Stevenson.

"Oh, yes," I replied. "I fancy every Englishman living abroad hopes to spend his old age at home. There's something that tugs at you no matter how long you've been away."

He looked at me again, with the hint of a smile on his lips. "There's nothing wrong with wanting a thing," he said. "The wrong is in not doing anything about it."

"It's easy to say that, if you'll forgive the impertinence," I said, "but not everyone can back his desire with the requisite energy—and coin of the realm. Sometimes one doesn't know what one wants until it is too late. For instance—I play a little game with myself."

"You do . . . ?" he said with a hint of amusement.

"Yes," I replied. "I went back to England for a holiday a few years ago, and I picked out a spot near Dorking. A perfect spot. A bit of land there, all green grass and shade trees, and a beautiful brook. Horses do love a brook. Every now and then I price that place—just for the fun of it, you know—but I know I shall never be able to buy it. I do get pleasure out of planning what I'd do with the place if I could."

"You're right," Mr. Stevenson said rather cynically. "You'll never get that place working for my father-in-law."

This rather embarrassed me. "No," I admitted, "I suppose not."

Again he glanced at me, and I noticed his look at this time was a bit on the speculative side, as though he were making up his mind to tell—or not to tell—me something. What he said, finally, nearly bowled me over.

"You and I, Evans, have a lot in common."

Fantastic! she thought. *Henry and this weary old man! Why would Henry link himself with a tiresome drudge? He sounds as if he might be a little queer.*

"But—but—Mr. Stevenson, sir, what rot! I thought . . ."

"Don't think, Evans, unless it's about your job and about that farm in England." He said that rather grimly. For a while neither of us spoke. When we reached my house, I opened the car door to step out. Suddenly I felt his hand on my arm. "Wait a minute, Evans, I want to talk to you."

"Certainly, Mr. Stevenson," I said and closed the door.

"Evans," he began, "I've got a little idea. If it's a good one, it'll mean that place in England for you. For me, it'll mean—well, never mind what it'll mean for me. You can tell me if it's a good idea, Evans. Nobody else but you can tell me." He wasn't smiling now. There was a look on his face as black as night. His eyes were drilling into mine. His grip on my arm tightened until it was almost painful.

"What do you mean?" I asked hastily, for his manner was certainly frightening.

"I mean you can buy your way to England, or anywhere else, by just making a few mistakes."

"Mistakes?" I gasped. "I'm afraid I don't follow you."

"Mistakes," he said evenly, "in the amount of dope you put into Cotterell products. Not more, Evans—less. Much less."

"Good heavens, no," I said, trembling. "I never heard—"

"No one but you—and me—would know, Evans," he said. "You know as well as I do that those cheap nostrums would really be better for suffering humanity if there were less dope in them. Nobody—certainly not the Cotterell Company—would ever know the difference. And the dope you held out, Evans, would buy that farm you were talking about—in England."

No! she cried inwardly. *It's impossible. This man is a lunatic. What's he trying to do? Who does he think will believe his ravings? To suggest that Henry would do such a thing! He's crazy. That's what he is. Crazy! But there must be something underneath all this nonsense. Henry must have had some dealings with the man. Miss Jennings mentioned that he'd called Henry several times.*

I was horrified—and fascinated. He'd struck so swiftly that I hardly could think. I wanted a bit of time to collect my wits.

"I'm not so sure it could be done as easy as all that," I said.

"What!" he said. "For a fine chemist like you it would be simple."

His flattery warmed me, I must admit. No one had ever bothered to show any appreciation or understanding of the miracles of chemistry that were so carefully produced under my direction in the Cotterell laboratory. Least of all, Mr. Cotterell himself!

"You really believe I'm a good chemist," I asked, foolishly.

"I know you're the best around," he said quickly, "I've watched you work. I've looked up your record. And I've hated seeing them pick your brains for peanuts."

I didn't know what to do. Temptation is a terrible thing, especially when what was wanted of me was so easy to do—for a good chemist. I hesitated, fumbling with the handle of the car door. But Mr. Stevenson had more to say.

"Come on—Evans, don't be a fool. I've already talked the whole thing over with someone else."

I was aghast. "Someone else?" I cried. "Good heavens, man, what folly!"

"Not folly," he said, grimly smiling. "Good sense. Someone has to sell the stuff after we get it. I wouldn't know what to do with it. Not yet—anyway. But the man I spoke to does. Name's Morano. He'll take everything we can give him—and split three ways."

Insane, she thought. No doubt of it now. Perhaps a discharged employee whose mind has broken down. This crazy tale. Sounds like a movie.

The cold-blooded enormity of the thing finally rang a warning bell in my mind. Had it been anyone but Mr. Stevenson, I would not have been quite so shocked. But that this handsome, powerful young man, living in the bosom of a millionaire family, could broach such a scheme was incredible.

"You—you've been pulling my leg, Mr. Stevenson," I said weakly. "Why would you—of all men—want to embroil yourself in the kind of tawdry affair you suggest? I do believe you've been testing my integrity—and I resent it, sir."

His lip curled, and the sneer on his face was not pleasant. "Evans," he said, "*you* want something—that farm. *I* want something, too. Money. My own money. I'm going to get it. And the sooner, the better. And the easier, the better. That's all. I want it. I get it. Now let's go up to that room of yours and talk it over."

"But wait," I pleaded. "What if we're caught?"

"We won't be," he said. "Let's go."

And we were not caught, Mrs. Stevenson. From the 15th of December, 1946, to the 30th of April, 1947, we were not caught. I carried out my part of the bargain with surprising ease. It was a simple matter to substitute harmless powders and liquids for considerable quantities of morphine alkaloids. I did it at night, usually, when my staff was away. No one paid me the slightest attention. And the packages of illicit drugs I turned over to Mr. Stevenson every Friday. He, in turn, gave them to Mr. Morano. Where, I don't know. I never saw Mr. Morano at any time.

By the 30th of April I had saved nearly fifteen thousand dollars. It was incredible. It was my dream coming true. Then, one day, I received a notice from the Cotterell Company telling me that I was to be transferred to the Bayonne, New Jersey, plant. Although, according to the notice, I also was to be in charge of the narcotics laboratory there, I was frightened. It seemed so unnecessary to move me to a place where I would do the same work, for the same pay. I went to see Mr. Stevenson at the first possible opportunity.

When we were safely alone in his office, I showed him my notice of transfer.

"You asked to be transferred?" he said sharply.

"No, never," I assured him. "That's why I'm rather upset about it. I'm sure something is suspected."

"Nonsense," he said. "You'd have been picked up by the police long ago if anything was wrong. This transfer must be a routine matter. I'd check on it myself, but why draw attention to it? There's nothing to worry about."

I wasn't entirely calmed by his cool assurance. Mr. Stevenson has a core of iron in his character, but not I.

"It's a sign," I said nervously, "a portent. I'm sure of it."

"A sign—of what?" he asked.

"To stop," I said. "This—this is a terrible business, Mr. Stevenson. I can't go on much longer. I'm not young, for one thing. I've almost enough money to quit now and go back to England. Perhaps I can do that after the transfer to Bayonne becomes effective."

Mr. Stevenson looked at me with that sly little smile of his. Not a very cheerful thing to behold, I assure you. "Evans," he said softly, "you'll stop when I say you stop. Let us be perfectly clear about that—when *I* say you stop. Not before."

He got up from his desk and walked to the door to make certain no one was within earshot. Then he came back, and sat on the edge of the desk close to my chair. He was still smiling, but his eyes were cold as ice.

"I need you, Evans, and I don't intend to let you go. Maybe you're interested in the chicken feed we've collected. But not me. I want more. A lot more, Evans, and I'm going to get it. And I think I know how to get it—fast. Faster than we've been getting it lately."

"What do you mean?" I asked.

"You've given me an idea, Evans, a big idea—the kind of idea that appeals to me. You were right when you said the transfer was a sign. It's the biggest sign you ever saw. And it's pointing right at the biggest pile of money you ever saw. When I get that pile—you can have out, Evans. It shouldn't be too long a wait— if you do as you're told."

He was talking in a low voice, but there was no mistaking his determination. His eyes were alight with a burning intensity that had something almost maniacal in it.

"Please, Mr. Stevenson," I begged, "are you sure it would be wise to carry this thing along any further? I'll admit it's been rather a simple thing so far. But aren't you permitting this initial success to topple your judgment? After all, how far can you trust Mr. Morano?"

He snorted. "Morano. A small-time gangster. He's been using us like a couple of stooges, Evans. We take all the risk, and he gets a fat share of the profits."

He got up and walked to the window, looking out over the huge plant. With his back to me, he said, "I don't see Morano in this picture any more. No, I don't see him at all—the little chiseler." He turned to face me. "With you in Bayonne, Evans, I think Mr. Morano will have to find someone else to supply him."

I hadn't any idea what he was talking about. "It's not too easy to stop dealing with such a man as Morano, I should imagine," I said. "These men work in groups, and are generally supposed to be rather difficult—rather *physical*—about such matters."

"I'll handle Morano," he said. "When he learns that you've been transferred to Bayonne, cutting off my source of supply, he'll never give it a second thought. He's a stupid man, Evans. And his whole mob hasn't got a brain among them. He'll make no trouble."

"Now," he said, sitting down at his desk once more, "here's the set-up. This narcotics racket is a big one. I've never realized how big until I saw what a small-time gunman like Morano draws down just from us. And he's dealing with others, too, don't forget. All right. We close up shop here, getting rid of Morano and his one-third cut. We start our own business out of Bayonne, peddling in New York, the richest market in the country. We'll do more business, at a larger profit, with larger shares for each of us. All you have to do is just what you've been doing right along. Except perhaps warehouse the stuff some safe place. We find another place for our—showroom. And we're in business!"

"But Mr. Stevenson," I said, "it's fantastic. Suppose, for the sake of argument, I were able to help you this way. How would you be able to—to contact the purchasers of our products? It's too risky, I tell you. It's better to stay small, and safe, than to tempt Providence."

"Look, Evans," he said, "when I was a kid, jerking sodas and wrapping up packages in a drugstore, I always managed to stache away a few compacts, bottles of perfume, all kinds of small things. There was always someone who would buy things from me, cheap, and no questions asked. I only got caught once. And an old guy named Dodge, who liked me and knew I was poor and had to help my family, got me out of it. I got caught because I didn't watch my step—and that taught me a lesson. You can get away with anything if you're smart and watch your step. Well, Evans, I'm smart enough to establish the right connections in New York. You leave that to me. And believe me, no one will ever dream that either you or I have anything to do with the business."

. . .

Good heavens, it was insidious! She was actually beginning to believe him. He made it all seem so real. Everything fit together so neatly. But she must not, she dare not, give in to him. It could not be true. She would not let it be true.

One and a half months later we began operations on Staten Island, New York. Our headquarters were in an old house at 20 Dunham Terrace. I bought the house for Mr. Stevenson. I managed to hire a couple of local lads—not too bright, you understand—who thought I was working on a scientific project for the government. One of the lads acted as a sort of lookout for me, warning me of strangers and so forth. The other, a hunchback, kept the house fairly tidy and ran the small motor launch I bought to carry me by water to the house. Both were very loyal and very close mouthed, although I had little to fear, for nothing was kept in the house for them to see. It was only a distribution point—the "showroom" Mr. Stevenson mentioned—and the drugs were brought there from the "warehouse" and instantly disposed of.

The warehouse has been my room, the room from which I'm calling you now. It is an eminently respectable private home—my landlord is a retired minister of great simplicity. My trunk has served well as a repository for the various substances we sold. It seems unlikely that a place could have been found safer than this pleasant room.

I traveled to Staten Island several times a week, where I would be met by clients whom Mr. Stevenson sent. How he solicited them I do not know. We had a code word to identify the clients until I got to know most of them by sight. These men—and a few women—were small dealers. They bought in quantity and redistributed the products to the—ah—ultimate consumer.

You might suppose that I was banking considerable sums of money each week and you'd be correct. But apparently Mr. Stevenson was not satisfied with my progress.

Several months ago—as you know—Mr. Stevenson arrived in New York, having somehow effected his own transfer to the New York office of the Cotterell Company. His real objective, as you may surmise, was to take over the supervision of our drug sales, for he believed that the mounting volume of our little business could be further stimulated if he were close at hand. I discovered a short while after that there was a far greater urgency than merely Mr. Stevenson's desire to make as much money as quickly as he could. The truth was that Mr. Stevenson had been quietly playing the stock market, using the proceeds of his less honorable pursuit as capital. Unfortunately he was less astute in his stock-market speculations than he had been in his unlawful enterprise. He was in rather difficult straits. What was even more unfortunate was that he continued, as soon as he reached New York, to pour more of his money into futile market operations, so that every penny he got from me was turned over immediately to his brokers.

Sally! Sally had mentioned a brokerage office. And that man—Freeman or whatever his name was—commiserating with Henry over losses. This was no coincidence. Evans hadn't made this part of it up. More and more the whole story was becoming rational, terrifyingly rational. Perhaps Evans was not insane . . .

This was all very shocking to me, for I could see no opportunity to free myself from Mr. Stevenson's grasp. His overwhelming vanity—which was really at the root of his anxiety to succeed in a legitimate field—drove him to repeated attempts to recoup his losses. When I suggested that he stop and simply accumulate funds while our business was in such excellent shape, he would stare at me with that cold contempt I'd learned to know so well, and tell me to save my breath.

One day I asked him, "Mr. Stevenson, why do you insist upon gambling in the stock market? Surely in these days the opportunities to make substantial profits on the exchanges are limited —compared to our own business, that is."

He smiled at me queerly. "You know I want money. Not any money. But money I can show around—money that will buy me a little respect. I want lots of it. And I don't want to wait all my life for it. Okay— How can I explain the money I get from this racket? The answer is—I can't. All I can do is use it to get me going in something respectable. So I play the market. When I hit it right, nobody'll know what it cost me to start. I can tell them I saved some of the dough old man Cotterell paid me for warming the bench. Then, when I've got this thing licked, I'm rich, respectable, a smart operator—and I can tell Cotterell what he can do with his tailor-made vice-presidency."

Mr. Stevenson was, as you can see, very bitter—and very vain. His desire to be thought well of would have been perfectly natural in another young man. But another young man would have been content to work honestly toward his goal, whereas Mr. Stevenson intended to reach the goal without the work. I can moralize tonight about Mr. Stevenson's lack of morals, because —as you must now suspect—I have finally extricated myself from bondage. I do not belong to him any longer. I don't excuse my own conduct. But mine was the weakness of a hopeless old man sorely tempted. His, on the other hand, was the unhappy product of a warped, degenerate mind in a strong and beautiful body. In other words: I am a bad man—he is a dangerous one.

Fortunately—or unfortunately, depending on how you look at it—the final chapter of our story was being written even as Mr. Stevenson set about improving the sales of the drugs I was supplying. About a month ago we had a visitor.

10:40

I was to meet Mr. Stevenson at the Dunham Terrace house one evening. I arrived a bit later than usual. This time I'd come by ferry from Manhattan, and fog on the river caused some delay. I hurred up the steps of the old house, and entered the living room. Mr. Stevenson was seated in one of the rickety chairs with which the room was furnished. An oil lamp stood on the table near him, and in its light I could see his face plainly. He was white as a sheet, and that queer halting little smile of his flickered about his face. He looked at me, then looked away toward the corner of the room behind the door which I was holding open. I stepped in, closed the door—and saw the man in the corner!

He was straddling a kitchen chair, his arms folded across the chair's back. In the rather dim light of the lamp I couldn't make him out too clearly. But I knew I had never seen him before. He seemed to be a small man, carefully dressed. His oily black hair reflected the lamp's beam. He was looking at me, and what I could make out of his face was not pleasant—sharp, regular features, swarthy complexion, tiny eyes that did not blink. For a second after I'd closed the door no one spoke. Then the little man turned his head toward Mr. Stevenson. "Him?" he asked.

Mr. Stevenson said, "Him." And then to me, "Evans, meet an old friend—Morano."

The small man looked over at me. "Siddown," he said.

I sat down—with relief, I might add. The shock of this unexpected meeting had unnerved me. I was thoroughly alarmed.

"Morano is not pleased with us," Mr. Stevenson said mockingly. "He is hurt to think that we have voted him off the board of directors."

I looked anxiously at Morano to note the effect of Mr. Stevenson's gibe. If there was any, I couldn't see it. He sat there in silence, waiting for Mr. Stevenson to finish.

"I have just advised Mr. Morano that we cannot consider his application for re-instatement," Mr. Stevenson continued. "He was about to comment on this when you joined us." He put the tips of his fingers together, pursed his lips, and looked at Morano with exaggerated politeness.

Morano stared a moment longer as though making up his mind about something. Then he began to talk. His words slurred a little as he slid them out between almost motionless lips. Nevertheless I'm sure both Mr. Stevenson and myself had no difficulty in understanding them.

"Climb down," he said. "Maybe this ain't so funny. Maybe if you button up and listen you'll learn something, Stevenson. Even a very smart gentleman like you can sometimes learn something. Something like f'r instance how to keep alive." He paused for a moment.

"What kind of business you think this is? The gocery business? Anybody can open a store? Anybody can just move in and go to work? Did that fancy brain of yours tell you that, Stevenson? Like it told you to cross me up? I wouldn't know to keep an eye on you?"

"One for you," Mr. Stevenson said lazily. "I misjudged you, Morano."

"That ain't all you misjudged," Morano snapped. "If it wasn't for me you'd probably be very dead right now. Every mob in the business knows what you're doing. Or maybe you thought they didn't? You were a cinch to be knocked off as soon as they figured how to get to the professor here. They wanted him. As soon as they had him in line, so they could keep the stuff coming in, something would happen to you, Stevenson. Something very sad. But I fixed that. I got plenty friends here. So they let you alone—for only a small cut."

Mr. Stevenson was no longer smiling. "I don't think we're interested, Morano. I think we'll carry on without your help. When we have to make a deal, we'll make it direct. You've got your Chicago business. That ought to be enough."

"It's funny," Morano said, "but it ain't enough. You are being very foolish, Stevenson. I don't think you have much choice in this deal. It looks like you ain't got any choice at all."

"Which means what?"

"Which means either I move in—or I blow the whistle on this joint. It's as easy as that. I take over—now—or there ain't any business."

Mr. Stevenson sat bolt upright. "You wouldn't do that, Morano. You were in the Chicago deal yourself. You'd go down with us."

"Na—" Morano said, "nobody'll bother me. Nobody's got anything on me that would stick. I never saw you guys before in my life, see? What's more, nobody's going to know who done the singing about old man Cotterell's drug-running son-in-law. A tip like that buys plenty protection."

Then it happened.

Mr. Stevenson sprang from his chair, livid with rage, and lunged at Morano. His fist hit the little man on the side of the head, sending him reeling backward. Like a crazed animal Mr. Stevenson followed him, flinging himself on Morano, clawing at his throat as they both fell to the floor. I have no doubt he would have killed Morano then and there—all things being equal. But as I had already discovered, where Morano was concerned, nothing was equal. As the two men hit the floor, the door opened and in an instant Mr. Stevenson was standing upright, his arms locked in the grasp of a couple of Morano's men. Savage-looking desperadoes, they were, and I feared they would beat Mr. Stevenson to a pulp. But Morano said from the floor, "Leave him alone, boys. I don't want him marked up. I don't want he should have to explain anything to anybody.'"

Morano got up from the floor, brushing off his natty clothes, straightening his necktie. From his pocket he took a comb and carefully restored his shiny black hair to its gleaming perfection. Then he said, "Sit him in that chair—and scram."

They hustled Mr. Stevenson back to his chair. I noticed one of the men run his hands over Mr. Stevenson's clothing—searching for a weapon, I suppose. Mr. Stevenson, white and shaken, sat down and the men went out of the room. Morano walked over and stood before Mr. Stevenson. "See what I mean?" he said.

Mr. Stevenson nodded sullenly.

"Okay. Now we understand each other. No need we should get in each other's hair any more. You do like I say, and I'll take care of you. That goes for the professor, too." He grinned evilly at me.

"Now," he went on, "from here on I run this show. We split fifty-fifty, half for me, half for the two of you. Not so good for you as before—but I got heavy expenses."

"It—it's not fair," Mr. Stevenson said weakly. "There won't be enough . . ."

"It's fair," Morano snapped. "It's fair because I say it's fair. If you don't like it you can always get out, just so long as the professor stays." He turned to me. "Maybe the professor would like that? A full share? The professor would not try to cross anybody—except maybe you, Stevenson."

But Morano's cocky humor didn't last very long. His cold gaze returned to Mr. Stevenson. "Now we know where we stand from here on. So there's only one more little matter to settle—a little matter of a hundred grand."

Mr. Stevenson stiffened in his chair. "A hundred grand? For what?"

"For the time between now and when you walked out on me."

"You're out of your mind," Mr. Stevenson cried. "I don't have that kind of money. I've lost every cent I made in this racket."

"That's too bad," Morano said sorrowfully. "That's really what you call too bad." Then his face froze. "You'll get it up. And you'll get it up in a month."

Mr. Stevenson paled. "You're insane, Morano. I couldn't raise that much in that time. I need a lot more time. Then maybe my wife . . ."

Morano said with contempt, "Your wife! You couldn't get a nickel from your wife."

"You don't understand," Mr. Stevenson said hoarsely. 'She's a sick woman. She's going to die . . . in a little while. She's leaving me everything . . . It's in her will. Wait just a few months . . . That's all, I'm sure . . ."

"I don't wait for nobody to die—ever," Morano said, "and you don't either—if you're smart. If somebody is supposed to die—they die."

"God God!" Mr. Stevenson cried, "I can't . . ."

"Never mind what you can or you can't," Morano barked. "You get that dough up in thirty days."

"But—"

"Look—" Morano grinned. "I don't want to be too hard on you, Stevenson . . ."

"Yes?" Mr. Stevenson asked hopefully.

"You have too much trouble, you come to me. Maybe I give you—some help."

That was on the night of July 17th. I haven't seen either Mr. Morano or Mr. Stevenson since. And now—as I've already given you the final message, I believe the rest explains itself quite simply . . .

The phone shook in Leona's hand. Frightened tears started in her eyes. Her body felt drained and empty and she could scarcely control the trembling of her jaw. "Explains itself—how?" she managed to ask. "Where's my husband? Where's Mr. Stevenson now?"

"I wish I knew, Mrs. Stevenson," the weary voice replied. "Perhaps if you were to try the Caledonia number . . ."

"The—Caledonia—number?" she asked.

"The number I gave you in the message," he told her. "And now—if you will check it all over with me . . ."

"I can't," she cried, "I can't. I've forgotten."

"Then I will repeat it for you once more, Mrs. Stevenson. Point one: the house at 20 Dunham Terrace was burned down this afternoon by Mr. Evans. Point two: Mr. Evans escaped. Point three: Mr. Morano was arrested. Point four: it is not necessary to raise the money as it was not Mr. Morano who tipped off the police."

"It doesn't matter," Leona mumbled. "It doesn't matter. Just give me that Caledonia number—the one for Mr. Stevenson."

"Point five," Mr. Evans said evenly. "Point five: Mr. Evans is at the Manhattan address, but he is leaving now and may be found at Caledonia 5:1133."

"Caledonia 5:1133," Leona repeated, scrawling the number on the bit of memo paper with her lipstick.

"After midnight—" Evans said quietly. Then, with something

that might have been a sigh, he added, "Thank you very much, Mrs. Stevenson. And good-bye."

After Evans had hung up, she continued to stare at the scarlet numbers streaming across the paper, as though if she took her eyes away they might disappear. Mechanically, numbly, she dialed. The first time she tried, the trembling of her fingers made her slip and she had to start over again. As she moved the dial, the tension within her mounted so that every breath was a painful effort. This time she completed the call, and after two purring rings the phone was picked up at the other end.

A man said, "Caledonia 5:1133."

Fear, fright, the approach of hysteria pitched her voice unnaturally high. "Caledonia 5:1133?" she asked. "Is Mr. Stevenson there?"

"Who, lady?"

"Mr. Stevenson. Mr. Henry Stevenson. I was told to call by—by a Mr. Evans."

"Stevenson, you say? Just a minute—I'll see."

She heard the thud as he laid the phone down. Straining to listen, she could hear his departing footsteps. Then silence. The seconds slowly passed. Her heart beat wildly as though it were struggling to fly from her breast. She clenched and unclenched her free hand, squeezing until her long nails bit into the flesh of her palm. Outside a low, moaning whistle drifted up from the river, and somewhere below someone—a policeman, perhaps?—rattled wood against an iron fence.

Suddenly the man was back. "Nope. He's not here, ma'am."

"Oh," she said, "Mr. Evans said he might be expected. Could I leave a message?"

"A message? We don't take no messages here, lady." The man seemed puzzled—and a little amused. "They wouldn't do no good here, lady."

"No?" she asked. "What number is this? Who—? What am I calling?"

"Caledonia 5:1133," the man said. "The City Morgue."

Now she sat motionless in the bed, desperately trying to piece together the macabre jigsaw of that night's happenings. Out of the dreamlike chaos of shock piled on shock she began to shape the truth. And as the stark outline grew more distinct, its enormity made her shudder. That such a thing could happen to her! That such evil could have found her out!

That awful phone call, she thought. Why had she been the one to hear those terrible criminals? Why had all her calls to Henry's office—the calls before she'd asked the operator to help—been answered by a busy signal? Who had been in Henry's office, if not Henry? And if someone, no matter who, had been using the phone in Henry's office, could one end of that mysterious crossed wire have been . . . ? No—she wouldn't think of it. She'd force it from her mind. There were other things to think about.

What about Sally's story? That Henry was involved in some kind of trouble with the authorities? She had to believe that—or at least part of it—for Evans had established the truth of it. If any of it was truth, that is, and not a plot to drive her out of her mind. Suppose Evans *was* telling the truth. Henry would then be hard pressed to find that money, that hundred thousand dollars. And he couldn't. Unless he told the whole sordid story to Jim Cotterell! Which he'd never do! She marveled at the way Henry had managed to seem so—so normal these past few weeks. And as she did, she found herself recalling Sally's talk, the talk of years ago, when Sally had tried to tell her about the strange depths of Henry's character. Sally hadn't been lying!

What then was left for Henry to do? She knew the answer, of course. She had known it ever since Evans had finished talking with her. She could no longer exclude it from her thoughts, any more than she could exclude the real meaning of those crossed telephone wires.

And as the awful realization tore at the foundation of her reason, she heard again the grinding, clanking progress of a train across the bridge. Wisps of remembered conversation now floated freely across her consciousness . . . *our client* . . . *Then I wait until the train goes over the bridge* . . . *in case she should scream* . . . *is a knife okay* . . . *our client* . . . *our client* . . . *she's going to die* . . . *I don't wait for nobody to die* . . . *our client* . . . *our client* . . .

Frantic with fear she snatched up the phone again and dialed the operator.

"Your call, please?" How smooth! How impersonal!

"Give me the police," she cried brokenly.

"Ringing the Police Department."

In a few seconds the phone was picked up. "Police Station. Seventeenth Precinct. Sergeant Duffy speaking."

"This is Mrs. Stevenson again," she said. "I called you a little while ago . . ."

"Yes, ma'am. Mrs. Stevenson did you say?"

"Mrs. Henry Stevenson, at 43 Sutton Place. I called you about a phone call I overheard."

"Why, yes, ma'am. I remember it very well."

"Well, I wondered what—what you'd done about it?"

"It's right here on the blotter, ma'am," Duffy said cautiously. "But—haven't you . . .?"

"We'll do everything we can, ma'am. If anything happens—"

"If anything *happens*?" she echoed. "Do you mean to say a thing has to happen before you do anything?"

"I told you before, ma'am, that when the information is vague there isn't much we can do."

"But . . ." She paused. She *couldn't* tell him. Even though it might be true, she couldn't. For in spite of everything, it might *not* be true. And if she told now, it would be irrevocable. She could never take it back. It would be the end of her dream. She couldn't tell the police. She'd have to find another way. . . .

"I'm sorry to trouble you," she said faintly. "I thought perhaps you might at least have sent out a radio call . . ."

"That's up to Headquarters," Duffy said. "We pass along the tip, and it's up to them to take care of it. So far there hasn't been a call."

"Thank you," she said. "I—I hope it's all a mistake."

She hung up, thinking fearfully of her next step. She must do something, something to protect herself in case . . .

A detective agency? That might be one way of getting some-one to watch over her, someone who could be sworn to secrecy. She glanced at the clock on her night table. Eleven! She didn't have much time. Trembling, she dialed the operator.

"I want a detective agency," she said nervously.

"You will find all detective agencies listed in the Classified Directory, madam."

"I haven't a Classified Directory—I mean—I don't have time —to look anything up—it—it's getting late."

"I will connect you with Information."

"No!" Leona shouted angrily. "You don't care what happens to me, do you? I could die—and you wouldn't care . . . !"

"I beg your pardon . . . ?"

"Give me a hospital," Leona said.

"Is there a particular hospital?"

"Any hospital!" she shouted. "Any hospital at all—do you hear?"

"One moment, please."

11:00

She waited while the phone rang, looking uneasily about the room, glancing nervously at the half-open door, the shadowy pictures on the wall, the elegant debris on her night table and vanity. Soon the ringing stopped and a woman said, "Bellevue."

Leona said, "I want the Nurses' Registry, please."

"Whom do you wish to speak to?"

"I want the Nurses' Registry. I want a trained nurse. I want to hire her immediately for the night."

"I see," the woman said. "I will transfer your call."

"Nurses' Home," another voice murmured.

"I want to hire a nurse," Leona repeated. "I need one right away. It's very important that I get one right away."

"What is the nature of the case, madam?"

"The case? Why—I—I'm an invalid—and I'm all alone—I—don't know anyone in the city—and I've just had a frightful shock—I just can't be alone tonight."

"Have you been instructed to call by one of our doctors, madam?"

"No," Leona said, her voice rising peevishly, "but I fail to see why all this—this catechizing is necessary. After all, I expect to pay this person . . ."

"We quite understand that, madam," the voice went on calmly. "But this is a city hospital. It isn't private. We don't send nurses on cases unless an emergency is certified by one of our staff physicians. I'd suggest that you call one of the regular Nurses' Registries."

"But I don't know any," she wailed. "I can't wait. I'm desperately in need of help."

"I'll give you a number you may call. Schuyler 2:1037. Perhaps someone there will be able to assist you."

"Schuyler 2:1037. Thank you."

Again she worked the dial, its clicking beating like little hammers in her head. The phone's ringing seemed interminable, although it was only a matter of seconds before she got her answer.

"Center Registry for Nurses. Miss Jordan speaking."

"I want to hire a nurse—at once."

"And who is this calling, please?"

"Mrs. Stevenson. Mrs. Henry Stevenson, 43 Sutton Place. And it's very urgent."

"Have you been recommended to us by a doctor, Mrs. Stevenson?"

"No," she said impatiently. "But I'm a stranger here—and I'm ill—and I've been going through the most awful night. I can't be alone any longer."

"Well," Miss Jordan said doubtfully, "nurses are very scarce now. It's most unusual to send one out unless the doctor in charge has specifically stated that it's absolutely necessary."

"But it is necessary," she pleaded. "It is. I'm a sick woman. I'm alone in this house—I don't know where my husband is—I can't reach him. And I'm terribly frightened. If someone doesn't come at once—if something isn't done, I'm afraid I'll go out of my mind."

"I see," the woman said reflectively. "Well—I'll leave a message for Miss Phillips to call you as soon as she comes in."

"Miss Phillips? And when do you expect her?"

"Sometime around 11:30 or so. . . ."

"Eleven-*thirty!*"

And then she heard the click. It was a tiny click, a click in the phone. It was a sound she thought she had heard many times before.

"What was *that?*" she cried.

"What was what, madam?"

"That—click—just now—in my telephone. As though someone had lifted the receiver off the hook of the extension downstairs . . ."

"I didn't hear anything, madam."

"But *I* did!" she gasped in a voice almost suffocated by fear. "There's someone in this house . . . someone downstairs in the kitchen . . . and they're listening to me now. They're . . ." Terror gripped her and she screamed, hanging up the phone with a mechanical movement.

Clutching the bedclothes in an agony of fright she concentrated on the silence around her. Suddenly she heard a quiet tapping along the floor—slowly—steadily. She started up with a shudder, eyes wild, her hand raised to her contorted face.

"Who is it?" she called frantically. "Who's there?"

She was like a creature at bay. As the tapping continued—slowly—relentlessly, she stared in horrified fascination at the door to her room—waiting—waiting. Suddenly she yelled, hoarsely, "Henry—! HENRY!"

No answer. The steady, remorseless tapping went on. She threw back the coverlet, trying to get out of the bed. But paralyzing fear sapped her strength. She stretched and strained, then collapsed against the pillows—frozen with terror—unable to move. Her wild gaze roamed the room, fastening for an instant on the half-open door, then darting past it for fear of what she might see. The sound of a roaring motor truck rolled up from the street, and looking toward the window she discovered at last the source of the tapping—the weighted window drapes stirring in the freshening breeze!

For a while she knew relief. The pounding of her heart subsided. Doctor Alexander must be right, she thought. It's sound as a bell. And suddenly she was tearfully glad. If she lived through this night, she'd never stay in bed again, never. She'd get strong as quickly as she could. But the odor of danger was everywhere. She must do something quickly. How could she escape that room!

Automatically she reached for the telephone. But in mid-air her hand froze. Whom should she call? Who would help her now? The silent listener somewhere in the house had heard her talking to that nurse. What chance had she of avoiding his frightful presence now?

She lay there in a mist of indecision, terror strangling her ability to sort out the teeming product of her brain. Then, as so often before, the brooding, massive silence was shattered by the telephone's sharp ring. She snatched it up quickly, clutching at any straw.

"Hello?" she said with pitiful expectancy.

The maddening, unconcerned voice of an operator greeted her. "New Haven is calling Mrs. Henry Stevenson. Is Mrs. Stevenson there?"

"Yes," Leona cried, adding with sinking heart. "But I haven't any time now . . . call back later. I can't talk—"

"I have a person-to-person call for Mrs. Henry Stevenson from

Mr. Henry Stevenson. You do not wish to accept the call, madam?"

Thunderstruck, Leona asked, *"Mr. Henry Stevenson . . . ?"* Almost in tears, she said, "Did you say—Mr.?—From New Haven?"

"Do you wish to accept the call, madam?"

And now the fantastic hope grew that it was all a lie—a terrible dream. Nothing so awful could have been conceived by the man whose life she had shared for so long. Yet she knew it wasn't a dream. If there was only some other answer to the whole thing—! Well, at least she could ask Henry to call the police. That would bring things out in the open.

"Yes . . . I'll . . . accept it," she said.

She waited tensely, hovering, breathless. She heard the Long Distance Operator's little ring, and then, "Go ahead, New Haven."

11:05

The railroad station in New Haven was a lonely place so late at night. The few people who walked about, or sat idly on benches, were mere specks in its vastness. Footsteps clicked on the stone floors and echoed to the high ceilings. There was an emptiness that could almost be felt, a strange unreality—as though the station, drained of its daytime bustle, slumbered through the night.

Under a huge clock a row of telephone booths extended along the wall, all save one dark and empty. Beside the door of the occupied booth stood a handsome valise—a pigskin affair, with the initials "H.S." neatly stamped in gold near its center lock. In the lighted booth Henry Stevenson waited to talk with his wife.

He was hatless. Under unruly brown hair his face was heavily handsome—an attractive face with wide-set, thickly lashed eyes, straight fleshy nose, powerfully molded mouth and jaw. As he stood there staring at the telephone, his expression was one of grimness and determination. He looked like a young man who knew very well what he was doing, knew that what he was doing must be done.

At last he heard the Long Distance Operator say, "Go ahead, New Haven."

"Hello. That you, darling?" he asked quietly.

"*Henry!* Henry, where *are* you?" He could almost feel her clutching at him over all those miles.

"Why—I'm on my way to Boston, dear. I stopped off in New Haven. Didn't you get my wire?"

"Yes. I—I got it . . . But—but I don't understand—"

"Nothing to understand, dear. I couldn't reach you before. Your line was busy so often. I thought I'd call now and see how you were. I was sorry—about leaving so unexpectedly—but I knew you'd be all right."

"I'm *not* all right—I'm . . ." she began wildly. "There's someone in this house right now—I'm sure of it."

An ugly, malevolent light gleamed for an instant in his eyes. His nostrils flared, and he drew in his breath sharply.

"Nonsense, dear. How could there be?" he said. "You're not there alone?"

"Of course I am," she replied, whining. "I'm all alone. Who else could be here? You gave Larsen the night off . . ."

"So I did," he admitted gravely.

"And you promised to be home at six sharp."

"Did I?" he asked innocently. "I don't remember."

"You most certainly did," she said. "And I've been alone here for hours. I've been getting all kinds of horrible phone calls that I don't understand . . . and Henry . . . I want you to call the police . . . do you hear me? . . . Tell them to come here at once."

He wondered at the panic in her voice. She was really frightened. Yet—it didn't make sense. What could she know? He could understand it if she were only irritated—Leona had an oversized capacity for irritation. But this kind of fear was another thing. "Now Leona," he said crisply. "No need to be so nervous."

"*Nervous!*"

"You know you're perfectly safe in that house. Larsen certainly must have locked the doors before she left."

"I know," she said weakly, "But—I heard—someone—someone pick up the phone in the kitchen. I'm sure I did."

"Nonsense," he said. "The house is locked. There's that private patrolman. And the telephone's right by your bed. What's more, you're in the heart of New York City, Leona. Safest place in the world."

"I'd feel better if you'd call the police, Henry. I called them.

They wouldn't pay any attention to me." She started to sob in self-pity.

"Look," he said, "I'm in New Haven. If I call from here, the police'll think I'm crazy. Why the police, anyway? Maybe if you call Doctor Alexander? . . ."

String it out, he thought, glancing at his watch. Let her run on—a few more minutes. What could she do then? He was smiling now, a queer half-smile that transformed his brooding face into a mask of glowering evil. Shifting his position in the booth, he glanced casually out of the door for an instant, then turned back toward the phone. He had scarcely noticed the burly, white-haired man with dark skin and the large liquid eyes lounging a few paces from the booth.

But what was this Leona was saying?

"Henry! What do you know about a man named Evans?"

"Evans?" he asked, taken by surprise.

"Yes," she said. "Waldo Evans."

"Never heard the name in my life, Leona. What makes you ask?"

"He called me up—tonight—I had a long talk with him . . . about *you!*"

11:10

The huge man with the white hair and the dark, permanently sad face had moved just far enough away from the booth to be out of sight of its occupant. Otherwise he might have noticed Henry grow pale as death—the pallor pointing up the defiant set of his jaw. But the man was not interested in Henry's telephone call. He was only interested in Henry. He waited patiently, observing the line of booths, absently fingering the badge in his pocket.

"About me!" Henry said as naturally as possible. "What could he have had to say about me?"

"He told me some terrible things. Some of it sounded . . . insane. But there were parts that sounded true . . ."

"A crackpot," Henry said. "You mustn't listen to every crackpot who calls. Now, just try and forget it . . ."

"He told me—you'd been stealing dope from Daddy's company. Is that true?"

Henry snorted. "True? Now see here, Leona, I'm a little hurt that you even bother to tax me with that kind of rot. You must have had a bad dream . . ."

"Dream!" she shrilled. "I haven't been dreaming, Henry. He left some kind of message for you. He said to tell you that the house on Staten Island had been burned down—and that the police knew everything. He said someone named Morano had been arrested . . ."

"What!" Henry snapped. "What was that you said?"

"And—I—I'd never have believed him—except there was that Mrs. Lord—you remember—Sally Hunt—and she told me the same things."

There was a silence for a second, and Leona called, "Are you still there—Henry?"

He wet his lips. "Yes," he said. "Yes, I'm here."

"They said you were a criminal," she babbled, "a desperate man . . . And Evans said—you—you—you wanted me—to die!"

"I—" he started to say, but there was no stopping the flood.

"That money—Henry—the hundred thousand dollars. Why didn't you ask me for it? I'd have got it for you—gladly—if I'd only known."

"Forget it," he muttered.

"Is it too late?" she cried. "I'll get it for you now—if it isn't too late."

"It's all right," he said. "Forget it."

Now the tears that had been threatening, streamed down her face. Her voice was hoarse and strangled.

"I didn't mean to be so awful to you, Henry," she said. "I—only did it—because—I loved you. I guess I was afraid you didn't really love me. I was afraid—afraid you'd run away—and leave me all alone . . ."

11:11

Henry remembered now the man he had seen standing near the booth. He looked through the door and, seeing no one, cautiously opened it to get a broader view. The man was there, not far away. He was watching the booths. Henry shut the door. He called into the phone.

"Leona?"

"Yes."

"Leona, there's something you've got to do."

"Will you forgive me—first, Henry?" she sobbed. "Will you?"

"For God's sake," he said brutally, "will you stop that nonsense and listen to me?"

"All—right," she whispered.

"Now do just as I say, will you? I want you to get out of bed . . ."

"I—I can't," she moaned. "I can't."

"You've *got* to," he commanded. "You've got to get out of that bed—and walk out of that room. Go into the front bedroom. Get to the window and scream—scream out into the street."

He waited, tense, fighting the fear within him. He heard her breathing heavily into the phone.

"I can't!" she mumbled piteously. "I can't move, Henry. I'm too frightened. I've tried and tried. But I can't move."

"Keep trying," he urged. "Don't you know I'll burn if you don't . . . I'll . . ."

"Burn!" she shrieked. "What . . . ?"

"You've got to move, Leona. Try again. If you don't you've only got three more minutes to live!"

11:12

"What . . . ?" There was a terrible gagging in her voice.

"Don't talk any more, Leona." His own voice broke with fear. Sweat poured over his body. He leaned heavily against the wall of the booth, to take the strain away from his shaking knees. "Don't talk. Get out of that bed. You've got to. It's all true, Leona. All of it, you hear me. I'm in pretty deep. I was desperate—I even tried—tonight I arranged—to have you . . ."

"Henry!" A great wail of terror tore from her lips. "Henry! There's someone—coming up the stairs!"

"Get out," he shouted madly. "Get out of that bed. Walk, Leona."

"I *can't.*"

"You must! You must!"

"Henry!" she cried again. "Henry! Save me! *Save me!*"

No longer able to control himself—the awful certainty of his fate and hers sapping the last remnant of courage—he shivered all over. "Please, Leona," he cried, "they'll get me—they'll *know* —they'll find out from Morano."

And then, through the telephone, he heard a sound—faintly —a sound that might have been a train grinding across the bridge. And above it Leona's bloodcurdling scream, *"Henry!"*

11:15

For one fleeting moment after her scream she clutched the telephone. Then she threw it back on its hook. Her eyes glazed with unspeakable fright, her heart hammering mercilessly, she heard the onrush of the pounding train. Gasping and gagging she tried to drag herself off the bed. But she might have been bound with bands of steel. She couldn't move. Louder and louder, rending the black stillness, came the train, until there was nothing in the night but its thundering roar. Nothing could be heard above it. Not even her last, terrible sigh.

The train passed, and in the room there was no sound except a coarse breathing—a stealthy movement away from the bed.

Suddenly the phone began to ring. Rubber shoes shuffled softly across the floor. A hand in a blood-stained glove reached down and lifted the instrument from its base. Henry's voice, trembling with desperate hope, floated up, "Leona! LEONA!"

There was a pause. Then a deep, guttural voice said, "Sorry, wrong number . . ."

11:16